Winespring Mountain

Other books by Charlton Ogburn

THE WHITE FALCON

THE BRIDGE

BIG CAESAR

THE MARAUDERS

SHAKE-SPEARE—THE MAN BEHIND THE NAME (co-author)

THE GOLD OF THE RIVER SEA

THE WINTER BEACH

THE FORGING OF OUR CONTINENT *(Smithsonian Library)*

THE CONTINENT IN OUR HANDS

Winespring Mountain

by
Charlton Ogburn

William Morrow & Company, Inc.
New York 1973

Grateful acknowledgment is made to The Viking Press, Inc. for permission to quote four lines from the early version of "Ship of Death" from *The Complete Poems of D. H. Lawrence,* edited by Vivian de Sola Pinto and F. Warren Roberts, Copyright © 1964, 1971 by Angelo Ravagli and C. M. Weekley, Executors of the Estate of Frieda Lawrence Ravagli; to New Directions Publishing Corporation for permission to quote the first stanza of "A Girl" from *Personae* by Ezra Pound, Copyright 1928 by Ezra Pound; and to Mrs. Norma Millay Ellis for permission to quote three lines from "Sonnet XIX" by Edna St. Vincent Millay, *Collected Poems,* Harper & Row, Copyright 1923, 1951 by Edna St. Vincent Millay and Norma Millay Ellis.

Printed in the United States of America.

Library of Congress Catalog Card Number 73-5325

3 4 5   77 76 75 74

For Isabel Stevens Knapp,
with whom others have always come first

Winespring Mountain

1

"I<small>T WAS</small> W<small>ICK</small> C<small>ARTER</small> striding along the highway."

A sense of being no one had been stealing over him and he spoke the words defiantly; unless he had to, he did not acknowledge his full first name, which was Sedgwick.

Hearing a car coming behind him, he turned. But it was barreling along too fast to stop for him. The curving road followed the slope of a hill on which two Appaloosas grazed in a scrubby pasture. Ahead was a small, low building, E<small>MMETT'S</small> G<small>RO</small>. S<small>TORE</small>, with a dull-red pickup truck in front of it.

He had no money other than a little change. He could have beaten his head against a telephone-pole for his stupidity in letting his wallet get away from him. The bus had stopped for twenty minutes at a little restaurant in a nameless town and he could have left it on the counter after he had paid the check. And perhaps one of his rear-seat companions had pocketed it while the other hurried him out to the bus. Or later, getting another pack of cigarettes from the luggage rack, one of them could have lifted it from his jacket, which was also up there.

They were two young fellows on leave from the Army—or so they said. They had all been together in line getting on the bus and after they had exchanged a few words it seemed natural to sit together. They had smoked and tossed out stories about themselves, mostly his companions' and mostly pretty far out. Not wanting to be left behind, he had let on to a good deal about himself—too much, maybe—and with improvements.

He had got off at Roanoke to put up overnight and take another bus in the morning. The hundred dollars in the wallet was to have paid for his hotel and his ticket to Harpersburg among other things. And, whatever had happened, all that money was gone.

He had walked the darkening streets of Roanoke grappling

1

with the question of whether to telephone home. He could hear his sister's sigh if she answered—for she would know at once that he had disgraced himself again—or his mother's voice, if it were she, in the high, helpless drawl it rose to in speaking to him. It was his father, however, who would have to be reckoned with. Less than twelve hours after he had been sent from home, banished to some miserable job, here he would be again, not even knowing how a hundred dollars had got away from him. He could not face his father again on such an issue—that biting disgust! "My son, a forger!" He had signed his father's name to a check, it was true, but only to meet a dire emergency not his, when there was no other way.

He had had no choice but to spend the night in the bus depot before setting out to hitch-hike in the morning. His two suitcases were in the baggage room, and he decided to leave them there and send for them later.

He had a hamburger special, with french fries, at the depot's all-night counter, then settled down under the glaring fluorescent lights, in one of a row of cupped, Fiberglas chairs. Across from him was a girl with a stout, erect woman, presumably her mother. Like many girls, maybe most, she was attractive. She had an impersonal air, as if being in an unfamiliar place made her invisible.

What would she be like? He put her mentally through one or two roles opposite him, but he knew, with habitual pessimism, that it wouldn't work out between them. His sister, Cynthia, told him that girls were put off by his stiffness and the dark way he had of looking at things. Maybe so. He was certainly different from the type that clustered around Cynthia. She attracted, and powerfully, the handsome, athletic young men of the Harwood circuit who made it without a hitch from college leadership to executive jobs that still left them time for golf and tennis and late nights at the club on week-ends. Their father's business guests, for that matter, melted at the sight of her, to their father's slight amusement and distinct satisfaction and to his own contempt. What they all knew, of course, was the public figure: the soft, feminine, eager way; the fragrance, the demure dresses, but brief and with a Message; the cascades of golden hair over which she spent hours and then continually swept back, as if she had been too heedless of it to restrain it. What an eye-opener it would have been for

2

them to see his sister as he did, in any old outfit—a shirt and panty-hose—striding around her room, a room that looked as if burglars had ransacked it, scowling as she yanked drawers open and slammed them shut, or as she turned on him because he had forgotten to give her a telephone message. . . . But why should he take his despondency out on Cynthia? He would give anything to be back eating corn flakes with her in the kitchen after they had been to the movies together when she had had nothing better to do—or had kept an evening for him—and he had been the envy of every male who saw them. . .

There was some coming and going of passengers through the depot. The girl had fallen asleep, her head on her arm. Her mother tried to pull her skirt down, but it did not go very far. The clock at the end of the room said eleven-eighteen. He had a cigarette from the half pack remaining.

. . . There was a time when he was fourteen that their mother had seen him in a supporting role. She had pictured her two off-spring, suitably attired, side by side on highly bred mounts where they would be seen, and had decided that he was to have riding lessons with Cynthia. He took to them and to everyone's surprise rode well from the start. But to his mother's annoyance he refused to wear the tweed jacket and jodhpurs until he felt that no one could consider them presumptuous. And he had a long way to go in his jumping. However the real trouble arose from the love of horses he had quickly conceived—their poised self-containment, their musculature, their fragrance. His attachment to the stables had been too close, or he had let it be seen. It gave his father, to whom riding was irrelevant, a lever: "Better grades in school, or no more horses." His grades had got worse. He had sat in his classes silently fighting his teachers. Why? He had known he was the loser. Given opportunities comparable to his own, his father could quite possibly have become President of the United States. It would have been the same, relatively, as his having got where he had after starting out as the son of a small-town grocer attending a public school where they had three classes in the same room. Anyway, that had been the end of riding. . . .

He had fallen asleep after all, for he came to and found that the seats the girl and her mother had occupied were empty. It

3

was nearly five o'clock. Feeling hot and achy behind the eyes, he washed his face and hands in the silent lavatory, then had coffee and a doughnut at the counter and went out into the street.

It was barely light by the gray dawn. Yesterday hung on in the refuse in the gutters, the shops that had not yet opened, the mannequins behind the plate-glass windows posing for a street bereft of shoppers. He experienced the kind of spacious loneliness he had known once on an empty beach. It might again have made him feel free, like the seagulls, but for the prospect ahead and having only twelve cents for food.

After eight or ten blocks he caught a ride to the edge of the city in a painter's old black panel-truck with a ladder on top, then walked for over two hours along the dual-lane highway while cars and buses went roaring and screaming by. When finally he got another ride it was only because he caught up with a tractor-trailer that was standing on the shoulder of the highway with its cab tilted forward. The driver, who emerged from its vitals wiping his hands on a rag, evidently had not the heart to let him trudge by and offered him a ride.

Wick had never been in such a rig before. Rocketing along in it was like going sixty miles an hour in a house. He sank back into the seat. Maybe this was the way to live, being by yourself, in your own cabin, cut loose from everything, with the highway rolling under you and the houses, towns and stretches of country slipping past you. The well-built young man at the wheel, whose smooth, tanned face might have been modeled of Fels-Naphtha soap, kept his eyes ahead even when he took a pack of cigarettes from the ledge beneath the windshield, flipped one partway out and extracted it with his lips. Wick got out one of his own, hoping it would blunt the edge of his hunger. The driver said, "I'd have offered you one, I'd known you smoked."

"Matter of fact, I been trying to cut down. Coach has been after me."

Now why had he had to say that?

"You an athlete?"

"Well, you know: football, basketball, track." He inhaled between his teeth and examined the cigarette through the smoke he blew out.

Said the driver presently, "You travel light."

He nodded, the other having turned to look at him. That was

4

it. He traveled light. "I sent some things on ahead," he deemed it advisable to add.

The conversation made him remember his friends. . . . It had not occurred to him that he could have called his friends at home and asked them to telegraph him a few dollars. He looked off to the side, past the driver. The country around them was growing steeper, with wooded hills rising back from the highway. . . . He could not ask them for that kind of help. He would never have admitted it before. There had always been his father's contempt to defend them from. "Is this one of your set who's been picked up for vandalism?" his father had asked negligently, handing him the paper. It was not, though it could have been.

But most of them didn't make much trouble. In good weather they hung out on the school athletic field or down by the river, at the boatyard, where there was a soft-drink machine, and talked about cars and sports and—unless there were girls with them— girls. When they had money for hamburgers, hot dogs, milkshakes —which usually meant when he had enough to provide for the ones who didn't—it was likely to be at a drive-in. More lately, now that they were all of age, it was apt to be at the Barn, where Joe Perucci worked—in the evening, anyhow. Draft beer was the special attraction there. There was much excitement, with voice pitched against voice, and the air filled with big ideas. However, as he looked back on it, these never seemed to come to much, unless it was the daring ones in the field of sex, for which you had to take the speaker's word.

He himself was not much of a talker. Maybe, with the clamor they raised, the bunch he went with appreciated having someone who listened. Maybe it was for that reason and not just because he was a source of funds that he had a place with them, though if he had *not* been a source of funds. . . . Anyway, they weren't superior and did not exclude him by their manner or seem to share mysterious qualifications that he somehow lacked. That was the answer to his parents' question: Why did he have to go to the town for his friends when there were boys and girls of his own sort in Harwood? But the answer would not have satisfied them, so he did not offer it.

In a way, the same question was in the minds of the crowd he went with. What was he doing with *them?* Wasn't he good enough for Harwood? He let on that the kids in Harwood bored him. To make the point that he was different, he had shoplifted an expensive AM.-F.M. radio set. Shoplifting was nothing out of the ordinary to his companions, but none had ever made off with so expensive an article or hit on employing a big hollowed-out book as a receptacle. He had gained a moment of glory. Upon Doris's admiring the set, he had presented it to her in front of everyone; "It's yours," he had declared. He was cool enough then though so sick with apprehension while carrying off the exploit that he feared he would betray his cowardice to Hank and Bob Stacey, who were watching from a distance, and later he could not rid his mind of the sad-looking man from whom he had stolen. In the end, fit to kick himself equally for what he had done and for his weakness in letting it get him down, he had borrowed the set back from Doris, smuggled it back into the shop and bought one like it. To do so, he had had to pawn his camera.

On top of that, the credit he gained from such escapades had to be renewed as occasion arose. It was he, when they were ice-skating on the river, who was looked to to cross the thin ice on the other side and retrieve a girl's muffler (a homely girl's) that had blown away. It was he who, when the police had been called to put the damper on a party that was getting out of hand at the Barn, had been put up to sneaking out and letting the air out of one of their tires.

His father had said of Doris Novak and Gwen Collier when they stopped alongside them once at a traffic light, "I wish you made as much of your assets as they do of theirs." The girls had returned his greeting only hesitantly, probably awed by the big Buick and his father at the wheel. His father automatically intimidated almost everybody. But the remark, on which he had closed his lips in a firm line, Wick had not understood until he had thought about it. He decided it could only refer to the girls' close-fitting sweaters and short skirts drawn tight across their bottoms. He was surprised and felt it not quite decent that anyone his father's age, and especially his father, should take note of such things.

Except for being a little short, Doris had the kind of figure that statistics are recited about. She was a natural blonde with hair that came straight down the sides of her rather square face and ended in a curl, like the hair of the jack in a deck of cards. She treated him somewhat offhandedly but with a kind of en-

6

couraging possessiveness. At least that was how it was in public. They were not alone very much—she found multiple dates "livelier"—but when they were she was inattentive and restless.

He thought often, both with longing for another chance and with despair of the time when they had been alone in her house, in the dark, rather dingy living room. He had not dared expect her to sit on the sofa, but she had, and had been cooperative, up to a point. But he could tell her heart wasn't in it, and he was like a dam trying to hold back a flood. His sister probably was right, and maybe if he had taken things as a matter of course they wouldn't have ended as they had, with Doris getting up to switch channels on the television set. It was like being jolted out of a dream. He had lighted a cigarette and launched into a fiction about a girl down the block from him and how. . . . But he wasn't going to let himself remember what he'd fabricated.

"All right, but you don't need to tell the whole neighborhood," Doris had said. "Anyway, you'd better go. Dad won't like it if he finds us alone in the house when he and Mom come back."

In the past two months there had been days when she was pale, with shadows under her eyes, and was short when spoken to. He had wondered about this, and more than ever after he had seen her one evening in a near-white Mercury, driven by a stranger with glossy black hair, a sallow complexion and a long, slanted nostril. He was instantly seized by animosity for that frozen face and by dismay at the expression with which Doris gazed up at it. When he saw her again two days later she seemed to him like a person who has been a long way off and is not yet used to being back. Then he had seen her once more in the white Mercury with the cruel-looking stranger. Only this time, to his astonishment, Joe Perucci was in the back seat, leaning forward, talking, with his hands clasped together. The next morning Doris had telephoned him, the first time she had ever done so, and asked if he could meet her at the Barn right away. She had said it was urgent, and he had known for sure that the call boded him no good.

Doris and Joe Perucci were waiting outside the Barn when he arrived on his bicycle, Joe looking down and working his fingers. Doris said Joe was in trouble, real trouble. She couldn't say what it was but he had to have seventy-five dollars. Right away. Seventy-five dollars! What about selling his car? He did not ask

7

Doris how she was involved. Joe's car had a cracked piston, she said. He couldn't unload it now. He'd sell it as soon as he could. But he had to have the money that day.

That was what had led to his signing his father's name on a check he made out to himself. He had traced the signature first and the bank teller, when he had identified himself, had made no difficulty. Nor would his father's secretary, who kept his personal books, have reason to be suspicious of a transaction between father and son.

These were all miscalculations. The check had been in a batch that reached his father's office three days later, the secretary *was* suspicious and his father had faced him with his misdeed that evening. He had explained, stolidly and hopelessly, that someone he knew *had* to have the money, for reasons that could not be given out. But what was the use? There were no extenuating circumstances. Work at the mines, his father said, would give him an opportunity to redeem himself, if he had it in him. He would leave in two days, and had only himself to blame for missing his high-school graduation exercises.

The tractor-trailer was turning into a sprawling gas station where other big trucks were scattered about. TRUCKERS, DIESEL FUEL, ICING, RESTAURANT said red-lettered signs. "Time to eat," the driver explained, pulling up in a vacant lot. "The way I go from here won't do you any good, but come on in. You must be hungry, and maybe we can find a jockey going in your direction."

Jockey? Another truck-driver, Wick thought. "I could use another lift," he said. "But I'm not hungry." He hitched his trousers up as they walked toward the restaurant. "I'm not much of an eater. I'm likely to forget all about a meal."

"Then you're not like me."

Half a dozen men were sitting at the lunch counter, waited on by a comradely girl whose plump arms filled her short sleeves. Wick dropped back and attached himself to a cylindrical rack of paperbacked books. The aroma of frying made him feel emptier than ever, but it was worth waiting. His companion found him a driver going on to Bluefield and, as he was leaving, pressed upon him a sandwich and a carton of milk. He did not give the boy a chance to think what to say. "OK, OK, you'll do the same for me someday. Run along or you'll keep the fella waiting."

The new driver, a chubby individual, made good time along the narrow swerving road. Steep, wooded ridges rose around them, and for a few miles they drove beside, and above, a broad, hurrying river—the New River. It was mid-afternoon when they came into Bluefield, where Wick was on his own again. It was an old-fashioned town and in its big railroad yards, its boxlike, brick industrial buildings, its edifices of rough-cut stone blocks, the broad window-sashes of the substantial older houses it resembled others he knew in the Alleghenies. However, that did not temper the aching disbelief with which he beheld himself there. Bluefield. *Bluefield, West Virginia.*

The town trailed out along the highway and he was a long time trudging through it. He looked with equal frustration at the food stores and the cars that passed him indifferently. Being consigned to nonexistence was new to him. As if someone else were in his shoes he walked up to a truck he had watched back up to the rear of a small supermarket and boldly addressed the driver. "If you need help unloading, I'll help, for something to eat, for a box of cookies." The other observed him disinterestedly.

"You get up there and carry the boxes forward to the tailgate while I wheel them inside."

He did more. Each time the driver returned with the empty handtruck he would leap down and help stack it. Unexpectedly, he felt joyful, and was sorry to reach the last, even though it meant he would now be eating. The driver returned from his last trip bringing him a box of figbars and a can of cold root beer. He attacked them at once, sitting on a flattened cardboard carton with his back against the building and looking on the unfamiliar scene with a touch of proprietorship about the world.

A feeling almost of buoyancy persisted as he resumed his journey. And it seemed to be justified when a convertible stopped for him at the foot of a long climb up a mountainside.

He was quickly to have second thoughts. The driver of the seven- or eight-year-old Ford was an odd-looking sort, not much older than himself, with a large head carried low between his shoulders. He took off with such abrupt acceleration that the tires yelped and Wick was thrown back in his seat. He was up to fifty before he shifted into high. From then on he drove with bursts of speed alternating unpredictably with slackenings off. To make it worse, he drove with one hand. "I'm Terp Smith," he

9

had said, "and people who don't like me . . . well, they just sure as hell don't."

He kept stealing sidelong glances at his passenger, who concluded that he was being observed for signs of fright. Wick's heart was in fact in his mouth, but he sat stoically. "She moves right out when you gun her, doesn't she?" he said.

They had entered a country of steep, closely packed hills, or small mountains, which were totally covered by forest. "This is as far as I go." The brakes were jammed on with such force that Wick was nearly thrown into the windshield.

The narrow valley they had been following was full of small, decrepit houses, many with a junked car or two beside them. On foot again, Wick felt an impulse to hurry, not to be caught there.

Most of the people he saw, even the most poorly clothed, looked as if they were meant for better things. The Southern Appalachians, he had heard, were still populated by descendants of the original settlers, a strain that, he realized now, predominated in the upper class at home.

He attracted no special attention as he walked along, looking continually back over his shoulder for a lift. Once he trotted forward to snatch up a ball that had got away from some boys playing catch and shied it back. A few of the towns had tiny parks with small beds of flowers beside the stream that flowed past them all. One had a wheelbarrow containing a large lump of coal embedded in concrete, the whole painted a bright silver.

It was coal country. He had already passed several tipples. Blackened, squared-off board towers, about two stories high, they rose above the railroad tracks on the lower slopes of the wooded hills. Now and again, moreover, a coal-truck passed, big, high-built, snub-nosed, its cargo-body braced by a cross-work of ribs on the sides. Wick got a long ride in one driven by an ex-miner, who said it sure as hell wasn't true that when you got coal dust in your blood you couldn't quit the life. This took him to the end of the afternoon. For the night, he had decided to put up in a junked car as far from a house as he could find one, but meanwhile he was ravenous and could think of nothing but food. *The next place*, he swore to himself. *Without fail.*

It was a depressed-looking roadside grill behind a bare, trash-strewn expanse; for weeks its patrons must have been eating in their cars and tossing the refuse out the windows.

10

Without fail.

The screened back door, at which he presented himself, was bulged and torn and the push-bar across it advertised Red Mule chewing tobacco. A broad, bald man in an apron was working at a stove in the untidy kitchen. "Some work in exchange for something to eat?" He echoed Wick's question. "Is that the deal?" He came to the door then, sharpening a knife on a whetstone. "Why aren't you at home?" Wick explained that he was on his way to a job. "If you want to work, you're an exception around here. But you clean up around the place—all the papers, the cups, everything—and I'll see what I can scrape up. You'll find trash cans at the corner of the house, by the crates of bottles."

It took Wick until after the lights came on, and his back and legs were sore when he had finished. The ignominious work had galled him, especially while he was being observed by a party in a car that included girls. But the grounds passed inspection and he was allowed to wash his hands at a rust-stained sink and dry them on a well-used roller towel, then was given a cheeseburger and coleslaw on a paper plate ("Don't let me see you chuck it on the ground") and his choice of a drink, which was hot chocolate. And though the proprietor had ascertained his plan for the night with a snort of mirthless laughter, he had pointed out a largely intact sedan at the edge of his property. As Wick was departing toward it with his supper, he said, "Come back for a cup of coffee in the morning."

Here I am, Wick thought. This is actually it: my life.

The back seat was vastly more comfortable than the chair in the bus terminal, and, exhausted, he fell quickly asleep despite the headlights and the noise of the traffic. Several times he waked, once to the sound of rain, but never for long. The darkness was lifting when he had slept himself out. Apprehensive about the weather, he looked up through a window and saw a pinpoint of a star in a blue-silk sky.

An amazing thing, he thought, for he was still considering his life as an object, like a display window. Here he was, standing beside the car wreck, beside the bushes and weeds and the trees that were acquiring form in the early light, and it was as if he and they had a bond between them.

He had been on his own for thirty-six hours and had not succumbed. Oblivious for the moment of his destitution, he stood

11

lightly on the balls of his feet, stuffing his worked-up shirt back into his trousers, then walked forward with an easy stride. He was Wick Carter walking toward the restaurant, where the lights were on and an early customer had already parked an old, dusty panel-truck at the door. He wished he could brush his teeth.

The proprietor stood by his offer and to a cup of coffee added a sweet-roll. With a motion of the head toward the dining area, he said, "The man with the truck outside is going your way."

He was, it turned out, going most of the way to Harpersburg and would be glad of company. Wick could have believed that he and his vehicle had grown old together. They seemed to be in accord, neither in any hurry, the elderly man bent attentively over the wheel, both ruminative. The conversation might have been between the two for all the part Wick took in it. Miles and hours passed. Between hills abrupt as camels' humps the highway ran up and down, curved this way and that. The hills crowded the houses at their feet, the houses crowded the road, the road crowded the smoky, littered stream or the railroad. Almost always there was a railroad and, where there were tipples, lines of gondola cars.

Several times the road climbed precipitous hillsides and crossed a ridge to the head of the next valley; shortly before noon Wick was set down below one of these ridges. He set his jaw and started off, visions of gargantuan meals before him. An hour later he was still walking and the same visions were torturing him. The road was a succession of blind curves on which there was no use expecting a car to stop. He marched with an indifferent horse's mechanical pace, recalling his departure from home only two days before as an event of his distant childhood.

On a straight stretch near the top of the rise he was picked up by a well-dressed man in a new car—a salesman of women's hosiery. The end of his journey and whatever awaited him was closer at hand than he had thought. At the foot of the long grade, before any evidence of Harpersburg, a green sign pointed down a side road to the Talbot Creek Mine of the Allegheny-Keystone Coal Company. The valley through which the road led struck him as fresher than those he had driven through. There were new brick houses among the shabby ones and also new cottages of blue or pale-green asbestos-shingle. The roadbed of the railroad that skirted the hills looked new, too. But newest-looking of all, when he reached them after a few miles, were the imposing silver-gray structures of the Talbot Creek Mine. There were two that were four or five stories high. One was like a narrow silo rising from a cone of coal; the other—the preparation plant—was the terminus of a conveyor-belt that emerged from an oblong black aperture in the side of the mountain behind the installations. A drift mine, and a model one, Wick thought. A shed, evidently the workshop, occupied a considerable part of the grounds. Separated from it by fresh black asphalt were the offices. All the buildings were of sheet metal and they shone in the late-afternoon sun. The scene could have been an idealized picture. But he did not feel reassured. There was the bank manager to be faced. And faced moreover— since he couldn't get by until payday without funds—with an admission of his pennilessness.

He put on the jacket he had slung over his shoulder, slipped up the knot of his tie and forced an outlook of nonchalance. What did he care what kind of place it was? They could take him or leave him.

There were lines of parked cars but few men in view, most of them in helmets of the same orange-yellow as the squat rubber-tired shuttle-cars in and around the workshed. Directed by a grizzled miner to the manager's office, he found himself confronting a Negro behind a desk. This was not the manager, however.

"Mr. Winstead," said the Negro, "is not in the office. He is not in the office because he is elsewhere. He may be in the shop. . . . He may be at a funeral. . . . He may be waiting for some whisky to age. . . . He may be—" He interrupted himself as the door opened to admit a gray-haired, sturdy-looking man in clean gray working clothes, a helmet under his arm, who made for a second door at the side of the office. "—Passing through this room right now."

Having grasped the doorknob, the newcomer turned and looked inquiringly but not very invitingly at the boy.

"I'm Sedgwick Carter." He tried unsuccessfully to sustain the mood of a few minutes before.

The other gave a slow backward nod, as if to say "Oh yes," his expression unchanged. "Winstead," he said. "Come in." He motioned Wick to a metal chair in the second office.

"I was told to expect you on yesterday's bus."

Wick realized that he had given cause for grievance. "I couldn't

13

get here any sooner," he ventured. Was this the moment for his confession, at the very start?

But no. Mr. Winstead flipped a switch on a gray-enameled box on his desk. When it crackled, he spoke in its direction, giving orders about a defective pump. Then there was a cigar to be lighted and brought up to a glow. Mr. Winstead's hands were puffy—big hands with fingers like sausages.

"I guess you know what to expect," he said, coming to grips with the evidently distasteful business between them. "Your father wrote that he wants me to put you to work and he says you aren't to be shown any favor. I mean, this comes from him. I want that straight. This is none of my idea." His look was questioning.

"Yes, I—" Wick cleared his throat. "I understand that."

"Your father evidently expected me to put you on the payroll here at Talbot Creek. But we're unionized here, of course. I don't know whether he figured on the explanations there'd have to be if you applied for a card—who you are, which he strongly thought ought not to get out." At the sound of footsteps in the next room he glanced at the door, hoping—or so it seemed—that there would be an interruption. "So I've arranged for you to work for a small outfit we deal with. We take their coal; there's a special arrangement between us. I've written your father about this. Another thing. One of DeSalla's employees—Michael DeSalla is the operator I'm talking about—has a room with a Mrs. Haney, a widow. She'll put you up and you can ride to work and back with young Jack MacDonough. But if you're getting money from home you may prefer fancier quarters."

Wick could not miss the conflict in the eyes that met his own —eyes that, perhaps because of the lumpiness of the face in which they were placed, seemed like upholstery buttons. He could guess the source of the mine-manager's unease and annoyance: He had before him a boy unquestionably in serious disgrace and quite probably worthless but who was nevertheless the company president's son.

Wick said, "No, I'm not getting any money from home. I haven't got any money at all. I mean I've only got twelve cents."

"You didn't bring any to carry you till payday?"

"I lost my wallet on the bus the first day. I think it may have been stolen. I hitch-hiked from Roanoke; my bags are still in the bus station there." His eyes burned with the effort of keeping them from wavering.

"What have you done for food?"

"Worked for some. But today I was in a hurry and I haven't had anything since coffee and a roll for breakfast."

It was written on Mr. Winstead's face that he had no patience with human situations that untracked the course of business; time was passing. Yet a trace of grudging respect appeared in his regard. "You must be hungry," he said. He took a wallet from his hip pocket and two ten-dollar bills from the wallet, then fished in his pocket for two dimes. "That'll get you some crackers from the vending machine. The twenty I'll deduct from your first pay—we'll be paying you here."

Footsteps sounded again in the adjacent office and this time the Negro opened the connecting door. "The inspector's leaving," he said. "He told me to tell you someone took a shot at the surveyor over on Bear Den."

"Hit him?"

"No, sir."

The manager made a sound of exasperation. "Maybe there's a still in there," he said, cutting his eyes at the boy. He stood and so did Wick. "We'll be shutting down at five," he said. "That's less than an hour. I'll drop you off at Mrs. Haney's, or in town if you'd prefer. You can go from one to the other by bus. It's not much of a bus, but it keeps a schedule."

2

LIKE BLUEFIELD, Harpersburg was an old town built around a railroad yard and bounded by hills. Near the top of the highest a large sign, illuminated at night, advertised a brand of home appliances. Along the main street were the choicer stores, a superior-looking hotel, a town hall with statuary, and the Chamber of Commerce, a small, over-shaped building most curiously constructed of shiny blocks of coal. The community's back was to an opaque river, which flowed sluggishly below brushy, rubbish-strewn banks. The brick houses near the railroad station were substantial but run-down. Farther off there were solid streets of small, identical frame houses, with porches, one section inhabited by Negroes.

Wick had arrived on a Friday and spent most of the time until Monday roaming the town, for the alternative was to languish at Mrs. Haney's. The room at the head of the stairs in which the landlady had installed him was a cubicle with scarcely room enough for the white-enameled iron bedstead with mended coverlet, bare table stained by rings, chair to match and ancient bureau that tottered forward when its balky drawers were pulled. A face towel on the bureau and two pictures completed the furnishings. One of these was a brown family photograph; the other, labeled "Innocence," showed two moon-faced little girls in voluminous skirts and striped socks playing with a bug-eyed toy dog.

"Mr. Haney always liked this room," the widow had pronounced with complacency. "He'd come up here to get away and think when the house was full of relatives." Mrs. Haney was in her sixties, a woman of comfortable proportions for whom, as Wick learned, everything was settled and her deceased husband the authority.

The house itself, originally of some pretension, resembled an

16

object that has passed through many hands and been well thumbed in the passage. Most of the houses of Kinston Hollow—or Holler—had a depleted appearance and the small grocery store, its bare yard paved with bottlecaps, made Wick think of a museum. He felt the inhabitants, like those of the country he had come through, should count for more than they seemed to. Among the many children scampering about, some had sores and most were dirty, but a high proportion were fair-haired and attractive—downright pretty. So was an equal proportion of the teen-aged girls. He could not keep his eyes off them, and they returned his interest with curiosity. But since they were always with other boys or girls, there seemed to be no way to take up with one.

At Harpersburg he arranged for his bags to be sent on and bought the stopgap necessities, some work clothes and a lunch box that Mrs. Haney would fill. He also ate. About every two hours on Saturday he became hungry all over again. He had written Doris, though hardly able to think of anything he could say that would interest her. That the letter required such an effort left him feeling more depressed than ever—betrayed and betraying. He thought of his room at home, the map of the two hemispheres on the wall, the posters, his desk, the Navajo rug, and wondered how he could ever have been unhappy there.

He had already got off the obligatory safe-arrival note to his parents and maybe he would just drop one to Cynthia—to let her know he wasn't going to scurry home as soon as he got a dose of the work, as he had seen she was concerned that he might. For that, though, he'd have to wait until he'd worked. That would be tomorrow. And tomorrow was coming. . . .

It was still early while he and Jack MacDonough were driving to the job. They had been on their way about ten minutes and Wick, a cold tightness in his stomach, was talking without pause. "He was pretty wild, all right, that stallion. He'd already thrown the stablemaster. There's a saying, 'A white sock fore and another rear;/And that look in the eye—you'd better stand clear.' I thought I could manage him, though." What crazy boast was he working up to? But by all the signs his words were scarcely ruffling his driver's consciousness. Jack MacDonough was a big young man with abundant, dark hair, large eyes and sculptured lips that naturally took the curve of a smile. He had appeared to find nothing out of the ordinary in having a boy of Wick's

17

kind for a passenger or in the newness of his passenger's shirt and trousers.

As they left the highway for a valley that looked as if God had cursed it, he cut short his saga of horsemanship. On the right, covering the whole side of a low hill and extending out from it, was a pile of shale forty or fifty feet high, black but for a dull, spent red on its lower side. A thin smoke oozed up from it, resembling phlegm.

"How long has that been burning?" he asked.

"Far back as I can remember," said Jack.

The floor of the valley was bare, dried mud and stony earth, much of it sooty. The stream at the bottom had not a blade of green near it. There were rusted pieces of machinery here and there, and the bare hillsides that cupped the valley were littered with the skinned, gray trunks of fallen trees. Higher up, however, growing denser with elevation, there were green bushes and young trees.

"Everything was killed here at one time, but the woods is makin' a comeback. When I was a boy there was a regular little town here. That was before the mine yonder was worked out." Cut into the foot of a hill on the left, its ceiling of concrete blocks sagging, was the broad, low entrance to the black galleries. It brought to his mind things he preferred not to think about.

The rutted road was climbing to the head of the valley; on the other side they would be where they were going. Jack had said enough about the operator, Mr. DeSalla, to sharpen Wick's anxiety. "Maybe he's got indigestion. He's sour enough. But if you do your job, he lets you alone. He's from somewhere in the East: New Jersey, I believe I heard."

He turned out to be short and chunky, short-legged especially, but with a look in his hook-nosed face that warned you not to make anything of it. His protruding eyes were unexpectedly pale under the dark brows. When they turned penetratingly upon Wick, he felt they retained an unresolved doubt about him. Mr. DeSalla was better dressed than would have been expected and, as Wick was to observe, was continually dusting himself off. "I want you to clean up that 'dozer over there," he said. "When you're ready to eat off any part of it, come tell me. Or tell Mr. Sims if I'm not here. Ask Mr. Sims for what you need." He walked

18

off without another word, picking his way fastidiously over the uneven ground.

The scene of operations was a cut high up on the side of a mountain. Bulldozed out of the slope, the cut could have been intended for a highway. A level shelf thirty feet wide, with a vertical inner bank, it followed the contour of the mountain clear around to the other side of the valley. And, as a fresh pile of earth and uprooted trees testified, it still was being pushed forward. The lower two feet of the cut's bank—which was anywhere from four to fifteen feet high depending on the steepness of the slope— were the face of the coal seam. The coal was being extracted by a contraption the like of which Wick had never seen, auger-mining being outside his experience. It was a framework of girders, stays, pumps, rods, chains, pipes, cables and hoses better than twice his own height and filling two-thirds the width of the shelf. A big Diesel motor in the middle of it turned an auger two feet in diameter that bored horizontally into the seam and brought the coal curling out. Falling onto a conveyor-belt, the coal was lifted to a height from which it could be dumped into a truck. The machine was an orchestra of mechanical noises, the Diesel emitting a stuttering roar, the auger grinding its way into the mountain, connections clanking, the coal clattering into the metal bed of the truck.

When all of a twelve-foot section of auger had been driven into the mountain, it was disconnected from the Diesel and another section was lowered between them from a rack overhead and coupled to both. Later, when the auger had bored to the full length of its combined sections, it was withdrawn and the sections were lifted out one by one. The whole huge machine, which rested on skids, was then pulled forward to a new position by a very large bulldozer driven by Jack MacDonough.

Wick observed all this from around the end of the bulldozer he was cleaning a little distance off. Its chains, tracks and wheels were caked with mud and dirt, and where the parts had been greased the grime formed a thick crust. When he had pried, scraped and brushed off the worst of it, he went after the rest with cotton waste soaked in gasoline. Any need to worry about the newness of his clothes quickly passed, for in his great relief at having a job off by himself to begin with, he threw himself

19

into it. From time to time, however, he looked across to where Mr. DeSalla sat in his pickup truck going over papers and more than once he intercepted a look in his own direction. He was relieved when in late morning his employer drove off.

At noon the Diesel puttered to a stop and the silence of the mountains descended. Jack called out to him that it was time to eat. Everyone had stopped whatever he was doing and gone for his lunch box. Wick joined them with his own, sitting a little apart. There were three besides Jack, including the driver of the truck that stood half loaded under the conveyor-belt. Their conversation mostly presupposed a fund of common knowledge he did not possess, but he learned that the shelf formed by the cut was called the bench and the bank the high wall, and someone referred to the shot aimed at the surveyor on Bear Den.

The truck-driver, whose name was Frank Allen, said, "I knowed all along there was goin' to be trouble up in that holler." He was a round-faced young man rather more animated and outgoing than the others. "They ain't anyones to fool with up there, if you ask me. I've seen 'em—seen how they look at you if you drive a coal-truck past there." A significant silence closed upon this declaration. The speaker looked from one to the other from behind the glasses straddling his sharp nose; he was from "outside," Wick was not surprised to hear later.

"Well," said Jack, staring at the sandwich in his hand, "I reckon it's natural to take it hard when you get a mountainside unloaded on your cropland." Wick was aware of glances cast at Mr. Sims, the eldest of the lot. A tall, lanky, graying man, as sparing of movement as of speech and expression, Mr. Sims only poured coffee from his vacuum bottle into a cup. He was not, it appeared, going to recognize the exchange, and nothing more was said on the subject. The fact was, however, as Wick reflected, that gouging out a mountain would beyond doubt make an unholy mess of whatever it was the soil, rocks, and trees were dumped on. It had surely made one of the woods below the cut they were working in.

He listened to the talk, to absorb all he could. They spoke a common language, these men; they were at home in one another's company, they knew the machinery, they knew the coal. As he sat eating with them, as he did at later times on the job, or when it was a matter of boys and girls his own age sparring with one

20

another on the porch of the Kinston grocery store, he felt that the next best thing to waking up and finding himself at home would be to be accounted one of them and have no feeling of being an oddity in their eyes.

Because he was alone so much in those days the habit of soliloquy grew on him.

'I'm off in the woods by myself most of the time now. I'm a lumberman. I cut down trees ahead of the bulldozer, trim off the branches and cut them into five-foot lengths for mine supports. I look around and there's nobody else in sight—nothing but trees, sawed-up trunks and tangles of bushes and sawed-off branches. The hillside is very steep. You have to watch yourself handling this saw; you don't want to slip.

'I'm off by myself all day, except when I'm carrying logs back to where the truck can pick them up, at the end of the bench the bulldozer's cut. The saw must weigh thirty-five pounds, and I can tell you, you sure feel it in your shoulders, and even more in your back. The first morning after I'd had a day of it I didn't think I could straighten up, the pain in my back was so terriffic. I decided I'd better use the axe on the branches until my back-muscles got built up. . . .'

So it would go if his soliloquy took the form of an imagined letter to Doris or Cynthia. He had had notes from both of them and had pored over them, especially the one from Doris. "We miss you," she had written, and he lingered over those words. She had written them just as he saw them; the paper had been in her breathing presence, just as he had been in her mind.

Looked at realistically, her letter represented, he knew, the minimum. And he would have acknowledged that the prospects of his actually writing her or Cynthia any letters except brief ones, or of their being received other than with groans if he had, were anything but good. However, his compositions took place in another and higher realm.

Sometimes he lived the contents of a book in which he saw himself as the central character, in the third person.

"Mr. DeSalla wanted to know if he had ever worked with one of these things. 'Not with this particular brand,' Wick said in an offhand way.

"Mr. DeSalla looked suspicious. But then he always looked suspicious. 'Jack, you see he knows how to operate it,' he said.

21

. . . 'And I don't want you to be cutting your foot off. I don't want no mess on the job. . . .'

"By now, Wick Carter could have given any of them lessons on the chain-saw. . . . He looked with practiced eye at the next tree that had to come down. A bad list, he thought. If the tree wasn't going to hang up in the crown of another, it was going to have to be brought down against the direction of the list. He'd have to make his cuts just so far in, then wedge the tree over against its tilt. . . .

"He raised one end of the log to his shoulder, bending to it, then straightened up raising the butt of the log, his muscles straining until the whole length was balanced horizontally on his shoulder.

"His muscles were taut under the crushing weight. Carefully he started back for the site. On the steep, tangled hillside a single misstep could send him sprawling with a hundred-and-fifty-pound log on top of him. But practice had made him sure-footed. He was springy and poised on his feet, like a prizefighter, his muscles like coil-springs under the load. When he came out onto the leveled space, he let the log tumble—another on the pile, another burden off him. And the sweat to be wiped away from his eyes. . . . His fellow worker, Jack MacDonough, had said, 'I don't know what that skinflint pays you, but I can tell you he'd have a time getting somebody else to do the work you're doing—hauling them logs.' "

Wick thought that that must also have been the opinion of Mr. DeSalla, when, at the end of the week, after he had given the others their pay envelopes, he called him over and held a last one out to him. "Charlie Winstead told me he was going to pay you to start with. I'm supposed to be taking you on as a favor. You're the son of a friend of his: that's the story I get." Wick resolutely met the marble-cold eyes until the speaker went on. "I don't like the arrangement"—only what he really said was *I doan like d'arrangement.* "A man works for who he's paid by, and anyone around here I want working for me. But I agree to give it a try. Depending how it works out, I'll hire you or fire you. So OK, I'm hiring you. You've earned a week's pay, I'm giving it to you. From now on you're working for me, you understand?"

So he was able to send Mr. Winstead ten dollars on account,

while in his next weekly letter to his parents—promised to his mother—he wrote in an altered tone, as one sovereign of his own life to another. The running saga of his exploits took a bolder turn. "He had showed he could do a man's work, and the crew began to look on him as one of themselves. . . ."

Of one episode the saga did not take account. A waitress in a Harpersburg cafeteria in which he had had several meals had a figure that was just about right, a friendly smile and a way of enveloping him in her atmosphere when she leaned forward to wipe off the counter in front of him. (He sometimes thought that if he became any more entranced by girls' breasts he would end as a mental case in an asylum.) She was rather plain, her nose too high up on her face, but that gave him courage, which he especially needed since she was evidently several years older than he. With a tremendous summoning of nerve he asked her one night if she would go out with him after work. She received the proposal and acceded to it—"I don't mind"—with an inattentive casualness that rather deflated him and proved an augury of the evening ahead.

He met her outside the cafeteria at nine o'clock, and suggested going to a tavern that he guessed would be open late. She didn't mind, she said. As a date, though, Gladys seemed more of a stranger than she had as a waitress. While they sat sucking their Coca-Colas—the drink she had ordered—he had difficulty keeping the conversation going, until the subject of a girl friend of hers came up. About Charlotte, who apparently brought out the most treacherous side of everybody, she could go on and on. He bought a pack of cigarettes for both of them, smoked too much and was glad when she had to go. At the door of her house, she said matter-of-factly, "I can't let you kiss me in case anybody's looking." He was left with the question of why he had not been able to get things onto that plane where girls had the same steamy kind of thoughts you had and everything happened naturally, almost of itself. He had to conclude once more that he did not strike the right note. And it was a fact that the imaginings he had had about Gladys, in which she had lent herself willingly to all his desires, had seemed outlandish as he sat across the table from her, the last thing in the world he could conceive of as happening.

The only bus running at that hour left him with over two

23

miles to walk and he was exhausted when he got to the house. But as if to compensate, word came the next day that his bicycle, which he had asked for in his first letter home, was at the freight station in Harpersburg.

Because of the bicycle his life was to be transformed, but not before other changes had taken place. These began in the morning with an accident.

An electric welding machine, mounted on a trailer that had been towed to the auger, caught fire when a spark from a short circuit ignited some spilled gasoline. This happened while the operator was filling the tank of the generator. Wick, switching off the chain-saw to carry back cut logs, heard the shouting and hurried toward it.

Flames and black smoke were pouring from the welding machine.

"Stand back, boy! If the fire gets to the gas tank . . . !"

It was one of those times. Wick knew it with a terrible faintness of heart. They had all drawn back. The motor of the abandoned auger was still running, the welding machine threatening to explode flaming gasoline over it. *You*, said that awful voice which there was no denying. Sick with fear, he raced for the tow-truck to which the trailer was still coupled. There was the truck's gasoline tank as well as the generator's. . . . Dimly, he heard shouts. The heat at the forward end of the truck was not bad but behind him the fire muttered and crackled. *Where was the choke, where was the starter?* He found them and the ignition switch. The motor revolved with a dead sound. How much chance should he give it? It caught . . . and off they went. . . . The auger was safe. *Finish the job*, the remorseless voice insisted. *'Close to the ground . . .'* He was out of the cab and, crouching, speeding to the back of the truck. Down nearly flat not only for safety but to escape the heat, intense so near the fire, he reached up, released the catch that held the handle of the hitch, turned the handle. Thank God the tongue flew up. Now for the truck. . . . They were off, and there was Mr. DeSalla's pale-blue pickup at the bend in the bench—and the trailer pouring out flame and smoke in the rear-view mirror, and it could explode all over the map if it wanted to, because he was safe, and it was all behind him, over.

He dismounted into a place of incredible tranquillity and bliss.

24

Mr. DeSalla had got out of his truck. He said, "That was good work, kid." Unbelieving admiration showed in his face. "You think the stuff you save was worth it?"

No, he did not. But that had nothing to do with it. "I don't know. I didn't stop to think."

Mr. DeSalla turned toward the welding machine and Wick followed his gaze. The fire was subsiding. Evidently it was not going to reach the gasoline tank.

"I come here a little while ago to bounce you," Mr. DeSalla stated. "I don't like to have things put over on me, see?" It appeared he meant to let that sink in, then evidently he thought better of it. "Carter is a common name, but on a hunch I inquire about the Carter who's head of Allegheny-Keystone and I find he's got this son, name of Sedgwick. That's all I need to know. But now here is this son taking a chance on his life to save me a pile of dough. . . . So what are you doing here? I mean here in this dump?"

Wick explained in the fewest possible words. It had not occurred to him that the confession would be greeted with skepticism, as evidently it was.

"Yeah, that's the story I get from Charlie Winstead. Frankly, I don't see you as a boy in trouble with his dad. But what-the-hell, I can't throw you out now."

"If nobody else had to know, I'd be glad. I mean, about my being . . . "

Mr. DeSalla understood. "Yeah, well, I don't know. I raise holy hell with Charlie Winstead. I can't take the responsibility." He called out to the group around the welder, "Hey, Mac, you want we should drag that thing back now?"

Not many minutes later Wick was driving the truck—a three-quarter-ton pickup—with the trailer behind it on the way to Harpersburg. "I don't give speeches," Mr. DeSalla had said. "But—you want to get behind a wheel for a change? You a good driver?" To make sure, he was following behind in his own pickup.

The elevation of his status and the obedience of the lumbering truck, combined with the way the others had looked at him, filled him with joy, and this was even keener when his employer turned off at the highway. The debilitating fear that so recently had gripped him, along with the even greater fear of giving in to it—and he was well acquainted with both kinds—had become

25

remote. He hadn't really been afraid, had only thought so, he told himself; it had been shown that he was not afraid. The welder-operator on the seat beside him was gazing morosely out the window and he was as good as alone with his thoughts, which was to say with scenes in which everyone was approving and glad to have him with them.

When he had delivered the welding machine he picked up his bicycle at the station. The thought of company had a new attraction for him and he planned to leave the truck at Mrs. Haney's (he was to return it in the morning) and bicycle, after dinner, to the roadhouse that Jack and Frank Allen went to. On one side of an illuminated sign hanging perpendicular to the highway it called itself LAST CHANCE and on the other side FIRST CHANCE. It was located, that was to say, just inside a jurisdiction in which liquor sales were permitted and beside one in which they were not. Jack had taken him there several times, though he feared only out of pity. Tonight when he got to the house, Jack seemed genuinely to seek his company, and the bicycle wasn't needed. Jack said, "Hell, I might have had to bring your remains down from Little Powderhorn, what we could have scraped together of them." It was his only reference to the afternoon's occurrence.

The public part of the Last Chance/First Chance consisted of a large room paneled in varnished knotty pine with a bar across one end and small tables occupying the remainder. It drew a mixed clientele, from the burly men who worked at the mines to quieter, less physical types from behind counters and cash-registers and free-floating youths eager to find something doing and ready to promote it. A few brought their women but most did not. As beer and some harder drinks were downed, voices rose and occasionally became aggressive. The owner saw to it, however, that any fracases took place outside.

For Wick, the Last Chance/First Chance had no stronger attraction than Roger Tenent, a man he could imagine following anywhere. The café's owner was good-looking to begin with. He had red hair, a straight nose, deep-blue eyes and a powerful yet light physique. He was in motion most of the time, and with a lilt about his movements as he purveyed drinks, cigarettes, potato-chips or chewing tobacco from behind the bar, stowed dirty glasses, slipped out for a word with a patron or to shoot a few

26

rounds of miniature tenpins on the tabletop Shuffle Alley. The way he kept in continual touch with the patrons fascinated Wick, the blue eyes making quick, vital contacts, keen with gusto and amusement and capable of flashing a warning like the flick of a whip. 'He's completely master of himself,' Wick thought, 'and he concentrates the life in this room in himself.' Most of what was left for Tenent's wife to do was to contribute to the tone of the café, which she did admirably from behind the bar. A handsome woman of stately stature, she had a cheerful, hospitable manner for all which yet drew a line and did so without frostiness.

She noticed Jack and Wick's entrance on the evening of the generator fire as did everyone. A spate of stares followed them as they made their way to the table at which Frank Allen sat with two others.

Jack was in hearty spirits. "My craw is sure full of dust," he declared. "If that beer makes me hiccup, I'll have a mouthful of mud." But there was no reciprocation.

"It's been a hot day," one of the men at the table agreed after a silence. And Wick was conscious of Frank's quizzical scrutiny.

"Oh she broke my heart for a laugh when I'd saved all year for a ring," Jack sang with the jukebox. "Frank, your nose is out like a bird-dog's, let's have it before you bust. What's on your so-called mind?"

Caught by surprise, Frank visibly fumbled for words, then blurted to Wick, "Is it true that you're the son of the president of Allegheny-Keystone?"

So that was it. "Did Mr. DeSalla tell you that?"

"It's all around."

The shock and astonishment in Jack's face gave him a jolt. Despite himself his gaze faltered. "Well, yes, it's true. . . ." He shrugged.

Jack said, "Well, I suppose there's a reason why you're here?"

Wearily he replied that his father did not approve of him. "He thinks what I need is hard work. He thinks I had it too easy at home."

"A coal-company president!" Frank exclaimed. "I'll bet he's so used to pushin' people around he don't know how to do any different."

"That's not so. He's fair with everybody. He got where he is

—he started as poor as anybody—where he is by working hard."
It came to him as he spoke, looking from one to the other of the
two men, that they had hoped he would take the out he had
been given: If he had showed enough resentment of his parent
he would have been at least partially cleared of the guilt of the
relationship. He could tell they were finding it hard to credit
that a coal-company president could be regarded as human by
anyone they had found human. "I've got to go have a leak," he
said.

There was the room to be crossed. And as he crossed it, he
knew what he was to those eyes: if not an agent of the enemy, at
least one of those who looked down on the people of this part
of the country as backward.

On his return, rather than force his company on Jack and his
friends or turn tail and flee, he took a stool at the bar. "Your
usual?" Mrs. Tenent, who was tending it alone, looked uncertain, as if she were dealing with a semi-stranger. Ordinarily, no
doubt unable to miss the absorbed regard he had for her husband, she acknowledged in her manner a special affinity between
them.

"Yes. No," he said, uncertain himself of the ground on which
they now met. "A real beer, please. A . . . " He consulted the
list on the wall behind her and named the first brand.

With his back to the room, his position was endurable. But
he had hardly wetted his lips when a highly unwelcome figure
appeared beside him. Wick thought, 'He must have arrived while
I was in the men's room.' Though they had never before been
closer than half a room apart, Bull Turner had from the first
marked him as an object for comment—comment shared smirk-
ingly with the three or four young males not long out of high
school whom he generally had in train.

Turner was no taller but much heavier than he with a dis-
proportionate amount of weight in his shoulders and neck. His
dark hair was matted on his forehead. His swollen bull's eyes
were shifting and watchful. But it was his habit of closing them
from time to time and sitting with heaving chest that made him
seem most menacing, as if he might come out of the spell in
some more awful form. According to Jack, he had been in bad
trouble a couple of times, and though nothing had been hung

28

on him, things had got so hot for him in his own county that he had left and turned up here in Garrett.

Now he was taking his time, looking Wick over.

"So you're the one we been hearing so much about," he said at last in a voice not for Wick alone. "Sedgwick Carter. *Mister* Carter." He made a smacking noise. "You know, I'm kinda disappointed. I was expecting something . . . well, more outa this world. I mean, the son of a coal-company president. One of the biggest companies, too. *And* a hero. That's something, ain't it?" Turner was facing him, standing, elbow on the counter.

Wick looked at him unprovocatively, in acknowledgment of the fact that he was speaking, then, trying not to make a point of it, returned to his drink.

"A real movie hero! Sure, we heard all about it. That valuable machinery saved. If the mine-owner's property is in danger, hop to it, boy—get in there and save it. Property's money—the mine-owner's money. That's what counts, ain't it?"

Wick glanced beyond Turner to Mr. Tenent, who had come back behind the bar. The latter's lips were closed in a half-jaunty smile and a sharper light than ever had been kindled in the intent eyes. Let him run on, Wick read the expression to say. Life's a funny business and we're too far above this sort of thing to be touched by it.

"And those fellows who were being just a *leetle* careful about their lives—boy, you sure showed them up, didn't you?" Turner appeared to Wick to have swelled. His voice was louder. Or perhaps it was that the hush had become general. "Well? You got anything to say for yourself?"

"Bull," said Mr. Tenent, "why don't you speak up so we can all hear you?"

Turner wheeled on him, but in Mr. Tenent's face there was nothing challenging, only sharp, relishful good nature.

"On second thought," he said, "I reckon maybe everybody did hear you. And now we know you stand foursquare behind the people of Garrett County. So how about the business left over from last week? Have you got the nerve to shoot me best four out of seven on Shuffle Alley?"

Turner cast a doubtful, hostile look at the boy. But he had lost his momentum. Confused, he tipped back his can of beer

29

and held it to his lips, everyone watching the performance, until he had drained it. "You've got yourself a match."

Wick finished his own drink, not allowing himself to gulp it. While most of the twenty or so customers were gathered around the contestants at the little bowling alley, he took advantage of the distraction to slip away.

Outside, he looked off to where the road disappeared in the darkness, beyond the lights, and faced the prospect of a walk that would seem even longer than it was.

3

THE WEEK'S END found him dead tired. Waking slowly on Saturday, he doubted that he could have made it to work. All morning he lay on his bed, reading a little. In the afternoon, however,
he got out his bicycle, swung onto it and from the first moment
felt restored, and more: set free. He decided that the next day he
would start out early and ride on and on, to new scenes.

An exchange he had had with Jack lay over him like a cloud.
He had awaited nervously their first encounter after the evening
at Tenent's. But Jack did not allow much to upset his comfortable
relationship with life.

On their way to work he had said, "Don't fret about yesterday
evening. The crowd wasn't as much on Bull's side as you might
think, even with you bein' who you are. He's known for braggin'
and showin' off, and not everybody cares for it. I'll lay a wager,
when you and Bull come to play it out you'll find more on your
side than his."

"When what?"

"When you come to play it out. Settle it between you." He
had not even looked around.

Wick was up on Sunday at dawn. Two rolls and heated-up
coffee served for breakfast and with his lunch box, provisioned
the night before, in his carrier he was soon on the road—his own
master. He had the world almost to himself, and one so palpably
made to be lived in and enjoyed he had scarcely ever known.
The drabness of Kinston Hollow and the broader valley it
opened into, the depressing, decrepit houses, with the fake-brick
siding and worn, grimy, painted surfaces, the old tires and enam-
eled basins in the streams and the everlasting car bodies did not,
this sunlit morning, seem to count.

Tomorrow, even later today, he knew that his troubles would

confront him as before, but clearly it did not have to be that way. Bicycling along, bathed by the light airs of morning, he reverted to the thoughts he had had persistently since leaving Tenent's bar-grill: thoughts of escape; removal to a place where there was happiness. The morning assured him that there was such a place, and that if he followed its path he would be led to it.

The quickest way to reach real country, away from all the ugliness, was, he judged, to follow the route he and Jack took every morning but to keep on past their turn-off. In an hour he had come to it and put behind him the blasted hillsides. There were side roads as he went along, but without any special decision to do so he guided on a ridge that stood out among the hills for both height and length and was further set apart by a crown of bare rock. It had been pointed out to him as the highest in this part of the state. Its name, which the mood of the morning caused him to repeat to himself like an incantation, was Winespring Mountain.

The resistance of the pedals grew as the valley walls came closer, but here the houses stood at wider intervals and had bigger garden plots. Where the road skirted the mountain he came upon two men working a narrow coal seam at its base, lying on their sides to hack at it with pickaxes: a dog-mine.

He had gone nearly five miles by his cyclometer from the familiar turn-off when the highway curved away from the mountain toward which he was headed. In order to keep it before him he wheeled onto a rutted dirt road. On its left, at the foot of the wooded hillside, a wonderfully clean stream swirled along. On the other, the road was shut in by a brushy bank. Soon the tangled growth on both sides closed in completely and, to his astonishment, the road turned into the firm sandy bed of the stream. He managed to keep in shallow water but was just as glad when the corridor through the vegetation widened and the road reestablished itself on dry land. After a hard pull, he came out of the constricted neck of a narrow valley to a fenced pasture where two small black-and-white cows were grazing, slashing at flies with their tails, and on the other side of the stream stood a small group of farm buildings, reached from the road by a lane that forded the stream and by a footbridge above it. The white farmhouse was a log cabin with a conventional addition. The other buildings, a barn with a roof that flared out over the open sides, a shed and a little hut on posts, were unpainted and showed their age. There was a motley flock of chickens under the last, washing on a line, and smoke rising from the rough stone chimney at the end of the house: a mountain farm of the Southern Appalachians. Only a hefty, flat-bed red truck was out of keeping. A rooster reared up and clucked aggressively as he passed. For the rest, all was quiet but for the liquid muttering of the stream and the sporadic singing of birds.

In a few minutes he came to another homestead more like those he was used to, run down, with pieces of junk in the yard. A red-spotted white hound barked, half-howling, and came loping toward him. "H'yar, boy!" A lean young man in overalls stood beside a shed that housed a saw-mill, its circular saw operated by a belt from a salvaged car motor. The dog trotted after Wick without closing in, head low, neck outstretched, while its master stood watching, a stick in one hand, a knife in the other. Self-consciously, Wick pedaled on.

He was nearing the base of Winespring, but as the woods closed in once more the road became overgrown and he turned back. He was hungry and thought he would like to eat his lunch looking at the white-washed farmhouse down below, with its smoking chimney, its vegetable garden and drowsy chickens. He coasted past the place with the saw-mill and the barking hound, eyes straight ahead. Above the Sherrod-Barrows farm—those were the names lettered on the mailbox—he found a stone to sit on.

He had no more than unwrapped his sandwich when a girl came out of the house, with a basket against her hip, walking slowly toward the clothesline. He noticed that a small chicken had left the flock and was tagging along behind her as fast as a maimed leg would permit, and that the girl paid no attention to it until it let out a demanding squawk. Apparently she had been waiting for this, for she turned and crouched down, smiling, holding out her cupped hand into which the chicken pecked avidly.

She was a beautiful girl. That could be seen even at a distance. Beautiful and young, less than his age, he guessed. She was slim, with brown hair that tumbled to her shoulders. She had an oval face and a mouth, he thought, accustomed to smiling, and when she stood up once more the awareness of her attractiveness swept through him so intensely as to be painful. There surely was something about her that was different from other mortals.

She went to the line and commenced gathering the clothes into the basket. The line was high, and reaching up to it raised her meager dress, exposing the loveliness of her legs. He was conscience-stricken at his interest in them, at his taking advantage of her unawareness of his presence, for she was doubtless of a far higher order than he. She seemed formed with such delicacy, with so loving a creator's touch, as to pierce the heart. A disquieting sound came to him of singing or humming in barely audible snatches. He could tell that her thoughts were not on what she was doing, for she gave the clothesline not so much as a glance, her mind being, as his heightened faculties told him, on something that made her glad; and what more natural that it should be someone she was in love with? To give him hope, she would have had to be in dire need of help. He longed to do her some dangerous service.

When she returned, at a dreamily lingering pace, to the house, his impression of one largely unaware of her surroudings was intensified.

He took up his sandwich but had only partly eaten it when a mud-spattered truck he had seen beside the saw-mill rattled down the road. As it came past him, fender flapping, both driver and passenger eyed him; either could have been the man he had seen. The truck halted, then backed up to where he was sitting. The driver leaned forward to examine him. "By God, you're right," he muttered.

They had recognized him. He must have seen them before somewhere. At Tenent's. Yes—those broad, low cheekbones and wild, gray eyes. . . . They were brothers, obviously.

"Watcha doin' h'yar?" The faces were hard.

"I been takin' a ride." Wick intended an even tone, but his voice had not been used since the day before. He slowly raised the last half of his sandwich and took a bite from it.

"You been takin' a ride. Well, you jest ride right back outa h'yar."

"And stay out!"

Since they had not piled out of the truck, they probably were not going to. Wick's eyes shifted briefly to the tranquil little farm. "It's a public road, ain't it?"

"Hit's a public road, yeah," said the driver in a raised voice. "Public fer people who live on it. But not fer no mine people, and sure as hell not fer no mine pres'dent's whelp!"

Wick swallowed—the mouthful went down hard—and waited. He was aware of a certain indecision in the others. There was nothing undecided about the animosity in their faces, though. It passed all reason.

The nearer one turned to the driver and murmured, "We gotta git." To Wick he said, "When we come back—and we ain't gona be gone long—we don't want to find you h'yar. And we don't want to see nor hair nor hide of you around h'yar agin. I don't keer how many deeds your old man holds."

The truck lurched forward.

They had some crazy idea about his father, evidently. It ought not to be hard to set them right, if they gave him a chance.

He saw that a man had come out of the house, one old enough to be the girl's father. He waited until his back was turned, then stuffed the lunch box into the carrier, vaulted onto the bicycle and pedaled off, without looking back.

At the end of the dirt road a sign in freehand lettering, which he had scarcely noticed on the way up, told him he had been in Oak Lick Hollow.

In the morning Mr. DeSalla said, "I don't want to keep you sawing these lousy trees all the time. And lugging them. But I got to have a catchment down below there if I want to keep out of trouble." He glanced at Wick doubtfully and then undertook, with a patience the boy had not observed in him before, to explain how trees and brush were to be cut and piled in the bottom of the draw to slow the rush of water from any cloudburst; the object was both to cause the torrent to drop part of its load of rocks and mud, thus forming a dam, and to lessen the further damage it was capable of.

Wick said he didn't mind the job. His muscles were toughening up, he felt with pride, and he was glad of work that kept him off on his own. Like a day in spring, the existence of the girl transfigured everything. He had only to turn to his picture of her and the landscape in his mind was permeated by a sweet and fragrant softness.

Between him and other people, moreover, there was now the wall of constraint. The exception was Jack, of course. On the

35

way home, Jack even proposed that Wick accompany him back to the roadhouse. "Got to have a little fun," he pointed out. "And you wouldn't want folks to think Bull Turner's got you on the run. That wouldn't do." Without comment, Wick watched him drive, head high and with undiminished speed, through a stop sign onto the main highway. "And I heard Gilley Huff is back, so he might be there," he resumed.

"Who is he?"

"Gilley Huff? He's a teacher at Thornton High. Teaches English or history, or something. Anyway, he's a talker. I mean a *reeeeee-al* talker."

Farther on Wick said, "When you were talking about Turner and spoke of 'playing it out,' just what did you have in mind?"

"Oh well. I didn't mean no fight to the death. Just a bare-hands set-to, to settle it between you. 'Course Turner's a lot stronger than you. But he's not too fast, and if you could work it for when he's liquored up, I reckon you might get him tired of it without you getting too much hurt. You wouldn't want to get him really riled, though." Wick decided not to ask why it had to come to such a showdown. Perhaps the less said the likelier the matter would be to blow over.

In the end he went along. Because it was true: If he was going to remain in Garrett County he would have to face people.

"That's him," Jack murmured as Wick held the Tenents' screen door open for him. "That's sure-enough Gilley."

Wick had forgotten about the promised talker, but he was glad that someone else had the crowd's attention while they made their way to their table.

Gilley was saying, "You can take my word for it. It's even worse-looking when you've been away." He was on his feet, a short, stocky figure with a small nose but a prominent one and red hair, sandier red than Roger Tenent's and almost kinky.

"Watcha come back for then, Gilley?" The speaker was grinning.

"Because I'm as dumb as you all are!" the teacher cried. That startled Wick. He knew you just didn't talk in any such way to these mountain people. But to his surprise, the assemblage appeared to be tickled by the insult.

"Even dumber! Because I ought to know better. I've been to college. I've been given opportunities. And why? Because my parents had the sense to get out of here when I was five years old."

"Where you done made your mistake to begin with was to come back!"

"And *that's* the truth! I came to have a look at the place I'd come from. And what did I find? All these Gilleys and Huffs scattered over the hills under dollar-fifty gravestones. Though it's a mystery why that should have given the place a hold on me. Considering how many of them were probably there with lead rounds between their ribs." He had on a tie and coat, but his tie was askew and his lightweight suit pulled out of shape and bulging in the pockets. About thirty, perky and full of gusto, he looked as if he would bounce if he were dropped.

"And jest as many with powder grains in their thumbs from lettin' fly with jest them rounds."

"I wouldn't doubt it! Great ones for killing and getting killed —that's us. Outsiders come in and make off with everything of value in the Cumberlands for a hundred years and we don't notice it. Cut off back in the coves and hollers, rubbing each other the wrong way—we couldn't get together on anything. Even religion. Especially religion. And the war. The rest of the country mostly stopped fighting the Civil War with Lee's surrender. But not us. Not we proud, God-fearing, independent, self-reliant frontiersmen of the Southern Appalachians. Union supporters and Confederate supporters and the sons and grandsons of Union supporters and sons and grandsons of Confederate supporters, letting each other have it from ambush or through a window at night. And if it wasn't that inherited bitterness, it was a dead cow or some timber cut on the wrong side of a property line. Talk about the Wild West! The Wild West was peaceable compared with the Cumberlands. How many got killed in the battle of the O.K. Corral? Three or four. Why, the Rowan County feud claimed eighty-five to a hundred killed before it ran its course.

"And all the while, the outsiders were skinning us. That was before they began to want our coal. It was the forests they were after then. Oaks, hickories, poplars, beeches, ash, six and seven

37

feet through at the butt. Growing so close together the sun never came through their tops. Hundreds of dollars' worth of prime, knot-free lumber in each one. And we let them go for fifty cents each on the stump. Till there were none left anywhere. We couldn't even hang on to just one stand of the old giants to remind us of what it was once like here. Oh yes, one time there was an appeal to set up a park to protect a grove of the survivors. Yes, and the state legislature laughed at it, and *we* sure didn't do anything. Better to get a few crumbs the lumber companies tossed us and let the trees go."

"All the same, our granddaddies missed some. They's still a few of them big sticks left over on t'other side of Winespring, hid away."

Wick looked in the direction of the voice. Leaning with their backs against the counter were the two brothers from beyond the Sherrod-Barrows farm. One of them threw back a glass and shot its contents down his throat, as down an open pipe. They did not appear at all baneful and seemed younger than Wick remembered them.

"Lead me to 'em, boy, lead me to 'em!"

Laughter followed this sally from the back of the room. But it meant no unkindness to Gilley Huff. Good-humored faces were turned expectantly toward him, and it was evident that he was held in respect and affection.

"Ain't no use cryin' over spilt milk, Gilley. Tell the menfolks how they kin make money *now*." The young woman who had spoken pressed farther back in her chair, flushed but exhilarated by her audacity.

The laughs died quickly this time, because it appeared Gilley Huff did not fully share in the mirth. He seemed to deliberate with himself, then to come to a decision. "Maybe you'd like to hear instead about milk there *is* a use weeping over? Some that's *going* to be spilt?" His tone had leveled. "Not that we haven't seen plenty of its kind spilt already. Enough so that maybe it won't bother us to see it go on—so long as it's over in another holler. The news was on the radio just before I came here. In case you haven't heard it." His small eyes swept the faces turned toward him with what struck Wick as a momentary sad detachment before he went on in an ordinary voice. "The Second Circuit Court has handed down its ruling on broad-form deeds."

His eyes rested on Wick for the briefest instant. "It has found them legal and binding."

The boy did not make the connection immediately. He had been thinking that a kind of game was going on. But the game had taken a serious turn; the silence was tense. While the teacher waited, apparently unfazed, some of his listeners sought the eyes of others and the rest seemed to avoid seeing anyone.

"Anybody expected anything else, he must be a fool!" a voice exclaimed.

"Well, damn them!" This came, at almost the same time, from one of the brothers by the counter, and Wick suddenly remembered what had been said of deeds the day before. Confused, he met the man's angry stare, then found that others had turned to look at him, including an older, drawn-looking man at their table, a friend of Jack's.

"Yes, sir, legal and binding in every respect." Standing with his hands thrust deep in his pockets, the teacher surveyed his audience with a seeming satisfaction. "So we know what's in store, don't we? More hills torn apart, and then more—bulldozed from top to bottom, back to fifty-foot highwalls, the spoil dumped off the side, onto cropland and pasture, into the streams. Anything that's in the way of the bulldozer—over the side with it, and good riddance. Down into the holler. A hillside lot a man's family may have planted for a hundred years—over the side if it's in the way. Down the slope in a landslide of dirt and stones!

"There's no use objecting to it, is there? Not if your grandfather signed one of those pieces of paper. To object would only annoy the strippers, and the strippers have the law on their side. The judges say so. And the judges are learned men. They're not like us backward hillbillies, half of whom haven't even got indoor plumbing. Besides, we're independent, self-reliant, God-fearing people up here, the purest Anglo-Saxon stock in the country. We can look after ourselves. We can grow corn and potatoes on the rubble that's left."

"Gilley," Mr. Tenent called from behind the counter, "when're you going to let the business of this place start up again?" But, as usual, the owner seemed to be enjoying life. He might have been the provider of a successful floor-show.

"When the customers are good and dry. When they'll be glad to pay even Tenent's price for refreshments. And by the way, boys and girls, some of you have been here quite a while, and if you need to be excused just raise your hands with two fingers up. . . . Roger, where was I when you interrupted me?"

"You had us growing corn and potatoes on the ruins."

"Including of course the ruins of the hills acquired outright from our gullible forebears at a twentieth part of their worth. If you like to see mountains ripped open, forests turned into kindling, and bottomland into mudflats . . . if you like to see that, stick around. See what the latest in bulldozers can do when they're given their head. With patience you'll find as much of Garrett, Clayton and Hawkins counties at the bottom of the Gulf of Mexico as where they started out."

"Huff, I say you're all mixed up." Bull Turner was sprawled back in his chair. He was like a monarch for whose entertainment this had all been arranged—and to no avail. "Ain't a thing wrong with 'dozers."

"Not a thing!" exclaimed the teacher, catching up the words. "Especially if you're in the driver's seat and aren't worried about what's in front of the blade."

As Turner pondered this, Wick thought: the Minotaur. He was glad of Gilley Huff and glad he seemed to belie his appearance of a comic Scotsman.

"Yeah. I'm a heavy-equipment man. I don't mind admittin' it. But you know as well as me: pay envelopes follows the 'dozer. Take away the 'dozers and what'd you have here?" He held up his hand to keep Gilley quiet. "You tell me how many more on the Welfare there'd be than now. All that talk about dirt and trees goin' down the mountainside! What of it? What's land for if it ain't to get some good out of? Man, I tell you, there ain't a piece a land in the world if I owned it I wouldn't be agreeable to see a 'dozer turn it upside down, if I was paid right." Turner's tongue was thick.

"You've convinced me." The teacher's head had been cocked at the ceiling. "And maybe you'll just let the landowners in on the secret of getting paid right. We'll take up some other time what we do when there's nothing left to bulldoze."

Turner held up his glass and, with one side of his face screwed up, sighted off across it. "If you want to know . . . if you want to know how the landowners can get a better deal, well. . . . That's one of them that runs everything in this part of the country. He's sittin' right over there."

Feeling like a spectator at a play who is suddenly made part of the cast, Wick saw the teacher turn to him.

"Anything you'd like to offer on the subject, Carter?"

Wick shifted in his chair. "I don't really know what you're talking about."

"Can't hear back on this side!" Turner was grinning at his followers.

Gilley Huff's expression was polite but noncommittal. It crossed Wick's mind that the teacher had known who he was. He said, "If a farmer doesn't want his land bulldozed, I don't see why he can't prevent it. If it's his land."

There was a whoop, a few laughs, some sounds of derision.

Gilley stared at him. "Do you mean to say you don't know what broad-form deeds are? Deeds to mineral rights?"

"I never heard of them." This reply received the same reception as the other. But he had managed to separate himself a little from the scene. Beside him, in his mind, stood the girl, the two of them apart from the world.

The teacher drifted over, examined Wick's face. Turning to the room, he said, "Maybe there are things in *his* part of the country *we* haven't heard of!"

"Well, tell him what the deeds are, Gilley. He's in this part of the country now." One of the brothers had spoken.

"I'll do that," Huff declared. "Landlord, the floor is yours. Look to your spigots! Put a slug in the jukebox." He took a chair from Wick's table, spun it back to front and straddled it. "If you're wondering where I fit into things," he said to Wick, "I can tell you that every Christmas, no matter where I am, I'm asked to dress up and play Santa Claus. One of these days I'm going to abscond with the presents. . . . I'm Gilley to everybody, as you'll have heard."

The boy replied warily, "I'm called Wick."

"You're an unexpected addition to local society. And if I've got it straight, you've accomplished a remarkable feat. You've succeeded in getting on the wrong side of the president of Allegheny-Keystone for un-Alleghenian, un-Keystonian activities while incurring the suspicion of the miners fraternity hereabouts as the agent of that very same president, not to say his son, and the suspicion of the farmers, to whom your bicycle looks like the first piece of invading mine machinery."

The boy stared. "I'm used to not caring what people think,"

41

he said, his face unconsciously reflecting the picture that had flickered across his mind of a resolute figure striding forth upon untrod paths. "Jack, could I bum a cigarette from you?"

But he had not smoked in over a week, and the effort not to cough brought the blood to his face and tears to his eyes.

Gilley said, "I've heard you've got plenty of pluck anyway."

"And that's the truth!" Jack spoke warmly. Wick realized that his coworker had assumed sponsorship of him just by not cutting him loose.

Frank, too, perhaps, for he concurred, "He's got nerve, all right!"

Wick drew a deep, exploratory breath; the spasm was past. The others were looking at him. "You're apt to do anything if you don't think," he said roughly, then asked the teacher, "Who were the farmers you were talking about? Was it those two up front there?"

Gilley tipped forward to see. "The Fergusons? Perhaps indirectly. But I wouldn't take any of it personally, including anything I've said." After a moment he added, "Of course, there's strip-mining pushing out into the next holler from Oak Lick, where the Fergusons live," and then, drily, "That naturally makes them a little excitable."

"I seen them with a bunch over there last week," Frank said, leaning forward, sharp-beaked, "if you're talking about Gorton Holler. I tell you, the way they looked at me, I was right glad to get out. You ask me, there's going to be trouble."

"Well, now, Frank," Jack said, "you go after trouble like a chicken after a worm. Things get worked out."

"They get worked out," said the elderly miner, who, it appeared, was convalescing from an illness and conserving his strength, "with the people in the hollers gettin' worked over again. Ask Gilley."

Wick said, "What're the deeds you were talking about?"

The teacher said after a second or two, "About the turn of the century the coal companies started waking up to what lay under all that shale in the Cumberland Mountains. And you can bet they weren't going to overlook it. Not with industry booming and the railroads and steelmills crying for fuel." He withdrew his hand from his coat pocket, a cake of unwrapped soap in it. "So they sent their agents in to buy it up. Coal was what they were after, and one way and the other they got it just about all sewed up. Where they didn't buy the land, or couldn't, they bought the mineral rights. The people who lived on the land and owned it were out of touch with the world, often couldn't read, and had no idea what the mineral rights would be worth. They let them go for a few dollars an acre—an acre containing coal worth up to fifty thousand dollars or more. But that was only part of it."

Not only were the others at the table following the speaker closely, though all he was saying must have been common knowledge, but their neighbors were making an effort to hear above the jukebox.

"In those days coal-mining was by shaft. So when they deeded away the mineral rights to their land empowering the purchaser to do all necessary to extract the coal—that's what's meant by broad-form deeds—what they had in mind was permitting the company to clear a road, sink a shaft and mine out galleries from the shaft underground. That was all the coal company had in mind doing, for that matter. And the landowner didn't stand to suffer much from that kind of invasion of his property. In fact, it almost seemed as if he were getting something for nothing. And several hundred dollars in cash, which is maybe what the total transaction amounted to, looked mighty big back in these hills, where even a horse and wagon could often hardly get through.

"Yes," the teacher interrupted himself, drawing the word out as Wick's expression betrayed that he perceived where this was leading. "Times change, and power-shovels and bulldozers appear on the scene. After World War Two it becomes possible and profitable to mine the coal near the surface *from* the surface. Extremely profitable. You just strip off everything down to the seam and shovel the coal into trucks or auger it out. The fact that the surface and anything on it—the value of the land—is destroyed in the process makes no difference. It's just too bad for the man whose land it is. The courts in this state, with Olympian majesty, hold that the deeds convey the privilege of destroying land and landowner, if that's what it takes to get at the coal."

Wick would not permit himself, or could not bring himself, to ask whether Allegheny-Keystone held deeds to much land in the vicinity. Instead, he said, "Why don't the farmers get organized and fight the strip-miners?"

The effect of his question startled him. The teacher laid his head back with his mouth open, as if he were struggling for air . . . and also looking to the Deity for witness. Lowering his head, his blue-gray eyes slightly red-rimmed, he spoke in measured words, "Here a coal-company president's son asks the question I am wearing my car out and wearing myself out driving around these hills trying to get the farmers to ask. He asks it right off the bat, as a matter of course." He turned an amused and ironical gaze on the boy. "How long are you going to be around here, Wick?"

"I? I . . . I don't know. All summer, I guess—anyhow."

The teacher consulted his watch. "I've got to run. Why don't you meet me for dinner one of these days, when you've got nothing better to do? . . ."

"I'd be proud to. Anytime." He paused, flustered. "I mean, anytime after tomorrow."

"Then the evening after that," said Gilley. "Lafayette café."

Looking after the departing teacher, Wick said to himself, 'I've been taken up by an insider, maybe the insider-most of them all.' But, left now to his reveries, he thought mostly of the next day. He had made up his mind to return to Oak Lick Hollow directly after work. Five hours of daylight would still be left, and he could meet the girl by presenting himself at the door and asking directions.

In the morning, accepting incuriously his explanation that he wanted to see the country, Jack let him stow his bicycle in the trunk of the car with the lid tied down on it. On the way home he let him out on the highway, from which there was only a forty-five-minute ride.

Trailing exhaust fumes, more cars were on the road than on Sunday, and the strong sun and inert heat made the scenes he passed seem jaded and dimmed the mountains with a bluish film. The day was sullied from usage. Probably he would find that the Oak Lick Hollow he remembered was mostly the work of his imagination. The girl, too. The very avidity of his dreams now made the expedition seem asinine. The grade felt greater than before and he was tired.

But the dirt road was as he recalled. The stream was still curling clean around the boulders in its path beneath the low-sweeping evergreens; these, he noticed, had closer, shorter needles and were more feathery than the scrubby, open pines that were common elsewhere. His spirits rose and he batted away a biting fly without irritation. When he reached the open pastureland and saw the farm in repose ahead of him, his expectations had recovered, compounded though they were with growing qualms. One of these was caused by the sound of a straining, unmuffled motor emerging from the woods behind him.

It could be, he thought, the red truck he had seen here before and which was missing today. But when he looked back he saw that the odd chance had befallen him and that it was the Fergusons'. Feeling almost unbearably exposed, he pedaled on, steering to the edge of the road. The truck passed him and pulled up ahead of him, almost at the lane to the farm. The doors opened simultaneously, like ears swinging forward, and together the occupants stepped out.

His way blocked, Wick dismounted.

"I thought we done told you to stay outa h'yar!"

"I'm not doin' you any harm." He felt, with no reason, more secure for having the bicycle between them, with the handlebars to hold.

"We never ast you if you was doin' us any harm," said one. "You ain't a-goin' to git no chance to do us none. We told you to stay outa h'yar. Now git."

Wick did not move.

"We'll give you a count of ten to turn that bicycle around and take outa h'yar as fast as you come. Faster."

"You got no reason to be unfriendly!" Wick declared. But he knew it was now past words. He watched the one who was counting—the older brother. His green eyes were hard as bottle-glass. As if there were all the time in the world he noted the scar on the side of the nose and the individual whiskers of the day's growth on the triangular jaw.

"Tin!" The man stepped forward and grasped the bicycle's handlebars, and yanked. Wick held on, bracing, then felt himself seized from behind by the second brother. There was a smell of alcohol and sweat. Rather than see his bicycle wrecked, Wick let go, and the older brother, tugging, went over on his back, the bicycle on top of him.

Throwing it off, he got to his feet "Why, you sonofabitch!" He drew back and swung, and the boy, held fast, caught the tearing blow on his cheek. Released, a blow from behind on the same

45

side of his face sent him spinning. Catching himself before he fell, he turned to face his assailants. To fight back, he knew, would avail him nothing, but he aimed a fist at an onrushing face. It was a short jab without much force, but his knuckles struck the other's nose and took the drive out of his lunge. Wick would have kept his feet but for a kick from the rear. His leg buckled, he went down and they were on him. Futilely bucking and twisting, he could do nothing to protect himself but cover his face with his arms. It was not their initial hostility they were venting on him now; they were aroused by the fight itself, he knew, and goaded by his helplessness. The weight on him was worse than the blow. He caught a glimpse of a strange face above his, a savage's—no, it was blood that transformed it. Then one grabbed hold of his hair, yanked his head up and slammed it back down. His skull struck the stone beneath it, lights shot across his blackened field of vision and a taste of metal filled his mouth.

That was all. The weight was lifted from him. There was quiet. He rolled over on his side, his head on his arm. His lungs were laboring. He could not move. Insofar as he was conscious of anything beyond pain and finality, he thought he was alone. Thus the sound of a voice close by confused him.

"Oh, Lord, h'yar comes Letty. . . . Let's git goin'. . . . We stay h'yar . . . you know what we'll be in fer."

"What about *him*?"

"What *about* him?"

"OK, let's go."

He heard the truck's doors slam and its roar and rattle.

As his mind cleared he thought of his life as it had been and as it was. But there was nothing he could fasten to and be hopeful about, nothing to offset the ache of body and heart. There was only the girl that had brought him here, and his thoughts drew back from her, as from the mirror of defeat. And two dry sobs broke from him, griping him.

"Are you hurt bad?"

He did not know what to make of the anxious, gentle voice.

"Cain't you h'yeer me? Cain't you tell me if you're hurt?"

He rolled partway over and opened his eyes. Blinking, he saw the girl from the farm.

"Oh." He pushed himself up and, ashamed, wiped his face on his sleeve. He stared at her. She was sitting back on her heels, her hands between her thighs, and was like a holy creature from another world. It was her eyes that held him. They were green around the pupils but otherwise a golden tawny, and soft—soft and shy; they did not quite meet his. From her face and position, her shoulders bent forward as if she were chilled, it seemed that a curious, helpless, anxious agitation possessed her. Taking courage from her evident timidity, he said, "I'm all right," bothered that his breath was still coming in gasps and wondering what he looked like.

"I h'yurd from the house what was goin' on. And the truck. I knowed hit was Hamp and Rafe." She clasped her hands together and leaned forward as if listening for something.

The dark hair, shot with gold in the late sun, fell lightly and softly and the face it framed—the straight nose, the delicately curved cheeks, the mobile lips above the pointed chin—seemed to be expressive of an ultimate truth. He proclaimed, "It took two of them. If there'd been only one, it'd have been different, I can tell you."

"Hamp come over and told us about you—about seein' you here on Sunday. You're Sedwidge Carter, ain't you—aren't you?"

"*Sedg*widge—Sedg*wick*, that is. Wick is what I'm called." With that lovely concerned face before him, he almost rejoiced in his pains and lacerations—wounds of a martyr to the faith.

"I'm called Letty. How old are you . . . Wick?"

Eighteen, he told her, and she said she was a year younger. "Hamp said they done told you not to come back h'yar. I know how mean they kin be, though they *are* my cousins. They don't mean to do no wrong—they're good boys, they honest-to-goodness are—but they git carried away. We thought with the warnin' they give you, you wouldn't be comin' back." She had slid off her heels and was sitting on the ground, her legs drawn up beside her, one hand pressed palm-down on the earth, the other clutching the hem of her skirt, her face lowered. "What brung you?"

"You did."

She started but without looking up. He waited, paralyzed. A stranger must have taken possession of him, for him to have spoken so. No, it was that the combination of her princess's beauty —her rough and shabby dress made no difference—and her mountain speech had thrown him off guard.

After a moment, her head bent lower, she said incredulously, "*I* did?"

He had committed himself beyond drawing back. "I was watch-

47

ing you on Sunday, when you were taking the clothes in from the line. I thought maybe I could make friends with you."

"We've mighty good well water!" she exclaimed, raising her eyes almost to the level of his own. "And if you're bleedin' anywhere. . . . Are you?"

He made a sound of amusement. "I guess you could see if I am better than I can. Am I?"

She raised her eyes the rest of the way but looked a little past him. She said, "Cain't you *tell* I'm blind?"

4

THE NEXT DAY he reviewed the scene repeatedly, but not because he enjoyed it. On the contrary, it affected him with miserable discomfort.

I'm blind. He had been overwhelmed with embarrassment and with pity, repelled, frightened. He would have liked above all not to have been there. From that moment he had been unable to think of the emotions he had nursed about her without an intense desire to hide from himself. He had been duped, not by her, of course—though deep inside he held it against her that, disqualified as she was, she had stirred such thoughts in him—but by fate. He had been made a fool of.

Can't you tell I'm blind? He had not known how to reply. He had said something like "Oh. No. I didn't know." What more could he have said? Her being blind was such an enormous, terrible thing. You could not talk about someone's blindness. He had left it up to her to break the lengthening silence; what a performance he had given!

She had said, "I'm used to it. I been . . . this way since I was ten." It was he, by the way he had sat tongue-tied, that had made it impossible for her to use the word *blind* again. He had asked her if she had always lived where she was and she had said no, they had lived some ways off till she was nine and then they'd moved to the city—Dayton. But after a year of it they reckoned the country was the place for them and they'd come here; the farm had belonged to her grandparents. Then she said they were forgetting about how bad he might be hurt. But his hurts, even the aching of his head, had come to seem not to matter.

When he had dismissed the subject she had asked him about himself. She had seemed to want to hang her head yet to feel that she should not, but when she raised it she did so only tentatively,

49

and he could guess why. If she tried to look him in the eyes, as was natural when you were talking to someone, she wouldn't know exactly where to look. It may have been, too, that she didn't want him to look into her eyes, now that he knew they were unseeing. Yet you would have thought she was almost smiling. She had a rather wide mouth, as he had heard generous people were apt to have.

He had told her where he lived and what kind of work he did, but though she seemed absorbed, listening with her lips parted, he felt driven to make an end. She still sat holding the hem of her skirt down to a little above the knees. He thought how it must be for a blind girl, never knowing where her dress was, unless she felt it—but then for a blind girl it wouldn't seem to matter so much.

A woman, her mother, had called from the porch of the house: "*Let-ty*!" Turning, the girl had answered in a voice that was clear and mild even when raised that she would be back soon. The mother had remained for a moment looking at them. Just then the girl had lifted her head and announced that her uncle was coming up the road in his truck. Wick heard it, too, when he listened, but could not imagine how she distinguished it from other trucks.

He had been about to say that he had to go, but she had spoken first. She was going to tell Uncle Tom to bless out those Ferguson boys and make sure they wouldn't give him any more trouble. It wasn't right for him not to be able to ride on any road in these mountains he wanted to. And there was lots to see hereabouts in Oak Lick Hollow. There was a big old coon that came out of the woods right up to their house to be fed, and when the cool air came drifting down from the mountain at sundown, sometimes the hoot owls would call to each other across the cove, human and inhuman at the same time, so that you wanted to laugh even while your scalp crept.

The truck had drawn up alongside them and Letty had turned and said, "Uncle Tom, you know about Hamp tellin' us about the boy he run into? This is him, Sedgwick Carter. Hamp and Rafe done jump him and he won't say how bad they hurt him. They run off when they seen me comin', and they was smart!"

It was a good deal for the man in the cab to take in all at once. He resembled the Fergusons, especially in his gray-green eyes and

50

the impression they gave of impaling you without really seeing who you were. But his face was narrower, more like Letty's, and the bones under it stood out more sharply. Beneath his gray shirt and blue overalls, his body appeared to be all long muscles and sinews. A young boy, dark-haired and dark-eyed, had craned around him to scrutinize Wick impassively.

"Evenin'," the man had said with a nod, his eyes on the side of Wick's head. Wick, who had got to his feet, echoed the greeting. He had not been able to tell whether the look in those eyes was apprehensive or fierce. And when the other had asked whether they had given him a bad time, he could not tell where the man's sympathies lay. Wick had said it could have been worse and then had added that he had been just about to go—he had to, to get home before dark. Addressing his niece, the man had said, "He don't look too bad. But I could put his bicycle on the back and drive him whar he's goin'." Letty had appeared a little crestfallen when he had insisted he didn't want to be a trouble and didn't need help. Perhaps he had been overemphatic, but he felt so ill at ease he was almost frantic to get away.

He and the girl had been alone again when the truck pulled off. "There's Winespring Mountain here, too," she had said. "I know you seen it lots of times from different places around, but I won't ask you what it looks like, 'cause you got to go. I been to where the trail up it starts with Colly—he's my brother; I reckon you seen him in the truck—and sometime we're goin' to the top." She stopped abruptly, standing with her hands clasped before her, her eyes masked by her lashes and with the faint, private smile that seemed to come naturally to her lips. "But you got to git started. You don't want to be on the highway after dark, with them cars like hornets goin' by."

He agreed quickly and when he had retrieved his bicycle told her goodbye and remembered to thank her for having come out to see if he was all right.

It was a wearisome way back to Kinston Hollow, though he broke the trip at Taulbee's combination gas-station-and-grocery-store, where he devoured some cold-cuts, crackers and milk. The beating he had taken no longer preyed greatly on his mind; there had been two against one, and even at that he had drawn blood. But he could not disentangle himself from what had followed. Often as he relived it, he could find no way of regarding it that would permit him to put it behind him as finished. It remained unsettled in his mind, yet to be worked out, and like something forgotten, something one knows is important but cannot think how, it gave him no peace. When he awoke in the morning, he had a moment of empty-minded foreboding—and then it descended on him again. It had nothing to do with his stiffness and soreness which, with his cheek as it was, made even smiling a little painful. ("You sure must have taken one hell of a tumble," Jack said, in almost the same words the grocery-store keeper had used the evening before.) Actually, he had tried imagining himself worse hurt and found that he might have been less out of sorts if he had been. But no matter how he tried to see the episode he could not make himself come out of it looking any better.

Ordinarily the day would have stood out as a bright one, for it was marked by Mr. DeSalla's putting him in with Frank to learn how to drive a coal-truck. Most of the trucks were owned by the drivers, but Mr. DeSalla had a few of his own. They were brutes capable of carrying twenty-five tons and costing thirty thousand dollars, and you climbed up into the cab by means of a ladder. " 'Jacobs Motor Brake'," Wick read on a plaque, and then . . . good grief! " '18-speed Quadruplex Transmission with Main Drive in 4th.' *Eighteen speeds!*" Yup, said Frank. There were, he pointed out, two gear shifts between the driver's and passenger's seats and a switch on the dash for an auxiliary range. Wick read the positions on the shifting-diagram: " 'Lo-Lo . . . Hi-Split . . . Lo-Split . . . Direct . . .

Said Frank, "It's not too different from drivin' any other car except you got all them speeds to get the hang of, and you gotta get used to the dimensions and the brakes. And you gotta remember every minute this baby's for real. Nothin's easier than bumpin' a telephone-pole over with her. When you're goin' up a grade with a load you feel you're haulin' a chunk of the earth up with you, and when you're goin' down you know she'd like nothin' better than to cut loose and plow through everything below. . . ." Wick bent his attention to what his instructor was doing; if not that day, his turn would come soon enough. . . .

Jack reminded him on the way home that he was to have dinner with Gilley Huff. Because it was drizzling, he took the bus and was first to arrive at the Lafayette Café—the one owned by an elderly Greek where Gladys was a waitress. The rain had stopped, leaving the sky still full of slow-moving clouds, and he waited outside by the door. In the light breeze, one side of his face was cooler than the other. Footfalls made a smacking, gritty sound on the sidewalk and tires sizzled in the roadway.

He heard, "Hey! Are you all right?" The teacher was standing in front of him.

"Oh. . . . I took a tumble. On my bicycle."

"You sure must have. I was wondering if it left you feeling sick, the way you're standing there with your eyes closed."

Wick's hand went to his forehead. He had been trying to tell what impression a person who could not see would have of a street corner after a rain. He said, "I was resting them."

He wondered what he was doing there, following the busy-looking, slightly bandy-legged figure of the teacher through the restaurant. He felt even more that this did not concern him when his companion, having saluted the owner, Mr. Marika, greeted two of the other patrons and had a short talk with one about his mother.

They had just settled in a booth, on either side of the silver-spangled Formica tabletop, when Gladys pushed through the swinging doors at the rear, spotted them and brought them menus. She said, "I didn't know you two knew each other." If she felt slighted by Wick's having dropped out of sight, she gave no sign of it.

"Of course I know him. As evidently you do," Gilley said. "And if I didn't I'd make sure I did." He thrust the menu at her. "Surprise me. Only keep it under a dollar and a half. And bear in mind that I want ice cream for dessert and not one of your baked apples."

"For a dollar and a half, you'll be surprised, all right." It was a sportiveness she had not displayed with him, Wick reflected.

Surprising himself, he said, "I'll have the same."

"Good man," said Gilley. "When my mother was a girl, she and Gladys were great friends." He dodged a saber-slice with the menu the waitress aimed at him.

When she had gone, he said lightly, "I hope I made it plain that everyone is expected to pay for himself. Which is to say that even though you undoubtedly make more as a mine helper than

I do as a high-school teacher, you won't be expected to sequester the check." He appeared about to change the subject when Wick inquired what else he did.

"I'm a stringer for a wire service. A reporter, that is to say. I cover whatever happens that might be of more than local interest. Usually that means it's sad, if not tragic. For every boy-saves-child-from-drowning, there are a dozen mine accidents, a destructive flood or two resulting from the pillaging of the hillsides and several houses catching fire from defective coal-stoves with three children dying." He looked away to the front of the restaurant. "We never go long without news of that kind. The people here are born to adversity and defeat. Or it would be easy to believe so."

Wick was startled when, at this juncture, Gladys returned to set down a plate of rolls and Gilley with a swift movement and a look of fiendish glee seized her wrist, picked up a roll, sniffed it and released her. "She's insanely jealous of me," he explained. "For a long time I've suspected her of a design to poison me."

The girl had raised her eyes on high in exaggerated patience. "It wouldn't be hard. You never know what you're eating." She turned to Wick. "Once he was eating by himself in here, reading, and after he'd finished his main course the other waitress gave him another customer's by mistake. He was halfway through it before we discovered what she'd done. He'd never have noticed."

"I'd have noticed quick enough if you'd tried to charge me for it," he called after her. He fixed his small, bright eyes musingly on Wick, and with genuine interest asked, "What's the president of a big coal company like? I've often wondered. . . . Probably not a fair question," he added as Wick, recoiling a little, sat silent.

"You mean my father?" His father just *was*. It was other people who were describable, in not being like him in one way or another. "He works terrifically hard. When he's in his study at night working on a pile of papers a cannon could go off next to him and I don't think he'd notice. I've had to go in to speak to him when he's working like that and he's looked at me to begin with as if he'd never seen me before. It'd have been the same if I'd been a giraffe. It's like," he declared, "you and that extra dinner."

"I never thought I'd be likened to the president of Allegheny-Keystone. Tell me, has he got much life outside of business?"

Wick pondered again. "He's the best golfer in the club and only a few of the members, the young ones, can beat him at tennis. Oh—and when there's a drive for a new hospital, anything in the community, they always turn to Father."

"And they think the world of him at the office—the men and women who work for him? . . . Thank you," he said with Wick as Gladys set down their dinners. "Join us, if you don't think it would lower the tone of the establishment."

"If you'll serve the other customers. . . ."

"Yes, they do. His secretary's been with him, well, since before I was born."

"A man like that wouldn't have any real faults or weaknesses," Gilley hazarded.

"No. If he had, he'd get rid of them. The way he gave up smoking."

The teacher regarded him fixedly for a moment.

"If you've got a picture in mind of a kid growing up delinquent because his rich, suburban father was too busy to have time for him, forget it," Wick pursued. "Father's always made time for family things. I'm the one who's always ducked out."

"Have you any brothers or sisters?"

"I have an older sister. She's beautiful. She could have her pick of any of the men around. You wouldn't guess it to look at me—I mean what a knock-out she is."

"Why, I. . . ." Gilley caught himself, screwed up his face scratched his head. "This is chicken. They must have cut the price for us. . . . You know something? I'd like to meet your father. I'd like to say to him, 'Forget you're a businessman.' . . . No, for what I have in mind I'd have to be President of the United States. I'd make him responsible for Appalachia. I'd tell him, 'Take your formidable talents and energy and your connections with the big guns of industry and devote them not to making your coal company an empire but to saving the people here.' "

Visualizing the dreary, cramped valleys, the miles and miles and miles of them, Wick said, "You'd have a selling job."

"And maybe I'd have some selling points. The people back up in the hills here are the nearest thing we've got to the frontiersmen. Here's where you'll find the purest American tradition—and the biggest failure of Americanism. The Southern highlanders are the children of adversity. Their forebears were English yeomen forced off the land into the slums to make way for the nobility's sheep herd. They were poverty-stricken crofters from Scotland, Dissenters who crossed to northern Ireland to escape the heavy hand of the Established Church and had to flee again from further tyrannies."

He went on, intermittently snatching mouthfuls. "Coming to America, they found the East pretty well taken up. So they moved westward, into the great somber wilderness of the Appalachians. They brought little with them besides their hunger for land—and the habit of self-reliance. Sometimes little more than the axe, knife, rifle, cooking-pan and Bible that the mountaineer has been able to make do with for the past two centuries, if he had to.

Wick felt the contrast between the man across the table, who was filled to bursting with so much, and himself as a weight upon him. His life was like so much fluid sloshing this way and that, depending on how the container was tipped. If he were asked what he was all about, the only honest answer he could give would be: sex-desire. Wick Carter was a package for an imagination that would take off for the wild blue yonder at the sight of a girl in one of those summer dresses. . . . And there was yesterday, leaving him restless as a person who cannot find a comfortable spot in bed or whose clothes do not fit.

His thoughts, hardly more than flashes, did not prevent his taking in the discourse aimed at him, under the nub of which he had a sense of being turned and shaped on a lathe. He was a listener by nature, and Gilley had continued. "Game was plentiful to begin with but probably didn't long outlast the Indians. Bottomland was fertile, but when the bottoms were filled up, successive generations were forced farther and farther up the valleys onto poorer and poorer farm land. . . . I'm not boring you with all this, am I?"

"No! Not at all." Wick's only concern was that the teacher had some preposterous hope in connection with his father.

As if in response to his misgivings, Gilley said, "I have a purpose in it. . . . All this time there was wealth in the Cumberlands, prodigious wealth in forests and minerals, waiting for the nation to need them. But the wealth was for outsiders to grasp—

operators with capital and experience and easy consciences or none at all. One of their devices—to give you an idea—was the quitclaim. A land-company agent would inform a mountain farmer that his company held a deed to the land that antedated the mountaineer's and was prepared to go to law to repossess it. The farmer would be intimidated by the prospect of a court fight in the unknown outside world. He'd be glad to settle by granting the company lumber and mineral rights in exchange for an agreement permitting him and his heirs to remain on the land—which was his all along.

"So outsiders looted the wealth, and the highlanders were left with denuded hillsides, wash-outs and floods, shale heaps, polluted streams and dismal mining camps. Yes, jobs for lumbermen and miners were provided by the pillagers. And the slim wages looked good by mountain standards. However, the forest once cut over takes a lifetime to come back. And coal, after the boom days of the First World War, was hit by depression. Unemployment came to the coal towns and came to stay. The union fought its way in to see that the miners got a respectable share of the proceeds from their work. But in return for recognition the union agreed not to fight mechanization. So fewer and fewer men have been needed. And what are the others to do? There's less and less place anywhere for unskilled labor. And these people haven't had any training in skills the world wants.

"Yes, there's been help from the outside. Our relief rolls are the biggest in the country, proportionately. Without the Welfare, as they call it, there'd be mass hunger up here—terrible suffering. But the price of welfare is loss of pride and self-respect—demoralization. . . . Are you resting your eyes again, or am I putting you to sleep?"

Opening his eyes, Wick missed his fellow diner's by about six inches. "No, that's not it." He had been trying to determine how much you missed of a person's conversation if you could not follow his expression. "I was excluding from my mind everything but what you're saying."

Gilley looked dubious. "What *was* I saying?—no, ignore that! Teachers are impossible. They take the classroom everywhere."

"You were talking about demoralization and loss of self-respect. And it made me think of all the trash everywhere, and the old car bodies that everyone just leaves where they are."

57

The other seemed surprised and pleased. "You can't work up interest in a public system of trash-disposal or in cleaning things up. Everyone dumps his trash down the bank of the stream behind the house and relies on the spring floods to wash it away. That's the custom and therefore it's right. And no one's bothered at living in a degrading mess. . . . Thanks, honey," he interjected as Gladys exchanged desserts from a tray for their plates and set coffee before Gilley. "If you stirred it with your finger I wouldn't need sugar." But Gladys only smiled.

Gilley attempted to hitch himself closer to the table—for the nth time—but seat and table formed a unit. "It's a bitter irony. 'Our living ancestors,' the Southern highlanders are often called, and justly. They have the qualities we like to think of as traditionally American—individualism, hardihood, simplicity, affinity for the rugged life. In fact, it's because the American people have developed qualities just the opposite of the highlanders' that they've prospered.

"Americanism is enterprise and organization, and the highlanders are short on the one and psychologically set against the other. It's American to pull up stakes when opportunity beckons. The highlander is strongly attached to his homestead, his valley. It's American to subordinate the present to the future, to put up with dull routines for the sake of rewards to come. The highlander is a creature of the moment. He'll shoot an offender with little concern for the consequences. He's amazingly superior to physical fear, and he needs to feel alive, in the way that only being caught up in happenings can make you feel alive. He'll stand by you if he's your friend, no matter what. And you can depend on his word, also no matter what. That's why the feuds have been so murderous.

"Of course there are those who don't fit the portrait I've been drawing. About two million have left Appalachia and lots of the seven million remaining have taken to life in the up-and-coming Appalachian towns like Harpersburg. But millions are still like fish trapped in shrinking pools."

While Gilley addressed himself to the remainder of his dessert, Wick sat with the echoes of what he had heard sounding in his head. The teacher, he reflected, could not have been trying to sell him on anything. 'If he had been, he'd be scrutinizing me to see how it had gone over.' Conscious, suddenly, of feeling an affection for him, Wick said, "What you're trying to do, talking as you did at Tenent's, is to sting the people around here into doing something for themselves."

"Well . . ." said Gilley with a gesture, his expression giving the boy cause to notice again that a comic face could be peculiarly melancholy—and didn't sensitive comedians take advantage of the fact to get under your skin?—"I can't reach many, and those I reach I doubt that I affect."

"I'll bet you're wrong! And I'll bet you have plenty of effect on your classes at school. I can tell you're used to teaching what you've been telling me."

The other grimaced. "The mark of the teacher! Actually, in this case it's the writer. I have to be careful in the classroom. The school board is leery of me at best. I'll be in serious trouble if the book I'm working on is ever published. I level in on everybody in it—the coal barons, the land companies, the United Mine Workers, the politicians, the churches, the mountain people themselves. No one is spared—except people as individuals. And by the way, if you're ever around when I'm laying into the coal companies, do bear in mind that—"

Here there came an interruption as the restaurant-owner and Gladys paraded up to them, the latter directly behind the former. Mr. Marika said to Gilley, "So. You enjoy your baked apple the way I have cooked it, Mr. Huff?"

The teacher stared at his empty dish with repugnance. "My God. I knew I wasn't enjoying it. I said to myself, 'This ice cream tastes just like a lousy baked apple!' "

"Then we will see how you enjoy something that tastes like what you ordered." Mr. Marika stepped aside and Gladys set a bowl of ice cream before Gilley. "The compliments of the house, of course."

The two were greatly enjoying their joke.

Wick had come to a decision. He would go back to Oak Lick Hollow and put things to rights, somehow.

'Everyone's fond of Gilley,' he thought as proprietor and waitress went off, still chuckling. He said, "The people from around here don't strike me as the kind you can talk to the way you do, and yet you seem to get away with it." He would have liked to hear what Gilley would say about Letty, if he knew her, and the terrible fact of her being blind, but he could not bring himself to mention his having met her.

Gilley, who had been looking sheepish, nodded his head. "You're right. They're not the kind. But with me. . . ." He peered at Wick with an alert yet timid look in his eyes. "Well, first, they take a sneaking satisfaction in hearing me come out with what's in their minds but improper for them to say. It's permissible for me for the same reason that the court jester could get away with impertinences that would have sent a duke to the block. I'm one of them, and yet I'm a freak and outside the rules. Since what I say doesn't count, they can be shocked by it and enjoy it."

Wick would not let the teacher drive him home. ("Next time we'll hear about you," said Gilley in parting.) After seeing him on his way and walking a short distance on his own, he turned back to a drugstore, where he bought a box of chocolates.

The clouds had parted when he descended from the bus and the moon shone through, nearly full, on the pallor-touched ghost of the world around him. He looked toward Winespring, hardly expecting to be able to see it, and was surprised at how its black bulk stood out in the moonlit night—but remote and apart, and unimaginable when you thought of being in the dark forest covering it.

What would he say if Letty actually asked him to describe the mountain? The question was in his mind the next morning, too, as he rode to work with Jack, his bicycle once more in the trunk.

5

IT WAS THE MOTHER who answered to his knock in the late afternoon. Her astonishment when she opened the door added to his self-consciousness. He asked, as if there were not a moment to lose, if Letty was at home. He took in enough to be aware that the woman was erect and had fine features, with dark hair and eyes, like the boy.

"Why, yes." She had quickly recovered herself, had taken in the parcel he painfully held. "We don't have many visitors come as quiet as you. Letty's—"

But Letty herself was beside her then, in the open doorway, drying her hands on a towel. Having come to doubt his first impression of her, he was struck by her beauty all over again, and by the life that shone in her face.

She said, "Hit's Wick, I know. I h'yurd your voice!"

Again as if there were no time even for a breath, he recited the explanation he had prepared, that he had thought he would come see where the trail up Winespring started from, and as long as he was going to be out this way he thought he'd just drop by and thank her again for coming out to the road. Extemporaneously, he added, "I had to leave in such a rush."

"Letty, why don't you take him around and show him the place?" the mother asked. "Comin' from the East, maybe he's never seen a real little old-time farm." She spoke without apology. Her build was a more mature version of her daughter's, her coloring an even tan, her face almost unlined.

"Would you like me to take you around?" Letty asked, shyly eager.

He said he would, though the feeling went through him that perhaps his coming had been a mistake. With that, he remembered the candy he had brought and held it out to her. "I thought you might care for this."

But she made no move to take it until the mother said quickly, "He's got something he wants to give you."

While he turned hot with contrition at his thoughtlessness, she extended her hand and he put the box in it. "It's just a little candy."

"Why, that was real kind of you!" she declared. "Warn't it, Ma?" She held the box gripped in both hands. "Kin I have a piece now?" she asked him. "I got a turrible sweet-tooth."

They all seized on the excuse to laugh, and each had a piece when she had carefully slipped off the string and removed the wrapping. "All my teeth are sweet-tooths, sweet-teeth," said Wick.

"Don't keep him on his feet too long," the mother said. "He's come a long ways and has a long ways to go."

"Let me git some seed. More than likely one of them little beggars will be around."

When she had returned, one hand in a fist, and they had set out from the porch, he asked her what she had meant, and she replied that maybe he'd see. She extended her arm. "Now over yonder on a fencepost there's some bluebirds nestin' in a box Colly made for them. It's the second time for them this yur. And over in the pasture there's a place where the creek widens out and gits deeper, too; you kin heer the fish jump there." Only she pronounced *where* and *there* more like *wh'ar* and *th'ar*. "It's swampy and bushy along the banks. That's one of the best places. There's Red-winged blackbirds that nest there. You know how they sing." She whistled an imitation—two low, hollow notes followed by a rising warble—that startled Wick with its birdlike quality. "And frogs! Peepers as soon as the ice is off fer good, in March." She imitated them too, and he recognized the plaintive little calls. "Later there's one that goes like this." And she made a sound a little like a wire snapping under tension. He had to laugh.

"It's so strange, hearing such sounds from a girl." he explained. "You can sure do imitations."

"I'm glad you think so!" He'd never seen a face to which a glow came so readily. "You'll have to watch out for them thistles we're comin' to, Wick." They were walking slowly toward the barn, the girl on a worn, bare path which he supposed she could follow without trouble. She was in tennis shoes and he was conscious of

62

a bruise on her bare leg. "Uncle keeps wantin' to cut them down, but I won't—"

She broke off as a small bird flew, whirring, close by her head and alighted in a low tree of twisted branches, with small green apples in it.

"That's one of the little beggars. If you just stand still. . . ." She held out her hand and, in a moment, the bird was back, hovering above her hand, then suddenly dropping down, clutching her fingertips. It cocked its head at her, seized a sunflower seed in its short, black bill and scooted off.

She asked him what kind it was and seemed surprised when he did not know. At least he was able to describe it—a small gray bird, nearly white underneath with a little crest and a brownish wash on its sides below its wings. It was perched on a twig of the apple tree with the seed clutched between its feet, hammering at it with its bill.

"Colly never told me about the brown on its sides," she said. "But I call it a peeto-bird from the way it sings—if you could call it singin'. Here, Wick, you take a seed and hold it out and it'll come to you, you'll see."

He put his hand out under hers, then when she failed to release a seed, thought to touch it. It was the first time he had touched her.

The bird that dashed in to take the seed when he offered it was not the one that had been to Letty but an even smaller one with a black cap and a black throat. "It was a different one that came—a chickadee!" he exclaimed, grateful that the name had come to him out of somewhere.

"That's one I know the name of too. I warn't sure—*wasn't* sure—he'd show up. This time of yur, you cain't be sure." There was a lilt of pleasure and pride in her voice. And they stood and fed the birds—the peeto-bird joined by a second—until the seeds were gone.

As they strolled on toward the barn he was struck by her alertness. Even as she explained how the birds were so tame—she had lots of patience, she said—quick little movements of her head indicated that she was sifting the air waves for sounds, and perhaps for scents. But her eyes remained soft and unfocused.

She said suddenly, "Let's git old Roof stirred up!" She clucked

ringingly, "Ta-*ka*, ta-KA-tuk!" and there was an immediate response in kind from behind the barn—identical.

"My gosh," he murmured, as the big rooster he had seen before came loping indignantly around the end of the building.
The girl's happiness at that moment was evident. And again he
thought, with a pang, 'Maybe I shouldn't have come.'

"Course he thinks it's another rooster, a rival. Poor old Roof.
Is he where you kin see him?"

"Oh yes!" He could not remember to make allowances for
her being blind, though he could hardly think of anything else.
"He's standing as tall as he can stretch. And he's glaring around
—with his gold eyes. He's furious. He's so furious he's red in the
jowls!" At the anticipation in her expression he went on. "Now
he's stalking off. He's in a huff. But he told that other rooster
off. He's nodding with every step. Yes, sir. He showed who's
boss around here!" And he could not help sharing in her laughter
of surprised delight.

She seemed to know when they reached the door of the barn,
for she put out her hand to it.

"Here's your little friend, for his hand-out," he said as the
crippled little chicken came hobbling up. When he told her
about having seen her feed it, she laughed, coloring a little. And
he watched with a queer stirring inside as she crouched to offer
the anxious creature a crust she had kept in her hand, her eyelashes long and dark on her cheeks, the skirt of her worn, red
gingham dress touching the ground. He wondered if she knew
what color it was, and if she could remember color.

The gray planks of the barn were so old the grain stood out
like sinews on an aging hand. Inside, there was a packed-earth
floor and a dank cavelike odor combined with one of sour milk.
Straws hung in spiderwebs from the rough plank ceiling above
which, Wick thought, there must be a loft. A pen, full of darting
piglets and a grunting sow, occupied one of the barn's open sides.
"I cain't let myself make friends with the little pigs," Letty
said. And just as he was about to ask why, the reason came to
him.

On the side of the barn opposite the pigs stood some stanch-
ions, the wood worn bright and smooth on the inside. As if
she had been following his eyes, Letty explained that they'd had
more than just two cows before her uncle went into the timber

64

business—spotting trees, buying them on the stump, cutting them down and taking them to the mill. He and Colly were off working now, she added.

She paused, evidently finding it hard to go on. "Wick," she said, as if breaking through an obstruction, "kin I ask you somethin'? It may seem kind of. . . ." She raised her head apprehensively.

Apprehensive himself, but trying not to sound it, he said she could.

"I don't know how you look, excep' for what the menfolks done told me, and that's not much help. And it makes you feel funny, not knowin' what another person looks like. I could tell, if I could touch your face."

Her embarrassment, vividly mounting, relieved him of his. He was saying he didn't mind just as she faltered, "I mean, you know what *I* look like." He was thinking that so long as no one could see. . . .

"You'll have to hold the candy. . . ."

When he had placed himself before her, in a curious suspense, her hands found his shoulders, then rose to his cheeks. He closed his eyes. Her fingertips moved over his face, lingered just below his right cheekbone. He felt the side of his face stroked lightly. It could have been a moth. "Those boys sure did hit you," she murmured. He replied in a croaking voice that it wasn't anything.

When the touch left his face and he opened his eyes she was so close to him, before she turned aside, that he could see the satiny sheen on the delicate blue-white skin of her eyelids.

"Well, Mr. Carter," she said, "I kin tell you one thing. You don't have no trouble gittin' yourself girls. Least you shouldn't."

Genuinely surprised, he scoffed at the idea, but not so vigorously as to put it beyond the bounds of possibility.

"I got a cousin who's real purty, Luellen, her name is. I'm goin' to tell her the next time I see her I'll introduce you to her fer five pounds of candy." She was frankly teasing.

"She'll ask for it back when she sees me."

"I'll take my chances. . . . Why don't we go back out? I reckon we've smelt enough hawg fer today." She waited but he did not comprehend until she confessed, making light of it, "I'm kinda turned around."

"Oh. It's this way." He took her arm, in a gingerly way, for her dress was sleeveless. But she gently disengaged his hand and took his arm instead, preferring, he understood, not to be steered but to go with him of her own accord.

When they were outside again and she had released him, she raised her face to the sky. "The sun's gone down."

"Yes, it's dropped behind the mountain."

"Are there still clouds in the sky?" When he said there were, she went on: "There were clouds going across the sun all day. What do they look like?"

"Well . . . they're gray inside but white all around and flat on the bottom. And they're lined up one after another, all down the sky. . . . You could imagine you're looking up at them from underwater and they're floating on the surface, without any weight."

"Oh, I can see them!"

"*I wish. . . .*" He wished that by closing his eyes and opening them he could see what was before them as she would see it if she *could* see.

What light there was!

He said, "It's in shadow where we are. The whole valley is in the shadow of the hills on the left, but Winespring is still in the sunlight . . . basking in glory. And behind it the sky is full of light. And blue. It's like a blue sheet of glass above the clouds with the light behind it. And it goes on far beyond the hills way off there at the end of the valley. It makes you want to follow the sky, on and on."

"Why did you sigh like that?" she asked.

"I didn't know I did. No reason." Because all that beckoned brought home to him his purposelessness. Because her tragedy fell darkly across it.

She sighed in her turn. With her hand at the neck of her dress, she said, "I'm lucky, livin' here where there's nearly ever'-thing I want, and more than I've a right to, so I don't always think how it may be with others. You're probably missin' your kinfolks and your friends."

She listened to his brief denial and said after a pause, "You know, you haven't told me what brung you here to Garrett County, so far from your home."

He repeated the explanation he had offered to others. "Hit warn't fair!" she protested.

"Oh, it was fair enough." He was touched and also a little uneasy at her seeming to experience and suffer his fate in herself.

"We're forgetting the cows," he observed.

On the way to the pasture she asked about the life he had left behind, her tone attributing a rare desirability to it. "I'll bet you got *lots* of brothers and sisters," she avowed, as if nothing less would have been worthy of so illustrious a family.

"No, I have one older sister and that's all."

"Well, I never! But your sister, I know she's purty."

He saw Cynthia breeze into a room with her certainty, never disappointed, of rocking a newcomer back on his heels, and he saw the enormous pride in her that their parents could never entirely dissimulate. "She's pretty, all right," he said. "After you, she's about the most beautiful girl I ever saw." The difference was that Cynthia . . . the difference was, he thought, the difference between a cultivated flower growing in a garden and a wild flower in the woods. It was only because Letty had halted that he turned to look at her.

She stood motionless, the color gone from her face; something was badly the matter.

"You're laughin', ain't you?"

"Laughin'? Why would I be . . . ?" Bewildered, he went back over what he had said. When it struck him, he felt his heart drain. "You mean about your being. . . . I just said it without thinking. But my gosh, Letty, you must be used to hearing about how you look!" Any girl as beautiful as she must be. His sister certainly was. . . . But Letty? In her world?

She did not reply. She had turned away and stood with her head back, her face hidden from him.

In his wretchedness he was tongue-tied. But . . . was it really so terrible, what he had said? He saw her bring herself back from wherever she had been. "Auto's comin'."

He could hear it himself.

"A old one. A-rattlin' and a-chuggin'. Could be friends of Hamp's and Rafe's. Or someone to get cures from Ma."

It was not very old in years, but cars aged fast in the Cumberlands. "There's a woman beside the driver and some kids in the back. And it's turning in. . . ."

The woman, clad in a dingy dress, got out and walked hesitantly to the house. Letty's mother was waiting with the door open and the two disappeared within.

"Yes, she'll be wantin' cures," Letty declared on the strength of his report.

"Your mother sells cures?"

"Or gives 'em away. Dependin'." But her mind did not seem to be on what she was saying. "Hit's Uncle Tom." She was looking in the direction from which the truck would come, but still absently. Suddenly her face came to life. "You know what? I plumb forgot to ask you if you'd keer for another piece of your candy! I'm mighty ready for one, myself."

That was better, he thought. "I wouldn't turn one down."

"Mine's creamy and lemony. What's yourn?"

"I don't know. It tastes like some kind of perfume."

"Then maybe we ought to save it for Luellen to put some behind her ears."

The worn sedan with the visitors, the children at the windows like so many unfledged birds in a nest, cleared the ford in its departure as the red truck reached the lane.

"Your uncle's got the horses with him," Wick said. There were two, both well muscled, between board sides that had been erected in the back of the truck. He had noticed the horse droppings in the pasture.

The girl led the way to the house as the truck backed up to a grass-grown, earthen ramp. The driver and the boy got out and let down the tailgate, which formed a bridge across the gap. They appeared to be too preoccupied with unhitching and leading the horses away to do more than acknowledge his greeting.

"I guess it's time for me to shove off," he declared.

She had been digging a little hole in the bare soil with her toe. Now she looked almost at his eyes, smiling; at least he still thought of it as looking. "I got a idear! I'd sure be surprised if there warn't one you left behind you're lonely for. What I was thinkin'—if there's a gal you're pinin' for, maybe it'd ease your mind to have someone to tell about her. I'm a real good listener. I mean, someday when you're on your way to Winespring. Colly could show you the trail."

There! he thought: it was all right. He had worried himself needlessly. She didn't think of herself as a *girl* after all, that was to say a *boy's* girl; that was the main thing.

Bicycling down the road he recalled that ten minutes before he had longed to be somewhere else, for good. And now, here he was thinking of the next time he would be at the farm. To talk about what Doris meant to him to a girl who would be like a sister, but one not thinking of herself all the time, in fact a sister to whom his problems would be like her problems because she had no life of her own to speak of—this inspired a scene in his mind that he was continually drawn back to.

He spent the next day with Frank Allen, much of it at the wheel, taking the truck over increasingly tricky stretches. He caught on quickly, slipping from gear to gear, with a feeling for what the ponderous, powerful monster wanted—its way of doing things. The final test was taking her down the mountain under a full load—with his instructor sitting forward on the seat, his hand on the door, most of the way.

"He'll do, boss," Frank said to Mr. DeSalla when they returned.

Their employer only grunted, but accorded Wick the full scrutiny of his large, heavy-lidded eyes. "I'm takin' a lotta crap on account of who I got workin' for me," he remarked.

Wick was a moment thinking this through. "If they mean me, all you've got working for you is an ordinary high-school graduate." He had received his diploma in the mail a few days before. "Anyhow, Mr. DeSalla, if you don't mind my saying so, I don't think anyone hands you much crap." He had his nerve, he knew, being so familiar.

The other did not blink, however. "It could be you're right." He turned to look down the bench where the auger had shut down. "That punk Bull Turner—has he got something against you?"

Wick muttered, "You'd think so. But I don't know what. He's just got it in for me." It gave him a sinking feeling to have it confirmed.

A sizable bubble of gas rumbled up from Mr. DeSalla's stomach and very audibly out of his mouth. Without any other recognition of it, he reached into a pocket for a small box and placed a pill from it on his tongue. "Well, you stick around, you'll probably become just part of the scenery. . . . Frank, you and the kid arrange for his driving test. Monday, I'm putting him on a front-end loader."

After work, if he let go of himself, Wick would have been

drawn right back to Letty's. But not to give the impression of tagging after her he told himself he would have to hold off until the week-end.

It made a long evening. He read until bedtime, which was early—nine or nine-thirty unless he were out. The book was a paperback novel he had bought guiltily for its lurid cover, which showed a girl undressing in a way that got under your skin. Several passages lived up to the promise of the cover, and these made trouble for him when he put out the light. When a girl took over his thoughts she could be of one kind or another. Sometimes she was a being much above him, to be served undemandingly and revered. At other times—and the aftermath of the paperback was one of them—she was a temptress who met him halfway in all his desires. Often this was a girl he knew whose readiness for his embraces, undetectable in actuality, was revealed to be ardent and daring in his fantasies. He considered himself a Dracula of sex and wondered that his true nature was not apparent to others, as it presumably was not since they did not draw back from him in horror. Even more surprisingly, it did not prevent his casting himself in quite different roles, in which his virtue was invincible.

However, one evening of this kind was enough for a while. So after a day back with the chain-saw, he accepted Jack's invitation to go with him to Tenent's. Moreover, he thought he understood what Mr. DeSalla had meant by becoming part of the scenery.

They arrived early. Apprehensive as he had been of running into Turner, who was not there, he had not thought of the Fergusons, who were—and with Gilley Huff, who called to him to come over. 'I've got nothing to be ashamed of,' Wick said to himself as he obeyed. 'It was two against one.' He thought it might be what the Fergusons had in mind, too, for they did not look up as he stood before them.

Said Gilley, "I understand you've already met, in a manner of speaking." But he repeated the names of the three in introduction. Hamp, the elder, had his legs thrust out before him, his hands in his pockets. Rafe, of the broad cheekbones, was paring paper-thin shavings the length of a stick of wood, the end of which was a mass of curls; a sharp blade, Wick thought. Gilley, who perhaps had been lecturing them, commanded him affably to sit down. "You birds might as well get to know each other."

Hamp unexpectedly added his voice, "Yeah, sit down." He looked up at Wick, a furrow between his wild, cornered-looking eyes. "You goin' to be around long?"

"We mean around the county," the brother explained.

"I've got no plans to leave," Wick replied, preserving his distance.

Hamp fixed his gaze on Gilley. "What I want to know is . . . I mean, maybe he's got on Letty's good side, but how does he stand?"

"Why don't you ask him?"

"He h'yurd me."

Wick said unsmilingly, "With a lot of difficulty. That's how I've been standing for the past few days." He looked them in the eye, one after the other.

"All right," said Hamp. Apparently this was meant to concede that they might have made a mistake.

"What'll you have?" Standing by his shoulder was the young girl who served as occasional waitress, superficially the kind known as a freckle-faced kid, but much cooler-looking than the type.

"Which still leaves the question of which side you're on," the younger brother said when Wick had given his order. He turned the stick in his hand to examine it. "And what we mean is between the farmers and the strippers."

Gilley fetched a sigh and put his Coca-Cola down. "Why does he have to be on either? He's a stranger here—a guest, if you want to put it that way." He did not seem quite himself this evening. Wick noticed that he was wearing his shirt inside out— so it was probably frayed on the right side. Jack had told him that Gilley was supporting a crippled sister.

"Hit's gettin' so he ain't no stranger to Oak Lick Holler," the older brother declared. "Uncle Tawm says he ain't to be hindered. All the same, hit looks damn funny to me. We all know what's in the wind for Gorton Holler. What I want to know is, does his makin' up to the Sherrods mean Allegheny-Keystone's got its eyes on Oak Lick?"

"And the president would send his eighteen-year-old boy down to prepare the way?" Gilley scoffed. "By fanning up you two firebrands? Oh, come on, Hamp!"

"He's workin' for a stripper, ain't he?" said Rafe.

"It's a job," Wick replied. "I don't tell the man I work for

71

what to do. Anyhow, there're no farms where he's operating. And if you mean do I think a farmer ought to have his land wrecked because of a deed that never meant . . . that's being taken advantage of to permit what it was never intended to, the answer is no, I don't."

"That's fair enough," Gilley pronounced, as if he would nail down an agreement before anyone could spoil it.

A long horn blast outside the open window grew almost deafening before it ended. The door was thrown back against the wall and in burst Bull Turner and his hangers-on. In the silence that fell on the room, already quiet with the customers' week's-end weariness, he looked around with his teeth-baring smile, his thumbs in his belt. His eyes alighted with satisfaction on Wick. 'Here comes something,' the boy thought. But the other, taking in his companions, tore his gaze away.

"Hey! Roger!" he called out to the proprietor. "This place is like an undertaker's. Put a quarter in the box for me."

Being with the Fergusons, it occurred to Wick, was like being in a patch of blackberries for the victim of a hunt: prickly, but not without advantages.

All the same, he had not been forgotten. He was eyed, first with puzzlement by Turner, then in lingering glances by the whole half-dozen of them, their heads bent in shared jokes over the two tables they had put together.

None of it was lost on Gilley. "Have you given Turner any reason for resentment?" he asked.

"Only by being what I am."

"Well . . . just don't let him get a rise out of you. He'll probably get bored with it pretty soon."

"Yeah, maybe," said Hamp, boldly returning the attentions of the double table. "The reason he don't cross me is 'cause he knows I'd have his hide if he did. Or Rafe would if he got me first." He spoke directly at Turner as if inviting him to read his lips. Above the ear-filling lover's complaint dinning from the Seeburg Discotheque there was little likelihood of his being heard.

Was it possible, Wick asked himself, that he had allies? But if he had, would it matter?

"Just how much trouble are the boys prepared to make at Gorton Holler?" Gilley asked, noncommittal eyes on Hamp.

"Just as much as it takes."

"Just as much as it takes to bring in a few carloads of County and State Police with riot guns."

"Now, Gilley, we ain't as dumb as you think. But there are things you just as well don't h'yeer about, fer yer own good." Hamp had put out a hand to the other's arm, giving Wick a different idea of him.

"I wish I knew . . ." Gilley mused after a moment. Then he said, much more lightly, "I hear that isn't all you've got going on in Gorton Holler you've been keeping to yourself."

A grin broke slowly across Hamp's face. "I wouldn't take to anyone else talkin' about it, Gilley, but it's a fac' there's a mighty fine little gal over there. Purty and smart, too. Don't rightly know why she puts up with me, but she does."

"It's because you're such a handsome specimen of manhood. You wouldn't know that because the only kind of looks you recognize are a pretty girl's and a prize coon-hound's, and for a coon-hound your ears don't hang right."

"Gilley, you're fuller of talk. . . . However it may be, she don't deny me her company."

Wick was astonished to see the dourly tense young mountaineer filled with glee. With a cry of "Hallelujah!" Hamp jumped up, seized the impersonal young waitress by her waist as she passed and, pumping her arm, danced with her vigorously.

"You going to pay for Sally's time?" Mr. Tenent, aroused by his employee's first startled yelp, put the question in a cheerful voice.

"I doubt I got that kinda money," Hamp replied, releasing his partner and resuming his seat.

The music had come to a booming close. The room was suddenly full of voices. Then, above them all, Bull Turner's rang out. "Gilley, what's the matter with you tonight? Allegheny-Keystone got your tongue?"

"Yeah, how about it, Gilley?" Jack MacDonough cried good-naturedly, taking the edge off Turner's spite. "Ain't we goin' to get no what's-good-for-us this evenin'?"

Other voices joined in.

"Sure, I'll give you something to think about," Gilley replied, getting to his feet. "It'll be short, and it'll feature responses from the congregation, I hope."

He spoke with his back to the table, fingers hooked under its edge, leaning forward. "This has to do with Appalachia. And you know what people have in mind when they call us Appalachia. We're the national hard-luck story. This doesn't bother the up-standing people who've taken out of Appalachia most of what's worth carting away. But it does bother some people. Only most of those who came down to investigate us turn out to have axes of their own to grind.

"That doesn't seem to be the case with half a dozen young men and women just out of college who came down last month. They seem to be asking only for a chance to learn what they can and what they think maybe everyone ought to know about. Last night the leader of the little band, named Emory, was beaten up. They had to take him to the hospital. You may have heard a mention of it on the radio. A mention's about all it got." Gilley was letting the facts speak for themselves.

"Nobody knows who did it. Emory himself didn't get a good enough look at the man to give a description. He'd answered a knock on the door of his motel room late at night and—wham!"

Gilley's hands were still hooked under the table and Wick could see the muscles in them working.

"So since we don't know who did it, we might be tempted to ask ourselves who would have arranged to have it done? Who would have felt it so important to scare off these prying out-siders? What's your guess, anybody?"

From beside Wick came a loud voice. "How about a minin' company afraid of the hullabaloo the fellows might start about strip-minin'?" Hamp settled back in his chair, having let loose his shot. He had that glassy-eyed wild look again.

"*Or* about black-lung disease." It was the ailing, middle-aged miner sitting once more with Jack and Frank Allen.

"Why not . . ." A man with a gray pallor and hollows scooped out above and below his cheekbones sat up straight to look over heads. "Why not one of the dog-mine operators who say the new mine-safety regulations will put them out of business? *They* don't want to have nobody around makin' a case for enforcin' them." A regular miner, Wick thought.

"Enforcin' regulations? That's a good one!"

The author of that interjection was a blond young miner Wick had once ridden with on the Harpersburg bus. "You don't know

74

how lucky you are to have got a education," he had said. "I quit school after the third grade, and now I cain't get any work only in the mines. And I hate every minute of it. There ain't never a time I go down but I'm scared." Uneducated, yet to look at he could have been one of Cynthia's young men.

"How about the union local?" put in someone else. "Would the boys stop at a little rough stuff with outsiders stickin' their noses into the way the last election was run?" Not a miner, Wick decided, or anyone the union could hurt.

"How about the national headquarters? The big boys have plenty to hide, if you ask me." This was a woman in her thirties out with her husband, Wick judged. "All they're interested in is keeping the coal coming out for the sake of the percentage that goes into the pension fund."

"Which they use to keep themselves in office gettin' big salaries and expense accounts," the tired miner, his head back against the wall, put in again.

Even the waitress entered into the spirit of the assemblage in which there was a certain wry amusement as well as bitterness. "Don't forget the governor and the charges that he's under-reported his income by a hundred thousand bucks. Maybe Gilley Huff's friends were onto something there."

"Or," said Gilley, his hands jammed into his trouser pockets, "one of our Congressmen. Maybe they don't want too much made of the illegal contributions they've received from mining companies."

Wick thought, 'He's pulling it off very well.'

His glance swept the room. Turner had been in that strange state of withdrawal he was subject to, sitting with only a sliver of an eye showing between the lids, drawing deep breaths. But as the boy's gaze rested on him he slowly opened his eyes and, as slowly, turned his head to let them rest on the speaker.

"Well, those are some of the possibilities, aren't they? And it shows what nasty minds we've got. . . ." Gilley's speech had slowed down; he was staring oddly at Turner. ". . . Suspecting the whole run of our betters. That's what comes of living around here. You get so mean you have doubts about the finest citizens."

He was not taking his eyes off the other, whose expression was charged now with irony and challenge and, it seemed to Wick, gloating. By now everyone was aware of something between the two men face to face across the room, each seeming fully to understand the other.

The teacher turned away, taking his leave of Wick and the Fergusons with a wordless gesture. But at the bar, having put down some coins, he turned back to the room and to all the eyes still on him declared, "Whoever put him up to it, I'll bet the thug who did the job on Emory thoroughly enjoyed it for its own sake." With a last glance at Turner, he left.

"There warn't no need to put him in the hospital," Wick heard Hamp grumble uneasily.

He observed that Turner was surveying the room, shifting his gaze from side to side without moving his head. It must have come through to him that the company, though subdued, was not with him. Raising his voice he said "I'll tell you what *I* think. Maybe you ain't heard the tales—what this college bunch been up to. I mean sleepin' around with each other any ol' which way. An' bringin' in boys and girls from roundabouts, to get them liquored up and join in in things I'd be shamed to talk about, with ladies present. You ask me, somebody"—with his tongue in his cheek, he cast his eyes about—"like a preacher decided that Emory feller needed a lesson. An' are you goin' to blame anyone who give him one? Mind you, I'm not claimin' credit." He sighted on the toe of his shoe. "I got an alibi. It's done been checked out, too." He looked up with a grin for the room at large, then turned back to his followers, who broke into laughter.

In a few minutes, however, he stood up and led the way to the cash-register. When the party had settled up and left, the rumbling bellow of a motor was heard, then the spinning of wheels and a shower of flying gravel.

6

WHEN WICK GOT BACK to his room that night, he sat on the sagging edge of his bed almost too dispirited to undress. He was in a place of accumulated wrongs and deep-rooted animosities, as comfortless as a frontier and as dangerous. There would probably be a shooting fight at Gorton Hollow. And there was the fate of Emory: that above all. His insides shrank at the implications for him.

Yet there was then beginning a time of tranquillity which would see him come to feel more at home where Winespring's shadow fell than he ever had in the town he had grown up in.

Two nights later, it is true, the giant bulldozer that had been unloaded at Gorton Hollow to prepare the way for the augers would be dynamited—"blown all . . . to . . . smither . . . eens," in Jack MacDonough's awe-truck testimony; "I tell you, it's . . . all . . . over . . . the . . . map. And they got no idea who done it!" But operations would be called off, at least for the time being, and there would be peace in the hollow. And Turner had perhaps decided that he had done enough for the present; the weeks were to pass with no other threat to Wick than a look when they chanced to meet that seemed to say he was biding his time and savoring it.

The morning after the disturbing session at Tenent's dawned fair and Wick was early at Oak Lick. To his distress he ran straight into Mr. Barrows, under whose flashing, dilated eyes he tended to quail; he had seen the same light in those of horses about to rear.

"Letty said Colly could show me where the trail up Winespring Mountain starts," he stammered.

"No reason he couldn't! Colly knows whar hit is!"

At the creak of the screen door they both turned, Wick with relief.

77

"Letty, Wicker's h'yar. He wants Colly to put him on the path up Winespring."

She walked toward them as anyone would have. As was her way, her head was up, her glance a little down and to the side. "I heard him," she exclaimed. "Only hit ain't Wicker. Hit's Wick Carter." She was wearing a short dress of small green checks, made, he was to learn, from two grainsacks.

"Hi, Letty." He knew to speak quickly so that she would know his direction. Where in the past had he seen that slim face, to have it so impressed on his consciousness? Had it been a picture in a magazine, or in a movie? Could his awareness of it go no further back than his first sight of Letty herself?

"I knowed it was you," she said, raising her eyes to his face, then turning them after her uncle, who had gone on to the barn.

"And how did you know it was me? Am I coming so often you can take it for granted it's me when that old rooster clucks up a storm?"

"You don't come often. You only been here four times. . . . I got my ways of tellin'," she declared complacently.

"And could you tell the first time when I was sitting out by the road watching you?"

"It may just be I *did* know."

"You lookin' fer me?"

Wick started, audibly. Colly, youthfully noncommittal, was standing directly behind him.

Letty laughed. "Colly's the Indian of the family," she said.

It was not Winespring that had brought Wick to the little farm, but there was nothing for it but to go ahead with his expressed desire. However, it developed that Colly had lots to do and could not set off at once.

"Come on, let's set down," Letty said. "We'll have some coffee. It won't take Colly long."

He was to be ashamed in later days at having seemed to take it at these times that she had nothing to do but be available to him for company.

She led the way to the log-walled part of the house, a single room with a door to the outside. As they entered, her mother, Mrs. Sherrod, turned from her work at an unpainted table. She was a widow, Wick had learned, and a younger sister of Mr. Barrows's.

"We're glad to have you," she remarked easily when Letty had explained his being there. "You probably never saw a kitchen like this one. Log-built and chinked up with cement. A wood-burning stove—coal in the winter." It was black and squarish and a dim red glow could be seen through a grating in front and between the sections of its flat top. "A sink with no faucets and no plumbin' but the drainpipe. . . . An icebox." She might have been performing introductions. "We cut ice from the creek in the winter and store it in a pit up yonder in the woods under sawdust. They've never brung the powry line up the holler, so we got no electricity. No television and no radio."

"We could have a battery radio, but Uncle's got no use for them," Letty said with a note of defiance.

"Hit makes him nervous to have a stranger's voice boomin' out of a little box. Particularly hit soundin' like hit had every right to say what hit pleased, in his own house." The mountain speech issuing from a person of Mrs. Sherrod's evident quality sounded so incongruous that Wick could hardly help feeling, as he had initially with Letty, that it must be put on.

He said, "I see you've got lots of plants. Are they the cures?" There were deep shelves across one side of the room, some stacked with dried plants, which also hung from the rafters, a few full of glass jars.

"So Letty's been talkin'? What's in the jars is vegetables—what's left from last summer. We do a right smart amount of cannin,' don't we, Letty? The rest is yarbs—cures. I'll tell you about them sometime, if you'd care to h'yeer." She spoke lightly, half-humorously.

"I kin tell somethin' about them right now. They're what gives Ma reason for gettin' off in the woods by herself. I remember when I was eight or nine how I'd see her go off with her sack, walkin' light as a bird and hummin' to herself. Where she goes, nobody knows. But sometimes she'll be gone half the day. And she'll come back with a sackful."

The girl's mother laughed. "You'll have him thinkin' I'm some kind of witch. When you ought to be rememberin' that he's a boy and cain't go for long without food and drink."

"I did promise him a cup of coffee. I don't know whether he'll like our coffee much, with the chicory root, but there's nothin' the matter with our cream, if I *do* sound like I'm braggin'."

"I'll like both. And," he added, "I like this kitchen. It's the nicest I ever saw." In truth it charmed him—the whitewashed log walls, the sun coming in through a small, white-curtained window, the clean, many-times-washed wood of the tabletop, the scent of the herbs and the tang of the woodsmoke. The kitchen was so entirely what it was, as the inside of a boat's hull was; and the oil lamp on the table reminded you that it had no connection by pipe or wire with the big world beyond and like a boat was self-contained.

"And the baskets in the corner: what do you do with so many?" There must have been twelve or fifteen stacked up, of several designs, woven of thin strips of wood, all seemingly new.

"Letty makes them! And every couple of months a man comes and buys them."

"But they're beautiful! Absolutely perfect!" He had gone over to look at them. The curves were as regular as geometry, the strips smoothly bound to the rim, the handles deftly affixed.

"I know the girls where you come from makes a lot harder things than plain old baskets." Her confusion plainly compounded both pleasure and diffidence. "Anyway, Uncle Tom cuts the strips, though Colly's gettin' good, too."

"Not a girl in Harwood could do anything like that." But as he went on, warmly, he checked himself. She had bent lower, reflecting, he realized, that the girls in Harwood did not need to.

Mrs. Sherrod poured their coffee from a marbled gray-enameled pot standing at the back of the stove and added cream from the icebox. Then following her suggestion, they carried their cups, and a plate of corn bread spread with blackberry jam, to the front steps of the house.

Coming out into the light, inviting air with a companion in whose regard he saw himself important, before them the narrowing grassy valley starred with yellow flowers, Wick had a sense of the moment's sufficiency. He knew himself happy. But the very realization was the mood's undoing. He could not have said what he was looking for in life. But he was sure he would recognize it when he found it. It would reveal to him what he was; through it he would justify his existence. He would be in tune with the great things, as though marching to a band. But he would not find it in this backwoods valley, on a farm that however appealing was an out-of-date curiosity. There was Letty, but Letty could not count and in the end he would only come face to face with himself again. And apart from this there was nothing but his job and the round of days each ending as it had begun, the room at Mrs. Haney's, with the rickety bureau and untidy drawers, and the superheated imaginings that left him demoralized.

. . . Was he going to return again to the corner in Harpersburg where the dressed-up girl had looked in the shopwindow, meeting his eyes in it unwaveringly with hers? He had gone cold and walked on, and later been sick with desire. Two evenings ago he had gone back and accused himself disgustedly of being as much relieved as disappointed to find she wasn't there. . . .

Describing for Letty the night at the Last Chance/First Chance but dealing only cursorily with Bull Turner, he thought of the dreary, straggling communities the patrons came from, the grim, bleak little churches—Tabernacle of the Christian Salvation, Gospel Tabernacle, Round Top Free Will Baptist Church—and he felt the flutterings of panic. As an alternative for him there was the life at home, where he had been more a misfit all the time.

"I wanted to get up early to come here," he concluded, "so I was glad when Jack decided it was time to go home."

She put her coffee-cup down. As though she were part of his thoughts, she said, "Why are you unhappy, Wick? I been feelin' it in you all along." She bent over, smoothing her skirt. "I reckon hit's homesickness. You want to be with your friends."

His voice was dead as he answered, "It wouldn't be any different. I don't belong where they are. Sometimes I think I don't belong anywhere. People have to find themselves—young people, that is; everyone says so. But suppose you're just nowhere." He quoted in self-mockery: "'How did you find yourself after the party?' 'I just looked under the table and there I was.'"

She turned to him in mystification. He could not have guessed she was not seeing him. "Why, how can you talk like that? Look how well you done here, comin' a stranger and used to fine things, and in a job you didn't know nothin' about. I bet you could do anything you've a mind to. You're good-lookin' and smart and

81

you been educated. I bet you'll be rich and famous. Look how brave you are!"

"*Brave?*"

"I h'yurd how you saved that weldin' trailer when you might of been burnt to death."

"But you didn't hear how scared I was. I came near to throwing up afterwards. If I weren't so scared I wouldn't do things like that."

"Hit ain't no disgrace bein' scared. But when you go ahead when you're scared, that's bein' brave."

"Maybe so. But when I go ahead it's because I'm even scareder of not going ahead. And even at that, if I stop to think, I'm licked." When he had fled from the girl standing idly in front of that shopwindow—now that had been the real Sedgwick L. Carter. Or, more: when his stomach contracted at the threat from Turner.

"I'll tell you what I think." There was an almost sad tenderness in her face. "I think you're runnin' yourself down 'cause you've been in love and been hurt."

A softer light fell on the scenery in his mind.

"It may be I have been." He did not add "several times," which would have made him a comic figure; and in truth the heartache had been as severe in each case.

"Why don't you tell me about her? What's her name?"

"Well . . . Doris. I don't know how to tell you about her. She's very pretty, but that's only part of it. She's *superior* . . . as if she were made of finer material than ordinary mortals, especially me. She might have come from a more spiritual world than ours. . . . You know, when you're in love it's like a religious feeling. . . . The thing is, I'm nowhere near good enough for her."

"Why not?"

"Well, it's as I was saying. You aspire to higher things in her presence. You feel your unworthiness."

"Is she in love with somebody else?"

The words he had spoken, which he had earlier recited to himself, he now recognized as the purest crap. Whoever they referred to, they sure had nothing to do with Doris. Doris was self-centered and shallow. But endowed—that was all. That was all, and it had been enough.

He answered, "Yeah. I guess so. I saw her a couple of times in a fancy convertible with a gangster-looking type, and from the way she was looking up at him you'd have thought she was in love with him." He spoke in a heedless voice. "Afterwards she seemed a little strange—dislocated. I wouldn't be surprised if he'd given her a shot of something."

He felt, for a moment, a hand on his arm.

"To be honest," he resumed, seized by ruthlessness toward himself, "it isn't just Doris I'm talking about. Or Doris at all. It could be someone else. And has been. If I find myself looking up at life from the bottom of a hole, dreaming up mirages, it's a hole I dig myself. I suppose because where something should be inside me it isn't. So I burrow down."

They sat in a silence in which he could believe that she shared the burning lump in his chest. He told himself that being less than a whole person she was able to be more part of another.

She said, "It must be that everybody's got to suffer. And them that seems to have the least cause maybe has to suffer more. On account of more's expected of them. Or they think so."

He felt his face turn hot with the realization of his selfishness. Talk about Doris being self-centered! "What a pig I am! Pouring out my troubles to you! You're the one who ought to be. . . ."

She seemed genuinely surprised. "Oh, that," she said. "Don't worry about that! I'm used to it, and there ain't nothin' can be done about it. Anyhow," she added with a peculiar stress, "I got no right to complain about it."

"You've got every right!"

"You'd have to know how it happened." She looked down, her hair falling forward to hide her face.

"And you'd rather not talk about it," he said, that monster of selfishness within him, instantly and desperately denounced, wishing she would not.

"No, it's better I tell you," she replied in a voice from which she had shut out emotion. She was leaning forward, gripping the edge of the porch, her head between her shoulders.

"I was ten yur old, and it was when we was livin' in Dayton. We was cooped up in one room an' a kitchen in a buildin' full of people and nary a bit of green nor a hill nowhere. But Pa didn't see no other way to make a livin'. His brother had come out before him and said he could get him a job where he worked, in a factory makin' plumbin' fixtures—as he done, too. But that city! We was miserable, the whole lot of us." She was silent for a moment. "I was hit by a automobile crossin' the street to school. It only knocked me outa the way, but I fetched my head a turrible blow on the tar. I come to in the hospital."

Wick froze.

"I opened my eyes and I couldn't see. I tried battin' 'em, and I couldn't see. So that's how it was. Pa said hit was a judgment on him for leavin' the place where his kinfolks was buried. But I knowed hit was a judgment on me. I hated that school. We was hillbillies to the other kids—warn't dressed like them, didn't talk like them. I was wishin' for anythin' that would get us back home. Every day, every hour, I wisht it. An' I got my wish. 'Twarn't two days later we got word from Ma's folks that Grandpa had died and Grandma would be pleased if she and Pa wanted to come back and work the farm. I h'yurd Pa say that night when I was supposed to be asleep—talkin' in a dead kind of voice—'Well, we done paid the price, and now we got our ticket back home.' Natcherly we took it. And I'd larned my lesson. Hit's never to wish for nothin'. If you don't get your wish you pine for hit, an' if you do you're likely to get somethin' with it will make you sorry you ever thought of it."

The lame pullet had come up and was cheeping. It pecked at Letty's shoe.

"I hyeer you." She extended her hand to the plate and picked it up. "I reckon there's some crumbs on this." She set it down on the step beside her foot.

"I can't understand what you think you'd done to call down a judgment on you. Everybody wishes things all the time. *You* didn't injure anyone."

It was as if she had not heard. But then she frowned and said, "I warn't goin' to tell you. I don't like to spread grief, and this will grieve you. But you won't understand unless I do." As he looked at her uneasily she gathered her resolution. "I had a little sister two yur younger'n me I was supposed to be lookin' out for. She run out into the street and before I could get to her the automobile run her down. Hit was the last thing I saw, the auto hittin' us, and she was kilt."

He was horrified. But alongside the pity he felt for her was a consciousness of his own acute discomfort at having to meet the situation—and that this should be so when he should have had

84

no thought of himself sickened him. He put his hand on her shoulder. "You still can't blame yourself. You didn't know she was going to run out. . . . And you almost got killed trying to save her. You deserved a medal for heroism." He could tell that she had heard it before.

"If I'd held onto her instead of dreadin' the school waitin' to swallow us up and wishin' *any*thing would happen to take us back home, she'd be alive now, in all probability."

He said, quoting an English-teacher he had admired, "Anyone can tear himself to pieces with *if*'s."

To his surprise, she smiled—wanly, to be sure. "Oh, I don't do that. I don't brood. If I did, I'd only make myself a pest. I been punished. And I'm glad. I couldn't live had it been otherwise. If more punishment is due, the Lord, or whoever, knows where to find me. For me to take it on myself and go mopin' around would be settin' myself up on high. An' I ain't important. It's knowin' that that makes it easier to bear when I get to thinkin' only about myself—an' I do!—an' how much I'm missin' out on. There's been a million mountain gals before me and there'll be millions more to come. So what difference do I make? With you it's different."

He looked at her curiously.

"There's great expectations of you. Not only because you're the son of a big man, but because you got it in you to go a long ways."

"I got it in me to go a long ways to nowhere."

"That ain't what I mean and you know it. An' I kin tell! I knowed another feller I could tell was marked out for big things. I only seen him once. He was sittin' next to me at a church picnic that Ma took me to, and we was talkin'. I could *feel* it with him. Hit was like sittin' by a stove, only hit warn't hot. And now Luellen says he's got the biggest Baptist congregation in Louisville. An' him under thirty yur old."

"Oh, Letty. . . ." He was glad she could not see him smile. He said with sudden cheerfulness, "Now if I could just have your opinion of myself, and if you could just know you're as little to blame for what happened . . . seven year ago"—he could not put that *s* on it—"as I know you are, then. . . ." He hesitated, asking himself why a shadow had settled on her face . . . and the answer came to him with a swift insight he was not accustomed to having. Her blindness was bearable to her only because she was

85

convinced it was deserved and was just. It would be no favor to her to shake that conviction.

"Your father's been dead about five year, I heard."

"He died of pneumonia, from workin' in a dog-mine. The farm by itself don't provide a livin'. He was never very strong in health. Playin' the dulcimore and singin'—he had a beautiful voice; that was the kinda thing he was meant to do. Ma was left alone with the farm, but lucky for all of us Uncle Tom could come. He was . . . well, he'd been in trouble with the law, through no fault of his'n—he'd only done what he had to—but he was free. And his wife had left him. Got tar'd of waitin', I reckon."

She cocked her head. Colly had appeared from around the corner of the house, walking in his neat, fast way.

"You two run along now."

Undeceived by her bright smile, Wick knew he could not leave her behind. She protested that she would hold them back but was soon won over, and for Wick the light in her face illuminated the expedition. Touching his elbow to hers as they started out, he said, "Latch onto me. And don't let go till I give you permission."

"Yes, sir." Her hand traveled lightly up his arm to rest on his shoulder. "Only I better hold onto the hand-rail crossin' the creek. . . . I look to you to tell me what we're seein', Wick. Colly don't take notice of scenery unless some critter's made tracks across it."

"When hit don't do no good since you won't stand for no critter bein' hunted nor trapped." Colly walked on her other side, a little ahead.

"I ain't got so many friends I kin spare any. . . . Kin we see Winespring up ahead of us?"

He was touched by the *we*. "Straight ahead. The trees on the slope overlap the way shingles do. There's a . . . it looks like a kind of crease in the mountainside where the trees are much darker and more pointed. I suppose they're evergreens."

"Hemlocks," said two voices together.

Wick laughed, reminded that trees were a family business. "Why am I trying to tell you about it?"

She gave an impatient little push at his shoulder. "I want to know what things *look* like. I kinda remember the way hemlocks look. I know the needles is short and there's a row of 'em on both sides of the twigs and teeny little cones at the ends of the twigs. But what's the tree look like?"

What did a hemlock look like? "There're two or three down the road," he said. "They're dark—dark-green—and a little mysterious. They're like, well, sorcerer-trees with arms half-raised—lots of arms, draped in hanging sleeves."

She clapped her hands. "I remember now! I kin *see* them!" Colly regarded him sideways from a round, black eye.

Stimulated, Wick went on. "A lot of trees down lower on the mountain are a yellower green and come to a point, but with rounded sides, like an Indian arrowhead."

"What'd they be, Colly?"

"Yeller poplar." Colly marched on a few steps in silence. "They're shaped like evergreens. That's a fact. And their trunks is as straight as any pine's. And the wood's as light as a scrub pine's or White pine's. Ain't no lighter wood. Though they do call Yeller poplars hardwoods."

It was the longest speech Wick had yet heard from him. Letty appeared to be struck by it too.

"Why ain't you never told me all that before?"

"Never thought to." Colly stopped. "See that big oak off yonder?" He pointed down a level, straight stretch of road they had come to. "I'll race you for it."

"What?"

"I'll race you for it."

Letty declared the boy plain bumptious, but Wick had his standing in Colly's eyes to think of. And he had, as he knew, a fast pair of legs.

And needed them. Colly shot off, all four limbs working like reciprocating machine-parts.

"You're fast," the boy said between breaths when they had slowed to a stop on the far side of the oak, Wick in the lead.

"So are you. And you'll be faster when you've finished growing."

When they had jogged back, Letty said, "I ain't goin' to ask who won!"

"It was pretty near even."

"He did."

She was flushed and her own breathing was faster than normal. Wick said, "Now *you*'re going to run with us."

She looked alarmed. "Oh, I darn't."

"Oh yes you dar. We'll each take a hand. You won't fall. Colly, take hold. We won't go any faster than you want."

But by the time they reached the oak they were running head-long. The girl's face, her hair swept back from it, was charged with excitement. Her strong, lithe legs seemed to have confidence of their own.

"Oh, that was . . . oh, it was . . . wonderful, like flyin'!" The absence of focus in her eyes and the radiance in her face: what did it make him think of? Someone seeing a vision.

They might have got by the Fergusons' undetected had not Colly called out to the brothers, who were hoeing foot-high corn in a hillside field; he admired them, it was plain to see. "Hey! You two comin' down to help with the shoein' this afternoon?"

They shaded their eyes, waved, and Colly, a man among men, strode erectly on. Wick was not sure that he, too, was not holding himself a little more erect than usual. The girl's hand on his shoulder made him feel like doing so.

"It seems strange to see those two doin' anything as tame as hoein' corn," he said.

"I ain't sure what they got in mind for hit's so tame."

Her reply puzzled him, but before he could ask what she meant, she was talking about the birds that were singing around them. One that warbled softly—*"Tew lew lew-lip"*—was a bluebird, Letty said. And peering in the direction of the notes he at length could see the light glinting on a small back of almost unbelievable blue. "That's the gentlest song there is. The robin's a happy one. . . ." It was hard for her to believe he could not recognize any of the songs.

"Now that one!" she said, marking one she could not picture with quick little squeezes of his shoulder. *"Chew chew, chee chee,"* it began, high-pitched and steely, then went on, continually repeating itself: *"chee wee, chee wee; chu-a chu-a, chew chew. . . ."* Colly quickly spotted the singer at the very top of a tree, but it was very small and looked perfectly black against the sky.

At the same place, from the brush-grown swamp at the head of the Fergusons' clearing, they could hear a spirited little *"Witchitu, witchitu, witchitu."* Letty said she often heard it down in the pasture below their barn where the creek spread out and the banks were all brushy.

"I'm going to go get a look at it," Wick declared.

Keeping his eyes on the spot from which the song had issued made the going difficult on the swampy ground. The vocalist flew off as he drew near—it seemed to be an olive color—but he marked where it put down and continued after it in his soaking shoes, picking his way among the hassocks. Once more his quarry flushed ahead of him. But he went on, more warily. And as if the little bird had been testing him, there it suddenly was, on a low branch in full view.

'It was the most beautiful little thing,' he anticipated reporting to Letty. 'Underneath it was the brightest yellow and it had a black mask across its face, like the kind in a masquerade.' Out of this mask the bird's sharp eye met his in the instant before it sped away. He could hardly get over the sight of the alert, brilliantly turned-out, tiny being—and, indeed, he never would. Such a uniquely designed little thing, to be singing unseen from the tangle of the swamp. You could tell at a glance it was just what it was supposed to be—though how "supposed," he could not say. He had seen books on birds, and now it was brought to him that each of the pictured birds existed, busy with its own life, in a swamp, a thicket, a forest, each with its special color pattern, exactly as it was meant to be, whether anyone saw it or not.

To all he could tell her, Letty listened, absorbed.

The road above the Fergusons' amounted to little more than parallel tracks through the woods, rough and mostly uphill. Feeling Letty's hand removed, he stopped. She was listening, to one side, then the other. She drew a deep breath, testing the air. "What's it like h'yur?"

He said, "The trees meet over the road, but you can see bits and pieces of the sky through the branches. There was a sign down the road that said 'Property of Triple Creek Land Company. No cutting of timber.' I reckon you know about that."

Said Colly, "They pay Hamp somethin' every yur to keep a watch on the land they owns."

"Yeller poplars," he said again when Wick remarked that some of the trees they were passing were of a kind that had had flowers like green-and-orange tulips when he first came to work. "The flowers is right purty," Colly conceded.

The trail up the mountain took off beside a rivulet that trickled down the slope, over rocks and across the road. They all drank from the little pool it had formed on the near side. Wick led the girl to the driest spot, where she knelt and cupped the water in her hands. He and Colly, almost prone, sucked it up horse-fashion. It had struck him that Letty had evidently determined not to be embarrassed when she needed help but to accept a service simply. He wondered if he would be equal to that.

Colly said he thought it was about two miles to the top of the mountain. "If you're goin' up, Letty kin come home with me. I got to git back."

"How about going on with me, Letty? Just maybe a little bit more. What do you say?"

Because there could be no mistaking that he meant it, she agreed; and because the trail was not wide enough for two, he proposed that she hold on to his shirttail.

She giggled, but the system worked well enough. The handful of shirt she gripped both guided her and gave her support when she stumbled. When there was a rock of any size in the trail he warned her of it. Before long he would come to believe that she was assisted by instinct.

In the deep woods now, they spoke in lowered voices. "Tree close on the right," he murmured, looking back and pausing to be sure she got around it.

She put out her hand to it, exploring its trunk with her fingers. "Has the tree got leaves with wavy edges, like little waves all around them?"

"Yes. How did you know that?"

"Hit's a Chestnut oak. I kin tell by the bark. Hit's hard and has big ridges, with deep valleys between. Probably there's a pack of 'em like hit around hyur."

There were.

Farther on he stopped her before a Yellow poplar. And after feeling the trunk she knew it too.

She said she had learned the feel of all the trees in the woods around their house and that her uncle had told her what they were. As they walked on he stopped her before different trees and only one did she fail to recognize. His admiration of her ability obviously made her proud.

"Very smooth. Got only the finest cracks. Sugar maple."

"This one's a oak. Bark's hard and got deep valleys between the ridges, like Chestnut oak. But flatter ridges. Are the leaves wavy around the edges but not so many waves and cut in deep between some of 'em?" They were. "Then hit's a White oak. Timber men'd ruther have hit than iny. Best for baskets . . .

"Hyur's one don't get very big. You could think the trunk had muscles. Bark's in narrow strips with deep grooves between 'em. Leaves are like mittens, most of 'em with two thumbs, ain't they? . . . Chew a twig and hit'll taste like root beer. Sassafras. Makes pretty good tea. Which'll cure some things that's wrong with you. . . .

"Oh—this hyur's another tasty one! Smooth as silk but's got tiny welts. Could be a Black cherry, but I don't think it is. Kin you break off a twig and chew it? . . . Tastes like wintergreen, don't hit? Cut down a Cherry birch and come back and you find ants drinkin' from the top of the stump, Colly says. In my grandma's day they used to chop them up and bile the chips and twigs for oil of wintergreen. If I had my way, they'd be no trees cut down. Or mighty few." Still clutching the shirttail, she had an arm around the black birch trunk. She laid her cheek against it, her eyes almost closed. "When I die they're goin' to plant a little Cherry birch over my grave, and that's what I'm goin' to become —a Cherry birch with the wind singin' in my branches and skin like silk and wintergreen sap in my veins." She opened her eyes and smiled. "If you had a tree planted over you for you to turn into, what kind would hit be?"

"Well, let me think." It was becoming second nature with him not to rely on his expression to convey a response to her. "I'd choose an oak. . . . A White oak. And someday they'd make the timbers of a ship out of me, a clipper ship, and I'd sail the seven seas."

"And the crew that sailed you would drink birch beer made of the sap they'd tap me for when the snow was meltin' on Winespring."

What if they were already adrift somehow, the mountain bearing them away? It would have to be through time that they were moving, to the past or to a future of new beginnings. The world seemed even now to be left behind, far off.

91

7

THE TRAIL BECAME STEEPER. They walked without speaking until it turned back on itself to zigzag up the precipitous slope. Here he suggested they call it a day, and they sat down to rest on one of several smooth boulders that seemed to have shouldered their way through the soil.

"There's only trees around h'yur, ain't there?" She could have been hearing things inaudible to him.

"Only trees and the rocks and the mountain rearing up behind us." The sun was high now and it was warm.

"Tell me more about what we kin see—if I ain't bein' a pest."

How could he convey the impression made on him by all these trees? There were trees wherever you looked, standing in silence, yet all alive. "You ought to tell *me* about it." They still spoke in low voices. "You know more about trees than I do—Cherry birch. You probably know what goes on among them."

"You think somethin' goes on among them?"

He certainly never had before that moment. But then he had never before had a sense of the life-force of trees. "Maybe trees are conscious in their own way, and . . . without having any speech are . . . are *in on things* together: you know. And yes, I think you *do* know, I think you're in on it too."

She drew her knees up and, holding her skirt up under them, laid her cheek against them. "Well, I'll just let you go on thinkin' that, mister!" She raised her head. "What's that?"

From the direction to which she had turned a large bird came winging, swerving swiftly through the forest with a whooshing sound, a mostly black bird but with white patches and a dash of brilliant red. Smack! It fetched up against a tree-trunk, erect, long-necked, with a flaming red crest above a black-lined face. "My God," he exclaimed softly. With stiff, almost violently abrupt tossings of the powerfully beaked head, comic and commanding at once, the bird looked this way and that. Then it lurched hopping, up the trunk.

"It's some kind of woodpecker," he whispered, "but a giant—the size of a chicken." While he was describing it, the bird took off on its big black-and-white wings. As it disappeared among the trees, back to them came a string of yelping cries, as wild and abrupt as the bird itself. The hushed woods rang with them, shockingly. Wick felt a hand on his arm. The girl's expression was exultant.

"Do you know what it was?"

She shook her head slowly. "Cain't be that Uncle Tom ever seen one, or he'd of spoke of it. . . . With a long bill and a kinda long neck and a pointed cap as red as blazes!" she repeated, drawing out the words.

On the way down, she held back just enough to maintain tension on his shirttail. Again, they talked little. But frequently, having in mind how dull it must be for her just walking, he would stop and describe some feature of the scene: a mushroom with a red top like the glazed coating on a custard he remembered; a slim, incredibly green and agile beetle; some plants that were like little, thick, white-wax walkingsticks with knobby, bent heads—"Indian pipes," Letty said when he guided her hand to one. It seemed she could never hear enough of things like these, which Wick had never particularly noticed before.

Talking was easier walking on the road, with her hand on his shoulder or resting on his arm.

"Do you believe in God, Letty?"

It took her a moment to reply. "Uncle Tom's a great believer in God. An' if believin' in God does to you what it's done to him, I'd ruther be like Ma. She said to me once she didn't believe nobody knew nothin' about it for sartin and them that talks the most about it knows the least. That was after the preacher come callin' and left Uncle Tom in a turrible state. He done took it in his head— No, that ain't right. And *ain't*'s not right neither. Wick, you got to larn me to talk proper. How'd you say hit about Uncle Tom?"

"Just 'Uncle Tom took it in his head.' Or 'He has taken it in his head.' "

"He *has taken* hit in his head. . . . I generally know what's right when I h'yeer it. He has taken hit in his head he's beyond redemption. The preacher tells him to come into the church and have his sins washed away in the blood of the Lamb, but he takes the view that if his sins was washed away and then he found hisself sinnin' again, as he might well, bein' a sinner by nature—so he says—why, he'd be in worse trouble with the Lord. Such a pint havin' been made of his case, an' all."

"Pint?"

"Pint. What you put on the end of a stick to make hit sharp."

"Oh yes. Pint."

"He'd be *askin'* fer hellfar. I h'yurd him tellin' the preacher— you couldn't help h'yeerin' him—how he'd keep out of the way of the Lord, and then when he died he'd have a good chance of gettin' by without etarnal damnation. So long as he didn't draw attention to hisself he'd be paid no mind. So he didn't want to put in for salvation when as like as not he'd be found wantin' and sent where the sinners go. All the same, hit eats at him. I think he's scared to let off punishin' hisself for fear of bringin' on worse."

Their pace had slowed to a halt. It was strange theology to Wick. "Why does he consider himself a sinner, especially?"

"Well," she said with lowered head, "since you ask me, I got to tell you. But I count on you—"

"No—you don't have to tell me just because I asked."

"Yes. You ast, and you got a right to know. I couldn't not tell you." She spoke not submissively but with head raised, as if she were fated but equal to it. He had a glimpse in her of the relative she had portrayed. "I was goin' to ask you not to talk about hit. There ain't no use gettin' a lot made of hit again. When he was young he kilt a man. He was let off. It was pure self-defense. But then he had to kill another—he's always been pretty quick-tempered—and this time they put him away. He was in a couple of yur afore he was pardoned. They was both wicked men he done away with and everybody knowed it. But all the same, hit goes hard with him. . . . You won't think the worse of him for hit, will you? Uncle Tom's a *good* man. He wouldn't kill a livin' critter if hit warn't right."

"If he's your uncle, I know he didn't do any wrong," Wick said. "And I'll never say a word about it." They set off again,

94

almost without his being conscious of it, and he added, "It does seem a terrible shame, though, that he has to torture himself so."

"Hit's a shame, all right. But if hit warn't that—warn't?"

"Weren't."

"If hit weren't that, hit would be somethin' else."

It was of the girl, however, not of her uncle that he thought as they walked. What did it signify to find yourself talking so naturally to someone? He had scarcely ever before had a *conversation*, now that he thought about it. His mind had always been on the problem of conversing and of not putting himself at a disadvantage. This morning it was easy going. . . . What paradise it would be if Letty were a real girl! But would he not in that case have been his old hopeless self; or, rather, have been unable to be himself, or not have had a self to be? It was galling to reflect on that. 'Hey, have you heard about Wick Carter? He's got a girl who won't look at any other boy. She's blind.'

He despised himself, that such a thing could have occurred to him. And looking hastily, guiltily, across his shoulder, he thought, 'But would they be so sarcastic if they could see her?' She seemed to have no consciousness of being flawed—incomplete. She walked along appearing to spurn the ground and the tricks it could play on her; and he could not help feeling expanded by her confidence in him.

"You never told me whether you believe in God," he reminded her.

She moved her head this way, then that, as one does in examining various possibilities. "Do you?"

"Not in a church God."

She smiled a little. He knew she was going to answer him though she continued on in silence for the moment.

She reminded him of . . . well, surely it was by association: of the morning as it had been when they passed by here going the other way, when all had been clear, mild and fresh. And she had a fragrance that went with it, a natural fragrance a little like the scent of mown grass in the sun or of bread just out of the oven. But . . . even if he felt at one with her, she was on the other side of an unbridgeable gulf. Except insofar as she could see with his eyes. . . .

"My great grandma, and she was half Cherrykee, told my

grandma—that is, my mother's mother—that when the white men come to this country they brung with them ways of worshippin' that went a way back to a far-off part of the world. That was their holy land, and they didn't see nothin' holy about this one. She said they won't never have peace in their hearts until they larned that the Great Spirit is in the hills h'yar and the trees and creeks, an' in the birds and critters, too."

"So you do have some Indian blood! You meant what you said about Colly." He turned to look at her with new eyes.

"Yes. Lots of mountain folks has. Most don't talk about it, though—them as knows it. . . . Maybe it'll make you feel different about me." The hand on his shoulder made itself felt.

"Not the way you mean. I'd be glad if I had ancestors who went back thousands of years here, who were hunters in the forest before the white man came." He had a sound of Indian music in his head. "Maybe you're an Indian princess, like Pocahontas."

"Is she someone you know?" As so often when she questioned him about his other life—he was to notice—her voice had an edge of apprehension.

"No, she died long before I was born."

"Well, tell me how you know about her, then."

Before he had finished, she had extracted all he could remember of Captain John Smith and the founding of Jamestown, of which she had only vaguely heard.

"Will you tell me when we get to the oak tree we run to? Maybe if you'd be willin' we could run again."

And so they did, her hand clutching his. The ground had never before seemed to speed of itself beneath his feet.

Though he had some picnic sandwiches in the carrier of his bicycle, he was prevailed on to bring them to the kitchen, and join the family for the midday meal. It was the first of many times he was to eat with them at that table. What would have seemed almost impossible when he unwrapped his lunch that Saturday and had been poured a glass of milk came to pass and he grew to feel at home there.

He was aware from the beginning of something like an undercurrent between Mrs. Sherrod and him that he would have been hard put to it to define. He could not have said what she was like, inside, or what her thoughts might be. Yet it was as if they had been known to each other from far back. The long acquaintance was in her way of looking at him, her dark eyes beneath her arched brows seeming to go to an essential him and to accept what they saw; and this was comforting and relaxing to him, as if there were nothing after all he need hide. It was in the slight smile, too, when their eyes met, a reminiscent smile, it occurred to him to call it. When it happened that they were alone together she questioned him about himself as she went about her work, and grasped much more of what his life at home had been than he would have expected. "Queen," he called her, not impertinently but respectfully, and to her amusement; she smiled readily, her teeth even and white, not like the teeth of some mountain women he had seen. The name came about because of Letty's having shyly referred to Wick's calling her an Indian princess. "That would make me a queen, wouldn't it?" she had remarked. Continuing to grease a pan for corn bread she had recalled hearing her grandmother say that some Cherokee women had held high place and were called "war-women" because their advice was sought in time of war. "Grandma did say," she added, "that we come down from a war-woman."

Brother and sister were very different. At the start of their first meal together, the tall mountaineer had turned his pale-grey eyes upon Wick. While the boy waited for some kind of lightning to strike he had proclaimed: "If you've a mind to say grace, you're free to go right ahead." Unprepared, Wick had stumblingly disclaimed any such desire. "In that case," Mr. Barrows had said, "none will be spoke. The good Lord knows we h'yur is grateful for every scrap put on our plates. Hit's not for us to pester him about hit three times a day." Then, seeming to lose himself in some inner vista, he extended an arm as long as a gibbon's, gripped a piece of bread in his two hands and began to break it up and eat it absently.

Mrs. Sherrod, serving her family from a pot containing greens, potatoes and bits of chicken, asked Wick if they said grace in his house.

He replied in the negative. "I, er . . . reckon my father feels the same way about it Mr. Barrows does."

"But you're members of a church?"

"Well, no. Though my sister sings in the Episcopal choir, and my parents usually go to hear her."

Mr. Barrows, though Wick had not supposed him listening, turned on him with that shying-horse look. "Your sister—she's a devout, God-fearing young woman who's accepted Jesus Christ?"

"Yes, sir," Wick agreed under the force of the other's approach. "That is . . . that's not really it." The truth was owed something, and so was Letty's self-punishing uncle. "She mostly goes to church to be in the choir. She likes to sing. She's got a good voice."

Said Letty, "I bet she looks real beautiful, too, standin' up there." Suddenly she turned red, obviously remembering how she had learned of Cynthia's beauty.

"Yes, she does," he said quickly. "One of the men who chase after her said it made him believe in heaven, seeing her standing there in that white gown with her golden hair." A rapt silence followed this, and Wick heard himself voice an opinion that came to him from he knew not where. "Maybe that's why she joined the choir: to convert the heathen."

Mrs. Sherrod's eyes widened questioningly, then she broke into her quick, light laughter—"*Oh*-ho-ho-ho-ho-ho-ho-ho!"

"*Wha-ha!*" A clap of laughter split Mr. Barrow's silence. He grinned, grinned a really beautiful, transforming smile and whooped again while the rest of them laughed beyond any cause.

Mr. Barrows, Wick gathered, conducted his work on principles governed by his peculiar religious outlook, and was the last man anywhere around who brought trees out of the woods with a team of horses. Others in his business used bulldozers or "skidders." Wick learned more about it one evening when Colly during a discussion of plans said, "I don't see why we cain't have a 'dozer. We could sure haul out a lot more timber."

"We ain't got the money for no 'dozer!" Mr. Barrows had hardly let the boy get the words out of his mouth.

"Mr. Potter and Mr. Freeman got 'dozers. They bought 'em on time, and the 'dozers has paid for themselves." Colly had reddened and looked stubborn—and stubborn lines formed around his uncle's mouth.

"If they want to tear up the woods, hit must be hit's all right for them," he declaimed. "You plow through the woods with a 'dozer and drag a tree with all hits limbs two hundred feet through the woods an' you make a mess of them. But if a man's a Christian and don't see no reason to doubt he's made hit, in the way of salvation, he don't have to care about hit. The earth and what's

98

on hit, the plants and critters, is here to serve him. But them outside the ranks of the saved has got no right to make free and easy with what's h'yur below." He paused, glowering, and drew a deep, hard breath. He was having out with himself aloud, it seemed evident, what he had had out with himself to himself before.

"You wouldn't see a bar nor a coon tearin' the woods apart, nor a heathin Indian when they was h'yur. Hit was all they was goin' to have. Come Judgment Day, all them that lived by the Gospel will be lifted up to heaven and them that has accepted the Gospel but kept a-sinnin' will be cast down to everlastin' perdition. But there'll be the souls of the Indians, who never h'yurd the word, and them like the Indians who never put in for salvation—never prayed nor ast favors of the Lord and never got counted one way or t'other. Their souls won't go up and they won't go down. They'll stay on earth, with the critters. So it ain't for them to go tearin' up the woods."

There was no denying that there was a kind of queer reasonableness in the speaker's ideas. Whatever their merit, however, they appeared, from the set of his face, to afford him scant consolation. Wick was aware of Mrs. Sherrod's looking at him expectantly, and that supplied the necessary impetus. "Well, sir, I'd say you could be mighty proud of not doin' any more hurt to the woods than you can help." It was a matter he had come to take so to heart that the nature of his own labors rankled.

"If you can get a rock to dance, you can get Tom Barrows to take credit to hisself." Mrs. Sherrod spoke in the way of a warm and charitable being who saw people from a goodly distance off. As for her brother, he seemed a little shocked, as if perhaps he had not heard aright.

Wick said, "Don't it bother you, Mr. Barrows, to see other people wreckin' the woods and hills by their kind of timber-cuttin' and by the strip-minin'?"

This time he towered to his feet. "Is there anythin' in Scripture says they cain't?"

"Well—"

"No, there ain't, so far's I know. I never h'yurd tell of no preacher preachin' agin hit. That bein' the case, who am I to be judgin' of hit?"

When they were alone Letty said, "I h'yurd you say 'don't it'

99

again instead of 'doesn't it.' You got to stop that. You'll be talkin' just like us folks next."

They were together on Saturdays and Sundays and on most other days he would bicycle out after work.

He had gone to the public library in Harpersburg to see what books could be had on birds and trees. The interior, with volumes in ordered rows around the walls and magazines on a table and a small woman with a long face in charge, took him back to the world he had left. And it made him realize how much older, more independent and rugged he had become. The librarian was so helpful in providing the two books he sought that he was emboldened to ask if she could find him something in the way of description. Description? Yes—of scenery. But might she inquire what he wanted it for? "Well . . . to learn how to put things I see into words. Especially things in nature."

"You want to write!"

"Not exactly. But something like that."

She had taken two books he had never heard of from the shelves. But his first thought when he left was for the bird guide, in which every species was pictured in color. He had no trouble discovering that his little yellow-and-olive bird with the mask was a Maryland yellow-throat and the giant woodpecker either an Ivory-billed or Pileated—probably the latter, since the former was feared extinct. Letty's peeto-bird was a Tufted titmouse. There was the fascination in this of solving puzzles.

He ate lunch by himself, leaning against the wheel of the front-end loader and began *The Outermost House,* the first of the two books provided for his improvement. The dignity and sonority of the language of the opening paragraph and the solemn grandeur of the forms of earth it called up awoke in him a feeling of awe. He read through lunch, as he was to read during unoccupied moments of every day from then on, finishing it and one successor after another.

When he produced his discoveries for Letty that afternoon, she marveled as he had known she would. Maryland yellow-throat and Pileated woodpecker! Did you ever? He went over the book with her, exclaiming over the variety of birds—*hundreds* of different kinds!—and trying to picture some of them for her to give her an idea of the range in shape and coloring among birds.

She was an insatiable listener. He had gone on to the tree book and read what it told of the trees she knew, beginning with the Cherry birch. . . . " 'The sweet sap is fermented to make birch beer and oil of wintergreen was formerly distilled from the inner bark and twigs.' "

She was dumbfounded by the number of trees there were—he read off to her the names of all the pines and oaks—and awe-struck by the redwoods: "If I had a wish come true right now, you'd see me where them big trees is." They were named Sequoia, he read to her, for the son of a Cherokee girl who had invented an alphabet for his people. Between her longing receptivity to it and the pleasure he found in unfolding it all was a kind of echo back and forth, a reverberation, which made for a sweetness of sensation unlike any he had known.

She was so full of curiosity about the other two books that he brought with him the next afternoon the one he had not yet begun. After supper he read to her from it while she washed the dishes and the others finished the work outdoors. The book, he told her, was called *Far Away and Long Ago: A History of My Early Life* and was by a man named W. H. Hudson.

Thus began an evening that stood apart from his life up to then. The light was still bright by the little curtained window where he sat, and the music of a robin came in with the pleasant, fertile odors of the farmyard. When he raised his eyes from the print it was to see the trim-waisted figure of the girl before the sink, her shoulder-length hair shaking with the vigor of her scrubbing, her tan legs pale in the hollows behind the knees, the black iron kettle squat and assured on the stove.

When he had read for a while he looked up again and discovered her motionless, her hands on the rim of the sink. She shook her head slowly. "My, that's beautiful," she sighed. "Who'd even have thought words could sound like that?"

"I've been thinking that, too."

"Go back, please, and read that agin about the growin' grass an' the birds' voices."

He turned to the page.

> Never have I felt confinement less—I who feel, when I am out of sight of living, growing grass, and out of sounds of birds' voices and all rural sounds, that I am not properly alive!

101

"Had he writ of the *feel* of livin', growin' grass, I'd of thought he was another blind person. . . . I'd of died had we stayed in Dayton."

When he continued, he thought that he had never really read before. He had never fully known how books could admit you to lives more vital and to worlds richer than your own, and, astonishingly, in so doing reveal you to yourself—as if you were discovering your own tracks in a country new to you.

> The ombu is a very singular tree indeed, and being the only representative of tree-vegetation, natural to the soil, on those great level plains, and having also many curious superstitions connected with it, it is romance in itself. It belongs to the rare Phytolacca family, and has an immense girth—forty or fifty feet in some cases. . . .

Here was a man to whom trees were important and, as it developed, everything in nature, plants and animals as natural to be concerned about as one's human companions. And of course it was not just a matter of the book. There was the effect of having such a listener as the girl, who, the dishes finished, sat near him resting her arm on the table, touched and agitated by what he read, as if it were all there before them and happening to them— the strange-looking lame dog with "a face of extraordinary length, which gave him a profoundly wise, baboon-like expression"; the brutality of the gauchos in slaughtering cattle (which caused her to cover her ears with her hands); the time that came "for us small children to feast on violets and run wild in our forest"; the death of nineteen-year-old Margarita, who had "the sweetest smile imaginable, the softest voice and gentlest manner, and was so much loved by everybody." At that, Wick had trouble keeping his throat from closing and could only hope that Letty, in whose eyes tears had formed, did not see herself in the girl, as he did. He avoided looking at Mrs. Sherrod, who, having unobtrusively joined them, sat sewing by the lamp she had lighted.

"I'm forgettin' *everything*," said Letty when he came to the end. "I ain't put the chicken bones out for the coon."

But Colly, who stood leaning against the door-jamb, said he had done it, speaking with indulgent patience.

Later Wick himself met up with the raccoon in the dusk, a little bear with pointed muzzle and monkey's paws that confronted him with close-set expressionless black eyes in a highwayman's black mask, and when he proved to be empty-handed strolled off into the shadows. 'It remembers the Cherokees,' Wick thought, fancifully. He was on his way to the outhouse—another step backward into the spare, unpampered past of his ancestors. He had largely given up the practice of measuring himself against the boys he knew in Harwood, which had helped him through the worst of the new existence, but it gave him some satisfaction now. He drew a deep breath of the night air, heard a whippoorwill strike up and looked to the black earth's shoulder of Winespring. The Cumberland Mountains. Mrs. Sherrod had offered him a mattress for the night. "It ain't much, but you'd be welcome to it, and to grits and coffee with us in the mornin'. Maybe you'd find it better than that long ride in the dark. And there'll be woods all around." She was right about his preference, and with local habits as casual as they were, he doubted that Mrs. Haney, let alone Jack, would be much concerned about his nonappearance.

8

FROM THEN ON he and Letty read a great deal together. They also walked, and he was kept occupied describing for her what he saw.

Letty liked to have things in her hands, of course—even frogs and salamanders. The latter he had learned to find under rocks and rotting logs. Some kind of Dusky salamander most of them were, as nearly as he could tell from the little book on reptiles and amphibians he had bought, but once there was a six-inch-long Spotted salamander, black with two rows of yellow spots so that, as Wick observed, it reminded you of a picture of a ship at night with lighted portholes. Their favorites were the little helpless newts they picked up from the road, dull orange in color with two rows of scarlet dots encircled in black down the back and eyes with horizontal slits of pupils.

Ordinarily he kept hands off snakes—it went without saying off the rattler they met on some rocks near the top of Winespring, head and neck erect above its coils in apprehension of the foreign presence. ("I ought to kill it," he said, thinking of the danger of poisonous snakes to a girl who could not see, but Letty forbade it: "It's his mountain as much as ours.")

A small Green snake, however, had no hint of menace about it. He happened to detect it above his head in an apple-tree and, carefully unloosed from its branch, it seemed actually to enjoy ringing itself around Letty's fingers. Slim as a whip, elegant, exquisite in coloring . . . Wick was even more than usually frustrated by inability to convey what he saw. And as the Green snake was irresistible in style, so was the Hog-nosed in personality.

They were sitting on a rock listening to the insects trilling when the girl called attention to a sound she said was like a toad's *weeeeeeeeeeeeeeeep* but more chirping. Catching it on the next repetition, Wick claimed it *was* a toad, "a strong, musical, very cheerful toad." But he went forth to investigate, and was able to trace the sound to its source without giving alarm.

When he saw a snake at the edge of the lumbering-road they had been following—a small, rather thick snake with its head up— he could not believe he had found the singer. Watching it through the binocular he had by then acquired left no doubt. The little reptile, which was yellowish-brown, dark in blotches across the back, strained forward as the trill came. 'I'll be damned,' he said to himself.

Instead of fleeing when he went up to it, it coiled and drew back its head, open-mouthed, to strike, flattening its neck like a cobra and hissing. Even its head was flattened, so that it resembled an open purse. A copperhead? Its browns were almost bright enough. But, remembering his reading, he looked more closely. The scales on the top of the head were large, the nose turned up. Wick said, "I know what you are, and you're a bluff." He poked it gently with a stick. Whereupon it keeled over and after a few convulsive writhings lay as dead as it had been deadly a moment before, yellowish-white belly up, mouth ajar—utterly unbelievable. Recalling that Hog-nosed snakes were harmless, Wick picked up the limp form and bore it back to Letty.

Her enchantment with his report lived up to his expectations.

"It's got quite a nice face," he observed as she ran her finger over its snout, then took the still-inert form in her hands.

"Let's see if it'll come to now," she said, laying it carefully on the ground, right side up.

"Darned if it hasn't tumbled itself on its back again!" he exclaimed. "Wants to make sure we know it's dead!"

"Well, did you ever?" She shook her head: it was too much! "I'd be for takin' it home and keepin' it, but they say snakes won't eat only live things, and I don't much like— You know," she interrupted herself, "I got an idear. I bet if you look in the book when we get back it'll say a Hog-nosed snake feeds on toads. That's why it sings like a toad—to draw its dinner to it."

And the book did say it fed on toads. Only it did not mention any singing and neither did a bigger reptile book in the library. Wick was inclined to credit them with a discovery new to science.

He had bought the binocular to make out more about birds, and the small, compact one that sang from the top of a tree on the way to the Winespring trail was a cinch once he had the full

105

sun on it. "It's a deep blue, the whole bird!" he exclaimed. "An Indigo bunting. It's . . ." What could he say to make her see it? "Try to remember how the sky looked after the sun had gone down but before dark, when it was a clear—a deep, bright blue. It's a blue like that."

But they were content with silence, too. The trails were mostly too steep and treacherous underfoot for conversation, and even when they rested they were apt to sit listening to the undercurrent of sounds he would mostly have missed but for her—a cricket, the faintly heard whine of a saw-mill, the crowing of the Sherrods' rooster, the muted roar of trucks, the rustling of a lizard in the leaves, "bummel" bees that led Letty to flowers: "Where they stop hummin' and where they start up again—that's where the flower is." Once, on an obscure trail, she murmured, "Remember me to tell Hamp and Rafe to be keerful how they bang them pots." He had heard nothing, but, having finally caught on to the nature of the Fergusons' sideline, was not surprised at her thinking it best to turn back.

Sitting on the rock they had rested on before, he picked up the thread of an earlier conversation. "When we're in a place like this, it seems to seep into you that there's a knowledge trees share of things beyond us, explanations and meanings that we don't know about, and maybe as important as any we do." He could talk to her, he thought again, as he could have to no other girl. Of course, he had never had such thoughts in any other girl's company. . . .

"I think you ought to be called Wick, not I," he said; and when she asked why explained, "You know how a wick draws oil or melted wax up so it can be burned. I think you're like a wick between the woods and me, like a conductor the way copper is a conductor of electricity. Only you're a conductor of the spirit of the woods. It goes through you and down your arm into my shoulder. One of these days I'm likely to turn into the kind of critter people used to see in the woods long, long ago—a satyr or a faun with legs like—"

She took him aback by laying her head momentarily against his shoulder. And when she raised it her eyelashes were wet. He had meant just to entertain her. They invariably treated each other as being, for all that it mattered, friends of the same sex. (There were the details of physical privacy, it was true, but over these

106

they made little. "Mister, you may not know it, but you got business up the trail ahead.") He was relieved now when she smiled. After all, a sister might have had such an impulse. "It must be," she said, "I'm turnin' into a birch tree before my time. I better keep my arm to myself. We don't want your legs turnin' into— What kind of legs was it?"

"Goat's legs. But I'll take a chance, for the sake of the way the woods ease a person when his insides have been knotted up."

She said nothing but her fingertips touched him lightly beside the collar; she was sitting a little above and behind him with her arm—which she had not removed—resting on his shoulder. He was used to having it there, if he did not have her hand in his, as after a run or while picking a way over rocks. She had once asked him timidly if it did not bother him having her always "hangin' onto" him. He told her he felt something was missing when she was being independent. If it gave her comfort, he thought, any bother to him was unimportant. And he could appreciate how it might, for sometimes a sensation of being Letty would pass over him and with it one of the unnerving isolation of a person in impenetrable, unalterable darkness.

But what were they, one to the other? The difficulty of finding a category for their relationship made Wick uneasy. 'She's not my sister, or my girl, or just a friend.' A satisfactory answer came to him one day. They were as two natives of a country that had no other inhabitants.

If that was so, the chief feature of the land that made them kin was one he had gazed on that morning rising like a lonely island from the ghost sea of mist in the valleys, like the goal of a voyage across the unknown. Winespring grew in importance for them. The climb to the top was taxing, but the difficulties kept the mountain heights remote and made the ultimate gaining of the summit an achievement. They brought their lunch with them in a canvas shoulder bag and a canteen they replenished at the last stream, one that trickled through a rhododendron thicket around mossy stones like green sponges. A cupful was as refreshing as cold cider and they were convinced that its waters were those of the Wine Spring itself.

From there on the trees lost stature and the forest opened up, and there were larger expanses and walls of bare rock. Most of the exposed rock of the mountain was smooth and hard—"sandrock," Letty called it. But in places, invariably undercut beneath sandstone sills, there were beds of layered shale, the most finely divided resembling rotted telephone books, or—what Wick tried to shut his eyes to—a black seam.

Two-thirds of the way up the mountain the hollowing out of an exceptionally thick bed of shale had formed a deep recess high enough to stand in and on their first ascent they took shelter there from a thunderstorm. These gave little warning. The wall of slate-gray cloud would rise out of the southwest and halfway to the zenith before a walker in the deep woods would have noticed it leaning over the earth, a mumbling apparition, sullen and solid, lightning flickering in its hollows.

"You can hear the wind comin' up," said Letty in the sunless gloom. The first heavy drops made splashes the size of saucers. And then the full downpour was on them. In thirty seconds they were soaked. Their hair was plastered to their heads, water runing down their legs, their feet squishing in their shoes. "That ol' thunder's comin' right up the trail after us!" Letty cried—gaily enough, Wick saw when he turned to look back at her. All the same, the lightning was close enough to make the recess under the sandstone ledge providential in his eyes, a refuge equally from the blinding, stinging torrents.

Letty was hugging herself. "Do you ever feel that we're people in a story, like the ones in the books you been readin' to me?"

"Yes, I do!" He was struck that she should have a sensation so familiar to him.

"I suppose hit's because so much of what I take in comes from your tellin' me, just the same as if you was readin' hit to me. Only . . . I don't think that's all. Hit's like the things happenin' to us was especially important like hit is with made-up people. You comin' here from so far off. And now our bein' up on the side of the mountain in the rain, all by ourselves. Hit's just the way it would be if you were readin' to me about a boy and a girl in the woods in the rain."

"If we're characters in a book, does that mean everything in our lives is all decided, as if it were all written down, and we haven't got anything to say about it? Or are we writing the book as we go along?"

It seemed to him that her face fell. "Oh . . . I reckon whether we're in a story or are just ourselves standin' here, hit's all settled the way hit's goin' to come out."

"But haven't we got the choice, say, of going on up the mountain or going back home?"

"Oh, we got a choice in little things, likely enough," she conceded. "But the way they turns out, that's all out of our hands. If you ask me. Whatever happens, hit happens because of things we got no control over or because we bring hit on ourselves by bein' what we are—which is the way we was made."

It was his own long-standing belief, and one behind his chronically pessimistic view of his own case. But to hear it from Letty unaccountably upset and aroused him. "We once had an argument about this in English class. The teacher said you could make out a perfect case to show that whatever happened was bound to happen that way. If I told you to raise your hand, you might think you could raise either one, but the one you *would* raise you'd raise because of the way you're made—just as you say. And that's the outcome of all your ancestry and of all evolution, from the beginning of life. Sure, you ve got the power of choice. But the machinery you make the choice by in your brain—it's all set and it's bound to decide as it does. So you raise your right hand."

She turned a questioning face to him, seeming to realize from his cheerful delivery of the fatalistic preachment that he had not yet said the last word. But her expression, at once a little pleading and apprehensive, he thought, checked him. He knew what was in his mind, however irrational: that because her eyes looked perfectly normal and no evidence of injury had been found by the doctors she was not necessarily doomed to sightlessness. What made the hope more legitimate, to his thinking—and he knew that this, too, was irrational—was his certainty that her recovery would take her out of his life. 'With her sight, she could have Prince Charles, if he saw her' was the way he put it to himself. He went on:

"But what the teacher said was that while he couldn't find any grounds for disbelieving that everything in life was decided in advance, the truth was that the people who *did* believe that and allowed it to govern their lives were apt to be always on the receiving end of things, and they weren't likely to make anything of themselves. Whereas people who didn't believe it, or acted as

109

if they didn't—they were the ones who could do anything in life they were determined to—just as if everything weren't settled!"

He finished on a note of triumph and his companion appeared no less taken than he by the provocative contradiction.

She said slowly, "That's somethin' I got to think about. . . . Oh, Wick, what you know!"

"What I *don't* know," he echoed, though his dark view of his future was in abeyance and he had, as he not infrequently, and with little logic, did have, a sense of great possibilities ahead.

As if to give license and encouragement to confidence, the sun swept in upon them. "You can see it rushing toward us through the woods. . . ." But fast as Wick spoke the radiance was upon them, and the shadow had fled. "We're going to have to move fast in getting out from under our roof." He took her chilled hand. "Water's still trickling off the edge of it."

Out in the open, the sun beamed warmly on them.

"It's still dripping all around—everywhere," said Letty. Hearing, in itself, seemed always to be a satisfaction to her. "After a rain, when the sun comes out warm and the birds is singin' again, an' the smells is all so fresh an' good, hit's like a second early mornin'. You want to give thanks."

The hardest part of the climb was ahead, and the sunniest, as the forest thinned out. They were damper from perspiration than from the rain when they reached the last switchback and the trail leveled out at the crest.

"Here we are!"

Before them, over the tops of the trees below, lay the panorama of the world they had left.

He took her by the hand again to lead her safely to the most commanding part of the rock ledge they had come to. While they stood there side by side, he tried to steady himself in the rip-tide of powerful and conflicting emotions. She was absorbing it in her own way, her head back, her eyes closed. Her hand lay so passive in his that he released it.

Could she tell, he asked, that they were on top of the world?

She ran her fingers into her damp hair and raised it from her head. "I kin tell there's space all around, and great distance. An' there's. . . . You know how a holler box sounds different when you thump it, to the way a block of wood does? Hit's like that. I

110

mean the quiet is—like a holler quiet, a big holler quiet, big as the sky." She had dropped her arms and he waited, knowing she was submitting herself again to the distances she was conscious of.

She said at length, "Hit's like your soul leavin' your body without you dyin'. Hit's that kind of peace. The sounds that come floatin' to you, they's all that's left of all the strivin'. Just the lazy sounds you mightn't hardly notice—a dog a-barkin' and a saw-mill a-whinin'. An' they got nothin' more to them than a memory." She gave his sleeve a little tug. "Now you tell me about hit!"

Though he scarcely felt like smiling he could never help doing so a little when she gave orders. "It's like being on top of a huge, steep wave, the biggest in a sea of huge, green waves—as still as if a spell had been cast on them. Off to the east, through a gap, you can see across Virginia to a range of even bigger mountains, dreaming of things beyond our knowing. They make you think that if you could know it, you'd know what the earth is at heart."

To the right was a very different scene.

"What's the matter?" she asked.

"Over through a bigger gap you can see where the strippers have been at work on a mountain. They've bulldozed a road up the side and they've been around it twice. It's like cutting a mountain up into steps, each one forty or fifty feet high and all the dirt and rock from each cut pushed off the side. The top of the mountain is like a big loaf of bread on a tray, though it's still got woods on top. There's a saying that a billy goat couldn't get up a highwall like those." He doubted that he was concealing from her his horror at the sight. "Well, one thing: mountains can't suffer."

Letty was fingering the top of a huckleberry bush. "I've heerd tell of hit ever since we come back from Dayton. 'A mess of the hills, a mess of the woods, a mess of the farms down below and of people's lives.' "

"There's a law that calls for restoration. It would be interesting to see them restore a mountain that's been carved up like that. But I mustn't get critical. That's what my pay comes from! Mountain-butchering."

But she interrupted him. "That don't make hit your fault. If they didn't hire you they'd hire someone else. But some day you're goin' to stop hit."

"I'm goin' to stop what?"

"The strip-minin' and all the like of that." She had raised her face to him to convey her resolution.

"*I'm* going to stop it!" He laughed. "Oh, Letty, what an idea you've got of the world." He put a hand on her shoulder and gave her a playful shaking, as if to wake her up. "I can imagine them, listening to *me*."

"Hit come to me while we was standin' h'yur. They'll listen to you. You'll know the words." In her face his incredulous scrutiny detected no trace of doubt.

He laughed again, but shortly. How many more years would the Cumberlands last, at this rate? he was thinking. And Winespring? No—that could not be! "You'd better rely on Gilley Huff and his persuasiveness. And . . . certain people and their dynamite."

"I'm lookin' to you."

"I'll be doing well if— Here, why don't we sit down, if you're dry enough. Anyhow, the rock'll be warm. We'll be each other's back-rest."

When they had settled themselves, back to back, she reminded him of the sentence he had left incomplete.

"People think that because my parents are well-off I'm going to be. But if any of it comes to me it probably won't for another forty years. And as I was going to say. I'll be lucky if I can just make a living and pay the children's doctors' bills."

"I thought you said you warn't goin' to have no children—any children."

"Oh, well. . . . If I have any." When he thought of children, he thought of wailing toddlers, diapers sagging. But Indian children couldn't have been like that. He thought of them scampering about among the rocks, like wild creatures.

"You know," he said in an hypothesizing voice, "if I were going to have a child, this is where I'd like to start it, here at the top of Winespring. Wouldn't this be the finest place to get a new life begun?" The back against his stiffened—perhaps not surprisingly. However, the idea had an impetus and he sailed on like a boat before the wind. "Think what a boy—or girl—conceived up here would be like. With the strength of the mountain entering into them . . . into the lovers. Maybe rain would overtake them, come pelting down. They'd let it. The child they'd create would be the child of Winespring, mighty Winespring, lord of the range . . . companion of downpours, summer sunshine, lonely clouds, winds and winter storms. It would be the . . . the fruit of all those."

What possessed him? "How do you think a mother—a mother-to-be, that is—would feel about the idea?"

"I couldn't say," Letty responded in a flat voice.

"Well," he said, a little disorganized. "What do you say we eat? I'm starved."

But it was not so easy to recover the ordinary heedless tenor of communication. She was not talkative and he remained confused for a time, his thoughts colored by what had come into his head, as thoughts will be by a dream.

"That's better," he exclaimed when they had finished their sandwiches, which for a wonder had stayed dry. "But I've still got room for some blackberries. I'll pick us a few."

"Don't get scratched up."

When he returned with a handful or two in the canteen cup he found her curled on her side, her eyes closed, a pucker between them. She opened them as he spoke but appeared momentarily at a loss. "I can't hardly believe it, but I must of dropped off. I had a dream. . . ."

He said, "It's this mountain. It takes possession of you."

After their next trip he could almost believe that might be so.

They were sitting on a bed of dry moss from which the rock ledge ran out when Letty observed, "The last time we were here you said, well, anyway, mountains couldn't suffer. Can you be sure of that?"

"To suffer, they'd have to have life, and . . ." He paused, looking off into the hazy azure of the sky. "Well, of course, as far as that goes, who's to say rocks haven't got a kind of life of their own? It could be as different from trees' life as trees' life is from ours."

She had her legs drawn up to her and could have been gazing, as he had been, into the vague depths of the sultry heavens.

He added, "You do feel there's *some*thing that suffers when a mountain is torn all to pieces. Even though nature itself can be pretty grim."

Which made it strange, he thought, that in the world of nature

113

there should be the softness of a girl's face, the cheek shaped with so tender a feeling, the upper lip rising delicately to the odd little groove that comes down from the nose.

"Tell me more about Winespring. How it looks."

"I think I've told you all there is to tell."

"Oh, there must be more. To begin with, can you see it much when you're off workin'?"

"From down in most of the valleys it's hidden. When you're in the bottomlands this is shut-in country, the hills standing so close and steep. But sometimes there Winespring will be, at the end of the valley or nudging up over the other mountains."

She leaned forward, her arms clutching each other across her breast, eyes tight shut. "And?"

"And? Oh, yes, I always look at it. And . . . just after dawn, the sun hits it in a way that brings out every tree on it. It does that, too, when it's high in the sky and shining down at just the same angle as the mountainside. It hits the tops of the trees so that each one stands out lighted up above the bluey shadow below." He summoned up recollection. "Then when there's a haze of heat, old Winespring seems far off . . . withdrawn into its memories, maybe you could say."

"And?" When he did not at once respond she nudged him with her shoulder, imperious as a child.

"It's always majestic. That makes it hard to think of our being up on the top as we are now. Especially at night. In the moonlight, up under the stars, it looks— I almost expect to see it move, as if I were an ant and it were a great old bear crouched there." He would not have thought he had so much to say about it. "It's grandest of all when it calls up the thunderstorm. Then there's a silver light on it, and the big, black clouds swell up around it. With lightning flickering like . . . snakes' tongues in their hidden valleys. It's like a wizard then. Exercising its magic powers. Monarch and magician, all in one."

"Then admit it's got life, like anything that's alive."

"I was just saying it's as if it were."

"You said it could get into a person. It would have to have *spirit* to do that."

"Well, I suppose that's so." If it was how she wished it, he would not dispute her.

"But you don't believe it!"

Her intensity caused him to regard her more closely. It still disconcerted him at times that they could not see into each other's eyes. He could not always, as now, be altogether sure what was behind what she was saying. "I don't know," he avowed. "It's beyond my knowing."

"You got to know. Maybe the mountain's trying to tell you something."

"And what would it be trying to tell me?"

"Maybe what I was tryin' to tell you."

Before he could bring back to mind what she might be referring to, she went on. "But first you got to know there's a spirit in hit, a great spirit." She was unresponsive to his half-teasing air. Plucking at the dried grass beside her, she seemed unnaturally keyed up.

"*The* Great Spirit?" It was not often that their moods were so unrelated and he could not forebear baiting her a little further.

"Hit could be. And hit could be you'd be surprised if hit was to show you hit's got a claim on you."

Though her reversion to *hit* was a sign of her being exercised, he thought that with a little push she might go over the line and break into laughter. "I'd be surprised all right." And he added, "He said with a smile. He enjoyed seeing her colored up so prettily."

To his surprise, she took him by the shoulders and turned him firmly away from her. He felt her pull aside the collar of his shirt and the next instant the warmth of her face on his neck. Almost before he had time to be mystified a fiery pain shot through him from its base. The cry that escaped him was less of pain than astonishment, though.

"You bite harder than you know!" he exclaimed, gingerly rubbing the spot and articulating his shoulder.

He saw it had not been in fun, however. She sat, her profile to him, stiff and white-faced.

"What was that for?"

"Hit warn't me. Hit was the mountain. I told you what hit was gona show you." Her cheeks mantled with extraordinary rapidity. "If Winespring can put an idear in your head about bringin' a gal up here and take possession of you while you get a baby started in her, why shouldn't it make me do what it likes?"

"Leaving me a marked man, at least for a while, probably." His voice was on the borderline between flippancy and ruefulness. The place hurt.

"And you ought to be." But she could not sustain it. Her color drained away again, the corners of her lips turned down and her eye grew large behind the lens of a tear. Shining, the tear overflowed.

Putting a hand on her shoulder, he said commiseratingly, "What's the matter, Letty?" He was still in the throes of astonishment.

"You know what the matter is. I hurt you." A sob came like a hiccup and she hung her head. "I'll never forgive myself."

"But it wasn't you. Don't we know it was Winespring?"

"Then hit's a wicked old mountain."

"It just wants to show who's in command."

Though remaining bemused by her seizure, he set about to bring her around, cajoling and recalling the kind of incidents of his life that entertained her. But she did not wholly give in until, on the way down the mountain, he succeeded in an endeavor he had failed at several times in the past. He captured a Fence swift. It had scooted off as had others in a bounding sprint, but he had cornered it among some rocks. The cool, mail-clad but soft-bodied little lizard struggled with uncowed vigor to free itself, pushing hard with its sharp-clawed, long-toed little feet against the encircling fingers. But when Letty held it and gradually relaxed her grasp it remained immobile.

"It has its head cocked and is watching you with the brightest little eyes. It's amazingly alive, to be so utterly motionless. Only its eyelids move, when it blinks."

She stroked its back lightly with her fingertips for a moment, then, smiling, set it down.

"You've got a way with reptiles," he said. "I'll bet you could outdo any of those crazy religious people who handle rattlesnakes."

"I don't know what would make me try."

9

CYCLING TO THE FARM one afternoon, Wick was met, where the road diverged from the stream bed, by the novel sight of a new, chunky, four-wheel-drive vehicle coming toward him. Mr. Winstead, the manager of Allegheny-Keystone's Talbot Creek Mine, raised a hand in a restrained greeting and gave him a steady, comprehending, not unfriendly look as he drove by. He appeared not in the least abashed at having been encountered in a spot where his ordinary concerns would scarcely have taken him.

Well, well. No doubt it was natural for parents to be interested in the company a minor son was choosing, and word would surely have got around that he was seeing a great deal of the Sherrods. Let them keep tabs—so long as his life was not interfered with.

In fact, whatever reports had been transmitted must have put him in a favorable light. From the changed tone of the letters he received he knew that his father was surprised and impressed by his standing on his own feet—as he would have put it—without asking for help. There was talk of college for the fall semester.

There was also a great deal in defense of the coal industry. This was not to be wondered at in view of the references in his own letters to victims of black-lung disease, the squalor of the mining communities, the resentment of the companies for their neglect of the miners' safety, the grisly destruction of the hills. He read with attention his father's answers to these charges, and, a company-president's son in his own eyes as well as everyone else's, he made the most of them. He could not in any case imagine his father as less than totally right with respect to the things of the world. "Unsatisfactory as the lot of the Cumberland people may be, it would be far worse without the mining companies," one letter said. The clincher offered was that "no one has ever suggested that the companies get out." Nothing in the

117

boy's eyes would have justified the devastation of the hills, but for that Allegheny-Keystone was not responsible.

He had had three letters from Cynthia, written in her round, sure hand on her expensive, stiff blue stationery. He learned from her latest that their mother was all for his early recall to Harwood but that their father opposed

> cheating you out of the experience. He says this is putting something solid under your feet that you'll be able to stand on all your life come what may. Hope that makes you feet better. To tell the truth, I think the old boy is getting a bang out of the way his son is handling this, and doesn't want to be deprived of the satisfaction of following it, installment by installment. He'd prefer you didn't come back a revolutionary, though. . . .

He tried not to think of the future at all. He could not imagine his present life continuing or his forsaking it for another. So he sought to lose himself in the passing days. He had more cause than ever not to look ahead after his next encounter with Bull Turner, this one at Taulbee's store where Turner was getting gas. What made his jeering malignancy far worse than usual was that he had beside him in his low-slung, overornamented old black Cadillac a coarsely attractive woman. And that when he invited her to share his derision, she regarded Wick with bold appraisal and remarked audibly, "I think he's cute."

Wick said to himself when Turner had slammed his car into gear and lunged off, 'That really does it.'

He had stopped at Taulbee's to buy groceries on his way to the farm, where he was having so many meals that he felt the least he could do was contribute his share. That he did not spend more time than he did there was at Letty's insistence. "You've got to go around some with other boys and men. It wouldn't be right for you to be up here whenever you aren't workin'—though we'd like it. If you do, it'll come to you one of these days that you've had too much. Then I don't know when we'd see you." Perhaps she was also thinking of public opinion. Anyhow, she was firm, and instinct told him rightly. So sometimes he went with the Fergusons or Jack to the Last Chance/First Chance bar or by himself to the library in Harpersburg, which stayed open late on two nights a week.

There one evening he ran into a familiar stocky figure. Gilley was at a table with books spread around him, making faces at a pad of paper he had half covered with writing. "So you're still here with us," he observed, and suggested that when Wick had finished at the library they eat together.

On the street, Wick asked his friend how the book was getting on. To his surprise, Gilley seized his arm and brought him to a halt. "What a perfect time to ask that!" He looked over both shoulders before going on. "And the answer is—great!" As they walked on slowly, he continued. "I sent three-quarters of it to a New York publisher with a résumé of the rest. And three days ago the reply came. You know, after I read the letter I was afraid to look at it again for the rest of the day for fear I'd misread it. But it said the same things in the morning. The editor was enthusiastic. If I can get the rest of it in by October the book will come out in May. Isn't that glorious?"

"Terrific!" Wick was joyful to the point of surprising himself. That success had come to someone who had the good of his fellows so much at heart was like a vindication of the world. "Can you finish it by October?"

"Oh, I think so. I'll have to. May would be just the right time for the book to come out. You've heard of people being fired with zeal? That's how I'll be fired when the school board gets hold of the book."

"Doesn't that worry you?"

"Of course. Everything worries me," he asserted with no diminution of the bounce in his step. "At any rate, I'm getting an advance on royalties of five hundred dollars in a few days and another of the same amount on delivery of the rest. Think of it!"

Gilley steered them to the Lafayette Café, where Gladys, after a glance at the inner door, said, "We have a surprise for you this time without your asking. Prices have gone up."

Surveying the menu, the teacher observed, "I see what you mean. Is bread and butter still free? . . . Then bring me five orders of bread and butter and a double water." Crouching over the table and taking hold of Wick's arm, he stole a sly look up at her. "Her self-control's beginning to wear thin. We can expect anything now."

"These things are sent to try us," the young woman murmured with upturned eyes.

"I'll tell you. Let me have as much as you can for a dollar fifty

119

in the way of scrambled eggs, sliced tomatoes, bread and butter, ice cream and coffee, with ten percent for a tip included—and not one penny more, you greedy thing."

When Wick had sheepishly asked for the same thing only with milk instead of coffee, Gilley sat back with a look at him of friendly appraisal. "So you're still with us," he observed. "I can't say I'm altogether surprised. You've a stubborn look about you."

"Do you think that's it?"

The teacher's eyebrows went up. "Can it be that you've come to like it here?"

"I like it when you get back from the built-up valleys and off the main roads to where there are fields and woods." He knew he sounded as if he had merely embarked on the subject but found himself unable to add anything. He watched Gladys return with the rolls and butter.

When she had set them down, she said, "That's all the bread there's going to be. So make them last."

Gilley said, "You've probably stuffed half what's due us in a bag to sneak out to your young man."

To Wick he remarked when they were alone again, "I'm glad there's something that holds you here. I hope it'll be good for some time to come."

As the boy only raised his hand to his head and ran his fingers through his hair, he resumed. "We need friends from the outside, to tell our story. All we can get. And there are some of us here who can call you friend, I've heard. Up in Oak Lick Holler, for instance."

Gladys, placing their dinners before them, received amiable but vacant stares in return. "You two are a pair, I must say," she muttered.

Wick replied cautiously, "Yes, I like them up there. It's a nice farm, too. I go up there after work pretty often. It's a relief after navigating a coal barge over nonroads. And after grubbing coal with a front-end loader in all the dust and racket. I'm even learning a little about farming. I've even tried milking, but it's not easy if you're not used to it. Gets you on the inside of your forearms. I'm more at home with horses, and if I'm there I help water them and all." Not having known how to proceed with an explanation, he found himself not knowing how to end one. "Of course, it's not a real farm. It's just a sideline for Mr. Barrows. . . ." Perhaps the way was just to stop.

"I understand there's a girl in the family—unfortunately blind, though quite pretty," said Gilley, looking off into a corner of the restaurant.

"Yes. Letty."

"Do you see much of her?"

The warmth in his face annoyed him. "Whenever I'm there. She likes to get out walking. You wouldn't think it would make any difference to someone who can't see, but it does."

"And you give her a chance to get out and around. It's commendable of you. I mean with all the girls there are you could . . . well, with whom your prospects would be very good."

Wick shot him a dark, almost unseeing look. "Letty's a good friend." The unspoken question, he knew, was what he got out of the relationship. "She . . ." He looked into a receptive face and took the plunge. "She makes me aware of things I'd never *been* aware of. A whole world. You've got no idea how . . . *remarkable* it all is until you're made to realize how it is not to see anything whatever. And when you're with someone who can't see and wants to know all about it."

Gilley, he could tell, was caught up by the idea. "Ye-e-es. I can see how it would make all the difference . . . But I was just wondering—what with your being together so often—if there is any danger of her conceiving a romantic attachment to you."

"A romantic . . . ?" Wick was forced to laugh. "She'd certainly be amused if she could hear that!"

"Would she?" Gilley appeared only partially to share the joke. "There is the question, though"—and he frowned—"as to how it will be for her when you have to move on to other things, other places. . . ."

Wick said with a suggestion of heat, "If people looked ahead to partings and brooded on them there'd be no friendships formed at all."

"Yes. . . . Anyhow, you must be welcome at the farm to the girl's mother." His tone dismissed the subject. "So she can't be worried."

He questioned the boy about his impression of the brother and sister. Apprised of Mr. Barrows's singular religious ideas, he observed, "It's the mountain religion, but sort of turned inside out," and undertook to elucidate the Southern highlander's Fundamentalism.

"Tell me," he interrupted himself at length. "You said you liked it here when you got away to the woods and fields. How do you feel about the rest?"

"You really want to know?"

"I wouldn't ask if I didn't."

"If it weren't for the Oak Lick farm and the hills I couldn't wait to get away. I'd die if I had to live in one of the towns strung out along the highways. It's not the poverty. That doesn't strike you so much. And the people don't seem unhappy especially. On my way here I was watching a bunch of boys racing a string of ponies down the road hollering and carrying on. It was the kind of scene you'd expect to see in the West. Anyhow, those boys bouncing their feet against their ponies and waving their hats didn't seem unhappy.

"But . . . you know yourself how ugly and run-down and sordid things are here. Yes, I know people are hard up and have good reason to be demoralized. But they seem to have given up, or a lot of them have. They dump their trash wherever it happens to be and let things slide and sit in front of their houses and watch people—or cars—go by. Then, on Sunday, to make up for it, there're the religious binges. Have you ever seen one of these revivals?"

Gilley nodded. "I have," he said shortly.

"I passed one once when I was bicycling. It was being held out in the open and a man in a white shirt was holding forth to a crowd on camp chairs. And I tell you it made my flesh creep—all those shouted exhortations. 'Oh, give your love to Jesus. Yes, I say give your *love* to Jesus. I want you to give your *love* to Jesus and glory in his name. I want you to *praise* Jesus. Praise him, praise him, praise him!' " From Gilley's quick glances to either side he could tell that his voice was rising like the evangelist's. Lowering it, he said, "They might as well have been getting drunk on moonshine. All this praising the Lord, and all around the mountains being wrecked by strip-miners and highway-builders."

"I don't think we're much implicated in the strip-mining. Most of us are bitter enough about it."

"But when the people here get up in arms about it it's usually friends and relatives getting together to keep their own farms from being bulldozed or buried. No one knows as well as you how hard it is to get people organized to fight it. They don't care about the mountains themselves."

"No, that's not true. That's not it. They do care."

"All right. But not enough. If there's anything everyone here wants it's more and bigger highways. And the highways beat anything for destructiveness. It's just that there's so much more strip mining.

"Wouldn't it make a difference if they could be stirred up more about the country here, that's theirs? If they could have more pride in it—in the mountains and forests and the beauty of them? Doesn't it say anything in the Bible about God's expecting human beings to love their land and protect it if they're aiming to be saved?"

"I wish it did."

Gladys, setting their ice cream down, said, "Twenty-five cents' worth of vanilla. You're tipping twenty cents each, by the way, whatever percentage of a dollar fifty that is. There was an extra nickel."

"Just so long as you're not exposed to undue risk at the hands of an unscrupulous fortune-hunter. . . ."

"If my beauty doesn't drive him insane with desire," she said as she leaned over to collect the empty plates, bringing her bosom, beneath a glossy white blouse, within inches of the boy's face and momentarily confusing his thoughts, "I don't suppose the extra nickel will turn his head."

When she had gone, Wick blurted out, taking the teacher by surprise, "I don't belong here. And in case I should forget, there's Bull Turner. Whenever I go to the Last Chance/First Chance I'm greeted with a general look of slight surprise. 'What, you here and still unmaimed?' Yes, I know they don't want me beaten up. Even though they resent what I represent to them—the rich outsiders who've always done them dirt and somehow can't be got at. They all dislike Turner, and they're afraid of him—except Roger Tenent. And he says to me when I'm sitting by myself at the bar—you'd hardly know he was talking to me, he keeps putting things down and getting things out, keeping in touch with everyone—'When you look around at these faces, sport, don't you wonder what's in it for you here? If I were in your shoes and had

123

the chance for something better than Garrett County has to offer, I'd go back to it. And that advice could cost me a customer.'

"But they all take Turner as a natural part of life. Jack Mac-Donough does, and Frank Allen and the Fergusons, the whole gang at Tenent's. It's like the West—a lot of things here are, or the way you picture the West. There have to be badmen and shoot-outs, or knock-outs. Otherwise there wouldn't be the action to give point to life that you told me about. Except taking a car around a curve with screaming tires when you're tanked up or going to look at the wreckage of someone who tried it.

"I've been telling myself that Turner's waiting for a chance to finish me off in circumstances that would keep it from being proved he did it but leave no one in much doubt. As in the case of that Emory. Now I'm beginning to wonder if he enjoys keeping me in suspense."

"I hope you're wrong about Turner. But if he ever goes for you, you get out, fast, and don't worry about appearances. If you're right about him, I doubt if it's to keep you in suspense that he's held off. It's more likely that he's afraid."

"*Afraid?*"

"You forget you've got the biggest power in this part of the world behind you—a major coal company."

Said Wick bitterly, "And that makes everything just grand."

"If your pride never has to suffer on any worse account than that," Gilley said, "you'll have come off pretty well."

10

THE NEXT AFTERNOON he arrived at the farm on a secondhand motorized bicycle. He had had great misgivings about buying a noise-making power-plant, but pedaling was simply too slow for the distances he had to travel in the time available. With the new machine he had made thirty miles an hour on the level and fifteen on hills, and had given in to the satisfactions it awoke in him, had even sung as he felt it pick up speed beneath him: *pup-pup-pup-pup-pup-umpa-pup-pup-pup-umpa-umpa-pup-pup*. . . . The *umpa*'s were when he let up on the accelerator.

With his new means of locomotion Wick was able to spend two or three nights a week at the farm. On a Saturday or Sunday morning—Letty had to put in one or the other working, and he chose to do as much—they could be away with the first daylight. She seemed always to wake when she wished to and could tell the hour by a clock he had given her from which he had removed the glass.

This time a whippoorwill was calling and he could not believe night was over. He had to make himself get up. "It was like dragging myself out of a lovely warm tub of molasses," he said, pulling his clothes on quickly in the chill kitchen. When he had made a wood fire in the stove—in September coal fires were still too hot—they poured water to wash in, then with practiced teamwork cooked a breakfast of grits and coffee with canned orange juice and sausage, the latter being the boy's contributions. While they were eating, Mrs. Sherrod came in, a light coat wrapped about her, and on Wick's insistence shared their meal. In the lamplight, with her dark hair falling behind her shoulders, she looked not much older than her daughter and, he thought, perhaps a little like her half-Cherokee grandmother must once have looked. "So you're goin' to the woods of the big trees," she mused.

125

Mr. Barrows had told them of it, a forest of huge old trees on the other side of Winespring, beyond Winespring Fork, the only woods he had ever heard of that had never been cut over. "You must come back and tell us what hits nature is," she declared. "Wick, I'm goin' to have to teach you yarbs. No tellin' what there might be where you two go—ginseng at fifteen dollars a pound for the root, Cherokee tea, *adisha*—what's it called?—meadow rue. . . ."

Mr. Barrows had sauntered in, easing the strap of his overalls on his shoulder. "You listen to me, Wicker, and you'll be keerful what you pick up and chaw on," he said. "They's some kinda yarb in these pesky hills that if you eat hit you won't have no peace of mind nowhar else and no matter whar you go to git away you'll have to come back." He spoke with severity though with less than full attention. He was looking about the kitchen—for his pipe, it turned out when he spotted it on a shelf. "She could tell you which it is, I don't doubt, but she won't."

She smiled, facing the paling oblong of night framed in the window. "If I could, I might warn him of it. But then again I might slip him some in his food unbeknownst. As 'tis he'll have to take his chances."

Their way lay along the overgrown road they took to Winespring but straight on, past the turn-off of the trail to the summit. The dawning day had a breathless expectancy and Wick, released from the dragging routine of the job, could feel himself flowing out to meet it. In the forest, half-lighted by the diffusion of the silver sunlight that glimmered on the nearly hidden opposite mountainside, the breath of life's mystery, the echo of its purpose, seemed instilled in the sharp, sweet air.

"You aren't *too* cold?" he asked the girl. He was glad she was in overalls, though their purpose was to protect her legs from scratches.

"No, just cold enough. . . . Listen to the crickets—tree-crickets, you said they were." Tiny, singing steam-jets they could have been. He had found one, by luck a little pale-green ghost of the common field-cricket fiddling away on a twig with wing and leg.

"We've come to an old stone wall, falling apart, with the remains of a split-rail fence running along above it," he reported after a mile. "The woods are lighter on the other side of it."

"Can we wait here a minute?"

He led her to some flat stones on the wall. "Hold still. There's that damned fly." With a light smack of her shoulder he crushed a small biting fly. Flies and gnats were a nuisance in the woods if you were bare-headed, but they were not bothered much under the farmer's straw-hats they had taken to wearing.

They sat in silence, given up to the quiet, which seemed the more profound for the weak, thin tremolos of the tree-crickets and the uncertain, distant song of a vireo, the only bird still singing. The stillness seemed to Wick to mount strangely in intensity. He looked at the trees receding into the shadows and strained to hear a whispered intimation of the truth at the threshold of audibility.

Letty murmured, "I never heard it so plain, the singing of the wildness my grandma told me of. You don't hear it in your ears but in your blood. Don't you hear it?"

He had said he did, was agreeing that that was surely it when she laid a warning hand on his arm. He listened for an interval in vain, then heard it—a rustling and snuffling from the direction in which they were headed. Fear leapt up in him despite himself, and his hand went to the claspknife in his pocket. He whispered, "Something's about to come around the bend up ahead."

What it was became apparent in an instant. His mouth against the girl's ear, he breathed, "It's a bear. Black. . . . Humped. Head low, swaying." He moved his arm slowly to put it around her and was glad they were twenty feet off the hulking black shape's line of march instead of on it as they had been. "Don't move." She did not appear likely to. She was following the animal by the sounds it made brushing against the vegetation and the padding of its heavy paws on the gritty earth. It came unsuspecting by them, its small, black eyes, separated by the high-bridged gray muzzle, opaque and seemingly unchangeable. It stopped once to raise its head and take stock of its surroundings, then disappeared as it had come, around a bend, its short-legged, shaggy hindquarters the last to be seen of it.

A bear—given to them to witness! They were transported by it, kept returning to it with incredulity. The girl declared it had been years since a bear had last been seen in Garrett County. "And it was killed. Wherever a bear turns up it can count on everyone being out to kill it." The thought caused a black bile to rise in Wick's mind. With no cage-bars between them, the animal

127

had seemed an engine of the wilds, and the knowledge that it was roaming the woods intensified their power for him.

In another half hour they reached a small stream that flowed in the direction of Winespring Fork. He said, "This looks like a place for a coffee stop."

"And none too soon. My blood's mostly turned to water."

The canteen nested in a capacious cup, and in this they brewed their drink. He enjoyed the whole process, breaking up dead branches, arranging them over twists of paper from the canvas bag in a fireplace of stones, filling the cup from the stream and holding it in the flames by a stick fitted to its handle. It put one in touch with the early settlers. A song from Letty, once she had been persuaded that he admired her accomplishment, had become part of the routine—a "ballard" from the repertoire she had acquired from her father and from friends. She sang in a rather high but sweet and true voice, and with a yearning intonation that touched him.

> A great lord lived by the Northern Sea;
> Blow, winds, blow;
> A great lord lived by the Northern Sea;
> The winds they blow so drearily;
> A great lord lived by the Northern Sea,
> And he had daughters in number three;
> I'll be true to my love and he to me
> True to our loves where e'er we be.
>
> A young man come a-ridin' there;
> Blow, winds, blow;
> A young man come a-ridin' there;
> The winds they blow so drearily;
> A young man come a-ridin' there,
> And his heart it went to the young and fair;
> I'll be true to my love and he to me
> True to our loves where e'er we be.

But an older daughter pushes the young one into the sea and a fisherman who pulls her from the waves robs her of her "gold ring gay" and pushes her back in, and both the fisherman and the older daughter are put to death.

"It's beautiful poetry and music. But they're grim, these ballads," Wick observed.

"I reckon they're like life usually is."

She spoke uncomplainingly but the verdict darkened his heart. Gilley's warning weighed on him. How else could it end between them but with a wrench and the swift, conclusive sadness of one of those songs? Letty, it occurred to him, never spoke of the future —except his.

But the sun was in the treetops, the stream was purring as contentedly among the rocks and a band of crows yelping as enthusiastically in the distance as if the present moment were all there was, and the water was boiling. . . . When the coffee had steeped and the grounds had settled they added sugar and milk and drank from the one cup.

Winespring Fork, a little farther on, was a rushing stream, bent by the hills, flowing through a gorge between banks of rhododendron. The road descended almost to the water's edge, and they walked out into the open for the first time on stones and gravel the little river had deposited. The water's turbulence was almost dazzling white at first sight. Inshore, however, there were quiet pools where every detail of bottom was as distinct as if seen through a magnifying glass. The scents were of sun-warmed wood and foliage, different from the cool, dank air of the shadowy forest and the damp earth flooring it.

Wick said, "This must be the only stream its size in this part of the Cumberlands that isn't silted from the stripping or poisoned by mine-drainage. And you know, when you come to a place that's open and sunny like this and you'd expect to find human beings and there's no one, no one anywhere near, it seems even wilder than the woods."

The steep, rocky vestige of the footpath led on from the end of the overgrown road and they followed it in single file. But with each step, while the boy held her hand, the girl had to feel the surface ahead with her foot before setting it down. Tears of humiliation and vexation came to her eyes. "I'd carry you on my shoulders," Wick said, "but there are too many low branches. They'd scrape you off."

She stood still and with a smile announced, "This is as far as I go. You keep on. I won't mind waiting. I want to hear about it."

"This is as far as either of us'll go. We'll turn back."

But she would not hear of it. And at length, reluctant as he was to leave her alone, he saw that she would take it out on herself if he did not go.

Within a hundred yards the last indication of a trail was lost among the rocks of a steep ridge that ran athwart it, apparently down from the heights of Winespring. It was probably this ridge, he surmised as he climbed, that had protected the primeval forest behind it when lumbermen were making a clean sweep of its counterparts.

He descended the far side of the ridge into the darkest forest he had ever seen, and the grandest. It was largely of hemlocks, and among them giants immense in girth. The ground was muffled in coffee-colored humus, soft underfoot, and the deep-green, leathery leaves of the undergrowth of rhododendrons added to the somberness. His eyes traveled from one of the great trees to another. The dark-brown and fissured boles, from which the branches jutted perpendicularly, were as massive and solid as pillars of stone— pillars raised by gods in a temple to an ultimate god, yet alive.

He went on and came to a stream that poured toward Winespring Fork. Above it the thickets of rhododendron gave place to growths of fern. There the glades were brighter, the vistas longer. Farther still, as the slope increased, oaks, Yellow poplars and beeches predominated, their trunks even broader than those of the hemlocks, close to six feet through at the level of his eyes. Through the interlocked and spreading crowns, upheld on limbs themselves the size of ordinary trees, scant sunshine filtered. Lesser vegetation was sparse and there was little impediment to movement except from the boulders or where, longer ago than he had been born, he imagined, one of the great trees had toppled and lay decaying, giving life to mosses, ferns and seedlings.

Towered over by the awesome patriarchs, he felt diffident about his brash intrusion and he refrained from sudden movement. If he could have expressed his deference he would have. And at last he did speak, though only after a recurrence of his doubts about himself. As he was preparing to leave, he leaned face foremost against the hugest of the venerable hemlocks. "Old king," he said, "old king, tell me how to know the way." He raised his arms to embrace the rough trunk and for the first time in days felt a sharp reminder of the brand mark of Winespring, as he thought of it, at the base of the neck.

While he described to Letty what he had seen there was the question he could never find an answer to: How could she conceal her despair at being unable to have the joys of seeing for herself?

". . . The little creek sounded like elves and goblins underground burbling away. . . .

"There were those little plants on runners you'd think were something between mosses and ferns. The one that's like a tiny fir tree and the one like a little green parasol. . . ."

One would have thought it was satisfaction enough for her to see through his eyes.

It was past time for lunch when they regained the bank of the little river, warm from their exertions.

"Swim first, food afterward," he announced.

"Swim?"

"Dip." Knowing that mountain conventions with respect to divestiture had not changed in a century, he watched with amusement as consternation spread in her face. "Where I come from, boys and girls don't think anything of stripping for a swim." No, it was cruel. "But you can keep on whatever you wear under your shirt and jeans. They'll dry out quickly."

Finding her voice, she said, "Well, thank you very much, mister! That's sure handsome of you!"

She would not be persuaded even to that, however. Instead, she proposed that he wear a blindfold.

In the midst of his laughter, he suddenly saw the matter in a different light. All right. Let *him* be helpless for once, dependent on *her* for apprehension. "You'd have to do the seeing for us. . . ."

"If you'll tell me just where things are. . . ."

He led her to the stream and turned her toward it. In that direction, he told her, there was a deep enough pool, and he cautioned her of the obstruction—a steep-faced rock and a big dead branch sticking up out of the water. She would have to lead them to the pool and back to their clothes. She nodded, her face upturned, and he knew that she was gauging the direction of the sun and slight movement of air.

He had to promise most solemnly not to look over the blindfold, for which he said he would use the strap from the canvas bag.

"I'd die of embarrassment, if you were to."

The strap in place, he emphasized to himself as he unbuttoned his shirt that she had said she would be *embarrassed* if he saw her. It was not that she feared the sex-hungry male in him. He was thankful there was no misunderstanding on that score.

He said, "About what's important, a girl actually hasn't got much to be embarrassed about." Forgetting the nude mixed

131

swimming supposedly commonplace to him, he added, "When I've seen my sister a couple of times by chance it's struck me that she looked like a boy with everything tucked away out of sight."

Her snort was, he trusted, mirthful.

When they were ready to go they bumped into each other while trying to locate each other's hand and recoiled apart. They did better on the second try.

The water was cold but she seemed not to be bothered by it. She led him so confidently over the slippery, stony bottom, past the rock and the branch that he wished there were sometimes a genuine need to reverse their roles for the sense of her value he could tell it would give her.

"This is it," she declared.

"I should hope so." The icy water was over waist-high and he was gasping.

"I'll count three," she said, "and down we'll go."

When they waded out again, exuberant in the warm sun, and ravenous, he proposed that they eat while they dried off. So sitting on one of the huge rocks encumbering the stream, using their folded jeans for cushions, they attacked their sandwiches before dressing.

He could raise the blindfold and look at her without her being the wiser, it occurred to him. Or could he? She was remarkably intuitive. But why should he be so conscious of her nakedness beside him? It was inevitable, of course—but not that he should be picturing her and wondering about her. He had only to lift the strap . . . but . . . a blind girl! There was a disturbing difference in his feeling about her and it came to him that it was because he also could not see, the effect of their being on a par. The horror with which he thought of taking advantage of a blind girl was lessened.

And with that intuition of hers she had detected the difference. She was less communicative and, as he could tell when they had dressed and he could see her again, more turned inward.

But as the normal order returned his unsettlement passed and with it the shadow it had thrown over her. He espied a prize new flower for them he had missed on the way out, a Yellow Fringed orchis glowing in the shadows. "You can feel how the cluster of little flowers at the top of the stalk almost forms a globe," he said as they squatted beside it. "They make me think of tiny little angels all launching out into space from the top of a pole."

She turned to him with a thoughtful expression. "Hold still," she said.

Obediently he waited with eyes closed, surmising what was coming and somewhat amused. He felt her fingertips as they touched on his temples and crept over his face to come to rest at the corners of his mouth, at the bottom edge of his eyelids and on his eyebrows.

"Are you happy, Wick?"

She had caught him, as obviously she had planned, unawares. His answer, spontaneous enough, was that he was; and judging by her smile, he thought she was satisfied—at least partly. And it was true. So long as he was engrossed in the day around it did not occur to him to question his happiness.

When she had dropped her hands he took her face between his own and raised it so that he could look squarely into it. "And you? *Can* you be?"

Flustered, she replied, "I? You mean happy? Oh yes!" Any other condition, her voice implied, would have been unnatural. But she must have guessed that he was looking into her eyes, for she quickly lowered them.

Releasing her, he said gently, "You know, no one could ever tell that your eyes were any different from anyone else's. Can't you see *any*thing? Not even light—the difference between light and shadow?"

She shook her head, then stood up. "I'll bet it's late."

They were nearly out of the heavy woods when they heard voices. They halted and the girl asked in a low tone, "Can you see anyone?" He replied, "No. They're beyond where the road curves ahead."

They walked on, Letty's shoulder against his. Coming to the bend, he murmured, "There they are. There's five . . . six of them. And in good clothes. Roughing-it clothes, but good. They're middle-aged. . . . One has . . . my gosh, they've all got binoculars! Or a camera. . . . Two are women—in trousers like the rest."

They were noticed at some distance off, and Wick returned the covert looks of interest he and his companion—mostly his companion—attracted. These were men and women of a kind he knew but had seen little of in recent months. A tall, gray-haired man, who had been addressing the others until he turned in their di-

133

rection, had a strong, clear, cultivated voice. And this incongruous stranger was standing there as if his presence were the most natural thing in the world and the mountain his, almost, to gesture at. Who could they be, with their binoculars and cameras?

As several of the strangers moved aside with small smiles to let them pass, Wick realized why Letty was attracting such deep attention. It was not because she was blind, which they would not have guessed, but because of her beauty, which even overalls and a straw-hat could not conceal. He had never before been in public with her.

"Good afternoon!" The tall man addressed them heartily. And he added as Wick was echoing his salutation, "I see that you're carrying binoculars. Can it be that you're members of the brotherhood—fellow bird-hounds?"

With an unobtrusive twitch at Letty's trouser seam, Wick came to a halt. His jealous mistrust was partly allayed by the intelligent and good-humored character of the faces around him. "We're interested in birds. But we're only beginners."

One of the others asked, "Do you find any special birds in here?"

Wick said, "I don't know how special. We've seen a Pileated woodpecker twice and a Great Horned owl." He surmised that they were finding it hard to account for him, coming out of the woods in worn work clothes with hayseed hat but Eastern speech and with a girl similarly attired who would cause heads to turn in the Golden Triangle. "We heard the owl first, on a gray day."

"We could tell it wasn't a Barred owl," said Letty, her head a little tilted, her eyes avoiding any encounter with others', "because its hooting was deeper and all on one note."

"Here in these hemlocks there was a Black-throated Green warbler singing most of the summer."

They were looking between the girl and him with what almost appeared to be fascination.

"What other warblers have you?" one of them asked.

"Well . . . where it's open, Chestnut-sided and Yellow warblers. In the woods, Black-and-white warblers, Redstarts . . . Ovenbirds . . . and a Hooded warbler down where the stream is. Also a Louisiana waterthrush. Maryland yellow-throats in the swamps. . . . What else, Letty?"

"Yellow-breasted chats. And don't forget the Prairie warbler that gave you so much trouble, with the little thin song that went up and up and off into nothin'." Her face, still partly averted, shone.

There were sounds of admiration and approval. And he knew that his companion, with her sidelong, shy way, even in her enthusiasm, was captivating these strangers. But he was wary. He could not understand why such people should turn up here all of a sudden.

Said one of the women, with fluffy, sandy-gray hair, "How about mammals—four-footed animals? Raccoons and foxes, I suppose; but are there any wildcats left?

"Colly—"

He knew why the girl had broken off. "You're not hunters, are you?" he asked, glancing from one face to another.

"On the contrary. Our aim is to save animals' lives."

"My brother Colly thinks he saw a bobcat cross the road just at dark. And if he thinks he saw one he most likely did. But— Shall I tell them, Wick?"

He hesitated, but, touched, realized that what was stirring her was eagerness to have her bit of homeland show to advantage. "All right."

"We've got a bear! We saw it this mornin', a Black bear walkin' down the old road back yonder. It came so close we could of tossed a pebble on it, couldn't we, Wick?"

The report made a great impression. The large gray-haired man said, "That's promising news indeed. Tell me— By the way, my name's Hugo Wright, and these. . . ." He went around the circle, citing names. "We're conservationists."

"I'm Wick Carter. And this is Letty Sherrod."

Someone had observed the name on the mailbox, and it was brought out that the farm was where Letty lived.

"I had a question," the man who had performed the introductions resumed, leaning forward slightly and clasping his hands together before him. "I was going to ask you about a stand of virgin forest at the other end of Winespring Mountain. Perhaps you know of it and how to get there. We've heard there's been no cutting in it and hope that's true."

The coincidence revived Wick's disturbance at the intrusion of outsiders, which now threatened to extend even to Letty's and his adventure of the morning. "It's true," he said, not to let the pause grow any longer. He would have to tell them how to get there, he saw, and he did so. He had meant to stop with that, but when they asked him he had to admit that he had been there. And then, questioned further, he spoke of the breadth and strength of the great trees that he could nowhere near half-encircle with his arms, of the spread of the immense limbs so high above the ground a squirrel among them was almost lost to sight. Prompted by Letty, he repeated things he had told her and went on to say that the trees made you think how they could remember the elk and bison and wolves and the Indians who'd had trails through here. He knew that the fervor with which he found himself speaking had an unaccountable challenging defensiveness about it. "The Indians were Cherokees, and they thought there was a Great Spirit that—"

No, he had delivered himself of too much as it was.

"That?"

In the silence, Letty said, "A Great Spirit that was in everything." She addressed the feet of her auditors, to whom her words could barely have carried. "It was in the smallest plants and critters and in the biggest mountains and highest clouds. All were children of the Great Spirit and all were kin."

The silence that followed this was of a different kind.

The woman with the sandy-gray hair spoke. "It's uncanny. But we've had our answer."

Mr. Wright appeared to pull himself together. "We shan't have time to see much more today, but we'll be back and perhaps you'll be our guides to the mountain and the forest." He spoke in the full, round voice one uses in speaking to a body of persons. "We've all, I know, been greatly moved by what you've said. It's plain that you have a strong feeling about these things. And so have we, though I don't think anyone here could express it more movingly." He glanced at the others as if expecting one of them to speak. None did. "In fact, we're here to help try to save Winespring Mountain and its forests."

"Save it from what?"

"From the strip-miners," said the second woman tersely.

He felt a block of ice on his heart. "Have the . . . has a coal company got deeds to the mountain, mineral rights?" The girl had moved behind him and gripped his shoulder.

"One owns it in fee simple—without restrictions. The company that has title, the Triple Creek Land Company—you've seen their signs—is just a coal-company subsidiary."

"They won't strip-mine Winespring!"

"You believe him, too!" Letty was holding tight to him. "He won't let them!" He could feel her breasts against his back.

"Let them remember Gorton Hollow, where a D-9 bulldozer was blown skyhigh. And . . . and Timmonsville, where a hundred-thousand-dollar Diesel shovel was dynamited." He stopped and stared at Mr. Wright's serious face. He asked sharply, "What coal company is it that owns the mountain?"

"One called Allegheny-Keystone."

The tension went out of the boy with an audible sigh. "Then you don't have to worry. They'd never strip-mine a mountain like Winespring."

Mr. Wright, looking puzzled and no less serious, said, "There've been strong rumors they were going to. So strong that several organizations have got together to try to have the state buy Winespring and make it a State forest. Why do you think it won't be strip-mined?"

His lips pursed in a smile, Wick was shaking his head emphatically. "I know. Allegheny-Keystone wouldn't do a thing like that. They'd deep-mine it, but they'd never strip it."

"This is too much for me," said the woman who had spoken last. "Mildred's right. It's uncanny." She dropped to the low bank beside the road. "Here we have two youngsters traipsing out of the woods at the precisely opportune time. The boy speaks as if he were right out of prep school and the girl, who is perfectly lovely, is from a farm down the road. They're accomplished observers of birds. They know all about Winespring. They have a deep feeling for nature. Could any more convincing sign have come from on high to tell us we're right in getting into this? Then, when the boy hears that Winespring is in danger, he offers to hold off the pillagers—a young David with a demure but impassioned nymph to back him up. And now, when he learns who the particular Goliath is, he promises us that it's not a wicked Goliath and may be trusted. My head's swimming."

"How can you be so sure, Wick?" It was an elderly man with kind eyes who asked.

When he didn't reply, Letty said, "I'm goin' to tell them, Wick. There s no use them worryin' for nothin'. His father's president of the company. That's how he can be sure."

"My God," said the woman.

"What are you doing here, Wick?" Mr. Wright asked.

The boy replied with a dodge he regarded as brazen. "Learning the business." For the sake of plausibility he added, "From the ground up. I haven't started the up yet."

The laughter suggested that they were convinced and were glad to be.

Mr. Wright said, "If I'm not prying—has your father said that Winespring would not be strip-mined?"

"No. But there's been no need for him to."

In the silence that followed, the elderly man took out a pipe and stuffed it from a pouch while everyone watched. It was he who spoke at last. "I'm not sure I've got this all straight. . . . No, let me put it this way." He paused long enough to strike a large match with his thumbnail and light the tobacco. "The campaign for the State forest will very soon smoke out Allegheny-Keystone's intentions. If you're right, it may not fight the forest if it's allowed to retain subsurface-mining rights. On the other hand, if the rumors are well-founded and stripping is planned, the company is likely to get started very soon—to forestall the State forest. In that case"—his eyes came up—"which side would you be on?"

In the silence he heard Letty breathing, but he was hesitating only to find the words. "Nobody's going to bulldoze into Winespring while I'm here. Nobody."

"There's nothing to worry about," he told the girl when they had resumed their way and were out of earshot. They were walking with his hand on her shoulder. Where the path was largely clear, all the help she needed was directional pressures of which she seemed hardly conscious.

"I'm not worried. If you say it's goin' to be all right."

As they passed a trucklike station-wagon drawn up beside the road, he described it for her and added, "Renton County plates. They're from the other end of the state. What I can't get used to is that people from so far away would know about Winespring. I thought it was only heard of around here. . . . What are you thinking about anyway, Princess?"

"Me? I was just wonderin' what 'demure nymth' meant."

To Wick's relief, the work at hand—shucking the corn with which Mr. Barrows and Colly had filled the single-horse wagon—could be done off the feet. They all took a hand in it, sitting on boxes or upturned pails and tossing the stripped ears into a wheelbarrow.

"Tomorrow," said Wick, "I'm going to paint that wagon."

He wondered who at home would have been as interested as Letty's family in their walk. Then in honesty he asked himself if he would have told his own family about it with nearly the zest. Or at all.

For the second time the bear made a deep impression. Colly's rounded eyes sought out the woods beyond them. Mr. Barrows thought the creature must somehow have come across from the national forest. "With people leavin' the hills, maybe the bars'll be comin' back." He cast an eye at the ridge of Winespring. "More bars, less people." He seemed more abstracted than ever, and restless.

To Wick's surprise, he had heard of the plan to make Winespring a State forest. "There's been talk of hit for yurs. Only more of hit in the past week or so, I reckon. But lots of things is talked about around h'yar, and not one in ten comes to pass. Not one in twenty." He stood up, frowning. "I got to settle some things with Hamp," he said.

"Kin I go with you?"

He looked down at his nephew, his frown deepening. "If you keep out of the way."

His sister watched them make for the truck and only when it pulled away did her attention return. Letty sat stripping ears in silence.

With her trace of a smile Mrs. Sherrod asked, "Did you two children go in the water at Winespring Fork?"

Jolted, Wick let Letty handle the question. Only slightly flushed, she said they had. "Wick bound his eyes. I had to do the seein' for both of us. And, my, was it cold! But I wouldn't of missed it." She spoke without reserve, but shortly.

"Well, that was good you were able to refresh yourselves. I kin imagine how it pleasured you. When I first left home and went to live in the city I remember how more than anythin' I missed the mountain creeks tumblin' down through the woods."

Evidently it was all right about the dip.

"You were going to tell me about yarbs, Queen. Can they really cure sick people?"

She laughed. "The juice of hemlock can cure well people of livin'. That's not the tree but a tall plant with a circle of little white flowers. It kin kill you. So can the berries and roots of snakeroot and poke, though the new shoots of poke is as good as asparagras. If yarbs kin be so powryful for bad, it's reasonable they'd be powryful for good, too. Pokeroot's said to help eczema, and bloodroot corns. Jimson root for ulcers. Sassafras for tonic. Yellowroot and boneset, too, though they're a lease bit bitter."

"A *lease* bit!" Letty put in, ironically.

"Yellow violet for heart trouble. Roots of Christmas fern for worms. Roots of foam flower for snake bite. Oh, I could go on and on."

"Ground-up root of partridge moccasin for a love charm," said Letty. But she seemed listless.

"So the Cherrykees believed. Oh, there's a lot of foolishness said about cures. I always counsel them that comes to me to go to a doctor. But if they want yarbs, I let them have them."

"And do the yarbs make them well?"

"I've seen many get well. Maybe they'd have got well anyhow, but in some cases I'd find that hard to believe."

As she seemed to gather her thoughts, tapping her thigh, he was struck anew by the beauty of her eyes, which were large and the dark brown of buckeyes. There was a term for her kind of profile, with the straight nose, the serenity, the hair done up in a bun low on the neck, but he could not recall it.

She said, "There's virtues in all natural things. It takes the city to teach you that. You kin look around you at the woods and pastures and see killin' and dyin'. Everything's got to die, when its time comes. But life is passed on. Trees die, but the forest goes on livin'. Life is strong. Growin' saplin's 'll split rocks. An' life gives strength to life. There's a world of difference between corn you planted, hoed and picked in your own patch and corn out of a can. Between drinkin' and bathin' in water out of pipes from a dirty river, with chlorine in it to make it safe, and drinkin' and bathin' in clean, clear natural flowin' water with live things around you."

Except in cold weather, the members of the family were accustomed to bathe in the creek behind a screen of alders, as was Wick, too. For Letty's sake, Colly kept the path clear of cow droppings.

Gazing at the road, she resumed, and he thought he had never known her so talkative. "All that's alive drinks from the same spring of life, but every livin' thing has its own nature. You have to respect that.

" 'Tis the nature of men who ain't been fully broke to the harness to be what men was in times long past. They need to have room, not to have people pressin' on them. They cain't stand to have somebody over them to tell them when they got to be where and doin' what. They cain't stand havin' life go on just the same day after day. It's in their blood to need excitement. And that means takin' chances—danger.

"I've larned it's men like that who'll stay with the hills hyur no matter how hard things get. They got to be free at any cost. They got to know themselves free, to respect themselves." She had resumed her shucking while her daughter had desisted from hers and, an ear of corn in her hand, was listening attentively.

"Such men was meant to be hunters. Every mountain man is a hunter at heart. He'd live by huntin' if he could, and he'd be happy. But there's no game left but some squirrels, and not many of them. All to speak of's been shot off. The game commission tries to restock the hills with deer, but they don't last a season. Too many guns against them." In a different voice she said, "Letty, why don't you get started mixin' some corn bread whilst we finish what few ears is left?"

Wick thought that ordinarily she would have gone herself on such a task and left her daughter with him to finish the shucking.

But Letty got up readily enough. "All right, Ma." She dusted the corn silk off her overalls and turned away toward the house without any word of leave-taking.

When the door had closed behind her daughter, she said, "One of the men I've been talkin' about is Tom Barrows. Him above all. The man in him is almost like an Indian hunter and warrior. It galls him past bearin' to have to go off to work every mornin' and do the same things every day, year in, year out. 'Like a mule hitched to a plow,' is how he says it. An' being looked down on for workin' with horses don't make it no easier. So once in a while he has to cut loose. I been readin' the signs, and they ain't

141

escaped Letty either. He'll go off with Hamp this evenin' or maybe some other men, and he'll work off some of what's eatin' at him, and we'll just hope there'll be no big row.

"But it'll be better if you don't stay this evenin', though we'll miss havin' you, and the readin'."

"I'll just empty the wheelbarrow first."

She went with him, walking, he thought, as if carrying a basket on her head. No, why not say a crown?

She helped him toss the ears into the corn-crib. When they had emptied the barrow she walked with him toward the house.

She said, "It's not easy to be a man, a true man, with all that nature has intended a man for, when that has to be denied. And for a young man it's hardest of all. He has to be a man and then some if he's to hold back what it is that makes him a man. . . . Goodbye, Wick."

They had reached the kitchen door, where his bicycle was. For the first time she offered her hand, holding it out at its full reach.

He called a goodbye to Letty. "I'll be back day after tomorrow," he cried, looking inquiringly at the mother, who nodded.

"Goodbye!" The girl did not come to the door. "We'll be lookin' for you," she added gaily.

Riding back he was gripped by thought. Mrs. Sherrod, at the last, had showed that she understood about desire. He wished he could open his mind to her, the whole Pandora's box that consumed him at night. . . . But no; he was beginning to make of her what was called a mother figure. Not that the figure was anything like a real mother, to whom you could no more imagine unburdening your soul than you could undressing in the reading-room of the Carnegie Public Library. It was more like a goddess of nature in mythology.

But if her intention had been to give him moral support in his contest with his sex-urges, her recognition of them had in fact lent them sanction. They claimed him now as by right. When he reached home he barely glanced at a message from Gilley before stuffing it in his pocket: something about meeting at Robinson Family the next evening to hear a speech.

It proved to be, as he had feared, one of those evenings. But mercifully sleep came quickly.

Mr. Barrows was not in evidence when he arrived at the farm in the morning. Not long afterward, while he was working in the barn, a new car drove up and out stepped a neatly dressed couple. The talked-of Luellen and her new husband, it proved to be; there had been a sudden marriage three weeks before, Wick had known. He learned now how it was that Letty could have said that whatever Luellen may have done—and she had led her own life—it was all right because it was part of being Luellen, and Luellen herself was all right. She was sunny and down-to-earth. Her figure, though by no means unshapely, was loosely organized, her nose longish, but her large blue-gray eyes would have improved almost any face, and they were quick with interest in everyone else. 'She'd be just as openly observant of you,' he said to himself, rather taken aback by the advance the notion marked in his thinking on the subject, 'if you were in bed together.' He could not help having sex on his mind in connection with her. Any couple fresh from the marriage bed was bound to bring its associations with them, but besides that she looked at him, he was quite sure, in a manner to gauge his natural history as a male. Her husband, who was an assistant manager of a supermarket in Wise, had combed and glossy hair, clean white shirt and shiny shoes. When, with the rest, he had taken a chair on the porch, he might still have been posing for the bridal photograph, hands on thighs.

While Luellen was answering questions about the wedding and honeymoon, gaily, cutting her eyes frequently at Wick, the man of the house appeared behind the screen door, a white bandage around his head. He resembled a martyr risen from the grave. He still did so when he stepped out into the open. A small cut in the chin, doubtless from the razor, was beaded with blood.

Luellen's light-colored eyes rounded and she whistled. "Aunt Em, why didn't you tell me. . . ." The boy, rather alarmed by the tokens of the night's transgressions, was relieved by the expression of feigned severity and reprimand that came to her face. "Uncle Tom, *what* have you been up to?" It seemed the matter could be taken lightly, at least by Luellen.

The stricken mountaineer threw her a desperate look, then with eyes closed stroked his forehead below the bandage with his fingertips. He uncovered his eyes to assist himself to a seat. "I was delayed on the way home last evenin' and didn't get to sleep as early as I'm in the habit of. Another cup of coffee might be just about what I need," he said, looking at his sister.

Wick sprang to his feet. "I'll get it."

As he departed with Mrs. Sherrod's thanks the mountaineer declared, "I come up against Satan last night, and thar was a set-to."

From inside he heard Luellen say, "If you mean Demon Rum, it looks to me like you got the worst of it."

"I don't mean Demon Rum. There was some corn drunk, I won't deny it. Hit was good corn, though, and good corn's got hits place like everything else."

Dragging his feet enabled him to hear that but no more.

Coming within earshot on his return with the coffee he heard Tom Barrows saying in a voice lacking its characteristic strength, " 'Twarn't much, but the feller that owns the place had done called the police, and that put a end to hit. Though not before some damage was done." He was leaning back with his eyes closed again, breathing in a conscious way, when Wick opened the door, and when he raised their lids it was to fix them on the cup the boy was carrying. "You kin never tell what kind of people you may come up against when you're tryin' to have a quiet evenin' with a few friends."

With that, the subject was dropped.

Luellen threw out her arms and stretched forth her legs. "Lord, it's good bein' back out h'yeer!" she exclaimed. "I ain't a city gal and never will be." She raised her hands to her yellow hair, which was caught up in loops around her head, and drew out a pin. "You don't mind, do you, Aunt Em?"

"Let it down by all means."

The newly-weds had brought the midday meal with them. ("You don't think we'd bust in just before Sunday dinner and not bring vittles, do you? With a food store in the family?") Sliced ham, salami and liverwurst were unwrapped and laid on the table, cole slaw and potato salad; rolls were heated in the ever-ready oven. Bottled soft drinks, even, were produced cold from a Styrofoam ice-chest.

Coming dimly and waveringly to the table, reminding Wick of an object seen through the heat waves rising from a highway, Mr. Barrows regarded the fare with initial despondency but warmed to it as the meal progressed.

Feeling he had intruded long enough on the reunion and wish-

144

ing to leave Letty free to talk to her cousin, Wick took himself off as soon as they had finished eating. He set himself to scraping the old wagon clean with a discarded plane blade and his pocketknife.

The two girls took chairs out under the apple-tree. They were hidden from him by the barn but from time to time he heard an eagerly raised voice and once prolonged laughter.

He was surprised when later Luellen appeared around the corner of the building, alone. Barefooted, she picked her way carefully on the rough ground as she approached.

"My feet are gettin' soft. We've got to go and I wanted to tell you goodbye."

But when he had thanked her for doing so and for the dinner, she developed an interest in his work on the wagon, which he explained that he was preparing to paint.

"You've sure fitted in here."

He looked around at the familiar sights, made aware of the odors of the farmyard—the sour smell of the sty, the warm fragrance of the horse-stalls, the dusty-woody odor of the old barn itself—and the comfortable clucking of the hens and the thump of an apple hitting the ground. "I don't know. It's all come to seem quite natural to me."

"Even us hillbillies?"

"I like you mountain people. Just as I like your mountains. People here have had it tough. But they don't complain. Maybe not enough. They haven't let it get them down or sour them. Sure, a lot have gone on the Welfare. If the Lord has seen fit to provide food stamps, why not take them? What else can they do anyhow? The Lord has provided little enough else. The people I'm thrown with are kind and never make a person feel like an outsider. A person knows he can trust them. I'm proud to know the ones who come visiting here on Sundays, especially—country people." It was not the way he had talked to Gilley, and what he had said in the Lafayette he was now feeling he had to make up for. "Mrs. Sherrod is a real lady and Mr. Barrows a real gentleman, and I could say that about lots of others. Now that Hamp and Rafe have decided not to kill me"—and here he prepared to draw on Gilley's testimony—"I know I could count on them. . . ."

After waiting to see if he would go on, she said, "All the same, you can't have been used to this sort of life. You must of changed since you came here. But it hasn't been all one way."

"How do you mean?"

"You've got Letty talking educated English. Even Aunt Em. She sounds almost like she used to when they'd been living in Dayton for a year. I hope," she said, feeling along the worn edge of the sideboard, "you haven't let the mountain way of speech fool you about her. She's smart, and deep—"

"I know."

"—and a great woman." She appeared to be going to add something, then to change tack. "If she lets you and Letty go off together so much, it must be all right."

A little nettled, he heard in this an echo of Gilley.

"I wouldn't doubt she understands you. What I'm not so certain of is whether she sees how Letty would look to a boy. I know how it is with boys, too. They're all right, till suddenly. . . . Well, they can't help it. They got that little kitten in them, clawin' to get out, itchin' so furiously. It's still true what they used to say about boys and girls under a certain age. That the girls are ready for love but not for sex and the boys are ready for sex but not for love. And Letty's not just like any other girl. She's got it in her to be hurt awful bad."

He said stiffly, "You've got nothing to worry about. We're good friends, and that's it."

She nodded slowly, in a judicial way. "I'm glad she's got a friend like you, who Aunt Em feels she can trust. All the same, if it was in my hands, I might want to do what would make it safer."

"And what would that be?"

"I'm not Aunt Em, so it don't matter."

And, though he knew the remark would prove a restless memory, he did not press her.

When he had a chance to, he asked Letty what had provoked the outburst of mirth he had overheard. She appeared aghast at the idea of telling him, but he would not let her off.

Flushed, but amused despite herself, she murmured, "It was something Luellen said. I didn't understand it till she explained it. . . . Do you promise you won't make me explain it?"

"I promise."

"Well . . . I asked her what marriage was really like, and—"

146

Her voice dropped to a whisper, "She said it was penal servitude."

He did not have to have it explained, but it took him a moment to get it.

Before he left, she said, "Don't forget you're meetin' Gilley Huff tomorrow."

A tract like a picnic ground, Robinson Family was so named because it was the site of an annual reunion of related Robinsons to the number of six or seven hundred. A crowd had already assembled before Wick came *pup-pup*ping up and cars were still arriving. Gilley, easily to be spotted up front over the heads of the others sitting on the grass, said the turn-out was possibly not all in attestation of interest in public issues; refreshments were promised.

"What am I doing here?"

With an inverse snort—his sinusitis was evidently bothering him—to clear his nasal passages, the teacher said, "You're here to give heed to a promising young politician, a State legislator who's beginning to make his mark. John Colman. That's him over there, with the dark hair and white shirt. You probably won't like what you hear, but you'll be doing your father a service to let him know what the voice of the future in the Cumberlands sounds like."

Colman was the one you noticed in the group standing by the platform—a door on two saw-horses. Was it, Wick asked himself, because he was the one who expected to be noticed? He had serious black eyes beneath straight, dark brows and appeared to be little more than thirty. The crowd was mostly of families. Many of the men Wick surmised to be miners from the drawn expressions and the look in the eyes of seeing things not before them, or before others. A few appeared to be farmers. Children played on the fringes. In the clear air the richly burnishing rays of the lowering sun lent the scene a quality of special, even august, significance.

The speaker did not wait long to mount the improvised rostrum. His delivery was to the point and dead earnest.

"You've heard it said," he began, "that I'm running against the coal companies. It's true. I am. It's not true that I'm against coal, as the industry spokesmen will tell you. My father is a miner. I picked up my first pay check with coal dust on my hands. What I'm against is the way the industry is going after

147

coal, ravaging the land, taking its profits out of the bodies of the miners below and the livelihood of the farmers above." He told of a farmer who had come home one day to find his family holed up in terror with a neighbor, the hillside above his farm torn apart, the house "busted through" by boulders, the auto flattened, a family grave laid open. "Twenty-three thousand miles of bench have been gouged out of the Appalachians so far." He said he would not stop fighting until strip-mining was outlawed throughout the State.

A murmur from the audience followed this. Colman let it rise and die. "I know what some of you are thinking. That strip-mining makes jobs and brings in money. It doesn't. It costs us jobs, it costs us money. For every strip-mine with five machine-operators you close down, you'll give work to about twelve miners underground. Because with the demand for power what it is, the industry is going to get the coal out one way or another. Only from now on the industry is going to have to show a lot higher regard for human life." There was hearty applause here.

It was, of course, an old story to his audience, who listened shifting and uneasy, but he hammered away at it—the disasters from collapsing roofs, explosions caused by methane gas escaping from the coal seams and by coal dust in the air. He made his hearers see mine tragedies of recent years in all their human details. "I know you don't want to listen. But you've got to. Otherwise these dreadful things will go on and on.

"And who's to blame for them? The government, the U.M.W., above all, the mine-owners, the officials of Peabody, Consolidation, Island Creek, Allegheny-Keystone. Yes, they grieve when seventy-eight miners die seven miles underground. They're sorry it happened. But they don't care enough to take a cut in their profit for the sake of better roof-support and control of combustible gases. Production comes first, human lives second. And when we get right down to it, when you're sitting in those fine offices with the mahogany desks, the deep-pile carpets, the underlings, the pretty stenographers in their little skirts—when you're surrounded by all that you're not in the same world as miners in the bowels of a mountain. The hundreds of miners killed in accidents every year and the twenty-five thousand whose lives are being shortened by black-lung, why, they're just figures. . . ."

Again there was applause.

148

"It's not true, it's not fair!"

There he was, standing before them all, the speaker, arrested in midcourse, staring at him. Time might have stopped, too, the heavens in a state of incredulous recoil. "They're just doing a job—just the way you'd do it if you were in their place." He was in for it. Gilley's head was bent, as if those same heavens were falling. "Sure, the company officials have good offices and people working for them. But they started way down on the ladder like everybody else." He was conscious of his own raised voice, of the white blobs of faces turned toward him. "Everybody has a fair chance at those offices. But a lot of work goes with those carpets. Work darned few people could or would do. Twelve hours a day of it sometimes. Or more."

The crowd, initially astonished, was showing an interest. The man on the platform was bent down, conferring. Feeling a pressure on him as on a diver at maximum endurable depth, Wick strained to recall the gist, the phraseology, of his father's letters.

"Mr. Colman talks about production. Yes, the coal-company officials. . . ." He could not think of a word. "They're after production. They'd be out of their jobs if they weren't. And you miners here, you'd be out of your jobs if they weren't. And so would you others who sell to the miners. What would Appalachia be living on without the coal companies? More Welfare?"

He looked back at the platform. The speaker was standing patiently with his arms folded across his chest, plainly meaning to let him have his say. The boy would have preferred, at that moment, to be shouted down. He did not know how to make the point in his father's argument.

But, as he faltered, a key sentence of it came back to him, and he said, "Maybe we think industries ought to be interested in doing good instead of in making money." As if a log-jam had been unlocked the rest began to come to him, and his father's words to flow.

"It would sound better. But making money is just the other side of giving people what they want better and cheaper than anyone else can do it. Isn't that the best kind of good? And isn't that the system our country has always believed in? That when everybody is free to make the best of his opportunities, it's to the advantage of everybody? And what country has a better system? Does any other country offer half as much as ours does, in the way people live? Would any of us be half as well off in another country?"

The astonishing ruffle of applause and one loud whistle of appreciation gave him courage to plunge into the harder part. So did the picture in his mind of his father. "Yes, mining is dangerous. Every miner has known someone killed in a mine accident. And every one of us has known someone killed in a highway accident. But we don't talk about motorcar-manufacturers and highway-builders as if they were criminals. That's not to say mining doesn't take special courage. It takes a real man to be a miner. But men go into mines knowing what they're doing. And because they reckon they can do better for themselves mining than in any other way open to them. Are the mining companies so evil, when they offer opportunities here in the Cumberlands, in the Alleghenies, that no one else does?"

He sat down to further applause, feeling heated and drained as though by a fever.

Gilley said, "That was brave going." He clamped his mouth shut, his lips turned inward.

The speaker had taken a step forward. "Thank you, Mr. Carter. I think," he said to his audience, "that the president of Allegheny-Keystone would be proud of his son." At this necks craned. "And I'm glad he said what he did. I accept every word of it. I applaud him just as some of you did. The mines *are* our jobs, our meal tickets, and we need the companies to capitalize and run them. *Only we need safer ones.*"

In Great Britain and Germany, Wick heard him say, black-lung disease had been just about eliminated. Overseas mine safety had improved much beyond the United States record. Other facts followed to discredit what he had said. He felt sick and humiliated. He had failed to make the case, after all his father had written, and had only set himself up to be brushed off by his father's enemy. And a new charge against himself now occurred to him: He had probably left the impression that he saw nothing wrong with strip-mining!

As soon as the address ended, he got up. With the most hurried farewell to Gilley, whose move to detain him he pretended not to see, he slipped through the crowd to his bicycle and went home.

11

THE EVENTS OF THE EVENING were put out of his mind by the experience of the night. This was a protracted, very real and intensely erotic dream in which a seductive and warmly responsive Letty lay entwined with him in mutual desire, a Letty whom he had divested of her clothes and was on the point of entering when he awakened. He remained as he was a long time, still charged with the illusion and incredulous—incredulous not so much of the occurrence of the dream as that his mind and imagination could have heretofore been so closed to the possibility that those occurrences could be real. He looked at his past self as a newly emerged cicada might at the shell that had encased it during its long, unseeing, molelike existence. All that a girl was, Letty was —and available. The scenes of the dream played themselves over and over again before him, his mind clammy.

And their atmosphere was instilled into the day. He could not think of Letty divorced from the figure of the night's visitation who had opened his eyes to the properties of the original. He still remained half in the dream while manipulating the controls of the lively front-end loader as one remained still half in an exciting journey through a day of dull routine succeeding it. Even when Mr. DeSalla came up to him he could not connect fully with reality.

He brought the machine to a halt, however, with the wicked, undershot jaw resting on the ground, the motor idling.

"No trouble with this?" his employer asked, letting his eyes rove over the machine as if he had not beheld it a thousand times.

The front-end loader freed the mining operation of dependence on the trucks. When none of these was present the auger could keep on pouring out the coal. This it was Wick's job to pile up and scoop onto a truck when one became available.

"Not very often. Though I think we're going to need a new clutch-plate before long."

"Yeah. . . . Say, that was a good day's work you did, answering back to that trouble-maker, Johnny Colman. Sure, you're who you are, but what-the-hell. That don't make it no easier to get up on your feet and tell him off. And you're a fella that works alongside of everyone else here. Too bad some of them miners making thirteen, fourteen grand can't speak up. Well, I just thought I'd let you know."

In his abnormal condition the thought of the spreading word of his fervid championship of the mining interests dropped quickly out of his mind.

It seemed a foregone conclusion, as though a superior power were impelling him toward it, that the dream would become a reality. At the anticipation, the blood drained from his heart, the strength from his muscles. The disability that had put Letty off limits even for thoughts of sexual contact had become irrelevant.

His fear as he rode to the farm after work was that he would betray himself to the family. He dealt with the danger by resolutely keeping his eyes off Letty while they all ate together at the kitchen table. Fortunately Mr. Barrows was in a talkative spell. He had managed to buy two walnut-trees, beating the competition because their owner did not wish to have his woods torn apart by a bulldozer. He had much to say of the difficulties he and the Fergusons had had in getting them out.

Dinner was almost over when Mrs. Sherrod said, "Something must have happened to you today, Wick. You been almost forgettin' to eat."

"I couldn't get to sleep last night. I've felt funny all day."

"I knowed—knew—there was something wrong." It was Letty's first remark of the meal.

"We'll have to send you home early this evenin'."

"Maybe Letty'd care to go for a walk first. We can't have much more chance on weekdays, with the sun setting so early."

He had a place in mind, not too far, a dry, grassy spot in the woods.

On the way he chatted strenuously of things they were passing. Letty was uncommunicative and he was nervous of silences. He did not know whether his heart was going to stop or pound its way out of his chest.

When they reached his goal she sat of her own accord. Upon his settling beside her she said, plucking at the grass, "I know why you brung me—brought me—here."

"Oh? . . . Why?"

She lifted her face to his with a shadow of a smile. "And why you couldn't get to sleep last night. You've met a girl, and you're mighty taken with her. You been broodin' on her and you want to tell me about her."

"Yes, I have." He grasped the opening. "And it's you." As he spoke he put his arm around her and drew them together.

Her astonishment clearly precluded any other emotion.

"You mean a lot to me, Letty." The declaration hung in the air, unnatural as a jack-o'lantern.

They could not sit there like that. The slim body firm against his own was warm and a girl's. He knew the program ought to be developed gradually, but, paralyzed for words and fearful of losing the ground he had seized, he planted his lips on hers. She was neither responsive nor resistant. Sure from the dream that his desire would stimulate her own, he laid his hand against her breast, pressed his mouth more urgently on hers. To his chagrin, she struggled to free herself. Perhaps for this reason, perhaps independently, the old barriers against any sexual approach to her began to reassert themselves. Seeing himself in danger of being defrauded of the dream, he strained her to him with the consequence that she tipped over backward with him on top of her. As he sought her mouth again with his own and laid hold of her raised, bare thigh she struggled harder. Using her fists, she pushed him away with a strength that surprised him.

Suddenly he was overcome by the enormity of his actions. The next instant he was apart from her, looking down at her, stammering apologies. "It was a dream I had last night. It was so real, so convincing. I was taken over by it. I couldn't help acting as if . . . that was really the way things were between us."

He did not know how much she was taking in. She was slow in pulling herself together and sitting up. Her head hanging, her eyes closed, she was breathing in gasps. At length she said brokenly, "It would of been different . . . if you had the feelings that should go with it. If you cared about me."

"I do! I *do* care about you."

"Don't say that!" she cried sharply. "I don't want you to say that." It took her a moment to get her breath again. "Oh, I don't mean to sound that way. I know you care as much as you can, things bein' what they are. And . . . that's a lot more than I have any right to expect. Maybe that ought to be enough for me, and I ought to let you."

He was thinking he should protest when she added, as if overcoming weariness to do so, "But it would take some gettin' used to before I could."

Reading in her face the magnitude of what was lost, he wished passionately he were miles away—from himself and from her, who shared the knowledge of his baseness.

Walking back to the farm he was shut up within himself, an outcast. The necessity of holding onto him as usual could only be a final ignominy to her, he reasoned, and excoriated himself the more. He discounted as forced her one or two attempts at conversation, which he could not reciprocate without seeming less remorseful.

Their parting was a kind of shambles. He saw her to the footbridge, where he had left his bicycle, and said goodbye. Her downcast and averted face, her nearness to tears, persuaded him that she wished most to be alone.

"It's thunderin' off in the distance," she said, half turning to him. "I hope you don't get caught in no storm—any storm!"

He gave a short and scoffing laugh. She was left to surmise that he considered a bolt of lightning much in accord with his deserts.

He might well have been caught by what he had asked for. The storm came up fast, and he was barely indoors when it broke. It came as a relief to him, a drastic change in atmosphere partially expunging the day. The rain was falling heavily when he went to bed exhausted, and just as hard hours later when he got up to go to the bathroom, feeling queer. It was still raining when his alarm-clock went off, and raining too hard for work in the open. 'Thank God,' he thought. He felt washed out, weak, dizzy and unsettled in his stomach. 'I need more sleep,' he told himself. But three more hours of it left him no better. 'I'm sick,' he thought. The toast and coffee he made himself was all he could manage. Jack MacDonough had gone out but not to work, he learned from Mrs. Haney, who was watching a television serial.

He reminded himself that he was sick and not supposed to feel cheerful. But there was no blinking the source of the murk that overspread all, like smoke: it was the shame of the day before. He curled up in bed on his side with his hands between his legs in a pose that offered as little access as possible to misery.

The rain had slackened off a little. He had his window open and could hear the clatter on the leaves.

In the middle of the afternoon, having been half asleep, half tossed by imagination, he roused himself to the sound of Jack's voice from below. Catching the drift of his words, he pulled on his bathrobe and went downstairs.

The persistent rain was far heavier in the north, it appeared. Jack's eyes shone with the reports of streams in flood and rivers rising, of Stokesville's main street under ten feet of water. He intended to drive as close to the scenes of excitement as he could without cutting off his escape route.

Bearing back to his room a bowl of crackers and milk topped by canned peaches, Wick opened *Birds over America* at his bookmark.

> Man has emerged from the shadows of antiquity with a peregrine on his wrist. Its dispassionate brown eyes, more than those of any other bird, have been witness to the struggle for civilization . . .

He needed only to be taken so far out of himself for the full panorama of his folly to be revealed. A child: he had plumbed the depths of infantilism. He had taken in nothing, understood nothing, except as it entered the narrow orbit of himself—his burrow. The result had been the imbecility of his assault on a helpless girl, whom he had been unable to distinguish from the nonexistent creature of his desires, and the almost comparable imbecility of rebuffing her poor efforts to put it behind them and recover their friendship.

He would make amends. They were already in his head and heart, pressing to be made. The thought of putting them off, of Letty's continuing under the impression he had left her with, was tormenting to him. But he could not possibly make it to the farm that day. He felt too rotten. Also it was still raining. He was astonished to see from the window that the far side of the back yard and adjacent back yards were under a lake of tawny water, sprinkled with flotsam. The steam had overflowed. The rain, luckily, had tapered off to a drizzle. He would see Letty in the morning. There could be no work where bare clay would be hub-deep butter.

After a long night of delirious, insanely repetitive dreams he came to in the morning with the knowledge that he was really ill. His heart was pounding, his head heavy and hot, his eyes throbbing. He could tell he had a fever.

Thus he remained all day, his thoughts going around and around in confusion, all but giving himself up for lost, commiserating with himself and visualizing the receipt by those he cared for of the tidings of his passing. The weather appeared to have cleared up; reflections of sunlight from the wet world swam on the ceiling. Mrs. Haney looked in on him several times, regarding him as she might have a sick animal, a victim of the way life is, but offering to bring him broth, the thought of which nauseated him. Jack, who had not gone to work, came in once to speak of flood damage north of them, of landslides, buried farms and deaths from drowning. It had not been so bad in their own neighborhood, though parts of the bench they were working on at Little Powderhorn had gone down the side. "You can hear the water rushin' by"—Wick had thought the sound was in his head —"but it looks like she's crested and ought to start goin' down."

Said Wick, "If you see the Fergusons, will you please ask them to let the Sherrods know I'm laid up?" He could not bear to think of the construction Letty would put on his absence.

Toward evening he dared believe he was beginning to come out of it. He got up and tentatively went through some ordinary motions, with reassuring results. Food became a possibility, then a necessity. He went down and had another bowl of crackers and milk.

After a good night he waked with the first light. Exploring himself, he found that, incredibly, he was almost back to normal. It was the day to shave. When he had done so he put away a heavy breakfast in the still-sleeping house.

The stream was down somewhat, but washed soil, vegetation tan-chalky with dried mud, tangles of weeds, branches and trash on the upstream side of trees, shrubs and car bodies showed how high it had risen. The water, soupy with silt, still covered the floors of houses along the bank and some of their occupants were wading around disconsolately, two paddling boats. Furniture was set out on the higher ground, mattresses, curtains and bedspreads were spread over the roofs. Below cuts of one kind or another in the hillsides, sandbars of gravel stretched across the driveway. At Little Powderhorn, he could see even from the road that as much as the outer third of the bench had given way under the weight of impounded water. With the flood behind it, and taking the spoil bank with it, the mass had plowed down the hillside cutting gashes the entire way and no doubt spilling disastrously across the bottomland. If it was like that here, what could it be to the north?

Oak Lick Fork was running so high he had to leave his bicycle behind and, taking off shoes, socks and trousers, wade the stream. It was a clear, early-autumn morning and despite the nip in the air he rather enjoyed pushing heavy-legged against the current. He had a right now to feel part of this world, and where Letty and Queen were, he was sure, a welcome and attention awaited him. Donning his clothes where the road rose out of the stream he struck out with a long stride.

This had taken him only to the foot of the pasture when the quiet was riven by a devastating crash—the near report of a gun from the side and behind him. Wheeling, very badly startled, he quickly then searchingly surveyed the woods from which the blast had seemed to come. Close as it had been, he could see nothing, hear nothing. Well . . . a squirrel-hunter, he thought, and one farther off than the shot had sounded. Unsatisfied, he went on anyway.

He had not gone much farther when another surprise was sprung on him. A movement of the vegetation beside the road was all the warning he had of Hamp's emergence from the woods, a rifle at the ready.

"Hi," Wick said uncertainly, halting. The other's expression froze any more confident greeting.

"Get the hell back where you come from. Fast."

Wick stared at him dumfounded. "I'm goin' to see the Sherrods."

"The Sherrods! Well, by God, that's a good one! If you think Tom'ld let you set foot on the place . . . ! Get goin'. I ain't kiddin', boy."

There was no arguing with a gun. Stunned, Wick turned and headed back down the road. The way of the Cumberlands! He had

157

dishonored, or nearly so, a girl of the country. But why had Letty told them, or how had they managed to get it out of her? Or was this some crazy, unrelated misunderstanding? He recalled the shot on the way up. When he reached the place he looked again in the direction from which it had come.

There was no question now about the source. Colly, his expression malevolent, was standing in plain sight among the trees, a shotgun held by the muzzle in front of him.

Wick did not even stop for the stream but forged in as he was. Waves of revulsion, heated by shame and humiliation, rose within him. It could not be that he had ever really known Letty or her mother. The mountaineers were an alien lot, not for *him*. 'Not for me, not for me!'

To get away, to put it all as far behind him as he could: the thought drove him as the bicycle bore him on. The first bus to the northeast. And then, no more of these walled-in valleys, no more of the shacks and trash and mobile homes on concrete blocks. He looked back over his shoulder to make good his rejection. There, serene and lofty, bright in the sun, saddled with a cloud shadow and dappled with the coming colors of autumn, was Winespring. 'Letty!' But he silenced the voice within him. His eye caught the movement of a sprinkling of birds fluttering, swooping, swinging across the fields. 'Barn—' No: their tails were too short, their builds too stocky and. . . . 'Cliff swallows! . . . ' But what did it matter? . . . And no more butchered hills; a truck with a WIDE LOAD sign in front was bearing up the highway toward him noisily hauling a flat-bed trailer with the biggest of bulldozers on it, orange-yellow, its enormous blade sticking out on either side.

To Mrs. Haney he explained that he had to go home for unexpected but important reasons, right away.

He would cram everything he could into the suitcase, roll the rest up in his raincoat. As for the bicycles. . . . The thought remained incomplete while he unloaded drawers and closet, setting his good clothes aside, and packed.

About the bicycles. . . .

"What the hell do you think you're doing?"

The last man he would have had turn up, Gilley Huff, was standing in the doorway.

"Taking off for home." Damn it, Gilley was not *his* teacher.

"You can't. Not today, anyhow. The Sherrods need you."

"*The Sherrods!*" Wick threw back his head and laughed immoderately and mirthlessly.

"I don't get the act."

"I've just been run out of Oak Lick Hollow." He put the facts of the encounter before Gilley while he gathered up his toilet articles. "And if you want to know the truth," he finished bitterly, "it was all because I forgot myself for a moment and offended Letty. Also the code of the hills, it seems. Your crazy highlanders were prepared to shoot me for it."

The teacher glowered with puzzlement. "Is that what they told you?"

"No, but there they were. With guns. All ready for me, with Colly to give the signal."

"You dope! They weren't ready for *you*. What you ran into were the outposts waiting for the bulldozer."

"Bulldozer? What bulldozer? And why did they turn on me?"

"Because Allegheny-Keystone is about to strip-mine the ridge above the Sherrod farm on its way to strip-mining Winespring Mountain. And I have no doubt they assumed you're part of the operation after your spirited defense of the mining industry —which everyone for thirty miles around knows about by now. At least they'd take it for granted you've known what was coming, all the time butter wouldn't melt in your mouth. You haven't, have you? No, I can see that. The point is, you've got to stop it."

"I've got to stop it?"

"Get on the phone to your father. Tell him he must call off this operation. *At once.* . . . Don't just stand there looking witless. We've got to move. They may have the crew out there already, and a carload of armed men from the County Sheriff's office. After what you've seen, you can be sure that the Fergusons, Tom Barrows and their friends are prepared to fight. They'll shoot if they have to, and those boys don't miss. And if Tom Barrows hits anybody, the *least* he can expect is jail for life." He was watching Wick anxiously. "I'm saying nothing about what stripping will do to Oak Lick Hollow and Winespring Mountain."

The boy's response came of itself. "There's no use calling my father. It wouldn't do any good." He did not give an instant's reflection to the reasons for that pronouncement. He simply

159

knew. "You've got your car, I take it. Let's get out there." Held by the other's disappointed and irresolute look, he urged, "We're wasting time."

They took the stairs two at a time. "I don't know what you think we're going to do," Gilley said. "Stand in front of the bulldozer?"

"If necessary."

"And kick the County Police in the shins when they wade in to remove us?"

"Let's get out there, first." The truth was, he had no idea what they could do.

He learned as they drove that Gilley had returned from Stokesville only late the night before with his story and his films: the wires were all down up that way. He had not known until this morning what was afoot. The operation was to have been sprung without warning, before any resistance could be got together, but word had leaked out yesterday and "spread like gasoline on water." It appeared that Allegheny-Keystone considered its hand forced because a public hearing on designating Winespring and its environs a State forest had been scheduled for five days hence —"and you might want to make a note to be there," the teacher added: "eight P.M. in the County courthouse in Harpersburg." The company was moving to deface the mountain and ruin it for parkland before legislation to protect it could be enacted.

"One more thing. I hear that Tom Barrows and Hamp Ferguson and a couple of the boys were out on the town a few nights ago and got into a tussle with Bull Turner and his buddies. Luckily the police broke it up before anyone was badly hurt. It seems that Bull had had some words to say about people who take in coal-company presidents' sons and even let them run around with the girls of the family."

Wick rubbed his eyes with the heel of his hand. 'My God, what am I going to do?' he thought.

"Sure you don't want to stop at Taulbee's grocery and put in a call to Allegheny-Keystone executive offices?"

"Keep going."

Oak Lick Road bore the tire marks of a double-wheeled truck. The truck itself and the flat-bed trailer Wick had passed on the highway were drawn up where the road entered the stream, on a flat expanse where everything had been leveled by the hauled-

160

in bulldozer, which could be heard reverberating up ahead. In picking this spot for a base, Wick had time to think, Mr. Winstead had reconnoitered to good effect. Two cars, one the County Sheriff's, and a pickup truck had been driven onto the matting of small flattened trees and left there, empty but for a man in the front seat of the truck.

Beside the cars and the truck stood a machine in which the boy saw the answer to his problem, if there was one.

"Drive as close as you can to the front-end loader," he said. It was an orange-yellow, like the bulldozer, and medium weight. "We'll walk up to it, in a matter-of-course way. And climb on. It's the only thing for us—to go after them. I'll drive, you find a place behind the seat and hold on."

"And if we catch them, what do we do?"

"You get off. I'll try to knock out the bulldozer."

Pulling on the hand-brake, Gilley stared at him an instant, then reached to the back seat for his camera. "Whatever else, it'll make a story."

As they climbed up, the man in the truck got out uncertainly. Wick found the ignition switch; the make was not too dissimilar from the one he was used to. The motor, still hot, caught at once.

"Hey! Are you two . . . ?"

The boy waved reassuringly.

"Hold tight. This may be rough." His passenger was well braced behind him. He swung the machine around and headed for the stream in low gear with a wide-open throttle. The man in the truck was running after them, staggering in the tangle of branches. He gave up as they splashed into the water.

"The stream's still muddy," the boy called over his shoulder. "We can't be far behind them." The heavy-cleated tires threshed the water like paddle-wheels. Overhung at both ends, the loader surged on with a rocking motion. Steering and ducking branches, feeling power in his hands, knowing that he could put his mount through its paces as well as anyone, he was exhilarated. To be after them! To be *doing!*

A shot rang out up ahead. "Colly's warning. We're catching up." The roar of their own motor drowned out the bulldozer's.

"The Sheriff's party must be riding with them," Gilley called over the noise. "They'll pull their guns on you if you interfere."

161

"I don't think they'll shoot. The loader, yes, but not me. I'll have to get close before they smell a rat."

Out of the stream they picked up speed. The woods gave way to the pasture . . . and there it all was. The bulldozer, looking to Wick like a tank, had stopped a couple of hundred feet away, facing the ridge above the farm. While they watched, two men in the brown-and-beige uniform of the Garrett County police jumped down from it and ran heavily toward the woods on the far side of the pasture, each with a gun. Two more armed men, from a uniformed party of half a dozen on foot, all soaked above the knees, started up the road.

Wick had brought the loader to a halt. "You'd better get off. There's one of them looking at us."

"I'm sticking with you till you're a lot closer. I've got to get pictures."

The boy started up again, following the bulldozer's tracks through a flattened section of the pasture fence. There was no sign yet of the Fergusons or Tom Barrows or any of their allies. The bulldozer blade was going down now, the motor surging as it dug in.

"The problem is going to be," Wick called to his passenger, it having suddenly come to him, "that he can operate on a steeper slope than I can!"

"And I think he's Bull Turner!"

The boy looked and had no doubt of it. Turner had still not noticed the pursuit. In front of him, the earth curled away from the monster blade like a wave from a ship's bow.

"Down you get."

"Good luck!"

Facing up or down the slope he would be all right—if he could keep that tremendous blade from bearing down on him. Sidewise to the slope, he might topple. But with a lead on the bulldozer, he could rush it up the slope and, if he could get in from the side or rear, bring the loader's bucket down on the controls.

Running below the bulldozer and parallel to it, he had passed it before a puzzled Turner noticed him. When he judged his lead sufficient, he prepared to turn straight up the hill. "Letty, Queen and Winespring!" he murmured. He heard a hammer-strike on the loader and in the same instant a scorching blow on the shoulder rocked him back. The crack of a gun resounded from up ahead, from the swamp or a clump of trees. One of his friends had fired at the loader and the bullet had ricocheted.

Several shots rang out behind him.

"Hold your fire!" he yelled toward the unseen source of the first report. "I'm on your side!" His left arm resisted painfully when he moved it. He could see blood where the shirt was rent. Never mind. . . .

Wheeling the loader around, he roared up the hill, bucket high. . . . 'I started too far off'; he knew it at once. Turner saw what was coming and took alarm. Wick saw him snatch at the levers. Sounding like an artillery barrage, the monster swung around exactly like a tank. He was charging a wall of steel. More —the wall of steel was coming down to meet him. Jamming on the brakes he shot into reverse and trundled backward down the hill. The distance widened; the bulldozer had stopped.

Snap! He had heard that sound close overhead once before, from a target pit. An instant later the report came from the Sheriff's side. 'A warning shot for me,' he told himself; he must keep in closer. Another report followed, this from the other side. A counterwarning from his friends to the police: lay off!

He was careening forward again, moving to circle the quarry —up the hill and around its rear to its other flank. His shoulder hurt as if a sharp weight were pressing in it, he saw himself as brainless, but there were those for whom this was his offering, and there was no time to think. . . . Only he dared not attack along the side of the hill, with the loader sideways to the slope. And the bulldozer, as he rounded it, swung with him, keeping the blade between them with Turner's face alert and watchful over the top of it. He was close to and getting above it, could glimpse Gilley crouching on the left now instead of the right. Down with the buckets to keep the center of gravity low as he came to the top of his orbit and would have to swing broadside to the slope directly above the bulldozer.

And now it was done, his heart in his mouth, the loader cornering on two wheels. Turner waiting with the raised blade toward him. Hold it: he brought the loader to a halt facing downhill but still well above the bulldozer. Up with the front bucket, not too far. Decide on something. But the bulldozer was coming at him. Out with the bucket and down the hill . . . and now pivot, swing at him.

163

And the loader with its heavy arm swung . . . and was short, missing by feet. Too far, he was still too far. "You little bastard, I'll kill you!" Turner yelled. He had come around to face his assailant. And was at him again. But Wick was already in reverse, bouncing downhill. When Turner stopped, so did he, a few yards away.

Damn, but the loader was precariously balanced! If it had roll-bars like a skidder at least he wouldn't be crushed if it went over on him. . . . If he could tempt Turner farther down the hill. . . .

He nosed forward, raising the bucket on high. Turner, watching it, raised his blade—probably as far as it would go. He heaved forward again . . . but the boy had already thrown the loader into reverse once more. "Come and get me!" he shouted, backing down the slope just ahead of the bulldozer.

When it stopped again, he did too. Face to face, the machines stood motionless. Both drivers snatched glances around them, Wick wondering if the field was going to be rushed by the armed men of the other side and assuming that Turner was wondering the same. The two forces must be holding each other in check, in a stand-off.

'Every time I threaten,' he thought, 'Turner will have to lunge. . . .' He advanced again, cautiously, right hand ready for the arm-control lever or the gear shift. And Turner did come at him. But the bulldozer with its immense weight could not match the loader's acceleration, and the loader recoiled un-scathed before it. A repetition taught Wick to keep just ahead of it, and when Turner stopped he was quick to threaten and force him to advance again.

They were getting down the hill. The frown on Turner's face indicated that he grasped the strategy. He tried to back up the hill, but the loader was at him so fast he had to throw the bull-dozer instantly into forward again. At that he lost his temper and kept on coming. With a mighty roar the huge machine gathered momentum. From near full speed in reverse, the boy whipped the loader around to the side. He spun it to face the bulldozer on the flank and brought the bucket down like a hammer. The clang of iron resounded above the racket of the motors as it struck the hood a glancing blow. But the bulldozer wheeled with appalling rapidity and, as Wick swung around, the edge of its blade crashed into the rear scoop, catapulting the loader forward and all but sending its driver backward off its seat.

Circling again, at a distance, shaken, Wick found that the loader still answered to the motor and controls. But a clout like that anywhere else on it would probably finish it.

To his astonishment, he saw that the onlookers had closed in from both directions and stood in an open ring around the arena. There must have been twenty of them, among whom he glimpsed Mr. Barrows and the Fergusons. He had been in this country long enough to know what was in their minds.

This was something like it!

It was not something like it for him. That wall of steel was still facing him.

If he could knock out the monster behind it, he would not care what they did to him afterward. If only it could not spin so fast, with one track going in one direction, the other in the opposite. With bucket up, he cantered forward. "Go to it, Wick!" he heard a shout.

He made a pass as close as he dared, past the blade, then turned. . . . But he was not fast enough. The blade was coming around at him before he could get it for a blow. He veered off.

There was Gilley, with his camera in front of his eyes. Others he noticed wore expressions of utter absorption in the spectacle.

The trouble was that Turner could see which way he was going and pivot with him. Maybe . . . he lowered the bucket, then bore down on the bulldozer, heading to swerve past it on the left. He saw the other move the levers to meet him on that side. At the last instant he put the loader sharp over to the right . . . and caught the bulldozer flat-footed. Wheeling to the left, he sent the bucket crashing against its back. The jar was terrific. Zipping off, he caught sight of crumpled metal where the bucket had struck and of a black liquid oozing out. He had got the oil-tank.

"Hit him again!"

Skirting the maimed Goliath, he called out, "Next time the bucket will be higher. When you see it coming you'd better jump!"

At the sight of Turner's face, he said to himself, 'I'm asking for the hospital.'

He turned off, then came back at his enemy. Only when he

165

was nearly on him could Turner be sure which way he was going. But he was not far behind in bringing his blade around. The boy had slowed down. Instead of swinging into the bulldozer as he had before, he swung away from it, simultaneously raising the bucket, and he kept on swinging, around nearly full circle. The bulldozer, pivoting in the opposite direction, presented its rear.

"Now, Turner!"

Turner had reversed his direction of turn, but with a look at the great scoop poised above him gave up and jumped.

Down it came where he had been, smashing the control levers and instrument panel. Wick knew he had little time, but he had less than he thought. Earth and sky suddenly reeled. The ground, above him, fell on him with a wrenching thud. He was looking up from it at the sky, and against the sky at a colossus.

But not at Turner alone. There was another, Rafe, with a rifle.

He got to his hands and knees, then to his feet. From his forehead, where it had struck something when Turner had yanked him off the machine, his hand came away bloody.

"Are you all right?"

It was Gilley. Wick nodded. Everyone was standing around. Rafe had grounded his gun. Turner, walking off, was hitching his trousers up.

"You're a traitor!"

Still unsteady, gripped by the pain in his shoulder and his head, Wick turned and confronted a face bloated with anger— Mr. Winstead's.

A tall man in the chocolate-and-coffee-ice-cream uniform inserted himself in the group, between them. "All right, let's have it calm." He was an intelligent-looking man, wearing dark-rimmed glasses.

Mr. Winstead declared, "Sheriff, I want this young man arrested."

Said Gilley, "Do you? Maybe you'd better be in compliance with the law yourself first."

"How do you mean?"

"It suddenly came to me that a new law has just taken effect. Getting a State permit for stripping's not enough. You have to post notice of intent a reasonable time in advance. There's no

166

use asking if you've got a broad-form deed on the Barrows property, though I doubt if Mr. Barrows knew it. You'd never make the mistake of coming on the place without one."

"That's right. We never knowed about it," the mountaineer declared.

"But what notice did you post?"

The mine-manager gave an ugly smile. "I thought there might be a bar-room lawyer around." He took a folded page of newspaper from his shirt pocket and opened it out. "There it is, Sheriff."

Both men bent their heads to look.

"You call *that* a notice? In that microscopic type, at the foot of a column of classifieds? I say that won't stand up in court even in this state. And another thing. As soon as the wire services get them these pictures are going to be in every important daily in the country. Can you imagine an editor passing up a photo story like this? A boy on a tractor who tackles the super-bulldozer to save the little mountain farm from rape? If anything can get national attention for the resistance to strip-mining. . . . Wick, we've got to get you to a doctor."

The boy saw what was coming and as the mine-manager lunged for the camera sprang on him. He had an impression of a powerful torso inside the jacket and a smell of cigar before he was thrown aside—to be caught by someone before he fell. In the confusion he had a glimpse of Tom Barrows's long arm extended and his hand around Mr. Winstead's face and saw the Sheriff step into the fray.

"All *right!* I said we'd have it calm!"

Gilley had stepped back and still had his camera.

Said the Sheriff, "Mr. Winstead, Allegheny-Keystone still don't altogether own this country. I think you'd better bear that in mind. As for all this"—and he signified the scene around them with a wave of the hand—"I think it's a matter for the governor to decide on. I'm takin' my men off and I don't want to hear of no provocation from either side. And you, boy, I don't want you leavin' the county for as much as ten minutes without the permission of my office, till I tell you otherwise."

12

It was his second morning at the Barrows house. After spending the day before as the Wounded Boy, lolling about in Colly's upstairs room, he felt like bestirring himself. He knew, moreover, that he ought to help Mrs. Sherrod with the work as well as he could. Colly was at school, and her brother had had word that his son, in the next county, had broken his leg and had gone off early in the truck, taking Letty with him. Wick suspected that her having been so much in his company since he had been brought back to the house had entered into her having been prevailed on to accompany her uncle.

The role of hero suited him better than he liked to acknowledge to himself. His reception when Mr. Barrows had brought him back from having his shoulder wound dressed and forehead taped, the half-jocular approbation of the men, the warm solicitude of the two women, had raised his exploit quite out of the ruck of chance, fear, bumbling and confusion in which it had taken place. "You had us fooled," Hamp said, "with what we h'yurd of your standin' up for the minin' companies."

The one discordant note was sounded when he thanked Rafe for having kept Bull Turner from kicking his brains out and his benefactor commented, "You warn't in no shape to stand up for yourself." And added, with Jack MacDonough's detachment, "Hit'll be different when your shoulder gets well."

There was, of course, his father. What would he say? Mr. Barrows had asked. "Plenty, I suppose," he replied. "But he's bound to see that A.-K. was in the wrong."

Though he considered his enhanced standing as fragile as a bubble, especially when he thought of Turner, he had felt able when he and Letty were alone to refer to the last occasion of their being together. "I don't know what got into me, except that. . . . Can you forgive me?"

She had said, "If there was anything to forgive, I forgived you right away," speaking as if the episode were to be hardly recognized as having happened at all. All the same, as she sat with him the next day, weaving a basket while he read to her, he had known that his consciousness of her had been changed for good and he did not see how she could fail to be aware of it.

Mr. Barrows had brought home a newspaper from Harpersburg that evening. On the front page were two photographs of "The Battle of Oak Lick Hollow" and a story under Gilley Huff's name with frequent mention of his own. The governor, it was announced, had suspended Allegheny-Keystone's permit pending a study of the situation. The manager of Talbot Creek Mine was said to be consulting the home office on possible legal recourses. . . .

He was up and easing himself into his shirt when he heard Mrs. Sherrod approaching. She was carrying the breadboard with a cup of coffee and corn bread with jam on it.

"Oh, how good of you!"

"I didn't know whether you'd feel fit to come down. Here, let me help you with that." She set the tray on the up-ended suitcase that had been picked up at Mrs. Haney's.

"I'm really all right." Getting fully into the shirt, he asked if she couldn't keep him company while he fell to.

To his surprise she agreed and sat down on the foot of the bed. No, actually he was more surprised by his presumption in asking. "I've been wantin' to talk to you. Or I've been wantin' to talk to myself in your hearin'." She looked down at her hands, palms down on her thighs.

He had not been prepared for anything serious, and this, which could concern only one thing, was going to be that. He looked at her gloomily.

She waited until he had sat down on the other end of the bed, by the suitcase. "I don't know what to do. So I'll talk to you as I would to someone a lot older. Probably I don't have to tell you it's about you and Letty. Maybe I shouldn't have let things run on as I have. But it's brought her happiness, a new life, havin' a friend like you. And I want her to have all the

169

happiness she can. . . . Don't," she interrupted herself to say with an almost impish smile, "let me take your appetite away. I'm not going' to say anything terrible. Let me see you start on that bread and coffee."

Her eyes lingered on him as he ate and drank.

"I've thought all along Letty would have too much sense to let herself get in love with you, seein' how hopeless it would be, and you only eighteen on top of everything else."

His rejoinder came of itself. "Why should it be hopeless?" At the level look she turned on him, he said, "If . . . that happened it would be because I was in love with her."

It was not what he might have chosen to say. But meeting her dark, receptive eyes, he felt in anticipation the relief of unburdening himself of what lay behind his words and made the future seem more than ever an unscalable wall not to be thought about. "You spoke about what it has meant to Letty. Two days ago, when I thought you had all turned against me and I was going to have to go away, I discovered what it means to me. On my way from here, I looked at Winespring in the sun under the blue sky and remembered its woods, and the waters of the Fork. I saw the goldenrod and wild sunflowers beside the road and smelled the hemlocks in the warmth. There was a Carolina wren singing while I was wading down the creek—nothing else so full of gladness. It was all in my heart and it was all bound up with Letty. It's all come to me through Letty. I've learned to see by telling her of things she can't. I've learned the words from the reading I've done because of her. All this was in my mind when I thought I was leaving. And I just didn't see how I could."

He raised his eyes to find her looking at him as if she were seeing more in him, other things in him, than he was aware of. "But that's all beside the point. There's no danger of what you spoke of, where Letty's concerned. She wouldn't want there to be anything romantic between us." He pronounced this as a fact reassuring to her.

"And you, Wick. What do you want? What are you looking for?"

He reflected as he munched his corn bread. It was easier to feel the void inside than to define what would fill it. "Some knowledge of what the purpose of it all is?" he hazarded. "To get through to the heart of things? No, I'll tell you. . . You have to think of life's being mostly meaningless sounds. But among them you hear snatches of music, from far off, barely audible. And they're tantalizing, you want to get to the source of it, to hear it all, and . . . well, you know how music can take you out of yourself, uplift you."

"That's a beautiful way to put it."

"With Letty I've felt closer to it than I've ever been before. . . . To me she's like a daughter of the hills and woods and streams—you know, that you said you missed so much in Dayton."

He added what he would not have presumed to say without the assurance the past two days had brought him, speaking as if they were on a par, and in the slightly wry tone to which she was given. "But if Letty's their daughter, you're her mother, aren't you? That makes you the hills and woods themselves. And I think in a way you are. You're in on what they mean. There are depths in you that are like—or . . . that are akin to the depths I feel in the woods."

She looked at him with widening eyes. "Because I'm an Indian gal?" Her whimsical-rueful smile forced a broadening of his.

"No, but it's true. You know what I'm looking for and where it can be found."

She surprised him greatly when she said she did. "I can tell you. But the answer will disappoint you. It's the only answer there is, though, as you'll discover in time—and maybe be content with it. What you're lookin' for is everywhere . . . and nowhere. It's nowhere . . . and everywhere."

He pondered. "Can you tell me what the *it* is?"

"You know what it is. It's what you're lookin' for. It's what we're all lookin' for. But some are driven to seek it more than others." She watched him consume the last of the cornbread. "And that brings me back to what I was going to say. Something—I don't know what—has made me fearful of what I should have been fearful of all along. That if you and Letty go on bein' so much with each other you'll lay together."

It was like having the air knocked out of his lungs.

"No! I wouldn't take advantage of her." The falsity of his assurance was, to his ears, self-proclaimed. "I mean even if I could."

"Can you tell me you never feel desire for Letty?"

"I can control it. In any case she would never—"

171

"Wick, you're an eighteen-year-old boy. As for Letty, even a stone if you leave it by a fire will take warmth from the heat playin' on it. She could even take the lead, thinkin' it's unfair to deny you."

"I wouldn't let her sacrifice herself for me. And if anything did happen between us, which it won't, it would be for good, as far as I'm concerned."

"Oh, Wick. You mean it, I know. But you've got four years of college ahead of you. You'll be amongst other young men and girls there, many of your own kind of folks. Do you truly think you could keep on carin' only for a little blind girl back in a holler of the Cumberlands? When the world is openin' out in front of you, and it a world she couldn't rightly share—maybe even if she weren't blind? No, let me go on. Whatever you say and believe now, it wouldn't be natural. And think of Letty. She couldn't let you have her even once and not lose her heart to you. I know her. And what would be left for her? There are fine mountain boys, but they're all poor. They can't afford to take on a wife who can't carry her weight. You wouldn't want her brokenhearted for life, I know."

A lump in the middle of his chest, he said, "To begin with, I don't know how you can be so sure I'm going off to college."

Some Blue jays were calling outside, carefree and excited.

"You've got to. You've got to make it up with your father, and go. You can't let yourself be caught and held in the poverty of the hills. You've got it in you to amount to something. It's in your nature, and you've got to obey that. And anyone who kept you from succeedin' by tyin' you down, you'd come to hold it against her. No matter how pretty she might be or how lovin'."

"Do you think success would be so important to me? Have I got to believe it's the purpose of life?"

"No, you don't. It's not. The purpose of life is livin'. But livin' means comin' up against hardships, troubles, dangers and overcomin' them, or doin' all you can to. Look at every livin' thing. It's pushin' on to the fullness of its ability. That's what the *feelin'* of life comes from. Didn't it come risin' up in you when you'd beaten the bulldozer, and you knew how much you'd done for us all, and for Winespring? I don't mean that life is all strivin' and fight. There are times of peace, like now. There's love, which is the greatest thing of all. But peace don't enter the heart of the quitter. It's what comes when you've put out your best. And so is love. You won't have them or keep them except as you've earned them."

She tapped her thigh, rocking her hand on its heel, looking sorrowfully, it seemed to him, at the bright window. "There are so many hard things to face. If I listened to my heart I'd tell you to leave here now." She turned to face him and laid her hand for a moment on his leg. "Wick, I'm thinkin' about that terrible, no-good Bull Turner. He's not likely to let it rest between you the way it is, with him havin' come off worst. Wick, I don't want you to get hurt. And if you got hurt on account of befriendin' us, that would make it all the harder to bear."

The sight of tears in her eyes moved him so much that he reassured her with a confidence he might not otherwise have mustered. "I can take care of myself."

She wiped her eyes unashamedly with the back of her fingers. "I don't urge you to leave. I tell myself it's because of what I've been sayin' about standin' up to the difficult things. The more we turn from the tests life puts us up against the harder they get to face. If I talked you into runnin' away, with everything still unsettled about Winespring, maybe I'd be doin' you a hurt. That's what I *tell* myself. But I *ask* myself whether it's because I'd like to keep you here and don't want Letty to lose you. You've got to go off to college, but maybe if you two stay just friends you'll be coming back to see us."

"I'd certainly do that." Distressingly, he sounded to himself merely polite. But she appeared to be in the grip of her own thoughts anyway.

"I have to come now to what will make me sound like a very foolish mother, but it's got fixed in my mind. It's been like a voice."

"What is it?"

"Letty's told you, hasn't she, how it happened she lost her sight?"

"Yes, when she felt she had to."

"The doctors could find no injury to her eyes. They said that a person can go blind from shock. They call it hysteria. Something will happen to the person so dreadful it kills the wish to see, without her knowin' it, and she goes blind. It's a way of cuttin' herself off from the world and all it reminds her of. I've

173

been feelin' all along that's what it was with Letty, and also it could be a way of punishin' herself. No one's ever been able to make her stop blamin' herself for her sister's death."

"That's it!" he exclaimed. He had full faith on the instant. "I'm sure that's how it is in Letty's case. You know, almost from the first I haven't been able to believe she *had* to be blind."

"The doctors say as far as they can *tell* her sight *could* come back."

"I've tried to tell her that, but she won't listen. She changes the subject. What do they think could bring it back?"

"They don't know. But it's in my mind that you might. Because of the different feelin' you give her about things, and herself. And when you said you'd come to see because of her, I could almost hear the voice sayin', 'There, what did I tell you!' Now do you see how I'm caught? If I come between you and Letty, I could be robbin' her of her best chance. Or so in my heart I believe. And if I don't, it could end with life bein' made even harder for her. I ought to be able to work it out myself, like a smart woman. But I can't. All I can do is make a plea for my little girl. And remind you that your expectations of life are a thousand miles ahead of hers."

He said quickly, "You don't need to plead. *Or* worry. There's nothing to worry about." Nervously upset, he got to his feet. "I promise."

He promised. So much for that. It left only the question of how to deal with the urgencies of sex. Not that he would do so, but he wondered what her answer would be if he asked her. She was a woman who had known a man's physical passion. She must understand its insistence.

He sat down again, feeling the thickening of his blood, just as she was preparing to rise. "Luellen addressed herself to the subject, too."

"Luellen? What did she say?" Obviously curious, she settled herself back again.

He told her, in a reportorial voice, as nearly as he could recall. At the comparison of the kitten scratching to be let out, her mouth twitched with the urge to smile.

"She said if she were you, she'd know what ought to be done about it."

Her curiosity gave way to uncertainty, presumably as to whether

174

she had heard aright. Expression faded altogether as she looked away.

"What did she mean by that?" He was provoked as he sometimes was by perversity—only it was not that. A sense of irony possessed him.

She shook her head slightly, in dismissal. Her coloring was darker and in her face he saw something like lethargy.

His surroundings had lost all substance. But it was still ironically that he persisted. "You must have some idea."

She stood up and looked down at him with arched brows, meeting his eyes, he thought, by an act of will. "Knowin' Luellen. . . ." She smiled, her eyes narrowing, "I'd say she meant she'd offer herself in place of Letty."

Mirroring her smile, he said, "But not being Luellen, you wouldn't."

"Not bein' Luellen's age, I don't have to think about it. I'm much too old to interest a boy." She spoke lightly and emphatically, closing the subject. But her voice was unsure. "*And* I've got to get back to work."

"But if you heard you were mistaken?" The world seemed darkened and contracted. Needs long combatted and suppressed were making their full strength felt within him.

"Why, I . . ." she began, preserving a light touch by perceptible self-command, "I . . . reckon I'd put it down to a stroke of fever, or some kind of attack like that. And I wouldn't think no more about it."

What he was asked to give up with Letty—for more than four years, wasn't it?—was so great and what she would be giving up not so very considerable, he should have thought: only a physical privacy she must willingly have yielded up many times. And yet, though it was sure to be ecstatically blissful for him and perhaps not unpleasurable to her, it was not to be. He could not even press her. That was the irony. If he did he would seem to be asking her to compensate him for what he was relinquishing by his promise—to pay a price in kind for her daughter.

She must have discerned the forces bearing upon him, for she sat down again on the end of the cot, regarding him compassionately, with no pretense of its being a joke. "I know it's not fair. . . . Wick, you've never had a woman, have you?"

He shook his head.

"If you had you'd have seen it's not so all-important, however it may seem at the moment. If you don't build it up in the mind too much, the wants of the body are less hard to bear. It's just part of nature. When it's over, it's the same old you, pretty much, and the same life, with all its troubles. When the longing's been taken care of, you can hardly believe it could have mattered so much."

"If that's all there is to it, why does it have to be such an issue?"

"Oh, but that's not all there is to it, except for coarse and unfeelin' people. You can't—"

"Especially," he interrupted, pursuing his own thought, "when it's part of nature. And for . . . anyone who . . . has a feeling about nature. . . ." An air of ironic detachment was not easy to preserve when the going was so hard. "Which would make it . . . not just something physical, but like. . . . Shall I tell you what it would be like?"

He was rewarded, if reward it was, by signs of confusion in her.

"What I was going to say . . . when two people are so joined together they each take the stamp of the other, the way wax takes and holds the print of what's pressed into it when it's soft. For a woman—but never mind that. For a man, the print he bears of her may be like a claim on him. He feels he don't own himself like he did. And the male in him rises up in rebellion. He holds it against her. He forgets how he coveted her—until the need arises again, and if she's handy. And because she has let him have her, and all that goes with that, she has lessened herself in his eyes. So the poor lady loses on both counts."

His slight smile, disabused, resigned, was intended to show how ready he was to accept any reason at all for her inflexibility. Because, of course, he had known that any aspirations he might permit himself were wholly unrealistic.

"Wick, if you could read my heart, you'd forgive me."

He wilted. "And you me, if you could read mine."

"I know."

"There's so much that gnaws at a person. Such longings."

"I know." Leaning toward him and taking his head between her hands, she kissed him beside the mouth.

He was afraid that, rising, she would say something brightly, like repeating that she had to get back to work, as if everything

176

had been taken care of. But she did not—only picked up the breadboard with the coffee-cup on it and departed with it.

He followed soon after and went out to see what jobs needed doing.

The great bulk of Winespring was in his eyes the measure of the job that had to be done to save it—and which he could not wash his hands of now. Talk of claims on a person! It was unknowable, what he might have let himself in for. . . . A chilly west wind had come up, bringing with it a succession of cold-looking, gray-bottomed clouds. Fall had come.

They had been through so much together during the morning that at lunch they were like an established married couple, or what he imagined one would be like. She produced two glasses of elderberry wine before they sat down and three cigarettes in a flattened pack which she said some visitor had left—if he would like them. He had not smoked in months, but he had one with the wine, though inhaling very little.

"I'm pretty sure I'm out of a job. To say the least. I'm going to have to start looking for something."

"I know Tom Barrows would be more than glad to have you in with him."

"You think so?" The idea appealed to him.

"I'm sure of it. There's always room for another man who knows loggin'." But she agreed to sound out her brother without letting him know anything had been said between them.

When they had eaten she changed the dressing on his wound with the gauze and tape the doctor had supplied. He would have been well content to have her ministrations continue longer.

His manhood and its potentialities for her had been acknowledged, she had treated him as an equal. He felt older, and remained conscious of it when Letty returned with her uncle. Yet oddly, she seemed older, too. The change in him could have enabled him to see in her what previously he had not, just as when you were raised higher you could see farther.

"I asked Agnes," she said to her mother, "if she isn't worried about Charlie's givin' himself a fit over bein' helpless. She said she was, more than anything. But what could he do to give him the feelin' of being important? Charlie bein' such a good hand with a knife, and rememberin' those walnut-trees Uncle Tom

177

hauled out, I thought he might put his hand to carvin' gun-stocks, little as I care for guns. Uncle Tom thought this was a good idea. I did say to Agnes I believed it might be the thing for her to nudge Charlie around to thinkin' of it for himself, so if he didn't take to it he wouldn't have to go against his judgment or turn down a job she'd asked him to do."

At seventeen and cut off from the world, she was a woman competent to deal with men.

She had no claim on him. Never had he given her cause to believe that he considered himself less free because of her to range among others of her sex. Yet, watching her as she talked so earnestly, and thinking how much his life was contained in their companionship, he felt such remorse as to be unable to comprehend the delay of its onset. In his desires of the morning he had betrayed her—and he could not let himself off with a plea of failing to differentiate fully between her and her mother. Her movements, the inexplicably awkward grace of her feminine gestures incited his protective instincts. Visually he traced the soft curves of her face. She was gentle and vulnerable. As fragile as glass, he reflected, and as clear . . . and as proof against the poisons that corroded and corrupted him. 'I love her,' he thought.

13

HE HAD LITTLE TIME to accustom himself to his new comprehension before Gilley drove up in his lusterless old maroon car.

The introductions over, the teacher produced two messages. These Wick passed around after he had read them. One was a telegram from his father: "TELEPHONE COLLECT AT ONCE IMPERATIVE." The other was a note signed "Hugo Wright." It congratulated Wick on his courageous intervention on behalf of the mountain, urged that his attendance at the public hearing the next day was vital and—causing his blood to run cold—announced an intention to list him among the speakers.

Gilley allowed that he had gone by Mrs. Haney's on the suspicion that Mr. Carter just might be seeking to get in touch with his son. That he might indeed had occurred to Wick, too.

"I'll have to go back with you, if you'll let me."

Said Mrs. Sherrod, "Oh, Wick, I hope he won't be too hard on you."

"He'll be proud of his son!" Letty declared, in a voice to rally the faint-hearted.

"It's having to get up and talk in public that I'm scared of." Panic was already overtaking him. "Maybe I can get out of it."

This only produced a chorus of dissent and encouragement.

"Just in case . . . I'd better stay in tomorrow and try to work out something to say."

Riding with Gilley down out of the hollow, Wick looked back at the slumbering mountain. 'If you can descend to helping mere mortals, old mountain,' he addressed it silently, 'now is the time.'

"I don't think you have any idea how famous you are." Gilley was saying. "You've been seen in the jousting match all over the country. There's never been a picture story of that kind. And the issue of strip-mining has been dramatized and personalized for tens of millions of readers."

"Maybe after I've talked to Father about Winespring there won't be any need for speeches at the meeting."

"And maybe there will."

Since his father might no longer be at the office, he waited an hour before repairing to the nearest telephone booth and then called his home. He heard his mother accept the collect charge, and then:

"Wick, what have you done? Why have you caused your father such embarrassment? Are you badly hurt?"

"It's only superficial."

He heard his father's voice in the background: "Let me take it"; and his mother repeat his words. Then, "Hello? . . . I'm glad you're not badly hurt. Perhaps you don't know the notoriety your incredible behavior has received."

"They were going to bulldoze above a farm belonging to my friends—my best friends. They'd have buried it under the spoil bank!"

"We were prepared to pay compensation. If Winstead didn't tell your friends that, he should have."

"Mr. Winstead was too busy trying to keep it all secret until there was no chance to stop it. Anyhow, what good is a couple of thousand dollars if your land is destroyed—when it's been in the family for four generations? And besides that, they were going to strip-mine the most beautiful mountain anywhere around—to wreck it."

"We proposed to do nothing that wasn't perfectly legal. Allegheny-Keystone owns that mountain."

"Legal! I know those deeds. They're pure robbery. The family that owns the farm didn't even know there were deeds until the day before. And what do you mean, Allegheny-Keystone owns the mountain? Did Allegheny-Keystone build it?"

From the silence he thought hopefully that his father was seeing the light. It appeared, however, that he was only getting a grip on himself.

"It may interest you to know that the news of your interference in the business of the company that supports you and your mother and sister arrived on the same day as a letter telling me about your courage in replying to a scurrilous attack on the industry

180

by that rabble-rouser who's running for Congress. How proud of you I was! And then this!" There was another pause before he went on in a different voice. "Son, I don't want you to think I don't understand how you feel. And it does you credit, within your lights. But the coal industry—and the country would be lost without it—the coal industry has to operate as it has to. It's out of the question for me to try to make an exception of any particular properties because you're my son and your sentiments are involved."

"You mean you're going to go ahead and try to strip-mine the Sherrod farm and Winespring Mountain?"

"If those are the names of the holdings, yes. The company has no choice but to proceed as soon as the nonsense about the State permit has been straightened out. And, son, I think the time has come for you to return home. Let's let bygones be bygones. Come on home. Tomorrow. I'll telegraph you the money for your fare tonight, if you need it."

"I can't leave here as long as the farm and the mountain are in danger."

Again a pause. Then his father speaking in controlled tones. "You'll find out there's nothing you can do. And if you try to mix up in it again, you'll be in serious trouble. And don't look to me to get you out of it, because I won't be able to. I won't speak of the awkward position you've put me in."

"I can't stay out of it"—and he sounded the words in quotation marks—"just because I'm your son."

"I ask you to think it over. Weigh your staying there to no purpose, risking grave damage to your future, against coming back to a pleasant home, beginning college in the second semester, if you'd like to, perhaps having a car of your own. Think about it. And now your sister wants to speak to you."

He heard the extension telephone upstairs lifted from the hook.

"Wick?" There was a wait after he had replied, then the click of the downstairs telephone being hung up. "Wick," said Cynthia in muffled tones. "I think you're wonderful. Or I think I think so. The father has been furious, but he's been impressed, too. Stick to your guns, whatever exactly they are. Only don't get hurt."

"I'll try not to."

"And don't stay away too much longer."

Queen was right, he thought on his way home. It was always back to the fray. Tomorrow at this time he would be at the hearing, would be having to get up and make his plea for Winespring, with all those eyes on him! But why did *he* have to do it? The world was full of older, more experienced people. He could well take ill and be unable. . . .

And what if all their pleas were in vain and the farm and the mountain left to their fate?

And Turner. . . .

He went to bed early and propped himself up to eat a bowl of graham crackers and milk and read some more of a book of poems Mrs. Draper, the librarian, had recommended.

> The gray sea and the long black land;
> And the yellow half-moon large and low . . .

"Meeting at Night" enthralled him.

The last he read before turning out the light he could not understand and in fact skipped much of, but some of it got inside him.

> Have you built your ship of death, oh, have you?
> Build then your ship of death,
>   for you will need it!

And:

> Oh lovely last, last lapse of death,
>   into pure oblivion,
> At the end of the longest journey. . . .

He would like to think of death, which he could imagine coming in the beautiful guise of an all-seeing woman like Emily Sherrod, as the ultimate union with the larger something he felt in the ancient forest of giant trees and saw in the reaches of mountains from Winespring's summit. Death was quite likely to be a violent one, though, full of the horror of pain. That was the form in which it could have come on the ridge above the Sherrod farm, under a heap of bent machinery. It was how it still could in a clash with a bull of a man who had vowed to kill you.

But it must be as Queen had said. You had to stand up to the worst to have a chance of the best. You had to pay your way. The people who *lived* were the people who played for high stakes. He would try to remember that. The worst that could happen was dying. And even in a violent death, perhaps in the end there would be a peaceful sense of drifting back into the original darkness, such as he was having now, with drowsiness stealing over him. If only Letty could be beside him!

He reached for his flashlight and in its beam for the book beside the bed, then turned in it once more to "Meeting at Night."

> Then a mile of warm sea-scented beach;
> Three fields to cross till a farm appears;
> A tap at the pane, the quick sharp scratch
> And blue spurt of a lighted match,
> And a voice less loud, thro' its joys and fears,
> Than the two hearts beating each to each!

He had plenty of time before the library opened in the morning to telephone his apologies to Mr. DeSalla, a duty which was not as painful as he had feared. His late employer spoke with his habitual positiveness but his view was not unfriendly. "I don't hold it against you. I understand there are circumstances. As far as I'm personally concerned, you could come back tomorrow. But that's got to wait till when, as and if you make it up with A.-K. That's an outfit I got to keep on good terms with."

He had hoped, sitting in the library, to be able to work out what to say that evening. The startling greeting he had had from little Mrs. Draper, whose smile bisected her longish face—"Well, you're quite famous!"—only heightened the altitude from which he saw himself falling flat. If he could somehow take off from the Bible, he thought, he might have the best chance of getting through to his hearers. He found a copy and sat down with it.

There was vastly more in it than he had realized. After reading the Book of Genesis and copying some useful things from it he decided he would have to skip to where Christ came in. An hour later, still floundering in the New Testament, he sounded out Mrs. Draper on her knowledge of it.

This turned out to be extensive. By the time he had finished he knew he could not have done without her.

Meanwhile he had been purposefully approached by a large, gray-haired man with a large way about him whom he had momentarily thought he had known back at home. "Hugo Wright," the newcomer had said. Of course. "The woman where you live thought I'd find you here. I wanted to arrange about picking you up this evening." He had recalled the boy's promise not to let them strip-mine the mountain and extolled what he had done to hold them off; nothing like it had been seen. "You'll probably be given between five and ten minutes to speak." Wick had been embarrassed by the evidence of preparations on the table. He would rather have had his performance regarded, and extenuated, as extemporary. Only the older man's hearty parting admonition could have made him feel worse: "Remember, you're our star witness!"

Mr. Wright arrived for him shortly after seven and they drove to the courthouse. This usually stood as forsaken by mid-evening as an Egyptian tomb, but tonight cars old and new were lining up along the curbs and people funneling in. At the door to the main courtroom, the boy asked his sponsor to excuse him: he had friends who had said they would be looking for him—"Letty Sherrod, you remember, and her family."

"Of course." said Mr. Wright, who planned to sit up front with his friends. Hesitantly, he added, "I must tell you that none of us guessed at her . . . misfortune. Perfectly extraordinary, how she keeps one from suspecting it. I hope nothing was said in our ignorance to cause her embarrassment?"

Nothing had been, Wick assured him.

Letty, her mother and her uncle were already there, sitting by the side aisle. He had seen Mrs. Sherrod before trimly turned out for town in her navy-blue suit and white blouse but never Letty in the pale blue-green dress, like a certain shade of seawater, that she was wearing. And nylon stockings.

"You all look grand," he murmured.

"*You* certainly do! Letty," said her mother, "Wick's got on a greenish-gray summer suit, pressed to an edge, a gray shirt with narrow white stripes and a dark-red tie. He could just have stepped out of a store window."

"Complete with glass eyes and a grin set in plaster."

Mr. Barrows said, "I could just have stepped out of a undertaker's, the way I feel. Down off the table, whar I'd been laid out."

"How do *you* feel?" Letty asked softly.

"Terrible."

Gilley, sitting in the row ahead, facing them with his arm over the back of his seat, asked how the conversation with his father had gone.

"Not," Wick replied, "good."

"Oh, Wick . . . !"

There was a light, passing touch on his leg. Letty's hand was hanging between them. He dropped his own beside hers and felt it clasped. "You're like a dessert," he whispered. "Cake and lime sherbet. It's a good thing I've had dinner." He did not know how he was able to form thoughts in the numbness of his mind.

The seats were all filled, even the jury box, and spectators were lining up against the walls. The judge's high-backed chair alone was empty but at the table beside it, on the same platform, a half-dozen men had settled down after some comings and goings.

Said Gilley, "Your friend John Colman's up there. He's the author of the bill to save Winespring."

He had not noticed him. 'The man I chose to jump on,' he thought: 'typically.'

"The proposed State forest is partly in his district," Gilley continued. "Most of it's in the district of that tall, smooth-looking fellow he's talking to. That's Walter Herndon. He's a lawyer who handles a lot of insurance-company cases. The way he goes on the issue will carry a lot of weight in the legislature; and the way he goes will be the way he decides will do him the most good."

"Will the hearing please come to order."

"The State commissioner of development and conservation, representing the governor," the teacher murmured over his shoulder.

The chairman, after introducing the other men at the table—the two State Assemblymen and members of his department—explained that the present hearing was to give citizens in the vicinity a chance to voice their opinions of proposed legislation to create an 11,000-acre State forest of Winespring Mountain and its environs. Formal hearings would of course be held at the capital before a committee of the Assembly. Each person as called should come up to the microphone promptly. Each would be restricted to five minutes.

Evidently the chairman had two lists, one of opponents of the bill, one of supporters, for the two points of view alternated. Thus, every other time a speaker was named Wick had a reprieve. But every time an enemy finished his heart would be subjected to such a squeeze he feared it would fail. He found himself transferring some of the pressure to Letty's hand.

The arguments raged back and forth. On the one side there was, again, the money and the jobs that the mining of surface coal, inaccessible from within the mountain, would bring the community; there were the nation's soaring energy needs, the requirements of an industry that made the nation strong and respected in the world; there were the rights of private property against the spread of a socialism foreign to our shores; there were the roads Allegheny-Keystone would cut through, bringing the blessings of the twentieth century to isolated hollows; there was the question of what else all these hills were good for anyhow; there was the pledge of Allegheny-Keystone to carry out to the letter the laws of the State requiring restoration of land disturbed in strip-mining. Mr. Winstead, when he was called, spoke scathingly of bleeding hearts and bird-lovers, reminding his listeners that the single biggest buyer of surface-mined coal was also the biggest agency for conservation in the entire world, the Tennessee Valley Authority.

On the other side there was the deprecation of the reputed benefits from strip-mining; there was the hideous scarring of the steep hillsides which was beyond man's power to put to rights; there was the question of *human* restoration (on which Mr. Wright dwelt) and the need of the multitudes scarred by the pressures of the huge super-cities of the future to escape and be healed by the serenity and beauty of unspoiled nature; there was the value to the State of an increasing tourism, amounting already to a third of a billion dollars a year.

In this connection, Gilley made the case for his personal vision of the future in the Cumberlands, with an economy based on deep-mining, forest products and the drawing power of a mountain preserve magnificently wooded, abounding in wildlife, laced with clear trout-streams, studded with man-made lakes stocked with bass, threaded by scenic roads sculptured to the shape of the land. His posture was a confident one familiar to Wick, hands thrust forward in coat pockets, head up and slightly back.

The applause following the speakers indicated an audience about equally divided in sympathies. They were all far beyond him in competence, Wick told himself. The line he had planned to take was grotesque. He would only make a monkey of himself and disgrace his friends. But it was too late now. In his cold sweat he looked at Letty, who was pressed back in her seat with an expression hurt, confused, resolute—he could not tell what. He could do nothing to save their mountain, which would go down, taking the farm with it.

She leaned toward him, gripping his hand. "*Sh, sh,*" she whispered softly, consolingly, to still the clamor of the thoughts she had divined.

He was good only as far as the reach of her whom his emotion bound him to. He had to be launched—like a kite—and insofar as he flew he depended on a cord held by a compassionate and steadying hand, tying him to earth—Letty's. Even if he could find it in him to soar . . . inspired by her—yes, that was it—he would come tumbling down if the hand released its hold. Were all men like kites, all fated to tumble earthward or flutter aimlessly in the wind if left to their own?

He felt his hand twitched. "Wick, he's talkin' about you!"

It was Mr. Colman speaking: ". . . not afraid to speak up for the mining interests when he thinks they've been unjustly attacked. So when he gets out there in front of those armed officers to fight for the farm and the mountain he's come to love, I say we ought to pay attention. If it takes outsiders to open our eyes to the value of what we have, by obeying the feelings we ought to have, then I say we ought not to be too proud to listen. And I know that many of you here this evening, whose families have lived on the soil of Garrett County for generations, have those feelings."

Prolonged applause followed this statement.

They were about to call on him, and it wasn't fair. They had just had a speaker on the pro-Winespring side. But it was what the chairman was doing. ". . . Sedgwick Carter.

"If you'll just step up to the mike, Wick."

He would never make it. His knees were jelly. It was like climbing up to the high spring-board. . . . And there he was, before the void, with nothing to fill it but his voice.

"You've all read the Bible. So you know how old Jesus was when he died. How old was he?" It took a moment for the audience to realize he was expecting an answer. It gave him a breather, during which he wondered if his trouser-legs were visibly fluttering.

A few voices were heard. Thirty-three. Thirty-four.

"And how long would it have taken him to say all he's quoted

187

as saying in the Bible?" He did not wait for any response to this. "Less than half an hour, I'd guess. So Christ must have said a tremendous amount we know nothing about. As a matter of fact, the Bible tells us that what is written about Christ is only the tiniest part of his life. You remember how the Gospel according to St. John ends." He looked down at the notes in his hand and read, " 'And there are also many other things which Jesus did, and which, if they should be written every one, I suppose that even the world itself could not contain all the books that should be written.' "

As he looked up from the paper he had a glimpse of the puzzled faces of his friends.

"Now we can be sure, can't we, that what Christ did and said was not just to keep on repeating himself. A man who . . . whom Peter said of, 'thou knowest all things,' which includes all that God expects of us, would have had more than twenty or twenty-five minutes worth to say." He glanced at Gilley, and the smile of dawning comprehension he saw on his lips helped give him a little confidence.

"What else can we believe he said that hasn't come down to us? And maybe we should also ask ourselves why such a tremendous amount we could know about Christ, who *knew all things*, has not come down to us. Could the Pharisees have had a hand in it, they who served Mammon, and were covetous?

"I think we can be sure he would have told us how we were to act not only toward our fellow men and to God but to God's great creation, the earth."

"But it says of what is written in the Bible," cried a voice—Wick could hardly see from whom it came—"if any man shall add unto these things, God shall add unto him the plagues that are written in this book.' "

Scarcely had the words fallen—like a knell—on Wick's understanding when Gilley sang out in the direction of the objector, "What you've quoted is from near the end of Revelation, and it applies not to the words of the Bible but—and here I quote, too—'the words of the book of this prophecy.' That's all."

His heart steadying itself, the boy nodded gravely. Where was he?

"I think Christ would have told us that we were to treasure

and preserve God's creation, the earth. Why can we feel sure of that? Because, for one thing, of what the Bible tells us God first expected of man. It's in the second chapter of Genesis." He could almost do without his notes now. " 'And the Lord God took the man, and put him into the garden of Eden *to dress it and to keep it.*' "

He paused and in the silence was startled by an acclamatory "Amen" pronounced by Mr. Barrows.

"That was God's intention, that mankind should live in the garden he had created, not ravaging it, not bringing destruction on it, but *dressing* it and *keeping* it. Yes, we lost the Garden of Eden, through disobeying God's command. But we still have the earth. And the earth is just as much God's creation as the Garden of Eden. It can only be God's intention that equally we should dress it and keep it. How can we look at the mountains, and the dark forest and the green valleys, the streams joining in mighty rivers to flow into the boundless ocean and not see that we are looking on the handiworks of the Almighty?

" '*And God saw every thing that he had made, and behold, it was very good*'!"

This time there was a scattering of *amen*'s from the audience.

"And do we see it when we look on every thing that God has made?" He felt equal to it now, and he knew his voice was stronger. "Do we see it was very good? Not so you'd notice. A lot of us don't give a hoot about God's concern for his creation. We look at what he has made and we don't care whether God made it or Satan. All we think of is the money to be made by demolishing it. Anyone who wants to know what I mean can go out and look at where the strip-miners have been. Or imagine what Winespring would look like if they got their hands on it.

" 'And God saw every thing that he had made, and behold, it was very good. And the evening and the morning were the sixth day.'

"Of course we know that the Bible doesn't mean actually six days as we would count them. As Peter tells us, 'one day is with the Lord as a thousand years'—which is to say equally a million years or a billion—'and a thousand years as one day.' You miners know there were forests here two hundred million years ago because it's their rotted remains that coal is made of; and you can see the print of their leaves and bark in the shale. For billions of years God's work of building the earth has been going on, growing more wonderful.

"And now we come along and think we have the right to destroy it. You remember what it says in Genesis. God saw that the wickedness of man was great in the earth, and he came close to destroying the earth and all living things with floodwaters. But he did not, and he made a covenant with man, with Noah, and with every living creature 'for *perpetual* generations,' that he would not 'curse the ground any more' because of man and would not 'again smite *any more* every living thing.' "

He suddenly saw Mrs. Draper sitting at the side of the courthouse and caught her pleased and congratulatory nod. Grateful, but thrown off his course, he consulted his notes. 'Some of us here. . . .'

"Some of us here take the Bible as a strict record of fact. Some of us regard it as a way of expressing the truth in the form of stories. But however we think of it, we can't have any doubt that God means for us to treat his works with respect. We have to make our living from the earth, yes. It can't be wrong to mine coal. But what must be wrong, and evil, is to act like vandals, to have no consideration for God's creation. How do we know whether what we are doing is right or wrong? I think the test is to ask ourselves whether God looking on what we had made would say it was very good. Would he say it was very good, looking on what we have done to the hills around here, looking on what Allegheny-Keystone would do to Winespring? He would say it was horrible. And what's going to happen to a people who keep provoking God to anger?"

"But it says that when the day of God comes," cried a voice— and it issued from a gray-haired, sunken-faced man who had half risen—" 'the elements shall melt with fervent heat, the earth also and the works that are therein shall be burned up.' It's not the earth God cares for but the salvation of the righteous."

As a murmur arose from the audience the chairman rapped the table. "Quiet, please! Let's let Mr. Carter finish."

"Mr. Chairman, Mr. Chairman!" It was Mrs. Draper. She was on her feet, standing not very high but smiling in a confident fashion. "Since an objector has been heard, I'd like to reply to the objection."

190

"If the speaker would care to yield for your reply . . ."

"Yes, I yield," said Wick, more than gladly.

"Science and the Bible are as one on the burning up of the heavens and the earth," Mrs. Draper declared. She swept the assembly with her eyes, as composed as Gilley and equally the school-teacher. "Science ascribes the event to the heating up of the sun and places it five billion years from now. From the Bible, too, we are to understand that it could take place very far in the future. The prophecy we have just heard the gentleman quote from the Second Epistle General of Peter is immediately preceded by the passage Mr. Carter earlier cited, that one day is with the Lord as a thousand years. In other words, we are to think of the burning of the earth as we would of an event a virtual eternity away."

With a silent but fervent thanksgiving for his two deliverances, Wick resumed with a vigor born of the approach of his finish. "If I willfully set fire to a church, I'm guilty of sacrilege. But what if we willfully destroy a mountain? For if a church is a place of worship, so is Winespring Mountain. Only it is one that God created that's been here millions and millions of years, the greatest of God's creations in this part of the country. We've done enough damage to the hills. If we want to be saved, let's show that we are worthy of it. Let's start with Winespring. *Dress it and keep it*. Winespring is a test of whether we care what God wants of us. If we turn Winespring over to . . ."

During his momentary hesitation a voice called out, "The money-changers in the temple!"

He picked it up. "To the money-changers in the temple, let's not complain about any disasters that happen to us."

The applause was the most enthusiastic of the evening. Oh, sweet it was, especially the warm exclamations of his friends, as he returned to his seat. "Hallelujah!" Mr. Barrows proclaimed, looking at him with eyes that had been afforded revelation. Letty took his arm and drew herself briefly against it. Gilley said, "The chairman let you run well over five minutes—and you were worth it."

A man had stood up in the middle of the auditorium and was looking around it with a smile, clapping his hands together at face level in a slow, measured way. The effect, as the general applause subsided, was less of approval than of an injunction to silence. A middle-aged man with sparse hair and a fleshy face, he had the authoritative yet familiar air of a master of ceremonies.

When silence had in fact been induced, he cried, "*Mister* Chairman. *If* you'll permit me. I have an important communication to make. . . . Thank you. I'm not competent to pass on this young man's theology." He looked around as if expecting the disclaimer to provoke amusement. "But I've been much impressed by it, as I'm sure you all have," he resumed in a brisker tone. "I think it ought to be heard by our religious congregations. If we have a duty we haven't been performing, I think they'll recognize it if it's brought to their attention and they'll want to make amends. . . . Ladies and gentlemen, I'm sure most of you have seen the big tent-fly put up by the Bible Interpretation Assembly on Truesdale Road. I feel sure I can arrange to have it made available at, say, five-thirty tomorrow afternoon if young Mr. Carter will agree to favor us with a repetition of his inspired remarks of this evening. I know the press is represented here tonight. If tomorrow's papers will abet my own efforts to get word around, I have no doubt we'll get a good attendance."

An ogre Wick thought he had laid low with much anguish had reared up again. But he had to agree.

"Does anyone know who that man is?" Mrs. Sherrod asked. "Mr. Huff?"

"No, but I don't like him," Gilley replied, staring after him with the tip of his pencil between his teeth.

Mr. Wright insisted on driving him back to his house. He sat beside the youngish woman with the sheared hair, now in a soft sweater and skirt and smelling like a pleasantly scented bar of soap, and was made much of.

Mrs. Haney was entertaining. That is to say, she and a guest were watching television, empty coffee-cups and plates beside them. As he passed the open doorway of the room, dimly lighted by a lamp mounted on a black ceramic panther, Jack looked out from just inside.

"Hey, Wick."

Mrs. Haney said, "There's a cake on the table by the stove."

Jack followed him into the kitchen. "This'll surprise you. A couple of the boys at Tenent's brought up the business at Oak Lick Hollow to see how Turner would take it. You coulda heard a pin drop. Everybody expected Bull would flare up like grease spilt on a hot stove. But he just laughed. Looked like it cost him something, but he did laugh. 'Got my picture in the papers, all over the place, didn't I?' he says. You'd never believe he'd be such a good sport about it, would you?"

Wick, who had stood with knife poised above the cake—a chocolate one—cut down through it. "No. I wouldn't."

The Harpersburg *Courant*, for which he had waited before leaving for the farm next morning, gave first-page coverage to the hearing, and quoted from his speech among others. And sure enough, there was the notice about his appearing at the Bible Interpretation Assembly—as proposed by Burton Keasley, a lawyer.

"You ought to be a lot prouder than you sound," Letty said.

His heart had tilted at the sight of her when he arrived—Truth, he thought, most delectably personified, companion and repository of what was worthiest in him. They were canning apples, Letty peeling and coring, her mother at the stove, where jars were steeping and a pot steaming with the tart aroma of the fruit.

"You all *made* me feel proud last night. But as Gilley Huff says, the Southern highlanders set great store by loyalty."

Mrs. Sherrod laughed. "You didn't need our loyalty. You should have heard us on the way home. I think my brother's seein' things different on account of it. 'We've heard the truth tonight,' he said, and not just once."

"We'd have told you the same had you been a stranger. . . . I think you're low in your mind this mornin'. Ma, how does he look?"

She turned to examine him. "Not quite up to his usual. Is it that meetin' this afternoon, Wick?"

That would do for a beginning. "Gilley thinks there's something fishy about it. That it's a trap. Anyhow, there won't be anyone there I know."

But the other two insisted that they would be, and nothing he could say shook them.

The chilly wind was in its third day. It came in gusts which swayed the trees. The stronger blows sent puffs of smoke into the room from the fire in the stove. He had a sense that the two women shared the mingled and oppressive premonitions that kept returning to him.

"I'm afraid your pa gave you a pretty bad time," Letty said.

Her mother said, "Maybe we ought not to pry into matters between him and his folks."

He hastened to deny that it was prying. There was nothing for it then but to report the gist of what his father had said. And lightly as he might treat it, the only possible response was silence. Indeed, when Mrs. Sherrod spoke after a moment it was tangentially.

"You can't let this keep you from goin' to college. We've been talkin' about it. And put out as your father may be right now, he's got to see it." She presented to him a clear and open face that seemed to ask him to be glad with her that their mutual regard could be altogether aboveboard. He did not, by his expression, deny it.

Bent over the apple in which she was twisting the corer, Letty said, "We got it all settled, except how soon you can go. When would that be?"

"I don't know. I suppose at mid-year. In January." He spoke as if the question were theoretical. More trenchantly he added, "But this is only October, and what I have to think about is getting back to work."

"Oh. I meant to tell you. I mentioned that to Tom and he said he wished he could get you to come in with him—on a sharin' basis." Mrs. Sherrod had stepped back from the stove, and was dabbing at her glistening face with a cloth. "He'll talk to you about it this evenin'." With eyebrows raised in a look perhaps of gentle remonstrance she said, "I had to tell him not to expect *too* much from your comin' in with him—if you do. Like walnut-trees turnin' up where nobody knew about them. After yesterday I think he believes you have a way of readin' the Almighty's mind better than most."

"Hah!" He shook his head. He wondered with a sickening pang if they might not all be attributing to him a power equal to saving their farm—marked now, and as if condemned, by the gash the bulldozer had left.

"I don't like the fall," Letty said. "It's the time of goodbyes, when most things that are alive go away—birds and leaves and flowers, bees and crickets and locusts. After them comes silence. Except when the wind blows. The wind has lots of voices, but the winter winds are all sad or cruel."

194

They were sitting on a favorite log at the edge of the woods, above the pasture.

She added, "I never minded it much before this year."

Though the wind had dropped at last and the sun fell on her she was hunched forward, hugging herself. He would have liked to tell her he loved her, was in fact as close as he could come to it, knowing he must not and would not. So easy it would be: the words would escape him if he simply relaxed. And if he did, he thought he could have her in his arms. And what held him back? His promise alone?

He was tugged this way and that, as the trees by the shifting winds.

There were birds overhead in the past few days, more than in summer. Blue jays straggled by, going southward above the tree-tops, and there were hawks similarly bound, high up against the wind-burnished blue of the autumn sky. Along with the migrants, other birds took wing from seeming restlessness. And the movement and the restlessness had their echo in him. The world was large before him—as Mrs. Sherrod had said it would be: he felt its pull. That he recognized this gave weight to her warning. Letty had to be protected. Yet he could not imagine life without her.

He said, "But the birds, the leaves and the insects will all be back. And friends, if they have to leave—they come back, too." His arm was resting on her shoulder.

"Do they? Always?"

"Always when they leave part of themselves behind."

The tent erected by the Bible Interpretation Assembly, of an orange-tan, was a huge thing, drawn tightly by guy ropes over two upright poles, its sides rolled up to leave it standing clear of the ground by several feet. Beneath it, the rows of varnished, folding chairs were beginning to fill up, mostly with middle-aged couples in clean but plain attire. Their faces were those of simple people who had seen the light and seen it once and for all. Sitting down up front, Wick bent to his notes. He would slog through his oration once more and that would be the end of it.

He looked up and saw the lawyer who had engineered the affair —Kelsey, Keasley—talking to a man with a dense covering of gray hair like carpeting and small eyes in a seamed and florid countenance. He shortly came over to the boy and expressed his gratification that he had been able to make it. He looked to Wick like a man who had to scrounge for a living. His curled shirt collar was not of the cleanest, his stubby fingernails when he took out a cigarette and lighted it were gray. "I'll say a few words of introduction," he explained, "then turn it over to you. There may be a few questions afterward."

He could believe it. His undoing would have been prepared. Mr. Keasley would be doing nothing not to his material advantage. And where would that lie in this controversy but on the side where the money was?

When the lawyer moved off he stopped to talk to the good-natured-looking, short-faced young man whom Gilley had pointed out the evening before as a reporter from the *Courant* . . . and who now held up a hand in greeting. Why couldn't Gilley have been here to help him through this? He had said he had to be somewhere. No Mrs. Draper, either.

His friends came forward reticently, steered by Mrs. Sherrod, who had prevailed over her brother's impulse to sidle into a rear row. The belief in him revealed in their faces dismayed him. To disabuse them of it, he made a confession at once. "I don't know anything about the Bible. I should never have pretended I did."

Said Mrs. Sherrod, "You sounded yesterday like you knew plenty." She leaned toward him across her daughter, who had taken a seat next to him, and added in a low voice, "If they back you into a corner, just repeat what you've done said, loud and strong."

"Anyhow," said Letty, "they'll believe you. They'll know you're tellin' the truth."

"They'll know it if you tell them so." His gaze lingered on that uplifted, sweet profile and the softly dreamy eyes under the long lashes. The thought of the abyss between it and the world came to him with such force that he recoiled from it. How could he ever bridge it for her?

"Now, what do they want that up thar for?" Mr. Barrows said.

A nondescript panel-truck had driven up beyond the forward end of the tent, pitching and rocking over the rough ground, and had stopped. After turning the motor off, the driver got out. Mr. Keasley, who had gone up to the lectern, regarded truck and driver thoughtfully.

Wick, his time about to come, replied, "It's to carry the speaker off in when they've finished with him."

The last mutters of conversation were being stilled and eyes were on Mr. Keasley, whose own had followed the driver of the truck to a seat beside the gray-haired man the lawyer had previously been speaking with. There was something odd about the newcomer, a man of stocky build—something in the combination of slow movements, dark, shining eyes in an upturned, glistening face, seemingly filled with an inner light.

The introduction was in fact brief, coming quickly to the purpose of the meeting—"to give us a chance to judge of what maybe as Christians we ought to hear."

His speech, which was forced enough at the start—he felt he was pushing every sentence uphill—was better received than he had expected. His quotations from the Bible brought forth increasingly numerous *amen's* of affirmation. No applause followed his finish, but the reason could be, he supposed, that the assembly was considered a religious one. The audience appeared well disposed, and as he steeled himself for the questions there was nodding and smiling.

Were there after all to be no questions? The boy was wondering if the event was indeed ending, rather flatly, when the truck-driver rose to his feet. He came up slowly, as if he were growing out of the ground. Holding onto the back of the seat in front, he cast his eyes slowly and inquiringly to right and to left.

What could he intend? The man seemed gripped by the excitement of a child whose long-promised moment has come. Some of it seemed to have been communicated to the audience, too. There had been a general stirring, but now there was stillness, all eyes on the truck-driver . . . who, staring over the boy's head, cried, "The Gospel According to St. Mark. Chapter sixteen. Verses sixteen, seventeen and eighteen. 'He that believeth and is baptized shall be saved; but he that believeth not shall be damned. And these signs shall follow them that believe; In my name shall they cast out devils; they shall speak with new tongues; they shall take up serpents; and if they drink any deadly thing, it shall not hurt them; they shall lay hands on the sick, and they shall recover.'"

"*Amen.*"

"Them that believe shall take up serpents and it shall not hurt them," the speaker reiterated. His eyes still rapt, he let the mes-

197

sage sink in. He surveyed the congregation. "Our young friend has asked us to believe that the commandment the Lord lays on us is what he says, picking from Scripture to suit his purpose. But does he come with the Lord's blessing, as a believer will? Is he one that believeth? That is what we seek to know."

There were expressions of approval such as those that had greeted Wick a few minutes earlier.

"Does he believe in what he preaches to us, or is he like unto the scribes and Pharisees that 'for a pretence make long prayer'?" He turned to Wick. "Young man, we want to believe in your belief. All we ask is that you show us *you* believe." He looked positively imploringly at the object of his address, even with love. "Will you in His name, in the Lord's name, take up serpents?"

With the dedication in that face there could be no reasoning. The boy saw that he was one of those whom the sight of rattle-snake-handling put into a kind of ecstacy. . . . Mr. Keasley, in his seat in the first row, was holding a pencil by its ends, revolving it and gazing down at it with raised eyebrows and pursed lips.

Out of the corner of his eye Wick caught an emphatic if narrowly confined shaking of the head on Mrs. Sherrod's part and a look of horror on Letty's. He said, "What serpents?" But the significance of the dingy panel-truck was apparent.

"Did you come h'yar bringin' a rattlesnake with you?" Tom Barrows demanded in a menacing voice.

The other turned to regard him with surprise at once guilty and gloating—or such was the boy's shrinking impression. "I come prepared. I was told one would be among us to speak in the Lord's name. The Lord made known to me what I was to do. If this young man believes, he'll thank me for—"

"The Lord and who else made known to you?"

Mr. Keasley partially rose and half turned to the congregation. He cleared his throat. "At this point, because the idea of our coming together here was mine, I ought to make clear that I have no association with these proceedings. If it was up to me I should bring them to a halt." His tone did not convey very strong conviction. "This seems to me too severe a test of belief to subject a person to, especially a visitor here who probably hasn't got the kind of faith we have. The law does not condone it. My advice to young Mr. Carter—unsolicited, to be sure—is to decline and rest his case on his, er, superior knowledge of Scripture and personal eloquence."

The damned hypocrite had put the cap on it, all right, Wick thought. An awareness of the actuality of the emergency was trickling coldly in his bowels.

"We ain't heard yet what young Carter wants to do," observed the big man with the carpet of gray hair.

"I'll get the critter while he's makin' up his mind, if you and maybe a couple of others will help me. It's a big box, with another box to set it on."

"Why don't you just pick the snake up and bring it h'yar?" Tom Barrows asked drily in his carrying voice.

The other turned his darkly lighted, seemingly unseeing eyes on him. "I've taken up serpents. In these hands!" he exclaimed, raising them. "Most everybody h'yeer knows that. Only this ain't the time for doin' it again."

"I didn't reckon it would be."

A murmur of assent had followed the claim just made.

The snake-man went off to the truck accompanied by several others. The back doors of the vehicle were swung open and the two boxes lifted out. There was silence as the men returned with these and set them down, one atop the other, a few paces from the lectern, beside which the boy still stood, his elbow on it. To Wick's critical ear, the box containing the snake was dropped on the other with a jarring jolt. Its owner unfastened the hasp and raised the hinged lid, letting it down against the back of the box. He had provided himself with a stick from the truck and he held it in readiness; the snake's prison was not a deep one. A dry and sinister buzzing was heard from within it for a moment.

Wick did not approach it. The next move was, however, up to him. He had a sense of time stretching out like an elastic band . . . and nearing the limit of its give. Then Mr. Barrows declared, "I want to see what you've got thar!"—and it slackened a bit.

The spare mountaineer, commanding by his mere stature, maneuvered himself past his sister and niece. The latter rose and to Wick's surprise and disquiet followed her uncle as he came forward, guiding herself by a light touch against his jacket.

He looked down into the box and stiffened. Anger came to his face as he stepped back. "Why, you . . . ! That's a giant in thar! I ain't never seen a bigger rattler. He's got enough pizen to bring a horse down!"

The snake-man looked at him with what could have been either guile or innocence. "He's a big one, all right. I knowed when I

199

seen him the Lord had somethin' particular in mind for him. I been keepin' him, oh, three weeks."

"An' all the while he's been gettin' hungrier and meaner. And now he's shook up, too, and primed to strike." Mr. Barrows's voice was enraged but tensely controlled.

"Don't anybody move or I'll pull the box over." While attention was fastened on the others, Letty had slipped around to the other side of her uncle and had her fingertips on the edge of the box. "And if I do, somebody's goin' to get bit. Most likely me. Don't anyone touch me or the box or over it comes. Uncle Tom, make everybody get back."

"Wicker, stand back thar! . . . Letty, get away from that snake. This ain't for you." His voice was still gauged to the necessity of not arousing the reptile.

The boy, checked in his impulse to snatch her away and not knowing what to expect, added his own. "Do what he says, Letty! *Get away!*"

"The man who brung the snake, whoever he is," said Letty, turned toward the audience, "talks about testin' a boy who's already risked his life against the people who're tearin' this country up. And you folks want a proof of his believin'. I'll . . . I'll give you a proof of *my* belief in what he's been tellin' you. That ought to be enough for you. . . . Uncle Tom, whereabouts in the box is the snake? I don't want to put my hand down on his head and scare him."

"Letty, *don't.*" Powerless, the boy was frantic. He could tell, if no one else could, how frightened she was—had to be. Tom Barrows and Mrs. Sherrod, standing, were pleading, too.

A murmur was going through the assembly—that she was blind.

The girl had turned her back. "Where is he, Uncle Tom?"

"She means to do it!" warned a voice from the audience.

And then there were others. "This ain't what the Lord had in mind. Not a blind girl." . . . "She'll do it if you don't call it off. She's proved to me she has belief." . . . "Call it off!" The voices were quiet but urgent. "Call it off": it was chorused from all sides. "Back away from that box, girl."

Letty waited.

The snake-man, who had appeared baffled by the turn of events, now seemed suddenly fearful, raising his hands before him, one clasped in the other. "Hit's called off," he echoed. "Get your hand away from the box."

"You ain't askin' him to take up no serpent?"

"No, you showed us. Get your hand away." His alarm seemed to be growing. "That snake could reach it easy."

The girl took her hand from the box.

As a collective sigh went up, her mother was beside her. Drained of color, almost lipless, she clasped the girl in her arms. "Letty, my dear, brave, sweet Letty!"

Said Mr. Barrows to the snake-man, "I don't know whether you just saved Letty's life. But I can tell you this. You sure as hell just saved yourn." But the man he addressed seemed to have attention only for the girl.

"You take that rattler back where you got him and let him loose," she said. Then, "Let's go away from here."

As they walked down the aisle, Letty on her mother's arm, a voice exclaimed, "Praise the Lord Jesus Christ, our Savior!" Others took it up. "Praise him! Praise him!"

When they reached the road Mrs. Sherrod said she and her brother would leave them and get the truck. Before she went, she turned a look to the boy that seemed both to lay bare her helpless love for her daughter and to renew more yearningly her plea to him of the day before.

Wick led the girl to the far side of the asphalt and kept hold of her hand. His feelings were beyond him to convey. He laid his forehead momentarily against her shoulder, hoping that nonetheless he might do so. "No one had a moment's doubt that you'd pick up that snake. I've never seen such courage."

"You'd have done it yourself."

"I don't know. I *had* to. I saw that. But I don't know."

The departing crowd was trailing down the other side of the road to the parking ground, casting curious looks at the young pair.

"One thing I do know—two things," he resumed. "I know I may well owe you my life. And when I think how it could be, owing one's life to someone else's courage, I know I wouldn't want to owe mine to anyone but you."

She gave his hand a convulsive squeeze. He could tell by the slight movements of her lips and brows that she was trying to pin down a thought. "You mustn't feel you owe me anything, ever. You *couldn't* owe me anything. Don't you see that?"

"If you want me to, I do."

When he saw the truck approaching, its parking lights on in

the dusk that gathered early in the valley, he said, "Didn't you think that even if you'd picked up the rattler they'd have expected me to do so afterward?"

"I was going to walk out with it, askin' you for directions, and let it go where it could get away."

"Good God!" He had told her she had a way with reptiles.

Before they parted, Mr. Barrows addressed him from the cab. "Maybe you'd like to start in workin' with us in the mornin'."

Wick said he would and was told where to find them. He promised to be there early.

He was not going to be, however. In the morning, joining Jack MacDonough in the kitchen after getting up at the old time, he learned that Gilley Huff had been waylaid on a back street in Harpersburg and beaten unconscious. The only words he had been able to utter were "I think—Bull."

14

THE MORNING WAS GRAY and rain threatened.

Garrett County Hospital, a long red-brick building, occupied a grassy site in a broad valley outside Harpersburg. The hour was very early and no one was abroad among the score of parked cars on the asphalt expanse. Starlings waddled about on the lawn, darting their bills into the turf—pushy, guttural-voiced, disagreeable birds.

Wick waited stolidly at a window in the lobby until an irritable nurse had time to direct him to the floor above, south wing. Here was a small, not very clean waiting-room with the nap worn on the chairs. One of these was occupied by a man who looked as if he had spent the night in it. A nurse, two nurses, passed and re-passed, both apprehensive lest they be intercepted. A few others passed: a young doctor in white uniform (twice); a white-clad colored woman pushing a wheeled table stacked with used breakfast trays; and two creeping patients in maroon bathrobes. Stronger than the smell of cigarette butts overflowing an ashtray was the germicidal-anesthetic hospital odor. In no condition to resist its impact, Wick was affected with horror by the hospital—the presence of cells upon cells of the sick, injured and suffering, all requiring unceasing care. Was this what life came down to?

One of the nurses walked to the stand-up desk in a corner of the waiting-room and he seized the opportunity.

"Mr. Gilley Huff? There's been no change since the report we gave to the *Courant* last night. He has a serious concussion of the brain and remains unconscious. There are facial lesions. The extent of possible internal injuries is not yet known."

"How . . . ? You say 'serious. . . .'"

"His condition is serious." The nurse could hardly be expected to take each case as a personal tragedy.

As he came down into the lobby, he recognized the man just entering it as the person he most wanted to see. Roger Tenent himself, however, appeared less than overjoyed at the encounter. When Wick had passed on his information about Gilley, however, he accepted the suggestion that they have something in the cafeteria.

The bar-owner could add little to what Wick had heard from Jack. Gilley had been found the evening before just inside an alleyway in Harpersburg. He might have lain there until morning had not a man in a car made a U-turn in the street and seen the prone figure in his headlights. This much had been learned at the Last Chance/First Chance from a late arriver who had heard it at the police station. Whether Turner (assuming it was he) had run into Gilley by accident and given in to a drunken impulse or had planned the attack, there was no way of knowing, or whether he had meant to finish the teacher off but had been interrupted by the turning car, which appeared to have arrived on the scene just after the slugging.

"About all you can be sure of is that Gilley was yanked off the street into the alley on his way to his car after dinner and there given the works." Tenent spoke impassively.

The boy tipped his head back; it would not do to let tears well up. Having little appetite, he had proposed the visit to the cafeteria in order to have the other's company and had taken only coffee and a doughnut. But Tenent had ordered fried eggs, bacon and toast and was going at his breakfast as if he bore it an animus.

Left feeling adrift by the man's taciturnity, Wick sought to bring himself to a focus. The terrible evil that had struck his friend down, the darkness of death hovering over him, distorted his mental processes so that they would not serve him. "I gather Turner tried to pass off the pictures Gilley took at Oak Lick Hollow when someone brought them up at your place, but he must have been sore as all hell about them. Though it was me he threatened to kill."

Tenent shot him a look. "He did, did he? Yes, he almost choked making light of the pictures."

"Do you think I'm responsible for what happened to Gilly?" The idea had just come to him.

Tenent put down his fork and considered the question. "No,

204

I don't," he said, drawing out the first word. "No, you're not," he added in the same slightly weary voice.

'He wishes I were,' Wick said to himself. 'Maybe to have things simpler.' It was not only to have a companion in sorrow that he had grasped the chance to be with Tenent, he now understood, but also to find out how he stood with respect to Gilley's near-murder, how people on the outside would see it. "You think I'm not," he said.

"It would have come to Gilley anyhow. He's had a charmed life too long. And now there's a rumor he's written a book showing up everybody who's added to the woes of this country. There's too many people around who'd be glad to see him disappear, and that, combined with those pictures, would make him a marked man to Turner—who likes to be in good with people who count. And likes to use those muscles. It's a lust with him, the way some men like to rape—Turner, too, if what you hear is true. He probably gets paid for his jobs. He's always got money."

"Won't the police be able to get him on this?"

"The police? It doesn't sound like Gilley will be able to identify him positively even if he recovers. Bull will make himself scarce for the time being. And he'll have two or three friends ready to swear up and down he was somewheres else at the time."

Tenent delivered himself of these remarks with unconcern, as if his thoughts were largely elsewhere. While he finished his toast they sat in silence. Things were not propitious for obtaining light on the question that preoccupied him, Wick told himself, even if he had known how to broach it. Seeing Tenent in these surroundings, where he was like a captain away from his ship, Wick realized how little he knew him. So why should he expect anything of him? With chagrin, he saw him push back his chair and tilt his coffee-cup to peer into it, as if he were about to go.

Looking indeed as if he were, he asked lightly, "So what are your plans now?"

"What should they be?"

"Well," said the other, "I seem to remember advising you to get out of here. It's still not too late." He appeared from his expression finally to be relenting. "Go on home, kid. This isn't any place for you. You can see that from what happened to Gilley. I can tell you, if it'll make it easier for you, that nothing can be done to save the Cumberlands. People come down here, full of bright hopes and determination. But as regularly as they come they get licked and give up."

"How can you be so cheerful, then, believing that? You were born here, weren't you? This is your home."

"Yes, but I've been away. I had two hitches in the Navy. It was Navy pay that bought the bar.

"I've learned that life's a sporting proposition. Not only that, it's a spectator sport. Sure, you've got to be in the game. But the more you can be in the stands, munching a hot dog and swilling pop and seeing it all for what it is—a game—the better off you'll be. Yes! I care what happens—as far as I let myself, or can't help it. I care which way it goes when I watch football on television, too—especially if I've got dough on it."

Even now, particularly now, he was clearly watching the game and his performance in it. The dark-blue eyes he cut at the boy had recovered their glint. He lit a cigarette, drew deep and released the smoke in a thoughtful exhalation.

"I could let myself get into a hell of a stew over the fleecing the people in the Cumberlands have taken. But it wouldn't do any good. Even if I could change it, just as much wickedness and cussedness and injustice would crop up in another way. The proportion of bastards in the human race is just too high to overcome, and to some extent we're all bastards." Estimating the effect of this discourse on his listener, his expression changed to genial hopelessness. "However, I see by the stubborn look in your face that I'm wasting my wisdom. You're set on saving that mountain and that farm."

Wick dropped his gaze. It sounded preposterously vainglorious.

"And you haven't done badly so far. Not by any means. You've made a big impression. . . . I don't know how to put this." He let his eyes shift for a moment to the food line, where a nurse was leaning over the counter, lifting a short skirt up tidy pink thighs. "We're a funny people," he pursued. "We see things in simple, direct terms. Your coming through two trials—that bulldozer and your talk at the courthouse—looked like a sign. Maybe for once the operators who're bent on lining their pockets weren't going to have things all their way. Maybe the wind was setting in a new quarter. You see, being who you are, you were laying a lot on the line. So people have been impressed. They're used to seeing their own kind pay the price."

He put a peculiar emphasis on that final statement, then sat in silence watching the smoke trail upward from his cigarette. It seemed to leave the thought for his listener to complete.

Wick said, "Gilley's a brave man. And last night he took the rap."

Tenent took an impatient draw on his cigarette. "I don't know that I'd put it that way. Gilley was, *is* a beloved figure." He looked at the boy with the impersonality that was so often, in the latter's experience, the vehicle for unpleasant truths. "And he's been in the front rank of the fight against the strippers. Moreover, it was his story of your scrap with Turner's 'dozer that put Winespring front and center. Now Gilley is upstairs here and may never recover. And Turner, the big bulldozer man, is probably in the clear and in the chips as well. You see how it looks. And public opinion in the mountain counties is going to have a lot to do with how the legislature acts on Winespring." He put his hands on the edge of the table to rise. "I mean," he added, "once again evil and greed will have had everything their way, as they always do here. So people will think, what's the good of struggling against them? It must be that God's not interested in this world, and justice has to wait till the next."

Brought face to face with the specter he had most dreaded, Wick said, "I get you."

"I doubt if you do." The other hunched forward and crushed out his cigarette. "If you did you *would* get. Get, get, get. That's my advice, kid—once more. And I wouldn't wait around as if nothing had happened till Bull turns up again. Things will go sour for you if you do—the way people look at you, all that." He regarded the boy from under his brows, admonishingly.

Nerving himself, Wick said, "I suppose if you gave out that I'm looking for him, he'd hear about it."

"He'd be only too likely to. Which is why I'm not going to do it."

"It has to be done. So you tell people what I said. I'll be seeing some others anyway to get the message out." He stood up and collected his coat from the adjacent chair. "I'm late for where I'm supposed to be this morning."

The other got up, too. "You're no match for him, kid! Unless you're thinking of a gun."

The boy shook his head. "Just tell people that I'm—"

"I know, I know."

Hamp said, "You'll need a good rifle. You can have mine."

My God, he was not thinking of blasting a man's life out in the style of a mountain feud. It would have to be bare-handed. Turner was strong enough to pull him apart, but he looked slow, and the way he lived might well have made him short-winded. 'I'll try to wear him down before he can get hold of me.' Hadn't Jack advised something of the sort? If he could put up a good show, if he could just do some damage to that sadist so he wouldn't seem to have got away with it, perhaps that would be all that was required of him.

He had found Mr. Barrows's truck at the designated place. The snarl of a power-saw had led him through the woods, up a steep hillside, to where its owner and the Fergusons were trimming a felled tree while the horses stood by. They had already had news of Gilley's injuries, and when they had digested his report of how bad these were, Hamp had come to the point, however regretfully. "And you're a special friend of his, with him havin' no folks around here to see that right's done." That was so, he had said in a level voice, meeting their eyes. It was then that Hamp had made his offer of the rifle.

He read in their faces their relief that he was not going to let them down, disgrace them, because of some unmanly city reasoning. "Thanks. But it'll have to be settled another way. And after all, there wasn't any shooting between Turner and Gilley. I'll be on the job tomorrow morning, but right now I've got some business to attend to."

It was pretty much the same at each of the three places he dropped in at—Taulbee's grocery store, the pool hall and a likely-seeming bar. "If you see Bull Turner or anyone who goes around with him, I'd be much obliged if you'd tell him I'm lookin' for him—Wick Carter," and, he would add significantly, a friend of Gilley Huff's.

And the proprietor, suddenly alert, would nod, comprehendingly. "Where'll he find you?" asked one.

"Oh—around. Particularly at Roger Tenent's bar on the Doane Road."

Where would he be found? Nowhere, he hoped in his heart. Yet at the same time he thought he would take almost any punishment if only he could drive his fist with all his strength into the face of the savage who had nearly killed that good-hearted, lively, lovable teacher.

If.

Anxiety about his friend could have been taken by the Sherrods as reason enough for his uncertain mood. But he felt sure that, knowing the spot he had been put in, they suspected the further cause of it. Furthermore, he was away every other evening.

They did not ask where, but he was at the Last Chance/First Chance.

As Tenent had foreseen, Turner had disappeared. Tenent had said, "I put your message in the p.-a. system. But if and when he turns up there can't be anything rough in here. That's what the outside's for." He had given the boy an unsmiling look. Wherever Wick sat, whether at the bar or at a table with Jack or the Fergusons, trying not to betray undue interest when the door opened, he was aware of being set apart. Not that anyone was unfriendly. On the contrary: he seemed to be the recipient of a marked gentleness.

By day he worked with Tom Barrows and one or both of the Fergusons, twice with an old, grizzled man who applied himself methodically and spoke little. He hated to see the trees topple; they were always the big ones, and the helplessness of the sky-aspiring branches as the despairing fall began was pitiable to see. But it was better than the other way; the forest went on living. And the hard work in the bracing air did him good. So did the companionship. So did being with the horses. The pitting of that great muscle power against dead weight awakened a response in him. It was a day's work, but it took him out of himself. And he had a couple of hours to rest before the time came to be at Tenent's.

Darkness came too early for walks of any length at the farm on work days. But they read a great deal sitting by the kerosene lamp, and much that they read was poetry from the book Mrs. Draper had lent him. Stirring the pulses of life within him, poetry seemed to be just what he needed at that juncture. And Letty was receptive to it with total exposure, as he thought of it, watching her. He sought especially poems that celebrated the world they shared:

> O wild West Wind, thou breath of Autumn's being,
> Thou, from whose unseen presence the leaves dead
> Are driven, like ghosts from an enchanter fleeing. . . .

"It's not easy to understand every bit," said Letty at the end, "but it's all beautiful."

"Ah, here's one for you!" he cried. "Called 'A Girl' ":

> The tree has entered my hands,
> The sap has ascended my arms.
> The tree has grown in my breast—
> Downward,
> The branches grow out of me, like arms.

"Not much as poetry, though," he commented.

When they were alone together on a Sunday he baited her—and indulged himself—with poems that scandalized and fascinated her:

> What lips my lips have kissed,
>   and where, and why,
> I have forgotten, and what arms have lain
> Under my head till morning. . . .

"Whoever told that on a girl should be ashamed of himself!" she declared indignantly before he had read half of "The Rigs o' Barley."

> Corn rigs, an' barley rigs,
>   An' corn rigs are bonie,
> I'll ne'er forget that happy night,
> Amang the rigs wi' Annie.

Despite her disapproval of the poem, the first two lines of the refrain enchanted her. And he found as she recited them, tears shimmering in her eyes, that the apparently artless words inexplicably pierced his heart:

> Corn rigs, an' barley rigs,
>   An' corn rigs are bonie.

But he could tell, though facing it only unwillingly, that she was being exhausted, and the cause was his own sheer nervous intensity, beleaguered as he was by uncertainties. The earth might have, but assuredly had not, swallowed Turner up; his very non-appearance was ominous. Gilley remained in a coma, his life in the balance. He had had a glimpse of his friend once through the open door of the intensive-care unit, recognizing the crest of curly sandy-red hair pushed up by the bandage swaddling his head, had heard the widely spaced exhalations of his breathing.

Without Gilley he was in the dark about moves affecting the mountain and with it the farm. He did, however, learn from Mr. Wright that hearings at the capital to determine the fate of the bill had been called for two weeks from the date of his writing. He urged Wick to be there to testify, or, if he could not, to write to the committee chairman setting forth everything he knew about the mountain "that commends it for preservation." Said Letty after hearing him out, "*If* you're not goin' to the hearin's, you've got to write the letter, and there's no use carryin' on about how you can't. Just write it as if you were tellin' me about it, the way you've had to all along."

They had spent much of a Sunday on it. When they had finished, and he had read it all to her, she pronounced it ardently as good as if it had come out of a book and made him promise to send a copy to his father. He said disdainfully, "I'll just tell him what we wrote it for and that I'm sending it to him so he'll know." He thought Mrs. Draper would let him type it out on the machine in the library.

"He couldn't be your father and have his mind so set against what you're tryin' to tell him. Maybe you're unfair."

"He could be and he has. And I don't think I am." The letter he had had from his parent since their telephone conversation had not shown any softening.

He had become pent up from confinement and could hardly wait to escape out of doors with her.

A fresh fall of leaves covered the ground and seemed to mirror, somewhat as the ruffled waters of a lake might, those remaining on the trees. The foliage, deep red, caramel and yellow, was translucent, like gems massed against the intense autumnal blue. Had the woods in fall always had this radiance? He could not remember it. The air itself seemed to glow. He was hard put to it to find words that would give her any idea of it. The world was so beautiful, and so treacherous. As they walked side by side he felt as if he were being wrung out inside like a garment between two great hands, one twisting one way, one the other.

"You're hurting," said Letty mildly.

"Oh! I didn't know." He let up and gently massaged the hand he had been gripping. She was wearing a heavy sweater he had given her, tawny in color to match her eyes and blend with outdoor shades.

They could not talk of what concerned them most. She was not supposed to know of the taunt he had broadcast to a killer. He could not admit his dire apprehensiveness of the forces threatening the farm and the mountain. He could not tell her he loved her—as she must have divined that he did and be wondering at his silence. And why could he not tell her? Was it altogether an ill-considered promise? Or was it also his cold suspicion that the promise had been wisely exacted because in fact he could not be trusted to sacrifice his world to hers?

"There's a crow going by overhead. It's flying with the wind and about all it has to do is keep up an easy kind of gliding, swimming stroke. It's very black against that very blue sky, and it feels on top of the world in every way."

He spoke of things around them as they walked on and they talked of past incidents. He told her more about Gilley. Automatically he looked ahead to take account of obstructions.

"There's a tree down across the trail," he said in time to allow himself to add, "and up we go over it," then sweep her off the ground in his arms before stepping up onto and over the trunk. He knew that while she made nothing over accepting a guiding hand it bothered her to be treated as helpless, but he fairly tossed her up, making a sport of it.

"Hey!" she cried. And when he let her down on the other side: "It's a good thing I've got no modesty left. I could tell my skirt was up to there."

"Down at the soda fountain in Harpersburg, where I hang around to help the girls up onto the high stools, I'm known as Conscienceless Carter, the crafty cad of the Cumberlands."

"Did you think that up just now?" she asked when she had done laughing.

"That's not a fair question."

Presently she confided in a casual voice, "I've been thinking what kind of things I'd like in a girl if I was a boy."

"Oh? And what are they?'

"First you tell me what kind of things you'd like in a boy if you were a girl."

He knew at once that this had been prepared and that his reply would be important to her. But he gave it virtually without reflection, so quickly had it come to him, with such inevitability: "A free heart." Then he added, "There's a poem—" Immediately he wished he had not. With great labor he had written part of a poem to recite to her in which she would be able to read a hint that he was not his own master. But he had seen that it was not only that his heart was not free; it was a question of what was in it. "Free of smallness, too. Free of selfishness."

Stubbing her toe, the girl stumbled and, before she could grasp his arm or he hers, fell full length.

"Letty!"

He dropped to his knee beside her. She responded so slackly to his efforts to help her up that at first he feared she was hurt. But from her averting her face and not putting her hand to any part of herself he guessed that the pain was not physical. Standing, she dropped her head and covered her face with her hands. "Sometimes it's so shamin'," she said hoarsely. "So shamin'."

"Oh no! It mustn't be!" he cried, gripping her arm. "Not with me! Not with anyone, but never with *me!* . . . Are you hurt?"

Shaking her head, she dropped her hands, drew a deep breath, held it with a grimace, then let it escape. "I reckon I'll need brushin' off," she said wryly, setting about it.

"You've skinned your knee." He got her to sit where the ground was highest and driest. Tying his handkerchief below the abrasion, he poured cold tea from the canteen over it. "I know it stings, but if it bleeds a bit, that'll help clean it some more. The damned tree-roots don't show up much with leaves on the ground, but I should have noticed."

"No—you can't do all the seein' for another person all the time."

He thought he would try one more time, and when they were on their feet again he took her by the shoulders. "I wish I could make you *believe* you were going to get your sight back. *See* that you weren't to blame for your sister's death."

"You think it's for nothin' that I'm blind?"

"It's that I think you ought to try believing you don't have to be."

"You know that bein' blind I'm not much good to . . . anyone.

So you can't make up your mind to it. I don't blame you. But it *is* what I am."

"None of that's how it is!" Feeling her breath catch he lifted her face. Tears trembled at the corners of her closed eyes. He removed them with the tip of his tongue, feeling the lids quiver. "I'll tell you something truly. I'd be the loser if you got your sight back. It would be the end of my having you to myself. You'd see when you went out in the world that you could have your pick of the males."

"Hmph! I can imagine!"

All the same, as they turned to go back, she seemed more herself again, or as much so as at the start of the walk. Without her usual good color and with shadows under her eyes, she looked drawn. He thought again that his unspoken demands on her for warmth, for feeling, for steadiness were keeping her physically drained.

"I wish you wouldn't go to Roger Tenent's," she blurted. Her face was defiant.

"I have to show I'm not afraid. We can't let them think we're ready to run because of what happened to Gilley."

He could see that she was unmoved but would say no more.

They had gone a few paces only when without warning she stopped and threw her arms about him in a passionate embrace, her face against his, a warm kiss on his cheek. As suddenly as she had done so, she broke free.

"There, I've done that, too."

Overwhelmed, he reached for her, but she pushed him away. "No! If you make anything of it, I'll fight like a wildcat."

"Oh, Letty, what am I to do, then?"

"Walk on while I hold onto your arm. And tell me that poem you were talking about. . . . Well, go on."

"I only know the beginning." He recited:

> Where the sunset gilds the cliff face,
> In the shelter of the rimrock,
> Sits the Great One of the mountains
> On his throne of ash and hemlock.
>
> Round him stand the forest people,
> Lithe and tawny, clean of feature,
> Born of hill, ravine and river,
> Blood kin to each rock and creature.

214

One there is brought here to judgment;
Youthful, he, to all a stranger—
All but one, a nymph most lovely,
Whom to love were mortal danger.

In response to her questioning he had to explain. The boy in the poem, who was not one of the forest people, has been brought before the Great One because he has been meeting the nymph. The forest people have learned that unhappiness befalls a wood-nymph who gives her heart to one from the outside. He said, "In the rest of the poem the boy refuses to give her up. So the Great One relents. They may go on meeting provided the boy promises not to tell her of his love or ask for hers until he has proved his constancy."

Their pace had slowed. The girl stopped to break off a switch that had scraped her leg.

"And does he?" she asked.

"The poem doesn't say."

Where the sunshine fell bright and warming the scent of the dead leaves rose like a light smoke.

"That doesn't seem fair. I'd like to hear the rest of it, when you see the book again."

The dried leaves underfoot made their progress unwontedly noisy.

"But—" There flashed through his mind the vision of exotic lands of white beaches, palm trees and pagodas, and of dark-eyed maidens wound around with flowered garments; of the streets of great cities glittering with lights falling on faces alive with secret knowledge and adventurous purpose; of palatial reception-halls hung with huge, sparkling chandeliers and beneath them men and women and girls in evening dress gathered to honor the successful—all that could await the free-ranger, unentangled and un-encumbered. "—When you read it you don't doubt that the answer is yes, he does."

15

LIKE SUMMER AGAIN! They both exclaimed over it, until it became a joke. And indeed it was summer that next Sunday—full Indian summer. Below the house and barn the pasture and bordering woods seemed to dissolve in the low-lying fog. The air was mild and caressing. Even in the twilight of dawn a sprite of a bird fluttered past their heads, looking to be fed.

The morning, so delicate and fresh, solaced and quickened his spirit as they set out for Winespring. Letty walked beside him with a light step. Her hair swayed as she swung her head one way or the other, savoring, he could tell, the fragrances, the shadings in the flavor of the air, the sounds—"A cricket!" she murmured. But it was not only her harmony with the infant day, he suspected, that made her more lighthearted. She was under less pressure from him. Gilley showed signs of regaining consciousness and the doctors were more hopeful. As for Turner—who knew? The benign grace of the morning was an anodyne to his worries on that score.

So in speaking of the day as like summer, he was sure she had in mind, as he had, not only its balmy temper but their recovery of the carefree feeling of months past.

About halfway up the mountain a large rock-slide offered good stones for a fireplace and to sit on and here they stopped to make coffee. As he set about it he joined in singing one of her ballads.

She said, "I should have brought along something to eat, but I wasn't thinkin'."

"Aha! But I was! I have a whole coffee-cake from Taulbee's."

"You haven't! Oh, you're wonderful!"

Her look of delight passed into one of alertness. She whispered, "What's that?"

He turned. Coming up the trail was a figure horribly out of place in the scene before them.

His blood congealing, he muttered, "It's Bull Turner."

Clad in Army fatigues, he came with a plodding, relentless step up the trail, a shotgun in his hand, carried by the balance. He had seen them, and as he came his grin broadened.

"A right homey sight," he conceded, halting a few paces away and eyeing the canteen cup suspended over the fire on a stick. "I thought I'd let you have a good walk before I caught up with you. So we wouldn't be within hearin' of nobody." He had put the shotgun down, its butt between his feet. His sleeves were rolled up above his thick, hairy forearms.

"So you wanted to see me, did you, Sedgwick?" he went on, a sharper look in his smoldering eyes. "But now I'm here you don't seem to have much to say." He glanced down. "Maybe it's this shotgun. Well, I could let you have a charge of buckshot through the middle, but that ain't my way. I only brung it in case you might have some kind of weapon, but I see you don't. So I tell you what I'll do. I'll leave it down the trail a piece. OK?"

With the gun in one hand again he went back a short distance. From the rear he had a triangular form, tapering from broad shoulders down through compact hips. Turning around, he said, "Not bein' sure I could catch you if it come to a run for it, I'll just unload it and pocket the shells." Breaking the gun at the breech, he did so, then leaned it carefully against a tree.

When he had left the gun well behind on his way back, Wick said quietly, "Letty, you start on toward home while I see what he wants. Go downhill for a bit, then turn right for the trail. If you miss it, keep going down till you hit the stream. That'll guide you back."

Said Turner, "I don't think I'd do that. Letty, your name is? I don't think I'd do that, Letty. You'd just put me to trouble, comin' after you when I've took care of your boy friend. I can be gentle, especially with a pretty girl, and you're even prettier than I heard you was. Or I can be rough. I enjoy it either way."

"Go on, Letty. Just start on downhill. Taking care of me will keep him busy for quite a while."

"Another thing," Turner remarked, leaning back against a tree and hooking his thumbs in his belt. "If you're going to be unfriendly, like tryin' to run away or settin' up a big holler, I might just cut your boy friend's balls off and give them to you for a souvenir."

217

"Go, go," Wick urged the horrified girl. He took her by the arms and impelled her down the slope. But Turner lurched toward them, and Wick released her. If Turner got hold of him, had him in his grip, that could be the finish.

"That's better. I put myself out considerable over this. Gettin' another car for the trip. Lettin' nobody see me for fifty miles. Then gettin' here early in the mornin' and waitin' for you two to come out for one of your walks I heerd about." He took a pack of cigarettes from the breast pocket of his shirt, extracted one and lighted it.

"From the time you showed up in Garrett County, I knowed I couldn't stand for it. I can't stand nobody who thinks he's above other people—and you higher'n mightier'n anybody." There was a flicker in the depths of his eyes as he drew on the cigarette. "I been bidin' my time—till others come to have a bellyful of you, too, with your interferin' and all the notice you been bringin' on these parts. Just like I waited with Gilley Huff. Then there was this pretty gal I heerd you was layin'. That don't go down with me. I ain't goin' to have no spoiled millionaire's brat comin' here and layin' our pretty gals, even one that's blind." He drew on the cigarette and turned his gaze on the girl standing numb, clutching a sapling. His mouth remained ajar when he had breathed out the smoke. "That's man's work," he said thickly. "If all she's had is a pup like you, she's got a big surprise comin'." He tore his eyes away and faced the boy. "So I reckoned that when the time come I'd kill me two birds with one stone."

Wick said, "While you're talkin', Letty and me might as well have coffee."

Neither had quite time enough. Wick had only taken up the cup of simmering water before the other grasped his intent. And the latter, though he managed to turn and dodge, still caught some of the scalding contents on the side of his head and neck. He let out a yell, and charged. Wick dashed for the rock-slide, pursuit hard behind him.

It was quickly evident that the older man was no match for the younger on the rocks. He came to a halt and straightened up, his cheek and the neck below it flaming.

"By God, you'll pay for that!" He looked about him and picked up a fist-sized rock. The boy picked up another. They drew back and let fly at the same instant. Both missed. Both rearmed themselves. Wick feinted and when the other had dodged, and started to straighten, he threw. The rock struck Turner on the shoulder without visible effect. And now, not daring to stoop for another rock or to take his eyes off the one ready to be hurled at him, he had to fall back.

It was coming and there it came and he succeeded in evading it but slipped and fell, his side striking hard on the corner of a block. Scrambling off on all fours, he managed to recover and lurch off the rocks on to the ground before his pursuer was on him. Quicker than the other, he ran around to the other side of the slide and took refuge on it once more.

And now it was rock against rock with neither pursuing nor retreating. Each took hard blows, warding them off the head with bleeding arms. Those Wick took were harder—he could not match the strength behind the rocks that cannoned at him—but the older man was breathing more heavily.

There came a pause and they stood watching each other, each with a rock in his grasp. Turner glanced at the shotgun down the trail, then speculatively at the boy.

Panting, the latter said, "Sorry now you didn't use it, aren't you? . . . Go ahead and get it. See what happens to you while you try to get the shells back in it." The eyes that glared into his he thought might have been a madman's. "You're headed for a lunatic asylum!" he cried.

As Turner made for him he threw. He hit him just to the side of the throat. Turner stumbled, caught himself, heaved his rock, missed and fell heavily. Wick leapt and landed full and crushingly on the man's back, then slipped and fell himself. Turner was pushing himself to his feet as he clambered to his own, his knee hurting. Turner's mouth was wide and blood was oozing from his nose as well as the side of his head.

Said Wick, "That was for Gilley."

Pain and fury in his bloated face, Turner gasped, "Got to get you off this goddamn rock heap. Know what'll do it, too."

Turning, shambling, he headed toward the girl, who still stood evidently paralyzed.

"Letty! Go! He's coming! Go! Go!"

This time she did, arms outstretched before her.

Following behind, Wick meant to land a blow on the back of Turner's neck, but a parrying swing of the arm sent him reeling. The earth spun beneath him, came up to meet him. Looking up at the foreshortened figure above him, he had time to think, 'I've been here before.' Then he was jerked to his feet by his shirt front and slammed back against a tree. Turner's face seemed to swell as his lips drew away from his teeth and his arm went back for the swing. Wick fell forward against him, bringing his knee up with all his strength. The threatening fist fell and Turner bent over, clutching his groin. Pressing back hard against the tree, Wick kicked out, his foot against the other's belly. It sent the hulking figure headlong backward. Wiping the blood out of his eye, he lurched toward the fallen enemy. He drew his foot back to kick him in the temple but before it struck it was grasped and twisted and he was sent crashing, clear over the body on the ground.

His leg could have been broken! . . . To lie there, if only for ten seconds to get a few breaths in: what bliss! That devil who had sent him down must have felt the same, for he had risen only to all fours when the boy had regained his feet. For the first time Wick landed a fist square on that awful face. It sent pain shooting through his arm . . . but Turner did not go down. It came into his head that he hadn't the strength left to stop the other, no matter what. . . . And now retribution was coming at him like a bear.

He fell back before it, keeping just out of reach up the trail, and when the bear stopped, chest heaving and face streaked with blood, he panted, "Come and get me!" He tasted blood himself and blood kept getting in his eye. Once more Turner rushed, but he had no chance against young legs.

"Come on! You givin' out? You scared?"

It was a wounded Bull and a winded Bull, but, standing there with a look of ferocity and slow cunning, it did not look like a Bull that was giving out or scared.

"No . . . you come after me, boy!" He turned and started back toward where the girl stood, flight abandoned, her fist in her mouth, eyes filled with terror of what she could not see, knowing as well as Wick that if the Bull couldn't be stopped. . . .

Overtaking him, Wick swung and missed as Turner pivoted around and with a fist in his chest sent him careening backward to trip and fall flat. Another tree saved him. Rolling over, he had it between them for an instant. But as he pulled himself up, two crushing hands closed on his throat. Strangling, panic seizing him, he clawed at the face before him. One of Turner's hands let go to pull off the fingers that were digging at his eyes. But again Wick had a tree at his back. Bracing against it as before, he swung his right leg around both of Turner's and yanked them toward him, pitching forward as hard as he could as he did so. Turner went over backward. Wick jumped once more, aiming to land, seat first, on the man's chest in the hope of crushing it, but his victim turned in the knick of time. He came down hard but glancingly and toppled off backward.

He *had* to be first up, but his tortured body seemed beyond his command. Panicked again by his weakness he thought Turner must surely be on him to finish him off. . . . But he saw that Turner was also having hard going. . . . And as, finally erect, they faced each other again, Wick knew it could not go on much longer for either, and almost certainly less long for him. If only, before he was finished, he could do enough injury to let the girl save herself. . . .

Again they went for each other. The stronger grappled for a hold, the younger writhed, struck, twisted, kicked, each time breaking free, each time with lessened strength. Blows fell less hard but did not need to fall as hard. A rushing sound filled the boy's ears, his body and limbs were heavy, were in vises of pain. . . . The face in which insane, blood-rimmed eyes glared at him was contorted by effort, and the blow that followed sent him staggering backward and sprawling again on the ground.

He could not get up. He could not escape the battering that would come. But nothing happened and when, with all the will he could summon, he got his hands and knees under him, he saw that Turner was plodding off. Letty. . . . She was off down the hill, seemed again to be trying to escape. Only Turner was after her. . . . Turner had caught her, was dragging her back.

Like an ape on its hind legs, he floundered toward them, drew back to drive in with his right, and was seized by the left, flung off with a fearful, wrenching pain. Fetching up against a tree, he did not fall. But he could not raise his left arm to ward off the fist that was coming. From his jaw a sheet of blackness shot outward. . . .

"Wick! Where are you? Wick?"

The small, mysterious sounds bored into his consciousness through the darkness.

"Hamp! . . . Hamp!"

The frenzy of the voice tugged at him unmercifully . . . dragged him from oblivion to a place of aching light and stabbing pains.

He could have been out only seconds; the scene was unchanged, Letty struggling in a monster's grasp.

"Yellin' ain't goin' to do you no good. You keep fightin' me, I'm goin' to have to hurt ya. . . . He's out cold, but I gotta. . . . Goddam you, you little bitch . . . ! Maybe I'll give it to you right now."

His left arm was helpless but he could move his other limbs. There was someone, once, in just this fix, with only one arm. . . . In a story. Would it work, what the man did in the story?

If Turner would keep his back turned. . . .

"Let him watch, if he comes to. He ain't good for nothin' more."

The boy unfastened his belt and pulled it free. It was a strong belt, one he had bought to hold his stomach in against the bouncing of the motorbike.

"I might even enjoy it more." Turner had seized her wrists. "Goddamn it, I tolja. . . ."

She had bent and bitten his hand.

He had passed the end of the belt through the buckle, forming a loop. He heard the sound of a slap and a cry from the girl. He slipped the loop over his useless arm, up to the shoulder and, with the end of the belt wrapped around his right hand, drew it tight. *Now. . . .*

From somewhere, from the frantic struggles of the girl, the strength came to him to pull himself to his feet. Stealthily he rose, quietly took a step, another, and again, and another. . . .

Now, over Turner's head with the belt, give it another loop around his neck, pull back hard, bear down on his shoulder, spring onto his back, scissors lock around his waist, and it's done!

Over they went, Wick giving the other a wrenching twist to keep the heavy body from landing on him. His fist, clenched grimly around the end of the belt that went once and a half around Turner's neck, dug into the windpipe. He was clamped to Turner's back like a shell on a turtle.

Hold on, hold on, and pull, pull . . . while the Bull thrashed them around on the ground and clutched at the wrist at his neck and the belt around it. *Hold on, hold on for everything, and tighten the scissors lock. . . And pull. . . .*

He could hear the breath rasping in the throat beneath his hand. But the neck chords protected it, standing out hard as wood, and the stomach was unyielding to his legs—legs too weakened for the task.

God, what strength there was in the man! With one hand disengaged to hold onto a tree he was pulling them both to his feet. . . . And now he was swinging around, crashing the burden on his back against a tree . . . hard, again and again. But he was weakening, too; and the leech clung tight.

He could not cling much longer, though: his muscles would give out. But surely those breaths were more rasping, harder drawn? And the hands clawing at his fingers and wrist less powerful?

Turner was staggering forward, up the hill . . . back to the trail. He teetered on his feet, his breath blasting in and out, steadied, then went on, foot after foot, to the trail.

One hand went to his side, pressing past the boy's hip to . . . to what? Into his pocket?

The shells! 'My God, the gun!' It was just down the trail.

He cried, "Letty, the gun!" He did not know where she was. "Letty, get the gun! It's down the trail! The light on it! *Look*, Letty, *look!*"

"I cain't see! I cain't!"

She was off to the side and behind them. He could glimpse her out of the corner of his eye, her hand to her forehead, her staring eyes wide with anguish.

The gun was only a few paces away. He had to abandon the scissors lock and drop his legs. With a frantic jerk he pulled Turner over backward and they landed together on their sides again. . . . But he could not match the strength of that bearlike body. Turner rolled them over . . . and now, on knees and one elbow, he hitched them forward, still tugging with the other hand at the arm pulling on the belt.

"The light on the gun! Look, Letty! You *can* see! . . . He's dragging me to it. . . . He's getting there! I can't hold him!"

Over the massive shoulder he saw the shotgun leaning against the tree a few feet away. If he let go it wouldn't matter whether he got to the gun first, nothing could save them. But Turner was almost ready to reach for it. He'd have to let go. . . . And now he saw Letty's legs in front of them, and as Turner's hand released his wrist and went out to it the gun was snatched away.

Exultation burst in the boy's breast. He felt Turner sag beneath him, every breath a battle.

Pull on that belt . . . though his hand was a ball of pain. *Pull, pull.* Another minute and the brute would be finished.

"Kill him if you want to, Wick, but I got him covered—if you done had enough."

"*Hamp!*" The cry had broken from the girl.

Wick let go and rolled off onto his back. The tall figure of the young mountaineer, dark against the sky, was standing over them, gun in his hands pointed down.

It was over, the danger was past, the danger of months, death escaped, all over, and the blind girl he loved had seen. She was on her knees beside him; she had *seen,* and while he could have believed a coal-truck had run over him, he might at that moment have been one of the immortals.

"Oh, Wick, you're hurt bad." Her hands were delicate as angel's wings on his chest and face. "But I kin see you. Hit's dim, but I can see you, and, oh, Wick, you're good-lookin'." And the eyes he gazed up into were eyes he *could* gaze into.

"Thank God, Letty. Thank God." He struggled to sit up, and with her hand behind his shoulders she helped him do so. She cradled his bloody head against her breast and laid her own against it.

When he roused once more in Colly's room, he said to himself that surely he would never again wake up here battered and bandaged. 'I've been through it twice. I must have paid the price by now.'

All the same, he was a lot better than he had been when he had reached the farm with Letty after the torturous descent of the mountain. If he was not a lot better than then, he would be dead. The doctor had given him pills, and a night of total extinction twelve hours long had made the difference.

This time they had brought the doctor to him. Two cuts on his head had required stitches, taken while Letty held his hand and did not look, and his left arm was bound to his chest to let the torn ligaments start to heal. The doctor had come out with the Sheriff and they had quickly been followed by some reporters from the *Courant,* one a female for the woman's angle on Letty. By the time they arrived Hamp had brought Turner down the mountain—a march Turner had not been up to for some time, Wick was gratified to hear. The prisoner had volunteered only one comment: "One thing you can't lick—age." The boy had heard Hamp's report through the open window while the doctor treated him.

Hamp had caught a glimpse of a figure clad in dull green slipping through the woods with a gun shortly after Letty and Wick had passed going the same way. A squirrel-hunter, he had thought and dismissed it from his mind. But it kept coming back to him that something about the figure was familiar. When it came to him whom it made him think of, he had reached down his own gun and got going. Only a hunch that his cousin and Wick would go that way had sent him on the trail up the mountain instead of straight on toward the Fork. He had not gone very far when he heard Letty's cry. "I ain't wasted no time after that."

When the doctor—who had been far more interested in Letty's case than anything else—left him to take care of Turner, the Sheriff replaced him and took his and Letty's story. The Sheriff kind of thought he'd lift the ban on Wick's leaving the county, though—with a glance of gallantry at Letty—it was hard to think of anything that would cause him to do so. After the Sheriff came the reporters, who, the doctor said, were to have five minutes, no more.

Wick thought it would always pierce him to the heart to recall the scene as they hobbled the last stretch before the farm. Queen had seen them coming with Letty holding his arm over her shoulders, and at the unnatural sight had come running. Wick had disengaged himself from her daughter. "Go on," he had commanded, and with a glance to make sure he could do without her she had hastened as fast as she dared. "Ma! Ma!" she had cried, "Wick's done near kilt Bull Turner and I kin see! Ma, I kin see!" And the girl had thrown herself sobbing into her mother's arms. "I kin see!"

She could not by any means see well, but as if a block had indeed been removed, she could see better by evening than when they had come down the mountain.

All that afternoon there had been visitors. He had heard the cars coming and going, through his torpor, the legacy of the first of the pills. Well, it was a wonder, all that had happened, and every relative and friend of the family's would have to witness for himself that the blind had been given to see.

He could hear Letty's voice raised in excitement and mirth, especially, he surmised, over the matching of unknown faces with long-familiar voices. The sound did more for his wounds than any pill. He was amused by the subdued, contrite expression Letty brought with her when she came in to show she had not forgotten him and to sit with him for a spell. He laughed as well as the soreness of his rib-cage would allow. "You don't need to be so serious about me. I'm all right. Just drowsy. Go see your friends and enjoy the incredible new Letty all you can." She was as he imagined a girl might be at a first, dazzling, incomparable party—Cinderella at the ball—trying to contain her riotous sensations.

She had come back later, peeking in to make sure he was not asleep. The last of them had gone, she reported. "And just as well. I couldn't of stood much more today." She was pale and when she dropped onto the edge of the cot her over-large eyes were shimmering with tears. "Oh, Wick, all I owe you! And it's all so beautiful, the grass, the silk in the milkweed pods, the old barn and the wooden planks with the grain. And people—their faces so kind and so changin', tellin' you so much how they're feelin'. It's like I been away all these years, havin' only memories with me, and now I'm back again. Only all afternoon I been not knowin' where to look next. Everything's so lively—so much goin' on. And the sky so big! I'd forgotten how big." She could have been an exhausted child of thirteen. "But here you are, havin' to pay for it all. After all that bravery. Oh, Wick, that Turner. . . . When I think of it, I think I'll die."

"You're not to think of it," he said. And added, both marveling and doubtful, "I can't get used to your being able to see me." He was praying that her first impression of him would not be nullified by comparison with others.

"Neither can I." She appeared at that moment at least content with what she saw. "I've got to go help Ma get some supper ready. What kind of thing would you like to have, to eat?" Anything that did not require much chewing, he answered. She looked him deeply in the eyes, before leaving. 'Wait,' her manner seemed to say.

And he waited, through a supper of soup and milk and for a time after Mrs. Sherrod removed the tray. Then Letty returned. "*You're* going to have to read to *me*," he said, rather at random, his heart pounding. The walls of the small room might have moved in even closer, the light of the kerosene lamp have grown even duller.

226

"It's terrible," she replied. "I'm goin' to have to learn to read all over again. Not to mention learnin' all else a gal of seventeen's supposed to know."

He said, "What's going to take some getting used to is that now you can have a pretty good idea of what I'm thinking."

Sitting beside him, she returned his gaze with one as steady and expressive as his own. "I reckon I can," she countered, barely audibly. She obeyed the arm he held out, leaning toward him, and he drew her the rest of the way. Her face came against his, their mouths together. Even his most vaulting imaginings had not prepared him for the rapture that flooded him, for the yielding softness, the warm smoothness, the fragrance and the taste of her as of a flower of paradise opening to him in a universe contracted to their blind mutual need and desire.

When she detached herself, he got out the words with what breath he had: "I'd die for that."

"You won't have to."

"Be beside me here for a moment."

"Just for a moment then."

He moved over and she lay down against him with her head on his arm. The gratitude that filled him as he gazed at the ceiling seemed to encompass the earth—enough to ransom a whole unregenerate planet.

"I love you so, Letty, I don't know how to tell you."

"I love you too, Wick."

They kissed again, absorbed, their bodies in contact as far as the arm he cursed would allow until at last she freed herself. She had to go, she said, as though already she had tarried overlong. Even by the uncertain light her flush was apparent, and it gave him new cause to marvel and to feel joy and pride: he had for a time possessed and preoccupied the girl he adored.

She turned to the small mirror on the chest of drawers and smoothed her hair into place with the same odd little off-center pursing of the lips he had seen in his sister when, as she would say, she was restoring the ravaged masterpiece. With a shame-faced glance at him, Letty said, "I'd hate for you to know how many times I've looked in a mirror since we got back."

In the morning, looking out on the bright, still, Indian-summer day, he thought that for now, if only for now, he was king of the world.

16

THE HOUSE WAS EXTRAORDINARILY QUIET. It might have been abandoned to the vociferating chickens and a whinnying horse. (Horses not with Mr. Barrows?) Sore and stiff as he was in every part, he could perhaps not have felt quite so lively and jubilant had he not known that Turner would be feeling at least as bad and would have waked in a jail.

Holding the collar between his teeth, he got his right arm through the sleeve of a raincoat he kept at the farm, pulled the rest of the garment around him and stuffed his feet into his old tennis shoes. Then with the expectation of a radiant, inexpressibly lovely Letty before him, he eased himself down the stairs.

Mrs. Sherrod was alone in the kitchen, in flour to her wrists. Letty had gone off with her uncle to Harpersburg, to begin to see the world. "She didn't want to go and leave you, just like that, but you were asleep and knowin' you, I told her you wouldn't want her to stay back on your account, when she was so excited."

He guessed that what had seemed perfectly natural to her when she began to speak made her feel awkward before she finished. "You did right," he declared. "Only you ought to have gone, too. You've missed out on seeing what it would all mean to her just so I wouldn't be left alone."

She had quit her bread-making to wash her hands and replenish the water in the kettle. "I wanted to stay," she said with agreeable finality. "Now what do you think you can eat?"

"The house, if you'll soften it with a little milk."

Outdoors, he lingered before returning, trying to imagine seeing the world with new eyes. When, with Mrs. Sherrod's help, he had washed his face and hands and had combed his hair he was glad to sit down. She sat with him and watched him while

228

he put away two soft-boiled eggs with grits and a quarter of a pan of corn bread in a bowl of milk.

He said, "I can't get over it. All these years that Letty had it in her to see but couldn't just for her own sake. It had to be for someone else—to save me from a charge of buckshot through the head. How right you were about her!"

She seemed to study his hand as it rested beside his plate. "A life for a life. That was what it took."

"One thing I ought to tell you"—and he in turn stared at his hand—"is that the moment I knew Letty was going to see again, I thought, 'The promise I made doesn't count anymore.' I hope I was right. I've told her I love her."

"I reckoned you had. It wouldn't be right for me to ask what she said."

"Would it be right for me to ask what you reckon she said?"

But she only laughed.

He had noticed that the clothes hanging over the stove were his. "You were good to wash those. You always take care of me."

"They were a sight. But they need mendin', too."

They proved to be dry; and finding him determined to get dressed, she turned until he had his shorts on, then helped him into the rest.

"Some more comin'."

When the house was quiet there was always several minutes' notice of an arriving car. As it crossed the ford, Wick went to the door. Opening it, he stared uncomprehending at the figure on the other side.

"Wick! We heard you'd been hurt!"

"Father! How on earth . . . ?" His eye went out to the chunky Jeep with the orange lettering of the Talbot Creek Mine.

"I flew down in the company plane first thing this morning. You did get banged up, didn't you?"

The mechanics of his father's transplantation to Oak Lick Hollow might be within the bounds of reason, but how in the name of heaven were the two worlds of which he himself was a part to be combined? Already Mrs. Sherrod was behind him, and there were introductions to make.

"You'll come in, won't you? You'll have some coffee with us? Wick, do you suppose we could take him to the kitchen? It's more cheerful there."

'This is impossible,' the boy told himself in dismay as the invitation was warmly embraced, and he followed his elders to the back of the house. He recalled the careless innocence his father could turn on, unrecognized by the victim for the trap it masked until too late, and he winced. In the bright light of the kitchen he observed that his parent wore a suit of soft, brownish-gray herringbone tweed with shirt, tie and shoes of equal elegance; he had once said that if you are known to have an income in six figures you only insulted the intelligence of those with a four-figure one when you dressed as if you could afford no better than they. He was surprised and somewhat disturbed—as if he were less himself than he thought—by Mrs. Sherrod's observation that she would have known they were father and son if she had only seen them a thousand miles apart. But he had to admit, grudgingly if with great relief, that there was something to being an adult. If either of them considered that they were treading a tightrope or, indeed, that the position was other than potentially enjoyable, no one would have known it.

"How badly hurt is he, Mrs. Sherrod?" his father asked, with a gracious deference.

And if Mrs. Sherrod on her side felt any diffidence, or loathed her visitor for his part in the threatened destruction of her homestead, she was able to conceal it as, having urged them to sit down, she prepared refreshments and gave a sympathetic and reassuring appraisal of Wick's injuries. "I reckon you've heard all about how it happened," she ended.

With a look at him that struck him as most uncharacteristically unsure, his father replied, "I had a long-distance call from the mine office yesterday and read an account in the Harpersburg *Courant* before I came out. Also the desk man at the hotel had a good deal to say when he saw my name. But of course I want to hear all about it from Wick. You've taken very good care of him. And this is not the first time. In fact, I'm beginning to understand that you've given him a home."

Could Mrs. Sherrod, the boy wondered, being new to his father's controlled tenor, appreciate how much that confession conceded? He looked the picture of composure. But to his son, used to those iron-gray eyes and those lips closed against any weakness or impetuosity, there was a hint of vulnerability in the face he could not remember seeing there before. Moreover, he had detected admiration in his father's way of looking at Mrs. Sherrod—for her harmony of feature and her bearing, he was sure, if for nothing else.

"It's been our pleasure to have him," she said. "He's been just like one of us. It made a great difference to my daughter, he brought so much of the world to her she'd been cut off from. She'd been blind for seven years, till yesterday. Maybe you heard about that, too." She did not lift her eyes from the coffee pot that she had set on the table.

"I did. It's being spoken of as a miracle—not surprisingly. I can appreciate the joy it has brought you. Wick's mother and I have been in the dark about a great deal. We have much to be straightened out about."

She had sat down and was filling the cups. "Your son has been a good friend to us," she said, looking up with a smile.

Wick speculated that adults find it expedient to communicate on two levels simultaneously, a speaking and an unspeaking. This now received a measure of confirmation from his father.

"And to me. He seems to have been instrumental in keeping the company I work for from an act of great inhumanity." A faint glow, another surprise to his son, overspread his face. "I knew when I saw this farm how grateful I was for that, and that I must do all I can to see that no harm comes to it from the Allegheny-Keystone Coal Company. I could not have entered this house if I had not decided that."

'Thank God for it!' Wick thought. He looked to Mrs. Sherrod and knew at once she had been aware all along that that was how it was.

She put her hand on his shoulder. "This is surely a time of great happiness for me, and will be for us all. I don't know how we can thank you."

The sound that perhaps afforded her and his father a welcome interruption was one he had awaited all morning with a burning in his breast. A truck was coming up the road.

"My brother and daughter. You'll let me put another place at the table for lunch, won't you?

But his father declined, pleading that he must borrow Wick long enough to have a meal with him at his hotel in Harpersburg, so they could talk over things that needed to be settled.

Wearing the frosty, pale-green dress, Letty wafted in like spring

231

after gray winter. Only, was it really the girl of last night, or
. . . or a kind of graduate of her? Perhaps it was the make-up—
the lipstick that made her seem so, while adding to the agitation
of his heart.

Brought up short in the doorway, she was looking with those
interested, gray-amber eyes from him to his father. Both had risen
to their feet, Wick as if released by gravity.

"This is my daughter. Letty, this is Mr. Carter, Wick's father."

Wick had seldom seen his father as noticeably caught unprepared. Amusement gradually dawned in him.

"Oh, yes," Letty had declared, with consuming attention. "I
can tell that!" She spoke as if the likeness were a matter of remarkable personal discovery—as of course it was for her.

Her mother said indulgently, "Letty, you've got to learn not
to stare at folks."

"She's welcome to stare all she likes as far as I'm concerned,
if she doesn't mind being stared back at."

The compliment from his father conspicuously pleased her.

"How was it in Harpersburg?" Wick asked. "How did it seem?"

"Heaven! It's all like heaven! I keep thinkin', if I'm lucky
I've got fifty years more of lookin' and seein'. All those colors!
They're comin' clearer all the time." They sat down again and
her elbows were on the table, her hands clasped, her eyes shining.
"I never dreamed there was so much colors. In the leaves on the
trees and in the clothes people are wearin'. In the houses and
the autos and the store windows. And the blue sky. It's there
anytime you want to look up and see it. So big and blue and
full of light." She was like a traveler returned from unimaginable
lands.

"And so much goin' on, autos passin' each other and turnin'
and people goin' every which way—all down the street. Everyone
with a shadow like a dark cut-out of themselves attached to their
feet. It's enough to make you dizzy!"

Her flow of speech was suddenly arrested and she flushed and
looked guilty. "I rattle on, and here's Mr. Carter just got here."
Her color deepened. "And Wick! I been so excited I didn't think
to ask how you are."

"I'm all right." In her eyes, as his momentarily held them, he
read an awareness of the evening before, but, he thought, disturbed, a resistant awareness.

His absorption in the girl was broken into by her uncle. Tom

Barrows was not one to rush in to meet the driver of a Talbot Creek Mine vehicle, but in the due order of things he now made an appearance with Colly. Wick watched the introductions nervously, without knowing what he feared, or on whose account. His father had risen and the two men clasped hands, their reciprocal scrutiny intense if quickly masked by decorum. Two men, Wick thought, not in the habit of truckling to others, and probably each immediately cognizant of it in the other.

Mrs. Sherrod said without delay, perhaps to let her brother know that no test of wills was in store, "Mr. Carter's told us he don't want the farm to come to harm and will do his best to see it don't, through his company."

Mr. Barrow's expression did not change beyond a quickened alertness in the eyes, though he may have stood even a little taller; he was not dependent on the favors of others. But he replied courteously, "That's right good news, and we thank you."

"*Oh!*" Letty cried. "It's the best news there ever was!"

Wick wished that look were for him. But, quite unmistakably, it was far from wasted on his parent.

Said the latter, "It should have come before now. I have much to thank this family for. My son has got a great deal out of being with you that I'm afraid he could hardly have found in a home like ours."

His father, it occurred to Wick, had known he must be at a disadvantage here. Yet he had come anyway. And he could not be finding it much easier than he had expected. He had surely not foreseen how close his son was to these people who opposed him. He took his medicine, if medicine he deemed it, in good countenance, and his son thought he did them both credit by it.

"Boys is restless, and sometimes nothin' will do but they have to be away from their folks for a spell. Wicker's a good worker and he's not afeared to stand up to whatever comes, as we seen."

"It's Wick, Tom."

He looked briefly at his sister and, as if having recognized his mistake in supposing she had spoken, resumed. "And he's got a gift of words. Hit'd be a bad day for sin if he become a preacher."

He broke out, and seemed to surprise himself, with one of his transforming grins.

Wick's father's laughter covered the quick grip he gave his son's elbow. "I don't suppose the devil need worry. But you make me proud of him. And now we've really got to go. We're just keeping you from your meal." He glanced at the girl, possibly to see if her reaction to their departure would give him the clue to the lay of the land between her and his son.

Wick was deeply anxious for a clue himself. She had seemed to take no special heed of him since her return, and as they all moved out he held her back a little. He might have asked her if anything had changed. But cornering her would be beneath them both. Instead he asked her if she had seen any birds since yesterday.

How was it she looked at him? With a brightness that held him off? Tantalizingly? Uncertainly? Whichever it was, her expression then softened. "Yes, I did. I've seen the chickadees and titmice, and nothing cuter ever lived. And Blue jays, just as beautiful as you said. *And* a towhee—all you said, too, as dressy and as dapper. I can tell them all from how you described them, Wick. And the hemlocks, and old Winespring, lyin' back there, so high and grand. All like you made me see them when I had no eyes but yours."

They had sauntered after the others, she setting the pace. He had to walk apart from her now; she had no need of his hand or arm. She seemed to have turned inward again, and he wondered if there was not a shadow of perturbation in her eyes, as he had thought there was at the end of her rhapsody over the glories of Harpersburg.

"Is there something on your mind?"

"Those people on the streets and in the stores—" She spoke as if his question had rendered her thoughts vocal: "Everyone of them seemed to know exactly what they were doing. They all seemed to know what it was all about and where they'd come out at."

They were nearly up with the others, at the Jeep. He had time only to say, "They're used to it. You'll be, too, sooner than you think."

She had stopped. Appearing to sweep her mind clear of its misgivings, she took in the farmyard with her glance. "To think that your father has given it back to us!" And he did come in for the kind of look, from the heart, that had so touched his parent.

His father seemed quite up to maneuvering the Jeep down the stream bed, Wick thought; he even seemed to enjoy it.

They stopped at Mrs. Haney's, where he changed his clothes and in the course of doing so unbound the injured arm, using the wrapping for a sling; the doctor had authorized the switch in a few days, so why not now? They had a late lunch at Harpersburg's good hotel. Because of his injuries he found himself attracting attention everywhere. There were also many smiles of recognition, sometimes with that sideways jerk of the head bespeaking approval. All this contributed to the marked change in his relationship with his father, who twice called him by his own younger brother's name, Cliff. He appeared to enjoy their nearer equality of standing, much as he had enjoyed driving the Jeep. The awkward conversational deserts Wick had anticipated their having to cross did not materialize. To his father's questions about his life since leaving home—questions which tactfully skirted the precise nature of his relationship with Mrs. Sherrod's beautiful daughter—he replied with growing ease and naturalness. And he was glad to be interrogated about the fight on Winespring. There seemed no need to be ashamed with his father of the terrible fear or the feeling he could not go on that he had had to surmount, or of the glory of pride and triumph that was his at the finish. "I could have killed him. He was paid back for Gilley. No one can say he wasn't." He was able to let this all pour out; and he had the satisfaction, too, of seeing that he had justified in his father's eyes what his father had done for him and would be doing before he was on his own. When he had talked himself out and his father was recalling his own younger days he was able to think of what he heard as the experiences of another human being familiar with quandaries and perplexities like his own and not be bored, as he would formerly have been, as by the irrelevant trials of a future superman.

They were in accord, too, on a looming practical issue. Wick was to apply for admission to college at mid-term and would aim at a career in forestry, if that was what he continued to desire. "Just be sure it's what you want to do," said his father. "Life's a kind of capital you can't hoard. You have to live on it, watching it diminish day by day. So be sure that what you buy with it is more important to you than anything else." It was also settled that he would come home as soon as he could. This was inevitable, in Wick's view, and the more readily acceptable because he pictured Letty's visiting there. The question was what was meant by "could."

It came down to the contest over Winespring. In that, the boy made plain, he was not going to give an inch.

"I understand how you feel about it," his father said. "You made the case for the mountain's preservation with remarkable persuasiveness in that letter you sent me a copy of. But you have to understand my position, too. I'm not Allegheny-Keystone incarnate. There's a board I'm responsible to and behind it the stockholders. I could be ousted tomorrow." A tacit bargain was struck. The boy would reserve his animosity and his father would let himself be shown the country the next morning. For the balance of the day the latter had company officials to see, which might run into dinner; he said with a smile, "You probably feel you've been away from the farm long enough for today, anyhow."

They parted at the company offices in Harpersburg. With his bad arm free for emergencies, Wick decided he could drive the Jeep and was allowed to keep it. He was to pick his father up at the hotel the first thing in the morning.

Anxious to learn what he could of Gilley, he drove first to the hospital, where he found to his joy that his friend was fully conscious, had been moved to a ward and could receive visitors for five minutes at a time. On the way to the ward he passed Gladys coming out. Beaming, she said, "He's pulling through."

The teacher's head was elevated on an extra pillow. Only his eyes seemed to have life in them. On the far side of his face, when he turned it, a huge, fading, yellow bruise extended up into his scalp, encompassing a newly healed cut across the cheekbone and another above the ear.

"We're a pair, aren't we?" he said in a voice that sounded filtered.

"I've heard about it," he went on. "Roger was here this morning." Each sentence seemed to require a renewed summoning of strength. But he managed a wink and a smile. "You were good to come."

He made a movement of the hand on the covers that led the boy to grasp it.

"You're going to be all right, aren't you." It was less a question than a determined assertion of fact.

"It's a cinch. Another week and I'll be out of here. High time."

"There'll be a big celebration at Tenent's."

Gilley's eyes were on the ceiling. When he spoke, he seemed to be measuring out his energy for what he most wanted to say. "An eye for an eye, a tooth for a tooth—for a friend. . . . You've become a highlander, Wick. Tell me . . . about it. He gave you a bad time. . . ."

"It was mutual." He gave a highly compressed report, treating the matter lightly and, when the ward nurse signaled that he was to go, promised to return soon.

There were three cars at the farm and a lively group on the porch. In the midst of this, reigning among some boys, was Letty, who waved to him. Detaching himself from the group, a man in business clothes came toward him with a broad smile and a hand extended as if to meet an old friend. Wick thought he recognized the regular features and guarded eyes, but the man had to introduce himself before he remembered him from the courthouse. He was "Wally Herndon, your State Assemblyman." He had come "to shake the hand of a mighty brave boy." Mostly, it appeared, he had come to have their picture taken together. He had brought a photographer, who fetched Letty from among her admirers to be included in it. The girl smiled and reddened at the cries of encouragement that followed her, but her pleasant excitement rather wilted under the Assemblyman's heavy conversational tread. "Yes, I can see how any red-blooded young man would be inspired to the heights of bravery by a young miss like you. . . .

"Suppose we just stand with Winespring in the background. . . . Is that right, Kenny? The flash won't kill the mountain, will it? . . . Yessir, Winespring's got a big following now—a lot of friends. We've been getting mail. . . ."

Mr. Herndon could be one of the fellas, too. ". . . So the boy says, 'No, I don't mind gettin' a hair-cut. Which hair shall I get cut, Pop?' "

When the visitors had headed back to their car, Wick said, "We can put our teeth back in our mouths now."

He was about to observe that it had been worth it for what the Assemblyman's visit said about Winespring as a political issue. Letty spoke first, however. "I'm so glad you come—came—when you did. Some boys have asked me go with them to where there's dancin' this evenin'. Couldn't you come, too? Even if you're hurtin' too bad to dance yourself?"

But the invitation lacked conviction. Halting just short of the porch, he said he thought he had better not. "I'd just be in the way."

Why was it he had to feel so self-conscious with her now, and she, by her manner, with him? What had come over them? In any case, she said she would be glad to go with him and his father in the morning. Her face had lighted up as if with relief—indeed with relief, he thought even while condemning his suspiciousness: relief from concern over forsaking him for the evening. . . .

It helped him when she had gone off with her three friends to have the morning to look forward to. There was the evening to get through and the strain of maintaining an unflagging cheerfulness, so as not to appear to begrudge Letty the diversion she had so long been denied. When he went to bed, he read until midnight but lay awake after blowing the lamp out. It was not until an hour later that he heard a car creep through the ford. Smothered sounds of merriment came from below before the car departed and he fell asleep.

They were both late in getting up, and at breakfast she pressed him with questions about the dinner with his father. 'She's interested,' he told himself. 'It's not just that she's avoiding having to account in detail for last night.'

On the way to Harpersburg she kept exclaiming over objects he had never grasped the singularity of—the pugnacious, flat-snouted faces of the coal-trucks; the bulging cheeks of two little girls with lollipop sticks poking from their mouths; a boy on a bicycle with colored strips of cloth woven among the spokes; all the colors of fruit displayed by a roadside vendor, from the snow-green of the palest apples to the black-purple of plums. Her excitement infected him and he was joyful for her.

" 'Corn rigs, an' barley rigs,' " he soliloquized, " 'An' corn rigs are bonie.' I thought of that when we passed the corn-shocks in the field a while back."

Her animation appeared checked. She said, "You must have thought I was childish to carry on so about that."

It gave him a cold shock. "Letty! You can't mean that. You can't believe I thought any such thing!"

She had lowered her eyes to her hands clutched together in her lap.

"*Can* you?" he reiterated. The horn of a car behind them blared. He had slowed down so that he was holding up traffic.

"No, I reckon I don't," she replied with a smile that seemed to put the matter in the realm of teasing. "You know what? I can't get over how beautiful the red and green lights are that tell the cars when to stop and go. I'd like to have a little one of each to set in a ring."

"To tell a boy when to stop and when he could go ahead?"

The remark had been offered humorously but without the expectation of its affording the merriment it did.

His father, when he joined them, was as taken as he by the girl's omnivorous enthusiasm, which was not long in reaching full flower again. For him, too, Wick could tell, she brought the world into new being. Even billboards had congenial parts to play in the transformation she worked in the commonplace. In fact, billboards and signs received much attention, for Letty was exercising her memory of the alphabet and word-formation, both of which were coming back to her well.

On a number of telephone poles, to Wick's surprise, cardboard signs urged in green letters SAVE WINESPRING! There were also fewer but larger ones on stakes countering in scarlet with PAY, NOT PARKS.

He had set a course for the strip-mined hills that were the rawest he knew. At the foot of the first of these, a workman stepped out to intercept them, then saw the origin of the Jeep and let them pass. A cut wide enough for five coal-trucks abreast had been laid bare, steeply ascending the hill to the site of operations near the top. There, where the mountain was being ringed, the bench was even wider and the highwall behind it all of four stories high. It was a scene of desolation. The roar and clang of machinery could be heard from the distance, from around the bend of the ridge.

The other two had fallen silent. Letty looked stunned.

Several loaded trucks passed them going down when Wick pulled over to let the view sink in with his father.

"No mere bulldozer dug this out," the boy said. "As you know. This took a power-shovel, and a big one. With a scoop that will hold four pickup trucks side by side."

He drove close to the brink and invited his father to take a look at the spoil bank spreading devastation. "I know you've seen this kind of thing before. But look at it from the point of view of the people whose country this is. Yours, for that matter."

239

Letty murmured, "It's worse even than I thought from what you told me." But she was inhibited in the feeling she could show, he knew, by the presence on the back seat of a man deeply implicated in the appalling spectacle of a mountain slain.

He drove on farther. "Look over there!" From the monstrous step cut in the mountain across the valley the landslides of the spoil bank reached far down the slope. Where they were thickest the trees were killed; their listing remains jutted through the spillage.

His father said, "I foresaw, of course, that I should find myself in the role of—what's the villain called?—the *heavy* this morning. But I had not anticipated how uncomfortable the backdrop would make me feel. Letty, I'm afraid it's a pretty strong dose for a girl whose home is these mountains—too sudden an introduction to the way the world works and the price of progress. I could argue that my son has been a little cruel to both of us in bringing you along."

It was true, Wick thought, that he had considered only his desire for her company.

"No," she said. "It's as well for me to see it now." She gazed cheerlessly out of the window.

As for his father, Wick had said that it would be nothing new to him. And he appeared to be regarding what he saw collectedly enough. Yet there was that in his face which made his son question whether he had ever before been brought so close to such earth-carnage, or had his eyes so opened to it. If Letty's presence, posing the little mountain farm against this soulless havoc, helped bring it home to him, then, however it sickened her, his bringing her was forgivable.

Back on the highway he asked his father if he would care to drive. His plan called for another twenty miles and his body was protesting the impositions on it.

"So you have more in store for us?"

"If you can spare the time and Letty can stand it. This is something I haven't seen myself—the area the floods hit last month."

On the way they stopped for coffee and muffins at a small road-side restaurant, and Wick was reminded again that Letty had the whole of civilization to discover. What the menu was, what the waitress expected of her, what people away from home did for toilets—all was outside her experience. Though self-conscious, her

240

inaptitudes were a succession of small jokes to her; seeing was so miraculous that no embarrassments could cloud it.

Wick's father cautiously brought up the question of his companions' plans for the future. Letty was prepared for Wick's starting college as soon as he could and knew he would have to go home in good time to do so. But he could not long look at her while discussing the subject—or she at him when she said that she was going to find paying work as soon as she could. "I've been dependent on folks so long, I've got to make up for it. I don't know doin' what, yet, but it's got to be something, not just makin' baskets. And I've got to make up for the schoolin' I missed. Maybe Gilley when he gets well can tell me how to go about it."

Letty out in the world, on her own, in the evenings, without him: Everything was breaking up, he thought as they drove along.

His objective was Stokesville. As they neared it they saw more and more damage done by the stream now coursing tamely enough beside the highway. There were the stubs of homemade vehicular bridges washed out, houses askew and some collapsed. At Wick's behest they turned off into a rutted road which a hand-lettered sign warned was closed in 1.3 miles. It led up a narrow valley between strip-mined hills rawly gutted at the valley's head. What had closed it, as Wick expected, was the mud, sand, gravel and rocks dislodged by the rains and swept down the slopes. This sackage of the hills lay across the valley, burying the road and part of a gullied field of dead corn-stalks beside it. "No doubt there was a farm back up there," Wick observed. A flock of black birds—grackles—rose from the field with a rustle of wings.

"Do you know a poem called 'The Rigs o' Barley,' Father? By Robert Burns? Say those lines for him, Letty, do."

" 'Corn rigs, an' barley rigs. . . .' " She stopped and drew a breath. "An' corn rigs are bonie,' " she finished in a hurried monotone, looking aside.

At Stokesville, they were told by a man at a gasoline station, the frothy, muddy river, swollen with the torrents pouring down from the denuded heights, had risen clear to the ceilings of the ground-floor shops on the main street. People had been taken by boats out of second-floor windows. Congressman Sykes and some Feds had come down from Washington. "Son," Sykes had said to the mayor when they jumped down from their helicopter, "you've got yourself a disaster area." And one of the Feds had said, "If it's any consolation to you when you come to dig out of the mud, think how much of it will have gone on to create hazards to navigation in the Ohio or Mississippi." Most of the damage had been repaired, but some shops still were lightless with rubbish embedded in the clay-covered floors; and piles of debris—planks, logs, weeds and trash—had not yet been removed from the warehouse yards above the river.

It had been a long morning. Letty remained subdued and met the question in Wick's eyes, when she met his eyes at all, with a small generalized smile he considered a screen. His father's predicament was plain. He could not give the occasion a gayer turn, as his regard for the girl would urge him to, without appearing to make light of the enormities they had seen and to be self-serving in doing so. He asked Letty about her ideas with respect to a job and they discussed the possibilities, none of which—salesgirl, waitress, seamstress—sounded inviting. Then, to Wick's delight, his father said what he would have, had he let himself: that she should put a job second, if possible, and plan to get all the education she could because it would matter more in the end. And he suggested that she do modeling for newspaper advertising. She should have no trouble getting the work, he said, and there should be enough of it in Harpersburg and one or two comparable nearby towns to give her an income while leaving most of her time free. From the light in her eyes, and her flush of mingled modesty and pleasure, Wick saw it happening, and taking her farther from him.

Where did he stand with her? Agonizing over the question wore him down more than his hurts and dully aching head. He tried to understand what it would do to one to see again after years of blindness, and concluded that it must be like running a low fever. You could be easily excited and overintense, or you could sink into preoccupation. And you would be easily confused. Fevers passed, and presumably these symptoms would in Letty. But where that would leave him he had no way of knowing.

When they stopped for lunch he spoke a short piece he had planned for his father. "What we've seen this morning isn't a patch on the full extent of the wreckage. I suppose when you flew here the pilot came down the eastern side of the mountains. Even if he has to fly higher I wish he'd take a route northeast *over* the mountains on the way back. They say that from the air

242

you begin to get an idea of what the statistics mean—over twenty thousand miles of mountainside strip-mined."

His father continued eating in silence long enough for the boy to wonder if he were going to acknowledge the speech at all. Then he set down his fork. "I could tell you how the coal has got to be extracted from the hills because the American economy requires it. I could tell you there's no other way than stripping to get at the surface seams. I could talk about restoration. What I *shall* say is that you've made your point. Something's got to be done to control, or stop, strip-mining in hills like these. I don't know what or how it's to be brought about. But the kind of operations we've seen this morning are intolerable. I only wish I had some say-so in the behavior of the many companies engaged in it."

"What about Winespring?"

To his surprise, his father seemed to relax. "Letty, my son here —and he is my son, though he takes my education in hand and sits in judgment over me—Wick tells me you helped him with that appeal for Winespring he sent the State legislative committee on development and conservation. As I admitted to him, it was hard to resist. I shouldn't mind having a pair of propagandists like you working for us instead of against us."

"It was almost all Wick's doin'."

"Don't believe her. And without her I wouldn't either have written it or sent you a copy."

"I'll do everything I can for your mountain. If I have my way, the corporation won't oppose the taking or require condemnation. We'll give the legislation our blessing. We'll put the lowest possible price on the land—lower than the courts would award—and charge it off to public relations. We'll ask only to deep-mine it, which won't harm it.

"And now, you two . . . ! Letty, have you ever had a banana split? They put three gobs of ice cream on banana slices, each a different flavor, with three kinds of syrup and marshmallow topping sprinkled with chocolate sprills and a maraschino cherry on each mound. It'll tempt the most finicky palate, I'm told. Come along. . . ."

17

After they had taken his father to the airport, Wick had picked up an Allegheny-Keystone driver to deliver him to the farm and bring back the Jeep. On the way, he cursed the man's presence in the car. More than anything in the world he yearned to kiss Letty. He was no longer sure a kiss would be granted, but at least he would have the evening with her and a chance to take a sounding of her feeling for him.

"Your father's a wonderful man," she was saying. "The way he's been about things here, the farm and Winespring—how can we ever make up to him what we owe him?"

"You've already made him feel rewarded."

"Not as much rewarded as you did. I'm not his son."

"Or I the world's prettiest girl. But I must say . . . you know, I've come to think a lot more of the old man." It was easy to: he was an asset with Letty. Shamed by his selfishness, he said, "So much that I'd hate to let him down."

Various people were at the farm. Without waiting to see who they were, Wick went off to lie down. Consequently, he learned only when they had all gone and he re-emerged at dinner time that his father had not been alone in his ideas for Letty's future. One of the callers had been a fashion photographer who had seen Letty's picture in the *Courant* and had come to ascertain if she would be interested in modeling. No decision had been come to. Mr. Barrows, knowing he had no proper voice in the matter, brooded somberly on it. "You'll be all over the place," he allowed himself to warn. "Thar'll be thousands of men starin' at you and passin' remarks."

To which Letty replied, "It'll just be a picture! They stare at *me* as it is and pass remarks. And"—flashing a look at the boy—"I wouldn't have my picture took in my underwear like some gals, with their pictures right up there in the store."

Her mother was inclined to treat the offer as not likely to bring about either the millennium or doomsday. "What do you think, Wick?" she asked, giving words to Letty's glances at him.

"I think the Moslems are right. They won't let their women show their faces in public at all." And, laughing, he raised an arm to ward off the cup Letty made as if to throw at him. But he was sure she could tell he was happy for her sake.

Halfway through dinner came the sounds of a car and the light of headlamps in the window. The voices carrying from the porch after Letty, bouncing up, had gone to investigate were those of mixed boys and girls.

She reported on her return, "It's Randy and Cal and another boy and two gals and they've asked me to go to the movies with them." If she had looked only slightly feverish a moment ago, she certainly looked more now. "I can't hardly remember what a movie's like. I can go, Ma, can't I? . . . Maybe you'd come too, Wick?"

She must have known he would not tag along even if he had been invited and were up to it. "You'll have plenty in the car without me. And I've had about enough shaking up for the day."

Eager, contrite, entreating his willing concurrence, ready for a warmth of gratitude if it were given and for willfulness if it were not, and withal a challenging sparkle in her eye—it was all in her face, and he could not help the pain in his chest. But above all it would not do for her to feel guilty on his account. He smiled. "Think of me dreaming peacefully. And enjoy yourself."

There was a knock on his door, and it was Mrs. Sherrod. He had been sure she would come when he had said he was going to his room to read, where he could stretch out. She would have known of his need for the relief of words.

"I just thought I'd find out how you were, and if there's anything I can do."

He lifted his legs off the cot and sat up. "You can congratulate me, Queen. My instructions, as I remember them, were that I wasn't to break Letty's heart. I think I've succeeded beyond anything we could have hoped for."

"You think she's changed. But she hasn't. She couldn't have changed so. Let me explain," she added quickly as he was about to speak. "Letty's a girl, and it's in the nature of a girl not to mind seein' more than just one man interested in her. Other girls Letty's age have had a few years to watch the nature in them work on boys, but Letty's never had a chance."

She confronted him squarely, letting him read a touch of humor in her regard.

"You shouldn't be too surprised, young man," she said, "if another youngster feels the little devil inside acting up some. Different as it may be in girls from boys—mercifully."

He brooded briefly on the distasteful picture of himself she had resurrected. "The truth is, I've always seen Letty in you, just as I see you in Letty." Would she accept this as a mitigating circumstance? Her expression was indulgent enough. "The truth is"—and he frowned: what a lot of truth he was proclaiming—"I haven't always known I love her. But I've found it out. I can tell you that!"

"And whether she loves you, it's not for me to say. Whatever she felt for you in the past, though, she still feels. I'm sure of that. But . . . up to now, Letty's been dependent on you, almost taking light from you like the moon from the sun. You have to understand that a girl could be ready to love a man all her life and still want to be something *herself,* as Letty wants to be now. She'd want to know she was givin' something that didn't *need* to be given, either. And she wouldn't be human if she didn't want him to know it, too. And he ought to. The more respect there is on both sides, the stronger love will be."

It sounded reasonable. He longed to believe it. But it was a limb he feared to trust his weight to. He stood up, though he had to put his hand to the wall. "So she's going to be a model. You know what's going to happen, don't you? The pictures of her will be seen all over the place, as Mr. Barrows said. The next thing you know they'll be after her in New York. New York! Men, successful men, sophisticated, handsome men with millions of bucks surrounding her. All greedy for her."

"Wick, you're driving yourself wild! Letty's been out twice with some boys who're old family friends. She's been asked to stand in front of a camera by a photographer in an Appalachian coal town.

And already you've got her modeling in New York with a drove of rich young men after her."

"You'll see!" If he was being histrionic, who wouldn't be, going through what he was going through? "With her beauty and charm it couldn't turn out any other way."

"Wick, you're makin' too much of her looks. There are plenty of girls just as pretty as Letty."

"I haven't seen them. Anyhow, I love her. And without her my life wouldn't be worth living."

Mrs. Sherrod persuaded him to take another of the pills.

"I'm going to see Gilley tomorrow morning. Then I'm leaving —taking the bus for home."

Watching the girl, he went limp inside, like one reprieved from exile; for her eyes grew round, the color drained from her face.

Bending her head over her plate of grits, she asked, "You mean you're going for . . . I mean, how . . . ?"

Sympathy gushing from a heart rent with relief, he went to her rescue, trampling over the resolutions he had made, "Oh, I won't be gone very long." Disturbed by the ardor of his retreat, he said, "Well, actually I don't know how long. I do owe my parents a visit."

"Have you got to go . . . so suddenly?" It appeared that, re-arranging the grits with her fork, she was trying to prepare a face to raise to his.

"The sooner I get started the sooner I can get it all behind me," he stated robustly.

The face she did raise, still pale, seemed both to seek to read his and to shrink from it. She said, "This is your last day then, for a while. How did you plan to spend it?"

By-passing his resolutions again, he replied, "I had thought per-haps of going up the mountain, if you'd go with me." To return to the world that had been so much to them and that they had shared alone, she would know he meant. "You haven't seen it yet, or the view from the top."

She asked—and there seemed still to be warring impulses in her response, "Are we going to bring coffee and things?"

He said questioningly, "If you'd like to go."

"Yes, I would," she answered quickly, as if there could be no alternative reply. Her eyes going from the bandage on his head to his sling, she added, "If you think it wouldn't be too much for you. . . . Wick, you've always been patient with me, haven't you?"

Startled, he replied, "I don't know. I've never noticed any need to be."

"Yes, you have," she affirmed softly but positively, as if, oddly, *that* were settled. And immediately she went off to get ready.

A tide of cold air had moved in quietly during the night. The pasture was sugared with frost, the sky a deep, hard blue. A chill nipped the face. The morning was almost windless, but in the sun's growing strength, with the least stirring of air, flocks of the leaves remaining on the trees released their holds and tumbled.

Taking his hand, she said, "I need it just as much as I used to to keep from stumbling. Not because I can't see where I'm goin' but because I'm too busy with all else there is to see."

Indeed, she gazed about her as they walked as if she would never have her fill.

"And there's old Hamp and Rafe's place! Where the sunshine that falls on the cornfield is made into another kind. I'm goin' to get after them to haul that rusty old truck off before people come to see Winespring State Forest."

And presently: "And yonder are the hemlocks where we heard the Black-throated Green warbler singin'—and could again next spring. They *do* look like dark spirit-trees, just like you said. . . .

"Everywhere I look, I see things you've told me about. How good to me you were! And even now I see them in your words! It keeps you in my thoughts all the time. . . .

"Maybe that's part of what the trouble is." She stood still, and took hold of his arms and brought them face to face. "Oh, Wick, I'm so dizzy in my mind! Ever since I got my sight back I've been like a cricket on a wood chip floatin' down a creek with the current spinnin' it around this way and that and the banks strange to it and different every minute. The poor, bewildered critter don't know where it is and it's not sure what it is." She sought to deprecate the unhappiness and need behind her words with a smile of sorts, but it was fleeting.

"I don't know what I am, Wick: Sometimes I feel like the same old me, and sometimes I feel like nothin' at all, no more than milkweed silk that any little breeze can blow any which way.

I been suddenly dropped into a world where everybody knows what they are and where they belong but me."

"Oh, Letty, a lot of us don't know. But it's far worse for you. I wish I knew how to help you through it. I curse myself that I can't when I think that it's because of you I've learned what *I'm* about." Letty, and this around them that he'd come to know through her, were what he was about.

"You do help!" The anxious exclamation broke into his thought. "I'd be lost without you. That's why I feel so miserable at behavin' as I do with you."

They moved with one accord into each other's arms. He freed his bad one from the sling to hold her. Clinging to him, as he to her, she said, "When you tell me you love me—you've only told me once, but I hear it over and over—I think, what would you be gettin' if you had me? How can you love me when even I don't know what I am?"

Her face, cool against his at the start, had grown warm.

"I know you well enough." He was surer of his love for her than of anything else in life. Yet how well did he know her, how well only his feelings for her? It had only gradually dawned on him in the past two days, really the past twelve hours, that a girl because you adored her did not become a heaven-designed answer to your needs and desires for fulfillment. She was a person equally, perhaps as oddly assorted within as you, with an equal right to weaknesses and shortcomings, with as legitimate a dependence on moral support. He was aware of how far short he probably fell of knowing Letty as she deserved to be known and how much growing he would probably have to do before he was able to. And as he saw now, a girl however lovely could have as hard and imperative a road to travel to self-knowledge as an oaf like himself.

He said, "I know I love you."

She made no resistance as he turned her face toward him and pressed his mouth against hers. Her hand even went to the back of his head to hold him to her. But she cut the kiss short. With her forehead against his shoulder, she said, "When we do that, I can't think. I'll have to go back and remember what I was goin' to say. . . .

"It was this. Not knowin' myself, I don't know how I'll behave when I'm up against all there is in life that's new to me. I don't know what kind of girl I'll find I am. I could be a terrible disappointment to you, or have to try to be something I'm not. Wick—" She pushed herself back and put her hand briefly over his lips. "What do you want of me?"

"I want to marry you—as soon as I'm able to."

"I believe you think so now. And . . . well, I know what would go with that that you'd want. Seems to me you didn't leave me in much doubt, with that talk about bringin' a gal to the top of Winespring, when the trees would be in bloom and a Wood thrush singin'— Wick, this isn't that trip!" she cried in alarm.

"I hadn't imagined it was."

"What else would you want? That's the question."

"I'd want to make you happy. I'd want to give you understanding. Long as it might take me to be capable of much."

His heart ravished suddenly by her infinite preciousness, he gripped her by the shoulders to look into her eyes. "I'd want to force the world to its knees at your feet for you to command it. I'd want it to know that if any harm came to you I'd tear it apart. I'd pull the universe down. The whole thing!"

"*Sh, sh!*" She covered his lips with her hand again. "I know you would, Wick. I know it," she said placatingly. "I saw what you done to Bull Turner—did to him—on account of me." Evidently feeling that she could safely do so, she removed her hand. "Did you used to scowl like that when I couldn't see you?"

"I scowl when things are scowl-worthy. Not otherwise."

"What you haven't told me yet—you said what you'd do for me—but what could I do for you?"

But he was not yet calmed down. "I'll tell you later—when we get to the top."

She took hold of his sleeve and bent her head. He could see nothing of her eyes but the dark lashes.

"Be patient, Wick. As you are. Give me time. After all, I'm only seventeen, and you're only eighteen." She looked at him pleadingly.

"Anything you want." He had an oppressive sense of the weight time could have. "Now and forever."

They walked on, up the trail. Seldom did they go a hundred feet without coming on some object to be commented on—one that had figured in times past, the trees Letty had named, places where Wick had reported birds or plants. The rock-slide they eyed in silence until Wick, recovering the canteen-cup, observed that he was afraid the coffee-cake had disappeared. There was the overhang under which they had taken shelter from the storms. Here they had coffee and jam sandwiches of corn bread.

"You've given me the most wonderful present a girl ever had from a boy. The farm, safe, and now this mountain."

"You can thank yourself for the mountain. Father couldn't have held out against you."

She shook her head impatiently. "You didn't hear what he said when you were in the men's room. It's because he's so proud of the way you've fought that he's doing what he is. And I don't think we have to worry anymore." She stood looking back the way they had come. They had little farther to go, and he knew that her heart was full of all they had passed.

At the top, when they had come out above the crowns of the trees, she was all but overcome by the argosy of hills around them, mottled gray, brown, golden, dark-green and oxblood, leading beneath the glory of the blue sky to the lofty eastern ranges, standing clearer now than he had ever seen them. "Yes, it's how I pictured it, but I never dreamed what it could be like—goin' so far on every side and so high above and all burstin' with light. . . . And there's this old mountain above all the others around, our godfather, sturdy and grand and noble."

'Old Winespring,' Wick thought, 'great chief of the Cumberlands!' It would speak for him, surely. It would plead his cause.

The gougings of the strippers had never looked more diabolical. Or the cut for the interstate highway, either. Even as they gazed across at this naked precipice a puff of dust shot from the top of it and a mass of rock and earth cascaded from it.

"They've made progress," Wick said. "They must have demolished a quarter of the hill by now, and filled the valley with it."

"You're the one to speak against it, Wick."

"Speak against it, yes," he said with a mirthless fragment of a laugh.

He led her to the smooth ledge where they could hang their legs over the side. When they had sat down, she said, "What was it you were going to tell me when we got here?"

"I once asked your mother where I'd find what I'm looking for: the truth at the heart of things; what you can believe in and hold

251

to, and that justifies it all. She said it is—nowhere and everywhere
. . . everywhere and nowhere. That doesn't sound like much,
but I think that's it.

"And I need you to help me bear it. The dread when I look
into the cold and dark and all the horrors there are and realize
the answer is nowhere. The ecstasy when I find it's everywhere.
As I have at times when we've been together. Without you with
me, they'll be too much for me. Only you will do. And I need you
to help me if I'm going to try to save places where it is right there,
everywhere you look."

She leaned back hard against him, her head on his shoulder, her
hair against his cheek. He could see that her eyes were closed
against the pain and division of her thoughts. "I don't want to let
go of this. But I have to know. Let me have a chance, Wick, as
I've asked. Only don't let me stray too far. Not too far!"

He tightened his arm around her. Looking out on the world,
so beautiful and so demanding, he knew that nothing would be
simple anymore.

"It's cold." Shivering, she shrank inside her jacket.

The intenser chill had come on stealthily in the still windless
and luminous clear air with the sun's descent.

He said, "It's just winter coming."

God knew if he could hold the girl who was his life against the
other claims and claimants waiting for her. God knew whether in
any case he could make a difference in the struggle for the woods
and mountains which had become his life, too. But he would try
to. With all that was in him. And as long as there could be hope
he would never give up.